Robert Wilder

The Sun Is My Shadow

G. P. Putnam's Sons
New York

1119332

THE SUN IS MY SHADOW

I

THE old man, propped against a high mound of pillows on the huge, canopied bed, kept his eyes closed. He had been swimming lazily in a dark pool, whirled gently and not unpleasantly in a murky void. It had been the sensation of lying in a deep, warm bath and he was reluctant to let it go. There was no point in opening his eyes since he knew what they would see. His sister Julia, in one of the brightly flowered organdie prints she always wore, sniffling moistly into a twisted handkerchief. Young Doctor Warren, from Court House, at his side with an inquisitive finger on the pulse of a bony wrist. Across the room, at one of the ceiling-to-floor windows that looked out upon the clipped perfection of a lawn sweeping to the edge of the North Anna River, his daughter Carol had her back to him. Nothing would have changed during the few seconds or minutes he had been away. Finally, because it was an effort now to keep them shut, he allowed the lids to raise.

"Thought I was gone, hey, Earle?" He addressed the doctor with a cackle that, even to his own ears, had an obscene, loony sound; an idiot rattling a handful of dry bones.

The doctor took the stethoscope from about his neck and dropped it into a black bag. "I'm damned if I know what keeps you going, Mr. Hillyard." It was a dispassionate statement of clinical interest.

"Me, that's what." The old man struggled against the pillows into a more upright position. "I keep myself goin' until I'm ready to turn loose an' there ain't a damn thing you can do about it." He half turned to glance at his daughter and the eyes grew foxily bright. "Sister." He spoke the word with pleasure. "In them ridin' britches I'm damned if you ain't got the prettiest behind in all Virginia. If I was a young man an' not your father I'd snatch me a handful of it."

The slender girl turned from the window. At the open throat of the oatmeal-colored shirt of flannel there was a twisted, chiffon scarf of purple. It gave her eyes the same tint.

"You're a dirty-talking old man." She winked at him and reached into her pocket for a cigarette. Lighting it she blew a jet of smoke in his direction.

He sniffed hungrily, eagerly and licked at dry lips. "Sister, you're tormentin' me a-purpose. I want a seegar an' some red whisky." He popped his tongue against the roof of his mouth.

"Doctor Warren!" Julia appealed helplessly.

The young man only shrugged and stood looking down at his patient with an expression of bemused wonder.

The old man grinned, his shiny dentures giving him a wolfish gleam. "I'm dyin', ain't I, Earle?" There was an almost fierce, challenging pride in the question.

"Yes, Mr. Hillyard."

"Then what the hell's the difference? Anyhow, I been sneakin' over there to get it when no one's around." He twisted about, thrusting a hand beneath the pillows, drawing out a wrought-iron key. He extended it toward his daughter. "In the cabinet there, Sister."

"Carol!" The word ended on a rising note. Julia's bosom heaved with breathless indignation and the printed flowers bobbed and tossed as though windblown. "Do you want to kill your father?"

The girl smiled pleasantly but ignored the question. She went to a highboy of exquisitely carved mahogany, unlocked a drawer and selected a half-filled quart from the bottles laid there. Then she took a cigar from a humidor, turned it in her fingers for dryness and sniffed its Havana perfume. The old man watched every move with alert pleasure. She poured whisky into a water glass, carried it to the bed and sat on the edge.

The old man accepted the glass and held it while she clipped the cigar end with sharp, white teeth. She lit it carefully and placed it between faintly blue lips. He drew upon it with deep satisfaction, allowing the smoke to purl from his mouth. Then he drank most of the whisky and leaned back, nodding contentedly.

"I'll be going now." Dr. Warren closed his bag. "Call if you need me. I'll look in tomorrow."

"There ain't nothin' more for you to do, Earle, but sign the certificate when the time comes." The old man waved the cigar at the retreating back and chuckled raspingly as the door closed. Then he bent his shaggy eyebrows, the color of dirty sand, and peered at his sister. "Julia"—he spoke calmly, puffing the cigar—"I want you to go back to Muncie. I want you to go before I die so I'll be sure you ain't hangin' around, makin' a nuisance of yourself an' botherin' Carol. I'd like you to go soon now because there ain't no way of tellin' how much time I got left."

"Well I never." The woman's voice trembled and the slightly protruding eyes floated in tears. "I never thought I'd live to see the day when my own brother'd speak to me that way." Indignation succeeded misery. "Don't you know you're waiting for the Call this very minute and when you cross over the Lord is going to have a lot of questions to ask Mark Hillyard. I'd be thinking about that, if I were you. I'd be thinking of what I was going to tell the Recording Angel to save my immortal soul, making my peace instead of swigging whisky and smoking cigars."

The old man ignored her suggestion and the pathetic quivering of a lower lip. He pointed his cigar at her. "I ain't being unpleasant, Julia." The voice actually softened. "It's just I know you. Carol's got her own life to live an' her way to go. I want her to do it without no interfering female relative. Now," he continued deliberately, "you know I've provided for you good in my will. There ain't never a money worry to cross your mind. You can go back to Muncie, Indiana, or live in Europe, California, Florida or with the Hottentots in Africa. I don't care what. All I'm sayin' is Sister here has got a

right to pick out the kind of life she wants to live. You'd be tryin'
to tell her. I ain't goin' to leave things that way, Julia. My mind's
made up."

"But a young girl needs taking care of." The protest was lifted
on a shrill note of urgency.

"If Sister needs takin' care of it can't be done by any old woman."
He was adamant but not unkind. "A real, stallion of a man now—"
He smacked his lips and finished the whisky. "That's the kind of
takin' care of she needs, maybe. By God!" His pale eyes fired. "I'd
like to be around to see that. I purely would." With a sigh,
reminiscent and regretful, he leaned back against the pillows and
stared at the ceiling.

Without expression Carol examined the ash on her cigarette and
then deliberately tapped it off into the V opening of the ruffled,
linen nightshirt. A small shower of sparks fell upon the mat of
grizzled hair, burning hotly to the skin. He pretended not to notice.

"I got some things I want to say to Sister, Julia." Mark nodded
toward the door. "Leave us alone for a while."

With a bewildered shaking of her head the woman moved in an
organdie cloud, pausing at the threshold for a moment to look back
unbelievingly.

"I don't know which of you is worse. A profane and blaspheming
old man or a quiet one like Carol who never lets you know what she's
thinking. You're a pair, all right." She closed the door behind her.

The old man looked at his daughter. "You believe that, Sister;
we're alike?"

"I'd hate to think so."

His face wrinkled into a smile, smugly pleased as though he had
been complimented.

"You want a drink?"

She scratched her back comfortably against the bedpost. "Later
maybe, before lunch."

He dug a finger into the hairy cavity of his ear. "Sister, when
I'm gone have you any idea what you got?" He didn't wait for a
reply. "You're like to end up as one of the richest girls in the
country. Maybe that five an' dime girl who's always gettin' her
name an' picture in the papers has got a mite more"—he made the
qualification regretfully—"but she ain't got what you're goin' to
have. Hers comes from little geegaws across a counter. Yours is
right out of the country's guts. It's power. It's pulp mills in Canada

and Oregon, oil wells in Texas and Oklahoma, spinnin' mills in North Carolina, coal mines in Kentucky an' West Virginia, a piece of a steamship line, half a dozen newspapers scattered around, some hotels an' insurance companies. Did you ever wonder how I collected such a hell of a lot of goods, Sister?"

"I always thought you stole what you couldn't get any other way." There was no rancor in the statement.

"By God you're almost right." He was mightily pleased. "I made some, stole some, connived, kicked and bit in the clinches. Let me tell you one thing. The minute you begin to get some goods in this world you got to spend a lot of time beatin' off those who want to take 'em away from you. Yes, sir! You got to carry a club all the time."

She stubbed her cigarette out on the heel of a boot and tossed the butt into a wastepaper basket. "Is that what you wanted to talk with me about?"

"No-o-o." He drew the word out. "It's just that I got a feelin' to know what's goin' to happen after I'm gone. Like Julia says, I'm waitin' for the call—which is a meechin' way of sayin' I'm about dead. If what Julia an' the preachers say is true, I'm goin' to have a lot of time on my hands in the hereafter. I don't want to spend it wonderin' an' worryin' about you. What's goin' to happen, Sister?"

"I suppose you're talking about whether I'm going to get married, settle down, raise a family."

"What's wrong with that? A lot of women have tried it. This here New York thing has been all right for sort of a joke or somethin' but you oughtn't to make it the end of things. You're twenty-two or thereabouts, ain't you?"

"I guess so." She shrugged. "You don't really know. Neither do I. I just guess at it from the time, as they say, a girl becomes a woman. It's as good a number as any."

"It's as close as I can come, Sister." There was a rare tone of apology in the confession. "When it happened, you I mean, we were in a little place called Silverlode, in Colorado. It wasn't much of a town then an' it's less now. You were midwifed. There was no doctor for eighty miles so there ain't no record. Your mother would have kept count if she had lived. Anyhow, twenty-two ain't a bad age to have. I'd take it sight unseen again right now. You know somethin'? I been a real mean sonofabitch in my time." He made the statement with complacent irrelevancy.

Studying him as he lay there, the wasted figure outlined beneath the light covering, her eyes softened. She wondered what she really felt for this tough, shrewd, vulgar old man. Affection. Affection and tolerance? No. Tolerance had a supercilious sound and implication. Understanding. That was closer.

"We've had a hell of a time together, ain't we, Sister?" He whispered the words without looking at her. "I'd like for it to go on. I'd like to be around for a while more. You scare me a little sometimes. But we've had it, ain't we?"

"You said it, old man. We've had a hell of a time."

"You goin' to maybe marry that Warrington fella that's been comin' around?"

"I don't know." She grinned at him. "I haven't felt the call yet, not really."

The eyes half opened. "He's too soft for you, Sister. You'll cut him to pieces an' not mean to. You'd ruin him and he'd never understand how it happened." The eyelids fluttered wearily.

She sat, looking down at him; listening to the rasp of a locust outside in the hot, midmorning sun; the voice of a yardman as he called to someone, the uncertain breathing of Mark Hillyard.

. It was impossible to remember a time when they hadn't been together. She had no recollection of her mother. There hadn't even been a picture to tell her what she looked like. If she searched the years it was as though they were pages in a book which had been skipped in the printing, leaving blank sheets to be thumbed over until, suddenly, the story, already begun and partly told, was resumed.

There was a day coach on a train. She sat on a seat facing this man who was her father. It was hot, sticky, and the air was foul with the strong odor of cheap tobacco and sweat. Her legs, in black, ribbed cotton stockings, itched intolerably where the band of elastic just above her knees made a welt. Her feet, short of the floor, hung limply and tingled painfully. She could remember the acrid, rank and sulphurous smell of coal smoke that seeped through the dirty windows and curled down the ventilators when they passed through a tunnel. The faded green plush of the upholstery was thick with cinders and they worked loose and fell down her neck whenever she leaned her head back.

There seemed to have been no time of beginning for this journey. They had come from no place she could remember. Suddenly they were on this train as though they both had been born there. She stared through the grimy window and watched an occasional calf or pony in a field as it threw up its head in fancied panic at the train's approach and raced wildly about the enclosure. She remembered wondering if they behaved that way every time a train passed and why they hadn't realized long ago the belching engine and rattling cars could do them no harm.

The man facing her made marks on a pad of paper with the stub of a pencil. Now and then, without looking up from whatever it was he was doing, he spat a thin stream of tobacco juice at the iron foot of her seat.

There had been a fat, red-faced boy who came through the car at intervals. He wore a tray suspended from his neck by a strap. On the shelf he carried sandwiches, apples, bananas, cake and souvenirs. He lugged a pail with pop bottles thrust into melting ice. Her father had bought her a root beer and a piece of cake. As an afterthought he selected a glass lantern from the tray. It was made to resemble the lantern carried by the train's brakeman who came with it through the car whenever the train stopped at night. The base and chimney were filled with small, red, buttonlike candies and the cinnamon of their flavor was sharp on her tongue. These years later she could never taste the spice without experiencing a slight nausea and the sensation of cindery grit between her teeth.

If this journey had no beginning for her now, it also had no end. At least she couldn't recall their leaving the train. What she remembered next was a long, jolting ride in a wagon. She sat on the seat between her father and a man who drove the team. He called her father Mr. Hillyard and the road wound and climbed through limitless forests where great trees, spicy and pungent, towered up to pierce white clouds. They passed through a covered bridge over a roiling river where enormous rafts of chained logs bucked and headed down the current.

There had been a settlement with dots of little houses, finished on the outside with rough, split logs, and long low buildings out of which bearded men came at daybreak to the sound of an iron tire hit with a hammer. They ate in an enormous hall and they climbed on wagons with saws and axes to disappear until nightfall into the woods. Long shadows from the trees slanted down in the afternoon to make paths up which she could walk or skip, balancing herself while pretending nothing lay below. Her father worked at a desk in one of the cabins and the men used to come in, pulling

15

off their wool caps when they talked with him. There were no other children and she was much alone.

Then there was a winter, but she couldn't be sure now whether it was of the same year or another. The snow piled high above the windows, almost to the roofs of the cabins. There was a woman but she was called Anna and not mother. She was a woman of strong breasts the size of melons, of apple-red cheeks, a warm smile and gentle hands. When she spoke, her sentences ended on a note a little higher than that on which they started. Carol used to imitate her and they would laugh together. The woman cooked, washed, sewed and polished, and the cabin sparkled darkly with her rubbing. She sang sad and lilting songs to the little girl while she made enormous pies with spices and dried apples that had been soaked in a crock of water overnight. After the evening meal her father and Anna usually sat about the table, which was covered with a green, fringed cloth. A nickel-plated oil lamp with a frosted glass shade made a puddle of yellow light. Anna mended socks while her father drew things on a pad and Carol lay on her belly watching the golden flakes fall from the logs in the fireplace.

When she attempted to pursue this memory the continuity eluded her. It was like gazing through a stereoptican where one picture was followed by another without any relationship. This time there was no snow, no forest, no bearded men in plaid mackinaws with ear flaps on their caps. No Anna. They were part now of a train of reapers, binders, threshers, as it moved through the great wheat belt; along highways and down country roads. Here the sun came up each morning as a dull red globe that changed with the hours to a dazzling and eye-splitting brightness. Heat shimmered over the fields like a filmy scarf waved, and the dust of the chaff clogged mouth and nostrils and made a cloud of yellow in a clear sky. They moved from great, lonely farm to farm and the wheat stretched in a sea to the end of the world. Sometimes they stayed at a hotel in one of the small towns or settlements or they lived with the farmer and his family while the crew made a camp of tents. At noontime long tables of boards on sawhorses were laid in the scanty shade and the men came from the fields to washtubs filled with mashed potatoes, fried chicken, steaks, milk and coffee. The men ate with a silent ferocity, wiped their mouths on the backs of their hands and returned to the machines. When they had left, she and the women would eat and sometimes they let her help wash the tin plates and cups in blackened iron kettles of steaming, greasy water.

Always they were moving and usually a woman became a small part of their lives for a while. They disappeared as mysteriously as they came, leaving in storming anger or with a cheery wave of a hand. They were sometimes young, dark or fair, slim and eager. They were friendly or ignored her and she finally came to accept this restless tide of women as normal as the seasonal or geographical changes. Her father would bring them to wherever they were living and say: Sister. This is Margaret, Enid, Lois or Helen. The new one, if she was young, usually said: Hello kid. The older ones patted her hair and called her Lamb or Dear, fussed and clucked over her clothing and took money from her father to buy her new dresses, shoes, underpants and stockings. Carol neither liked nor disliked them, knowing they would never stay long and weren't actually a part of her life.

They moved from Montana to California, from Texas to Florida and Maine. Always this restless man who was her father found something to which he could turn his hand. He seemed to know how to do or fix an astonishing number of things for which strangers would pay.

There had been a town, a village, where a line of trees ran down the middle of the main street. They had lived in a house there and the furniture had been upholstered in a shiny black stuff her father had called horsehair. Where it had been worn, small ends protruded and when you sat down they prickled your behind through the thin muslin underpants. You could pull these hairs out, stiff, brittle and slightly curved, and when you stuck them into the spaces between your teeth they made a walrus face.

A man and a woman lived with them at that time and the man owned a garage at the far end of the main street. At a bench at the back of the long room her father worked on a thing of metal and tiny screws. Sometimes he would let her go down with him in the morning and sit on a high stool at the bench to watch. Now and then the man who owned the garage would come and stand at her father's side and they would talk and nod their heads. She understood then the thing her father was making was called A Patent. When it was finished "Old Deering" or "Old McCormack" or "Those International Harvester Bastards" would pay a lot of money for it because it would make their machines work better.

Then, one day, her father left her and she didn't cry or even

17

wonder where he had gone but continued to live with the garage man and his wife. Once, after the garage man had been drinking, he and his wife had a terrible fight. They yelled back and forth at each other and the man said he knew she had been going to bed with that son of a bitch Hillyard in the afternoons while he was at the garage. She couldn't understand why he was so angry and wanted to tell him it was all right because all the women went to bed with her father. She didn't, though, and after a while they quieted down and went to sleep as though nothing had happened.

When her father returned it was in a new, red automobile and the back seat was piled high with packages tied with ribbon and colored string. There were presents for everyone and a blue coat of nubby wool with a white fur collar for her. The man, his wife and her father laughed, cried, shouted and sang. They got so drunk they could barely walk without tipping over and they were all rich or would be and the man was going to "get the hell out of this goddamned town and go to California." She could remember that night well because her father had suddenly looked at her, swaying a little with a bottle in his hand.

"By God, Sister," he had said, "you're growing up. It's time you went to school and had a decent home so's you can be a lady. I'm going to send for Julia."

So Aunt Julia came to live with them and they went to Houston, Texas. Aunt Julia wasn't like the others. She didn't go to bed with her father and she didn't drink or get mad or do much of anything except to see she always had clean clothes, took a bath every day and went to school.

"What the hell are you thinkin' about, Sister?"

The old man's voice startled her. She had been so far away, across the years and back. He was looking up at her with a small frown.

"I was thinking about you, me." She stood up and tucked the shirt into her breeches. "I was thinking about Texas and the first well you brought in, the Carol Number One."

"By God, I had it made that day, Sister!" He was suddenly animated and pulled himself upright, punching the pillows into a solid heap. "I just stood there in a hundred-dollar suit and let the damned stuff fall on me like rain. I even stuck out my tongue and tasted it. I licked it like it was molasses. It was the bounty of the world showerin' down on me."

"It did, too, didn't it?" She went to the highboy, poured a small drink and took it straight without water. She lit a cigarette and gazed across the room at him. "As you said, we've had a hell of a time."

"It was like I had a big funnel to hold up." The tired eyes were suddenly young again. "I just stood under it and the riches poured in. There was nothin' I could touch that didn't turn into money. That's the kind of excitement you ought to know, Sister." He relaxed slowly. "It's hard for a man to bring himself to know it's all over; that he ain't never again goin' to make a big gamble, love up a woman, get roarin', fightin' drunk just for the hell of it. I ain't really afraid of dyin'. It's just that it's takin' so damn long. I'm havin' too much time to think."

"What do you want for lunch?" She smiled at him.

"Not that damn puke Julia's been sendin' up." He was indignant. "You come an' eat it with me. We'll have a few drinks together. I want some fried chicken with gravy an' mashed potatoes."

She nodded and started toward the door. "I'll take a swim and get out of these clothes. You stay away from that jug." She glanced at the bottle. "If we're going to talk I want to be able to understand what you say."

"You goin' to keep this place, Sister?" There was a pleading note in his voice. "You goin' to live here some of the time?"

"I don't know. Does it make any difference?"

"Well, now"—he was so blatantly piteous she began to laugh— "a man would like to know things were goin' to go on. It'd be a fine thing to have grandchildren in a frolic around this big place."

"You're about as sentimental as a wolverine." She wiped at her eyes. "I have a real, good picture of you dandling a grandchild on your knees. I'll tell you what I'll do. I'll turn it into a home for unwed mothers. It'll be crawling with kids."

"Sometimes you don't talk nice, Sister." He made the statement with hypocritical piety. "If you're thinkin' how it was when you were young, you've got to remember I was a man well past fifty when you were born. I was set in my ways an' didn't know anything about raisin' a child. I could be a fine grandfather if I had the chance."

"It doesn't look as though you'll get it. If I started today it would still take nine months."

"Then there ain't nothin' for it but for me to go to my grave, like they say, unwept an' unsung." He seemed immensely cheered by the idea. "Hurry back now an' we'll have us a drink before they dish up the chicken. Don't forget the gravy."

She closed the door and went down the long gallery with its gracefully curving staircases winding from each end to the central hall below. In her room she changed her mind about a swim and took a hot bath instead. She ordered lunch on the intra-house telephone to the kitchen and added a salad for herself to the old man's selection.

Standing before a mirror, rubbing herself with thick, soft toweling, she studied the lean strength of her body and the flat muscles of her abdomen. She winked at the reflection in the glass.

"Don't let it go to waste, Sister." The tone was a startling piece of mimicry. It was the old man speaking. "It'd be a sin an' a shame to let it spoil. Use what the Lord give you for the pleasure an' delight of man. It ain't goin' to last forever."

A maid bringing newly cut flowers for a table at the center of the gallery wondered at the whoop of laughter coming from behind the closed door.

II

FROM the center columns of gleaming white the two great wings seemed to hold the structure in flight above the low ridge. Sometimes, in the moonlight or in the early morning when the mist steamed from the river, it appeared to hang suspended in shimmering beauty.

Mark Hillyard could have explained this house to no one; not even to himself. Years before, in his wandering, he had ventured deep within the plantation country of Mississippi. There, all but hidden in a grove of towering, moss-shrouded oaks and magnolias, he had come upon the shell of a manor. Time and the weather had stained it. Lichenous streaks of gray, unhealthy green soiled its pillars and damp rot had eaten at its cypress boards. Empty windows gaped with dark vacancy and enormous vines had writhed upward to hold it in a tangled grasp. In lonely decay it brooded here over what the years had brought. Staring at it, Mark had experienced a strange feeling of excitement and he carried the memory of its ruin with him. Later, when money ceased to be something a man pursued but spilled from the horn of its own accord, he had sent an architect and a photographer into this mosquito-ridden back country. They took a hundred or more pictures, sketched every detail of the abandoned plantation. Here, within the arms of the North and South Anna rivers of Virginia's Piedmont it had been recreated. It was true to the original from mounting stone to the slave quarters stretching in a double line of whitewashed cabins on the edge of the lower fields.

Mark threw himself into the project with the enthusiasm and vigor characteristic of everything he did. It was extravagant, far too large for his needs. There was nothing like it in the county and, probably, not in the State. It was a museum piece, saved from pretentious vulgarity by the sheer beauty and perfection of line. It belonged with the faded gray uniforms folded and packed away in round-topped trunks; the torn battle flags of the Confederacy in glass-fronted cases. To the man it was an expression of permanency. The gypsy strain that had carried him so restlessly up and down the country had run out. He reached back into the earth for roots which were not there.

From five miles away the town of Court House watched the construction with wonder and, in some quarters, condescension. Although the words were not spoken outright, this was Northern, Yankee, money; a rude, abrupt and sometimes angry man attempting to cloak himself in the graciousness of another age. It was even suspected the house was a form of mockery; coarse laughter over a distant glory and shattered tradition.

Court House had yielded little, and reluctantly, to time. It had survived the rigors of colonial days. Its men and boys had fought Indians, the British, the Yankees, the Spaniards and, an ocean away, the Germans. Many of its houses were of mellowed brick brought from England. The Green was as it had been laid out by the original settlers of the Virginia Company two hundred years ago. In places the sidewalks were the worn and sunken cobbles as placed there by forgotten hands. The tavern, reduced in this day of prohibition to near beer and Coca-Cola, carried its name, The Pipe and

Bowl, on an iron-ringed oaken board hung there by its first land-lord. Court House drew its sustenance from the land, the fields, the farms and the forests. Off the main highways which traced the State it moved slowly in its own warm, backwater current. Without too much readjustment it could have returned to the days of barter and survived. It was an elementary tenet that Virginians were in-disputably superior to all Northerners, and those of Court House set apart from other Virginians save, perhaps, a few families in Richmond. Its young persons grew up in the comfortable and re-assuring intimacy of a town where everyone knew everyone else. They went to the public grammar and high school and attended each other's birthday parties and weddings. Some of the boys went on to VMI or Charlottesville, whose University of Virginia was spoken of as *The University*, in italics, and no Virginian could possibly misunderstand or confuse it with any other institution. Most of them returned to the businesses or professions of their fathers. A few went to New York, or worse still, to Chicago, and they were quietly mourned. Some of the girls attended Mary Baldwin or Stuart Hall, in Staunton. They came back to marry and raise their children in the warm friendliness of the town they had always known. It was a community of soft and pleasant speech, of easy, sun-drenched tempo, good manners and a graciousness surviving in subdued pride. A few innovations were unavoidable. Rotary, Kiwanis and Lions made alternate Tuesdays, Thursdays and Fridays boisterous with their luncheons. A country club with eighteen holes of fairways, greens and traps became a social center formally dictated by the Daughters of the American Revolution and the Daughters of the Confederacy. Parking meters sprouted where hitching rails once stood and asphalt covered the ruts worn by farmers' carts.

Mark Hillyard had been a shock. If Court House didn't recoil, it at least braced itself. He came as an alien wind, sharp and tem-pestuous. Few persons had ever heard his name before, since the man wasn't given to the philanthropies recorded in newspapers or the extravagant splurges that caught public attention. Charles Porter, president of the Colonial Court House Bank, knew of him and from there the word was quietly spread that a great fortune was repre-sented by the gaunt, questing figure. The first knowledge Court House had of his presence was the sale of a large tract along the river. Real estate didn't change hands often here. Then Mark Hill-yard began buying up smaller pieces until he acquired almost six hundred acres. He was no profligate spender but bargained and haggled to the final dollar. He was an impatient man of no particular charm and made no attempt to ingratiate himself or become a part of the community. No one in Court House actually disliked him but no one liked him either. When he started building, a small flood of dollars was loosed upon the local contractors, skilled and unskilled labor. He became a one-man wave of unexpected prosperity. As the masons, carpenters and laborers spread the word as to the size of the manor slowly taking shape, local astonishment lapped over into adjoining counties. In the bank one day Charles Porter left his desk behind the low railing and walked to where Mark Hillyard was writing out a check. He attempted a few pleasant words with the institution's largest depositor.

"Everyone's wondering what you're going to do with a house that size, Mr. Hillyard." It was part question, part statement.

Mark scrawled his signature without looking up. "Tell the damn fools I'm goin' to live in it." He stamped away to the teller's window.

Hillyard was away for months at a time, leaving everything in the hands of his construction superintendent. When he returned he went over every foot of the work with a microscopic attention to detail. From old and impoverished estates he purchased fully matured hedges of boxwood and they came to Court House wrapped in burlap, their roots in the original soil. The formal gardens were laid out by professional landscapers and took on the appearance of great age. Crape myrtle flamed and spread. Oak and maple trees threw their shade over the dogwood and dwarf white cedars. What wasn't on the land or wouldn't grow and thrive quickly was imported from older beds to take root. The house and the land took form beneath Hillyard's driving hand and on Sundays the more openly curious drove out from Court House to stand and gaze in silent wonder. In all things, save in the matter of the slave quarters, Mark Hillyard was confident. He stubbornly refused to alter the architect's plans and the cabins rose in a neat whitewashed line, but Mark displayed an impatient embarrassment with their building. He finally pretended they weren't there, or if they were, he had no idea of their original purpose. A corps of painters, finishers and decorators followed the building crew and in the year of 1928 the house was completed. It rose in grace and dignity as though it had occupied this site for a century.

Carol, at their own rough guess, was nineteen and it was the spring of her being graduated from Miss Parkinson's Academy for Young Ladies, at Tarrytown, New York.

With the other parents, none of whom he knew, Mark sat stiffly and uncomfortably on a hard bench beneath the trees at the outdoor ceremony. He hardly recognized as his daughter the blond girl who walked with poised beauty in gray cap and gown to receive her diploma. There had been little contact between them. Aunt Julia had timorously accepted an apartment at the Plaza Hotel, in the city, and there Carol had come for the holidays, spring and summer vacation, during her first year at school. Later she made friends and spent most of her summers with them at their homes on Long Island or Westchester.

After the graduation exercises Mark and Carol were driven back to the city in a cream-colored Lincoln with red Morocco leather upholstery and a Negro chauffeur. They were silent, ill at ease as strangers might be when thrown together in limited space. They were not quite sure they liked each other. Small, inconsequential talk was made and answers carefully given. She and Aunt Julia were sailing for Europe at the end of the week. The subject was quickly exhausted since Mark had little interest in, and less knowledge of, the Continent. Each stared fixedly out of his and her side of the car, then Mark reached across and took her hand. She glanced up quickly, surprised. He smiled and it was an expression difficult to resist. In it were shyness, embarrassment and pleasure.

"We're not gettin' along very well, are we, Sister?" He had always called her that, never Carol. "I mean, here you are grown up, a young lady, an' I don't know how I should do with you. It would be a hell of a time for me to begin actin' like a parent. You want to be friends?"

She studied him gravely, understanding he was honestly offering her a choice and not pressing her into a corner.

"It'll be a lot easier if we are," he continued slowly, searching for the thought and the words with which to express it. "I suppose we could get along, sort of putting up with each other if that's the way it is goin' to be. Either way you decide, it ain't goin' to be easy at first."

"You ought to stop saying ain't." There was subdued laughter behind her eyes. "It ain't elegant. Elegant is a real elegant word, don't you think?" Her fingers suddenly twined with his. "Friends." She made the statement with simple directness.

25

"That suits me fine, Sister." He sighed his relief and lit a cigar, relaxing. "You know there really ain't any reason why children should love their parents or parents their children. There are bound to be things on both sides the other isn't ever goin' to like. About the best you ought to expect is some give an' take on both sides."

"Then you should have asked me first if I wanted to go abroad with Aunt Julia." The challenge was delivered coolly.

He mulled this over and then nodded. "I guess you got somethin' there. I figured Europe was a proper finishin' off for a finishin' school. Maybe I should have asked you."

"If we are going to be friends, that is how it ought to be. I won't ever take you for granted and you'll be the same way with me. I have as much right to my privacy, opinions, likes and dislikes as you." She wasn't being unpleasant. This was a fair exchange which she expected him to understand.

There were a few moments of silence before he spoke again. What she said was reasonable and right.

"I've built a place down in Virginia, Sister. When you get back from Europe, I hope you'll come down an' look at it. What I'm tryin' to say is I hope you'll like it well enough to live there with me."

"I'd like a home, Mark. That was the hard part about school in the beginning. All the other girls had homes. They had families and ties. At first I made up stories about my family and where we lived. After I'd been there a year or so I learned enough not to give a damn. I told them the truth. My father was a wool-eared, wild-eyed promoter, a wildcatter who used a cave for a home. It gave me a certain status for a while until some of the girls mentioned your name to their fathers. It seems you're pretty well known as a shrewd and unscrupulous sonofabitch. But," she held back a grin at the astonishment on his face, "since their fathers are also shrewd and unscrupulous sons of bitches in Wall Street, real estate, Mexico and South America, there was a common bond of respect sons of bitches bear for each other."

Mark reached forward and cranked up a glass partition between them and the chauffeur.

"Did they learn you to talk that way at school?"

She nodded calmly, took a package of cigarettes from her purse lit one and inhaled with obvious pleasure while he gawked.

26

"It wasn't included in the curriculum but the pupils introduced it among themselves."

"The only women I know who smoke cigarettes are whores."

"That was another thing." She inclined her head with agreement. "Most of the women I knew, the ones you were always bringing home, were whores. It gave me quite an advantage in the whispered conversations when the lights were out. I always had an audience and was considered an authority on the subject of S-E-X, if you know what I mean. Never underestimate the curiosity of a child. I used to peek through the keyhole."

"The hell you did?" He rubbed at his mouth with bony knuckles. "I was a randy dandy in those days, Sister." He made the statement proudly. "Do all the girls your age talk and act the way you do?" He was doubtful still of the cigarette.

"Few of them have had my advantages." She winked at him and they both laughed quietly and with understanding. She linked her arm with his. "Tell me about the place in Virginia."

"It's somethin' to see. It's the most beautiful goddamned house in the world, I expect. It's got a yard bigger'n a cemetery an' looks over a river called the North Anna. Ain't that a hell of a name? The town nearby is Court House an' the nearest city is Richmond, if you don't want to count Washington." He paused almost hopefully. "You could come right down now an' forget about Europe if you want."

"No-o-o!" She spoke thoughtfully. "I really want to go but I would have picked a better traveling companion than Aunt Julia. She isn't exactly lively."

"I figured for her to take care of you but it looks like it'll be the other way 'round."

With Julia in a flutter of apprehension, clutching her passport and guidebooks as though they were a breviary, they sailed for Southampton on the *Aquitania*. Julia regarded the ocean crossing as only slightly less adventurous than a trip to the moon. She was convinced the extravagant letter of credit would prove to be valueless when presented and the book of traveler's checks worthless slips of paper. She searched vainly for prices opposite the selections on the menu and wondered audibly how they could give all that food away.

Carol found her own companions, friends of friends, acquaintances of schoolmates. She danced and necked enthusiastically with a sophomore from Princeton and restrained him from further adventuring because there was "no real good place." This shocked the youth so that he regarded her warily for the rest of the trip.

After London came Paris, and Carol decided the only way she was going to have any fun was to be firm with Aunt Julia. In the everyday courtesies of the French, Julia saw sinister plots of white slavers to spirit Carol and her into a life of shame. The French were notoriously loose and decadent and she broke into tears when her niece joined a tourist party bent upon seeing the night life of Paris. Carol was frankly bored by the excursion. She had seen more through the keyhole of Mark's bedroom door.

Through the American Express they rented a Renault and engaged a chauffeur, a sleekly dark and handsome man with a fine mustache and roving eye. With chauffeur and maid and Mark's unlimited letter of credit they toured Spain, Italy, the provinces of France. Throughout the trip the chauffeur indulged himself, as only a Frenchman can, in airy and fanciful flights of amour with the daughter of an American millionaire. He would charm and captivate her with Gallic fervor. She would succumb to his limpid eye and gallantry and then, his complete slave, they would spend Papa's millions. He raced to her bidding but performed the services with the dignity of a man. None of this was lost on Carol. In Normandy she permitted him to believe he had at last seduced her. He smelled of pomade, cologne and cheap wine and during the act called her names which were never included in *French I & II* at Miss Parkinson's. She discharged him in the morning with a balm of five hundred dollars in American money. In a fury of humiliation and frustration he spat at her feet, but not until he had pocketed the ten thousand or so francs.

Aunt Julia whimpered and pulled at a handkerchief, moaning they would be lost in this inexplicable country without a chauffeur and tearfully wanting to know why Carol had dismissed him.

"He was," Carol told her, "inadequate." She left the woman to puzzle this out as best she could and drove the Renault herself back to Paris and without incident.

They returned to New York on the *Île de France*. During the summer she had made no attempt to correspond with Mark. He, in turn, contented himself with a cable now and then in care of the American Express Company. In them he hoped they were having a good time.

The months abroad had given Carol a new maturity. Where,

before, a natural reserve had concealed the small indecisions, the panicked flights in fear of doing or saying the wrong thing, she now drew upon an unsuspected source of self-confidence. She had learned what a magic key money was to most doors. She had discovered people liked her and a small amount of calculated charm dissolved the barriers of language, customs and inbred caution. With a keen ear and a talent for mimicry, she had picked up the idiom of at least three languages. She no longer wondered if strangers would like her. Instead she coolly appraised them and made her selection.

Mark met them in Richmond with a car and they drove to Court House instead of taking the spur line. The great, free sweep of the Virginia countryside excited her after the neatly clipped divisions of France. She felt at home.

"I don't know what made you pick Virginia," she told Mark, "but it was a good idea. I'm glad to be home."

"You look different somehow, Sister." He had been studying her. "Maybe it's them French clothes. It hardly seems possible that you could'a grown up so in a few months." He turned to Julia who sat between them, chubby arms crossed contentedly over her bosom, beaming happily. "I hope you didn't give Sister any trouble, Julia," he said seriously. "A middle-aged woman like yourself is bound to get herself undone with them hand-kissin' Frenchmen."

"Ask her why she fired the chauffeur." Julia had been struggling with this for weeks and had arrived at a complacent conclusion.

"I told you," Carol interposed sweetly. "He was inadequate."

Julia sniffed. She had her own opinion as to what had happened. "Just to be sure," she said, "I looked that up in the dictionary. It means deficient and not inefficient, like you expected me to believe. The sins of the fathers," she intoned dolefully.

"What the hell you talkin' about, Julia?" Mark was mystified.

"She's trying to tell you I had an affair with the chauffeur."

Julia squeaked her outrage and Mark studied the etched profile of his daughter. The wind caught at her hair, throwing small strands back and giving her face the appearance of racing eagerness. She was a classical figurehead on a clipper ship.

"Well"—he moved cautiously—"did you, Sister?"

"Did I what?"

"Did you get yourself laid by a French chauffeur?" He was angry.

"That's none of your damn business." She regarded him evenly for a moment.

There was only the singing of the tires, the muffled beat of the engine. Carol rested her head against the cushion and stared at the great marshmallow clouds. Mark chewed pensively at a corner of his lower lip.

"Sister?"

"What?"

"You're damn right it ain't."

They looked at each other and laughed quietly and with complete understanding.

As the car traveled down Gloucester Street, in Court House, Carol sat up and looked about with interest. The patina of time was unmistakable. The sun broke through the massed leaves of the rows of trees to mint golden sovereigns on ancient brick and stone. There was a fresh softness in the air and the bloom of late summer on hollyhocks and trailing fences of Cherokee rose. As they drove slowly she could read the names lettered on the curbs at intersections. Queen Anne. Suffolk. Dorchester. Essex. There was a pattern of leisurely well-being. A jaunting cart, with a young girl driving, didn't seem out of place at it spanked brightly past rows of parked cars, and in the business district the A & P had yielded and subdued the traditional garish red and gold of its front. She could feel the subdued pride of those who lived in this town. It was reflected in the easy lifting of a hat in greeting or an unhurried halt in the middle of the street to exchange a pleasant comment on the weather.

She looked at her father, wondering how he had come upon this place and of the unsuspected longing for permanency and order that had made him select it for his own.

"It's shook 'em up some here," he broke in upon her musing.

"What?"

"The place I built. They don't know what to make of it. Sometimes," he confessed with a quick grin, "I don't either." He chewed thoughtfully on a cigar. "It's hard to believe but they still sort of fight the war here, in their minds at least. They talk about Yankees as though they really were a kind of breed, set apart. They figure I'm upstart, Yankee money makin' a splurge. It ain't decent, the way they look at it. Of course, nobody's come out an' said such a thing."

The miles passed swiftly beneath the wheels and then the car swung left from the highway to move along an unpaved road through a tangle of oak and beech, locust and redbud with scarlet

30

berries sparkling in the scrub. The landscapers had wisely left this section untouched. When the drive curved out of the woods the broad, formal gardens and the manor broke upon the eyes in a gracious picture, startling because it was so unexpected.

Carol stood up in the car when it drew before the entrance and looked around with astonishment.

"It gives you kind of a feelin', don't it?" Mark waited for her to speak.

"If somebody rides up and says Jeff Davis is calling for volunteers, I'm not going to be at all surprised." She dropped to the ground, mounted the broad sweep of steps to the porch and looked out over the river. "What time do we go down to beat the slaves?" she called to him as he followed with Julia.

"It's against the law." He was panting a little from the exertion when he joined her. "You know somethin', Sister? Down back of the place, where you can't see 'em from here, there's the slave quarters like they used to be. I got a feelin', sometimes, to move in some colored families, rent free, just to see them around. Now," he took her arm, "you're old enough to take a drink with me. I been waitin' a long time for that. Let's get to it an' then you can say whether you like the place enough to stay."

Arm in arm, with Julia plodding heavily behind them, they entered the empty, waiting house.

III

IF Mark Hillyard had jolted Court House, rocking it out of a placid orbit, Carol first stunned the community and then swept it with honest and appreciative laughter. In it most of the resentment the man's impatience and rudeness had caused was buried for all time.

On the day after her arrival she drove into town, stopped at Denton Brothers long enough to order herself a blue convertible and make an inquiry as to the nearest lumberyard. When she left, Horace Denton stood at the window and looked admiringly after her, never questioning her authority to make the purchase of a five-thousand-dollar car.

At the lumberyard John Mayberry filled his pipe with rough

strands of tobacco, glancing over it to the girl who sat on a corner of his desk swinging a long, bare leg casually while she told him what she wanted. She took a pencil from a cluster in an old jelly glass and made a quick rough sketch on a pad, handing it to him with a quick grin of conspiratorial mischief.

"I can have it done for you"—Mayberry studied the preposterous drawing—"but somebody better leave town afterwards. I have a feeling I'm the one. That old man of yours is likely to tear up this yard and its been in the family for a long time. We'd hate to lose it."

She slid from the table and he walked with her to the car. This, he thought, was the damnedest thing he had ever heard of, but it was worth getting into trouble for. The warm sun splashed around them and the stacked lumber filled the yard with the aromatic perfume of pine in the day's heat. He closed the car's door after she had slid into the seat and stood, half leaning through the open window. Her eyes were bright with suppressed laughter.

"Will you get started on it right away?"

He nodded, reluctant to have her leave. "I'll have some men and the material out this afternoon. You'd better keep your old man in the house for a couple of days though."

She flipped a hand in good-by and he stood watching until the car crossed the railroad tracks and made a turn on Gloucester Street. He shook his head and wondered why he had agreed to do the job. There was no telling how old Hillyard would react and it wouldn't do any good to say he had just taken a job and followed orders.

At the intersection of the main highway and the road leading to the manor the sign went up quickly. The carpenters and painters, having had experience with Hillyard's temper, wanted to get finished and away.What they had erected was a billboard some sixty feet long and twelve feet high. At the top a red arrow pointed to the winding road. Below this in bright and eye-compelling paint was lettered:

HOORAH PLANTATION
See The Old Slave Quarters
Watch the Pickaninnies at Play
Listen to Old Black Joe on the Banjo
Eat Watermelon and Chitlins
M. HILLYARD—*Overseer*

Mark, on one of his rare excursions of inspection beyond the house and gardens, had come upon the sign just as the painters were stacking their gear in a truck. At the roar of outrage they had dropped buckets and brushes and run, scrambling for a place as the truck lurched away. Incredulous at what he saw, the man backed off and reread the still-wet lettering. Then he sat down on a fallen log and began to laugh. The chauffeur, waiting in the car, eyed him apprehensively as he trumpeted into a handkerchief and wiped at the tears between uncontrollable whoops of choking laughter. That Sister was the damnedest girl a man had ever whelped. This was the kind of thing he would have done himself if he'd thought of it. He watched with sly interest as a car on the highway drew to a slow halt, the occupants stretching their necks from the windows to read the sign. Even from this distance he could see their exchange of puzzled glances as they repeated the words, not knowing whether to laugh or believe what the sign said. Finally, with a shaking of heads, they drove away to spread the word of what they had seen and to speculate on the crazy people who must live up that country road.

He never gave Carol the satisfaction of appearing to know of the billboard's existence. Even when they were in a car together and came to the intersection he managed an airy unconcern, pretending an interest in another section of the countryside. Now and then, though, she caught him watching her with a bright gleam of interest in his eyes and his mouth twisted with stifled mirth. It became a customary morning's diversion for him to be driven to the intersection and sit there, half concealed behind a bend in the road, watching the cars of tourists as they braked to a halt while the occupants wonderingly read the sign aloud and debated a side trip to "Hoorah Plantation."

The effect of the billboard on Court House was surprising. Until its appearance Mark Hillyard and what he had built were regarded with an insular disapproval. He was rude and the manor ostentatious. It was vulgar Yankee showing-off. Now, though, there was a subtle change. A man and his daughter who could laugh at themselves in such a gusty fashion were worth knowing. Strangers smiled at Carol on the streets. Girls she had never met waved a casual hand when their cars passed. Although he pretended not to notice—and if he did, not to give a damn—Mark was not insensible to this social thaw. He even unbent a little himself, although he was a man of few social graces. An invitation to join the country club was delivered by hand to the manor, and Charles Porter asked him back to the paneled room in the bank for a drink.

They finally had to have the billboard wrecked. Too many strangers and tourists took it literally and came wandering up the road, not quite knowing what to expect but eager to see and be entertained. From behind a curtained window Mark would watch their perplexity and indecision with a gleam in his eye. When they began breaking off the plants and bushes to carry away as souvenirs he finally, even reluctantly, ordered the sign broken up.

"It was a real funny caper, Sister." He stood above her where she lay on a pallet by the pool. "But it's got to go. They're tramplin' the hell out of the place."

"You mean them Yankees?" Her expression was innocent.

He grunted and dropped into a chair beside her. She didn't, he thought wonderingly, have much more on than a diaper an' a little titty rag. "You got hips like a boy," he mused irrelevantly and knuckled his nose. "But I'd say that's about the only point of resemblance." He whistled vacantly. "You know anything about horses, Sister?"

She had become accustomed to his speaking in rambling, disconnected sentences. Some of the things he said required an answer. Others were simply statements made as they occurred to him. The question about horses needed no reply. It was merely a prelude to something he had in mind. She plucked a long blade of grass and nibbled on it.

"There ain't a chance in the world," he continued seriously, "of our roundin' up any slaves to put in them cabins but we could get some horses for the stables to sort of fill out things." He stared at the pool as a light breeze scampered across its surface. "When I was a young buster ladies all rode side saddle. Ladies didn't have any crotches in those days. It's a miracle they ever got knocked up."

She rolled on her back and yelled with laughter while he stared at her with a puzzled frown.

"What the hell's funny about that, Sister?"

She shook her head, refusing to look at him. This was the damnedest old man a girl could ever have as a father.

"I read in the paper. There's a fair in Wayne County. Along with a lot of other things they sell stock—pigs, cattle, horses. We could drive over an' look around, just the two of us."

She stood up, tugging on a tight bathing cap. "I'd like that. We

35

could pack some lunch and a jug. Take our time. Come back whenever we feel like it."

She dove from the edge of the pool in a tight arc. He watched with open pride as she came up in the center with the easy movement of a porpoise rising. She was a pretty one. Pretty and sharp. There was an edge to her, keen as a honed blade. Secretly he wondered how he could have produced this blooded stock.

"When do you want to leave?" She swam toward him and climbed up to pull the cap away and shake out her hair.

"In the mornin'. You see to things."

In the bright haze of a late summer's morning they drove through the countryside where the fields had yellowed and lay bare, waiting for the fall. The far-distant horizon was smudged where the mountains rose, and reed birds scattered from the ground like thrown shot, to settle and disappear after the car had passed.

On the seat between them was a large wicker picnic hamper. From it Mark drew a bottle of rye, swallowed a mouthful and stamped the cork back with the heel of his hand.

"You know, Sister," he brooded, "I've about come to the end of my string."

She didn't turn from her driving. "You look healthy enough to me."

"I don't mean it that way. I got some years to go yet, I guess. There ain't much left for me to do. I made more money than you an' I can ever spend. This country is in for one hell of a big bust. It's bloated up like a sick pig, filled with gas an' ready to pop. I been liquidatin' a lot of stuff. When the panic comes, if I ain't around, you step into the market with ready cash an' buy up the blue-chip stuff—things like A. T. & T., Standard Oil, public utilities, DuPont. Things the country can't get along without no matter how much jumpin' off the roof they do in Wall Street. You hang on to them for the long pull. I hope I'm here for that. I surely do. The way I got things arranged now, they sort of run themselves. There ain't no excitement left like there was when I woke up every mornin' lookin' for somethin' to claw."

"Why don't you get yourself a woman?" She glanced at him.

"I'll swear to God, Sister, you don't talk nice." He sucked at a tooth. "Anyhow, I ain't got the juice left to be servicin' no woman. I'm dried up like an old persimmon. I don't even think about it no

36

more." The thought depressed him. He peered bleakly at the rolling land. "You got to meet Jim Haney." He was off again on a sudden tangent.

"Who's Jim Haney?"

"Jim's kinda like a general manager who keeps an eye on all the goods I collected. He bought me a newspaper out in San Francisco last week."

She was surprised, lifting her foot from the accelerator. As the car slowed she turned her attention from the road. Of all the things this man might be interested in, a newspaper, she thought, would be the last.

"What in the world are you doing with a newspaper?"

"Lettin' other men run it. Them." He amended the statement. "I own three: one in Cincinnati, one in Charlotte an' this one in San Francisco. We write 'em off as tax losses."

This astonished her further. She didn't think it was like Mark Hillyard to hang on to properties that didn't show a profit. Newspapers. She felt a stirring of interest and touched the gas pedal with her toe.

"Why don't they show a profit, the papers?"

"I expect because they ain't run right." He wasn't concerned. "Like I said, we use them for tax write-offs. I figure to get me some fine obituaries when I die. In three places anyhow."

They covered some twenty-five miles before either spoke again. Mark, his eyes half closed, leaned his head against the soft leather cushion. He was satisfied with this girl. Without effort they had reached an understanding. He wondered some about her; the way she talked, saying things you wouldn't expect. He'd read a lot about this young generation. They helled around in their automobiles, drinking bootleg whisky out of flasks at football games. They screwed, or so everyone said, like wild rabbits. Maybe she did too. It wasn't a thing a man asked his daughter. He really didn't know a lot about Sister—what she thought, what she liked, how she felt about things. He had an idea that behind a bright serenity lay a metallic vein, a rocklike core. That's what you had to have to get along in this world. People might not always like you for it but, by God, they tipped their hats and stood to one side when you passed.

"You know," she spoke abruptly, "I'd like that."

"What?"

"To run a newspaper. To take one that didn't amount to anything,

37

build it up, make it important; a big voice to yell with when there were things to yell about."

"There's always somethin' for someone to yell about." He was unimpressed. "An' usually someone to do the yellin'. All they get is a sore throat."

"Maybe after you're dead I'll take one over." Her mouth twitched.

He snapped upright in the seat and stared at her. "For God's sake, Sister. Is that any way for a girl to talk about her blood kin father?" He reflected moodily on this for a moment. "Anyhow, who the hell ever heard of a girl runnin' a newspaper?" He was relieved by the obviousness of this statement, since it also negated the idea of his dying. "I'm gettin' hungry. Let's pull off the road somewhere an' eat."

The fair was an annual event held on the rolling acres of the Harkness farm. It was strictly local in character, not listed on the State or County's calendars. It was a small social affair, drawing families and friends of close ties and long standing. To it came the county's gentry, the horsy set from as far away as Warrenton, the well-bred and well-to-do. The gathering was listed in the society pages and never in the news columns. They held a steeplechase and a judging show, stood about in easy groups to trade breeding lore and studbook statistics. There was a hunt and a barbecue and an outdoor dance on a platform set up for the occasion. The families who gathered here each year were interlocked by marriage and distant kinship. The fair offered a pleasant reason for getting together. To it they brought their horses, their boars and sows, their prize bulls for judging. A Harkness, the senior of the family, always made the awards. Now and then sales were made but usually to friends, relatives and neighbors. Uninvited visitors were rare but not unwelcome. Pavilions of brightly striped awning were set up and some of the guests brought their servants. They visited back and forth, sampling each other's whisky and hard cider, exchanging gossip and recipes, cuttings and seedlings. It was a pleasant custom, an institution of over a hundred years' standing, interrupted by the years of 1861 to 1865 when the men were busy at Manassas, Fredricksburg, The Wilderness, Cold Harbor and Petersburg.

Carol turned the car in at the open gates. At the end of a long, graveled road some three-quarters of a mile away they could see the low, gabled outline of the Harkness house. At the left of the whitewashed stables she could make out the parked cars and the canvas of the tents.

"Are you sure this is a public fair?" She turned to Mark.

"Said so. Read it in a paper. Forget where. What's the difference? If we ain't wanted they'll let us know." He tilted a floppy Panama hat down to shield a sunburned nose. The food and whisky of a roadside lunch had made him sleepy. "After all, we only want to buy some horses. Never seen a fair without a Ferris wheel, though."

Carol eased into a slot between the parked cars and slid up from the seat to sit on the folded top with a view of the leisurely scene in the meadow below. A man turned from closing the trunk compartment of a nearby roadster. She smiled at him almost questioningly.

"Hello."

"Good afternoon." The voice was softly accented, courteous and a little inquiring. He slammed down the lid and walked toward them. "May I help you?" The word, Carol thought, was almost "hep" but not quite.

Mark pushed away his hat. "Want to buy some horses." He whistled between his teeth, eying the man suspiciously. Good-looking men, particularly when he was on strange ground, aroused a small antagonism in him. This one was tall with an easy stride and manner in faded corduroy slacks and a tweed jacket with leather patches at the elbows. He was young but a little gray where the hair was the color of burnt gunpowder. "Read they were sellin' some here," he added.

"Any particular kind of horses?" John Harkness glanced at Carol but the question was directed to the man.

"I'm Carol Hillyard." She extended her hand. "This is my father. Don't pay any attention to him. He likes to have people think he's woolly and homespun. He's an old fraud."

The old man grunted but brightened a little.

"I'm John Harkness." The handclasp was firm, decisive but friendly.

"Got some stables I want to fill up." There was a rakish gleam in the old man's eyes now. That ought to fix him.

"That isn't much of a reason for buying horses, Mr. Hillyard." John Harkness leaned on the car's door. "I wouldn't sell you any just to fill up the stalls."

"The hell you wouldn't?" The old man was agreeably astonished.

"The hell I wouldn't." Harkness was amiable but firm.

39

"Good." Carol slid to the ground to stand beside Harkness. She was tall but her head just reached his shoulder. "I ride pretty well if that is any help."

"It's a start." He was pleasantly reserved with her but continued to regard Mark with tight speculation.

Inwardly the old man chuckled. The young fellow was mad. He liked to dicker with any angry man. His mind was never on his business. He was too busy being sore. He took off his hat, leaned back and stared blandly at the sky.

Suddenly Harkness laughed and relaxed. He turned to Carol. "I think you're right. He's an old fraud. It's late, but would you like some lunch? The barbecue was pretty good this year."

"We ate on our way down." She reached for a cigarette and he struck a match for her quickly.

"Let's walk over to the stables then. I have a chestnut filly with a lot of spirit but good manners." He smiled at her. "The two of you ought to get along just fine."

"Coming, Mark?"

The old man shook his head. It wasn't going to be any fun, no real dealing. Sister was softening him up already. Hell, he'd like enough give the animal away if she really went to work on him.

"I'm going to take a nap. That cold chicken made me sleepy. You look around an' pick out what you want." Almost as an afterthought he added slyly, "If he don't want to sell, we'll go some place else. The country's full of horses."

"And horses' asses." She was angry with him for the first time. Turning to Harkness, "That didn't slip out either, Mr. Harkness. I meant to say it. You'll have to excuse us both."

"The same thought had occurred to me, Miss Hillyard." He reached in his coat for a pipe. "If you hadn't said it I would."

The old man actually smirked as he fitted his back into a corner of the seat.

They walked together toward the stables. In the meadow some of the tents were coming down, collapsing like spent balloons into untidy mounds.

"This is the last day." He saw her glance. "You should have come earlier in the week. We don't get many outsiders." He apologized quickly. "I didn't mean that the way it sounded." He packed roughly cut tobacco into his pipe and lit it.

She liked his voice and easy manner. He carried with him the not unpleasant smell of horses and freshly cut hay warming in the sun.

"How well do you ride?" He drew on the pipe and it fired quickly.

"A little better than fair."

He nodded gravely. "I like to know where my animals go. Maybe that's why Harkness isn't as successful as it should be. Sentiment on a breeding farm can be expensive."

They moved beneath an overhang. A couple of Negro boys looked up from the tack they were working over with saddle soap and smiled shyly. Here and there a sleek head was thrust out over a half-door of the stalls at the sound of a familiar step and voice. Harkness slid his hand along a velvet muzzle as a man might caress a woman he loved. He opened the gate and led the filly out. Light danced on her coat as a nervous tremor rippled over the burnished flank.

"She's a dancing lady." There was rich affection in his voice. "You and my wife are about the same size. She could let you have some riding things."

Carol shook her head. "I don't think you would sell anyone a bad horse, Mr. Harkness. I'd like to have her."

There was a faintly quizzical smile about the crinkles of his eyes. "You're not much of a horse trader, are you? Wouldn't you like to know how much I want for her?"

"Let's be vulgar and say it doesn't make any difference." She smiled. "Could you send or bring her to Court House?"

"Oh!" The surprise was unmistakable. "You're *that* Hillyard."

"What's that supposed to mean?" There was a faint edge to the question. She turned to face him.

He wasn't embarrassed. "Nothing. Just that I have heard of your father. I guess everyone in the county has." He let one of the stable-boys lead the filly back into her stall.

"You needn't make it sound like a dirty word, the name."

"As a matter of fact," they began retracing their steps, "I not only heard about your father but the daughter as well. It seems you had a sign put up." He chuckled quietly.

"It was a thing," she admitted proudly. "It was a real, sure enough thing." She caught herself in the act of taking his arm and frowned. Why did she want to touch him? The idea was oddly exciting. She could feel it somewhere in the pit of her stomach. With an effort she put the thought aside. "We had to take it down." She fought to keep

41

her tone normal. "There are too many literal-minded people in the world."

"John."

They halted at the sound of the voice and turned.

There was a dark and vivid beauty about the woman who came toward them. She was in jodhpurs and walked with a free, swinging stride of animal litheness. There was a rich ripeness in her body and watching her, Carol felt immature and almost skinny.

"The Parkhouses are leaving," she called while still a few yards away. "Do you want to say good-by?" She joined them and her quick glance covered Carol.

"Martha, this is Carol Hillyard. Miss Hillyard, my wife."

"How do you do?" She smiled but did not offer her hand. Carol would have sworn that for some reason there was a tiny glint of amusement in her eyes. She turned to her husband. "They decided to go back tonight instead of staying over."

"Miss Hillyard is buying Black Dancer."

"Oh!" The dark eyes again swept over Carol, this time with more interest. "I wish we could keep her." She pushed jet hair away from her forehead with the back of a hand. "If John and I weren't scratching for feed I'd never let an animal go. But then," she concluded brightly, "we'd be up to our ass in horses, wouldn't we?"

It was a crude and unnecessary flippancy and Carol wondered why. It also shocked her a little because she felt the vulgarity was contrived and spoken for her benefit. She was puzzled. The word in itself meant nothing. She had used it herself only a few minutes before in speaking to Mark. It was as though Martha Harkness had sensed something and was saying: See, I can meet you on your own level if I have to.

They walked toward the Hillyard car. Mark was brightly awake. He was even politely interested in Martha Harkness when Carol introduced him.

"Find what you wanted, Sister?"

"Yes. Mr. Harkness is sending her or," she turned with open inquiry, "bringing her tomorrow."

"I'll bring her."

Carol caught the momentary surprise in Martha's expression and had the feeling John Harkness didn't usually deliver in person the horses he sold. She nodded and slid into the seat beside Mark, starting the engine. Her last impression as she swung the car out of the parking space was of John and Martha standing, their arms about each other's waist, watching them drive away.

As the car disappeared down the driveway Martha Harkness glanced up at her husband.

"I think I ought to go with you tomorrow."

"Why not, if you'd like to." His arm dropped away.

She shook her head. "No. I was only joking. But you be careful of that one, Johnny-Boy. She's a man-eater."

He slapped her on the bottom with easy, good-humored affection. "She's only a youngster, eighteen, nineteen."

"That's more than old enough, in case you don't remember." She cocked her head a little to one side. "You know I'm intuitive about such things."

"You're a suspicious old hag." He took her hand. "She's a child."

"A baby shark is still a shark, Johnny, and you can lose a hand pretending it's a fan-tailed goldfish. Now, let's say good-by to the Parkhouse gang. I'm glad this is over."

Now and then Mark glanced from the corner of his eye at Carol. The car streaked down the broad, empty highway and she was driving faster than usual. In profile her face was a mask, hiding her thoughts behind a chiseled perfection. Then her foot eased on the gas pedal and the needle on the speedometer dropped back until it settled on an easy forty.

"What made you so mad, Sister? That black-haired woman?"

She was almost startled by the man's acute perception of her mood. He was sharper than she had thought or she was obvious.

"Did it show?"

"The hair on your back was bristling." He laughed dryly. "An' that fellow didn't even know what was goin' on." There was a moment's silence. "He's too old for you, Sister, an' married to boot."

"That never stopped you, did it?" Without taking her eyes from the road she fumbled in her purse on the seat for a cigarette. After she replaced the dash lighter, she exhaled. "You don't happen to have a stud farm along with all the other goods you've collected?"

He snickered. "That there's a department I always took care of personally."

"From what was said, the Harkness place is having money trouble."

43

He whistled without melody. "Sister," the word came softly, "there are cheaper ways of gettin' a man than that."

Her foot slammed down on the accelerator and the car leaped forward, throwing back into his teeth whatever else he might have been going to say.

IV

AT THE intersection, where the road into the Hillyard place swung off from the highway, John Harkness drew up on the shoulder and turned to look back at the trailer. From within the padded compartment Black Dancer's head lifted, her ears snapped nervously as she nickered a question.

He had been late getting away from the farm and a balky engine in the old convertible he drove had delayed him. He was hot, irritable and, having come this far, was not sure now that he wanted to sell the filly. There was no question about the need. He and Martha were being pressed from a dozen directions. Small debts had unaccountably grown into larger ones and their credit was strained. Even the fact that they were dealing with a Harkness no longer stayed the merchants from writing coldly polite letters demanding payment. The inescapable fact was, he thought wearily, he had failed at running Harkness Farms. The land lay as it had for a couple of hundred years in Harkness hands but he had been unable to wring a living from it as had sturdier forebears. He turned the motor off to let it cool and leaned back to catch a small breeze within the trees' shade.

The horse, he mused gloomily, in a mechanized age was threatened with extinction. It would go with the mastodon. In the dizzy wave which swept the country, people bought automobiles and stocks on margin. He had failed to breed an outstanding colt for racing. His hunters were sound, but half a dozen farms in Warren County did better. He wondered why he had been so relentlessly unsuccessful. To make things worse, he had waded timorously into the current of speculation which raced out of Wall Street. Everyone, or so he had heard, was making spectacular profits. They talked knowingly of mergers, new highs, stock splits. Instead of going to a reputable broker for advice he had listened to a friend and bought heavily into a Brazilian diamond mine venture, the stock of which seemed to sink lower with the digging. Now, he was pinched and apprehensive. The sale of Black Dancer was only a short breather.

He whistled with moody tunelessness. The annual fair at Harkness, instead of being a small source of income, was an unbearable expense. The master of Harkness was supposed to provide a full measure of traditional hospitality. Old friends and relatives must be quartered and fed. The hunt breakfast was a custom of long standing; the supper of the night of the dance, the almost unlimited quantities of food and drink that disappeared during the week. He wondered why he hadn't been honest and had the courage to say Harkness couldn't afford the occasion. Vanity and a stubborn pride wouldn't let him. Harkness had been part of an original grant of the London Company. It had seen periods of robust prosperity when the proprietors exported a golden wealth of tobacco and conducted themselves with the extravagance of feudal lords. It had survived two wars. The men had fought and the women had spun for their clothing and taken their places in the fields. It had endured the searing humiliation of the Reconstruction and remained intact. It was the knowledge of these things that had made John Harkness unwilling to admit he couldn't afford the fair.

Martha Hampton, who had brought a small inheritance to their marriage and saw it dissolve magically in repairs to the house, barns and stables—new cars, blooded stock and trips abroad every spring—had refused the conception of *noblesse oblige*. "If there is any obligation, Johnny," she had pointed out, "it is to ourselves. Now I know they are all wonderful people and some are distant relatives, but they are free-loaders. They are a luxury we can't afford."

He had been unwilling to admit this. Besides, Martha couldn't be expected to understand. Born in Ohio and raised in Florida she was inclined to be a little scornful of the heritage that was Virginia's. John had met her in Jacksonville where, from 1917 to 1918, he had been stationed at Camp Jackson, and they were married after the armistice. She brought with her a gay and easy companionship, a brightly flippant nature and some money. She had been delighted with the gracious antiquity of Harkness but neither she nor John had the slightest idea of management and the operation was both extravagant and wasteful.

"Mars' Harkness," she had made her imitation of a Virginia accent sound like something from a minstrel show, "we all are goin' to have to sell off some of the ol' plantation if we all are goin' to eat regular. An' we all are goin' to have to stop settin' out the jug an' a ham for every tenth cousin of yours that stops by for a few weeks' visit."

The burlesque and the truth of her statement had made him unreasonably angry. She was, he told her, a Yankee and couldn't be expected to understand a traditional way of life. This had erupted into a scene.

"Since my crass and vulgar Yankee dollars are going down the drain," she had reminded him, "I'm going to plug it up where I can."

He lit his pipe and started the motor now. Part of Harkness would have to be sold. He was pretty much of a fool. He recalled his resentment at Mark Hillyard's statement that he had "some stables to fill." A gentleman didn't buy horses that way. Neither did a gentleman sell for such a purpose. No, and he was impatient with himself, a gentleman sat a little threadbare in the afternoon sun, wondering what profit gentility and whether the bank would give him an extension on his note. He eased the car into gear and moved slowly forward.

The road changed abruptly from its rutted, back-country character where the woods ended. A broad avenue of well-raked bluestone chips swept forward between the hedges of box, to divide into encircling arms which enclosed the formal gardens. He whistled his astonishment and grudging appreciation. He had heard of the place, wild and extravagant stories had been passed around the county. Nothing, though, had prepared him for what he saw. The house and grounds were out of another time and place. There was the beauty wrought by skilled craftsmen working with gracious proportions. There was, he admitted almost grudgingly, no reason why a man should not have created this luminous thing if it pleased him and he could afford it. And, he added to himself, no man could want this and be quite as insensible and deliberately ordinary as Mark Hillyard made himself appear. He was, as the girl Carol had suggested, an old fraud who found a certain sly pleasure in his boorishness.

He continued along the main entrance looking for a turn-off that would take him away from the house. You didn't deliver a horse to the front door. The sharp beep of a horn solved the problem for him. He turned to glance back and then pulled to one side as Carol's blue convertible slowed.

"I waited for you at the Corners," she called. "When you didn't show up I decided you must have changed your mind about selling her so I went into Court House for a few minutes. How are you. How is she?"

"I'm fine, tired, dirty and hot. By she I suppose you mean Black Dancer?"

"No." She exaggerated a thoughtful expression. "I meant your wife, naturally. I can see the filly is all right."

It was such a deliberate bit of small insolence that for a moment he was angry. Then he had to admit he had almost invited it by his question. Martha, also, had not attempted to conceal an immediate suspicion and antagonism at their meeting. The girl had merely reacted. He supposed that was it.

"Where do I take her?"

"Follow me." She drew out ahead.

A few hundred yards down, concealed by a curving hedge, a road branched away. He could see the stables now, the broad, fenced pasture, the rows of cabins. He whistled and then laughed; not condescendingly but with honest pleasure. Only a man who was completely sure of himself, who didn't give a damn what anyone thought when he liked and wanted something, would have carried his re-creation this far.

At the stables a young Negro came quickly to help. He had a warm smile and a knowing hand on the halter. He led the filly from the trailer and took her to the pasture where bars were down. At the release of a restraining hand she tossed her head and raced down the stretch of heavy bluegrass with excited pleasure. The man replaced the bars and stood, leaning on them watching her run.

"She suah a pretty one, Miz Cahrl." He turned with a pleased smile.

"You take good care of her, Samuel." She glanced at Harkness. "One groom, one stableboy, one horse. All new. Want to walk back to the house? We can leave the cars here."

He fell in beside her. An early twilight was moving upon the river. A flight of birds came rocketing out from the opposite shore and sailed over their heads.

"Why don't you stay for dinner, spend the night and go back in the morning?" She stooped to nip off a bluet between her fingers and touched the flower to her mouth. "It's a long drive. I'd offer you a swim but the only suits around the place are mine."

"I ought to get back." He made the admission reluctantly. It would be a long drive and in the dark.

"I keep forgetting you are married." Her eyes lifted.

The small, deliberate goad made him angry. "No you don't." He was immediately angry that she was able to provoke him, to prick him into a display of temper. "You remember it very well and you're too fresh for your age. How old are you, anyhow?"

"How old did your wife say I was?" Her glance was wide with innocence.

He made no effort to check the appreciative grin. "She said you were old enough."

"I wouldn't think of questioning her experience." Her eyes were demure pools of innocence.

She had, he thought, a trick of keeping a person a little off balance, sparring with delicate precision. It was a trait, he suspected, inherited from the old man.

"I'll call Martha when we get to the house." This, he knew, was a form of adolescent boasting; kid stuff, showing her he wouldn't take a dare. He was ashamed of it and wondered how she had managed to maneuver him into a ridiculous position.

"I thought you would." She would give him no satisfaction; never letting up for a moment. There was a controlled ruthlessness about her as she kept unswervingly on the target. He wondered where it would lead her. "I was so sure of it that I told Mark you were staying over."

* * *

Mark Hillyard was seated within a deep, wicker rocking chair on the front porch. He read a paper through oddly old-fashioned glasses with square bifocal lenses in gun-metal frames. He put the sheets aside as they mounted the steps but made no effort to rise.

"I brought the horse trader." She sat on the arm of the old man's chair.

"How are you, Mr. Hillyard?" Harkness did not offer his hand.

Mark grunted, bent his head and peered almost belligerently over his glasses. It was the suspicious squinting of a man who expected to be out-traded. Secretly, Harkness was enjoying the meeting. The old man's bluntness was so much in a character, assumed or molded, that it no longer struck him as rude.

"What do I owe you for her?" The question came wheezingly, it was the plaintive query of a man who expected to be milked of his last dollar. It asked for sympathy and understanding.

Harkness laughed. "Seven thousand is a fair price."

"The hell it is." Hillyard almost upset Carol from the chair in his effort to sit upright. He glared at Harkness.

"That's too much." With a hand Carol pushed against her father's chest, forcing him back gently. "It's too much and you know it." There was curiosity rather than argument in the statement.

"That depends on who wants her. You do and you can afford it. It isn't every day I get a chance to stick a Yankee." He wondered why he was risking a sale he needed so badly to make.

"That's a hell of a way for a fella to talk who's goin' to eat my food an' sleep in one of my beds." Oddly enough the old man no longer seemed outraged. He was curious.

"Your daughter asked me to stay. I didn't ask you to buy the filly."

"You ain't goin' to to knock off a few dollars for bed an' board?" Hillyard rose from the chair.

"No."

Mark was alertly amiable now. "If that's the way it is let's have a drink an' I'll make out a check." He turned to Carol. "Sister?"

She nodded and moved ahead of them across the porch.

Hillyard's rye whisky was good enough to sip. It was bonded and uncut and certainly not something delivered by a local bootlegger. John sniffed its heavy perfume with appreciation.

The old man wrote a check and waved it in the air like a tattered

50

regimental flag. He handed it to John, who folded the slip and put it in his pocket without even glancing at the amount.

Carol was on a couch, one leg tucked beneath her, and she was studying Harkness interestedly. Hillyard glanced at her. Sister's takin' him apart, he thought. She's layin' him out piece by piece, tryin' to make up her mind if she wants him. Her intentness made him uneasy. He did not concern himself with his daughter's virtue or lack of it. It would be pretty late for him to start behaving like a parent. What really made him uneasy was a singleness of purpose. He could admire it in a man but a woman, he felt, should have a softness about her. When she didn't she became a monster. She could be beautiful and smart but she would be a sport, the way a black sheep would stand out in a flock of white ones. He turned to John Harkness.

"What would you have done if I hadn't bought the filly at that price?"

"Taken her back to the farm."

"Even though you need the money?" The question wasn't offensive although it should have been.

"I don't know how you could know that." He swallowed a little of the whisky. "But even though I need the money, I would have taken her back. I had you on the hip. Your daughter had already said the price didn't make any difference. She couldn't or wouldn't hedge on that."

"You'll end up sellin' pencils from a tin cup, Sister." Hillyard snorted his disgust.

Carol shook her head wisely. "The horse trader is being ordinary. What he is saying is that new money, Yankee money, having said the price didn't make any difference, couldn't back down. He's being pretty offensive about it, too. Isn't that it, John?" The use of the first name came naturally.

"That's close enough." He finished the whisky with pleasure.

"Why?"

"Because it ought to teach you not to throw your weight around."

"I doubt it." She looked up and smiled. "Now, why don't you call your home before it gets late."

She took him into a room which the old man evidently used as an office. It was scattered with old copies of the *Wall Street Journal* and letters were stuck untidily on an iron spike for filing.

"I'm going to spend the night here." He tried to make it sound casual when Martha was on the phone.

"I thought you probably would." There was a tiny, smug satisfaction in her reply. "Did you really ask seven thousand for Black Dancer?"

He couldn't keep the triumph from his voice. "I asked and got it."

Her whistle was long, low and appreciative. "She must want you worse than I thought, Johnny-Boy. But then," and this was deliberate malice, "you always were expensive."

Before he could explode there was a sharp click as Martha broke the connection. He stood, frowning at the receiver. That was a hell of a thing to say. It hurt more than he wanted to admit. He had brought as much to the marriage as she had; maybe not in dollars, but the intangibles. His resentment faded as his sense of humor caught up with him. Martha was jealous. Martha Hampton Harkness was in a burn over a youngster. Having decided this, he felt better.

For reasons which John couldn't quite understand, Mark Hillyard seemed to put himself out to be friendly and hospitable over the dinner table. He talked easily and with humor of his early days of wild-catting. There seemed to have been no job to which he had not put his hand. He had prospected and speculated with a devastating energy that had carried him half around the world.

"I don't know when I decided I wanted a lot of money." There was no boast in the statement. He actually seemed to be puzzled. "After Carol's mother died there was just the two of us an' Sister sure didn't need much more than a flour sack diaper an' a can of milk. So, I didn't want a lot of goods for her. I guess it was for the fun of it, like provin' I was smarter than the fellow alongside of me; like winnin' a checker game or pitchin' horseshoes. You want to win. There's no real trick to it. Most people don't never make real money because they honestly don't want to. Oh, they'd like to have it, all right, but they want it to come easy; somethin' they dream up lyin' with their backs against a warm wall in the sun. You got to want it the way you want a woman, a drink, a belly full of food. It's got to be a hunger you never satisfy. You got to make up your mind to crawl a little when you have to an' stomp 'em to death when they ain't lookin'. It maybe ain't a real noble way to go through life but it pays off in goods if that's what you really want." He belched softly and reached for his glass of whisky and water.

This was, Harkness decided, a strange family. The aunt, Julia, ate hurriedly as though she was afraid someone was going to snatch her plate away before she had finished. The old man, putting himself out to be entertaining for a stranger who had not only been rude but had overcharged him outrageously. He actually had seemed to warm to Harkness with the deal. There was no other explanation for his effort at the table. Throughout the meal he had felt the steady, penetrating glance of Carol on him. She had lynx eyes without a flicker and he had the feeling of being watched by a predatory animal from cover. Girls on the make were nothing new. He could recall several with pleasure. This one, though, if she was on the make, went about the business with the composed certainty of a skilled technician in a laboratory. He was being dissected, evaluated with clinical thoroughness, and it made him uncomfortable.

They finished dinner and Aunt Julia excused herself with a nervous flutter and vanished.

The old man watched her disappear. "Julia feels as immoral about this as if she just woke up in a cat house." The snicker was lewd. "Be a damn good thing for her, too. But I guess it's too late. I got some papers to read." He left them abruptly without a word of good night or apology.

Left alone with Carol, who smiled with an ancient wisdom, he wondered at her ability to make him feel uncomfortable.

"Let's sit outside." She pushed back her chair.

They stood for a moment on the porch. A pale quarter moon sliced through low and ragged clouds. She took a seat on the second step above the porch level, and turning to look back, motioned to a place on the one above her.

He took it and she leaned against his leg, resting on it with a deliberate regard for her own comfort.

"What did your wife say when you called her?" She was indifferent to the bad taste of the question.

"She sent her regards."

"I'll bet." She rubbed her shoulder blade on his knee. "You have a nice animal smell about you. You think I'm a nymph, don't you?"

"I'm not sure what I think. You're pretty obvious but then I have the feeling you know you are and so it probably isn't obvious at all. Let's call it a devious obviousness."

"My, but you do talk something grand and I'm ever so impressed." She whistled her admiration on a long, derisive note.

"You're making a career of being a brat, aren't you?"

"I'm experimenting," she confessed innocently. "I think," the words came slowly, "you ought to know that what I have in mind isn't a quick bounce in the hay."

Because he had no ready answer for this he reached for his pipe and took a long time packing and lighting it. I'd like to know, he told himself, just what it is you do have in mind. He cupped the worn bowl in his palm and blew softly upon the coal.

With her head partly turned she watched him. "A pipe is supposed to be so masculine. Does it affect your glands or stimulate those of a woman?"

"What does it do to you?"

"Nothing. Absolutely nothing." She lifted her face thoughtfully to the sky. "You know, I may decide I don't want you at all; not that way." She made the statement sound regretful. "What you have to understand is that I'm not an oversexed schoolgirl. I know very little about this business that seems to go on day and night between men and women. My experience with it was cheap and shoddy. I expect that was his fault as much as mine. Men and women kill each other over it. The Greeks fought the Trojans for Helen but the act itself, somehow, seems grotesque."

"You ought to get yourself booked on the Chautauqua Circuit for a lecture."

"With colored slides?" She laughed quietly and swung about to face him. "We're getting along better, aren't we? I mean, now that you know I have no immediate and foul designs on your body? I imagine, though, it is slightly wounding to your pride."

He laughed with her. The constraint he had felt—an uneasiness, really, which he hadn't wanted to admit—was gone. There was character and force here coupled with real beauty and a quick mind. Five, ten years; he wondered what she would be like then. He shifted a little until his back was against a pillar. She moved with him to keep her place.

"How old are you, Carol? Really. I mean it."

"Really? I don't know. I guess I'd better be nineteen. That's past the age of consent, isn't it? I'd like to have a free hand with no complications if the occasion should arise. The number of years means nothing. Mark and I led a pretty unconventional life. The layers of time were put on with a heavy brush. I can be thirty just as well as nineteen. That's pretty convenient. I'm adaptable."

"What do you do with yourself, here with just your father? I don't imagine Aunt Julia is much company." He was honestly interested.

54

"I read a lot, talk with Mark or to myself, hell around the county in a blue convertible, a picture of the jazz age."

"No friends?"

"I haven't tried to make any." She made the statement, not defensively but simply. He believed her. "When I want to I will."

"Court House, Virginia, may be a little hard to understand at first."

"I understand it, them, well enough. There is a cult."

"I guess that is as good a word as any." He found the idea openly expressed a little surprising although he had unconsciously subscribed to it all of his life. "There is a cult of colonial aristocracy. It is real. As real as the War Between the States is today. It is kept alive without effort; generated in the womb. All Virginians, from birth, feel superior to other Southerners. Northerners don't count. And some Virginians, because of the circumstances into which they were born, are elevated above the level of other Virginians. This superiority doesn't rub off. It can't be acquired by osmosis or marriage. It is mystical, inexplicable and a little wonderful, wonderful in the sense that it survives in a changing world. The miraculous thing is that it doesn't result in snobbery or condescension. It is simply a fact of life, as immutable as the stars. It is accepted by Virginians as indisputable. The sun rises in the east and sets in the west. Who is going to deny that?"

"Not the carpetbaggers. The Hillyards." She grinned at him with almost impish pleasure.

"We have old friends here." He worked slowly toward the suggestion, realizing he would have to be careful with her. "Ties bound by the years and kinship."

"Thank you, no." She was emphatic and stood up. "I'm selective, also. I'll choose the ones I want. If they're hard to get," she winked at him, "I'll soften them up by admitting I'm an old friend of Mars' John, but I'll try it on my own first." She extended her hand and he took it, rising from his place against the pillar. "Anyhow," she was perplexed, "I don't see how an introduction from a horse trader could be of much social value in Court House. Mark once sold mules in Missouri. That ought to do just as well."

He kept her hand in his as they crossed the porch. It seemed a natural thing to do. There was a solid, warm pressure of her fingers locked with his. There was an unaffected pleasure in the contact.

"Would you like a nightcap?"

He shook his head.

"I know you didn't bring anything with you." They mounted the staircase. "Mark sleeps in nightshirts. You'll find one spread out on your bed. I bought a safety razor and some brushless shaving cream along with a toothbrush and paste in Court House this morning."

"The hell you did?" He broke his step to stare at her.

"I thought you'd stay. If you didn't, someone would eventually use them." She opened a door on the long corridor.

The room was softly lighted, the bed turned down, and a fine linen nightshirt spread at the end.

"I'll see you in the morning." She stretched upward and brushed his cheek with her mouth. "That wasn't exactly a sisterly peck but I'm not leching for you either. Good night, John."

"Good night, Carol."

At the door she turned to glance back with a quick, uncertain smile. For the first time he saw something gentle in her expression, a softness he hadn't suspected was there. In that moment she was very young and vulnerable.

"Sometimes," the word carried with it a wistful sound, "I forget I have a name. Mark always calls me Sister. I really don't like it." The latch nicked into its slot as she closed the door.

Alone, he picked up the nightshirt and held it to his chest in a measurement for length. Dimly he could recall his grandfather wearing one of these with a tasseled, knitted cap that was supposed to keep the noxious vapors of the night from the head. They were of heavy cotton or flannel, though. What he held could almost be crumpled into one palm. It was of sheer, Irish handkerchief linen and the hand stitching was so fine it could barely be seen. Mark Hillyard, he thought as he undressed, was an individual of surprising contradictions. For reasons of his own he turned a rude face to the world. He liked to be thought of as a man of few sensibilities and little appreciation. It amused him to be accepted as someone who probably slept in his underwear and wore socks on his dirty feet to keep the sheets clean. Yet in privacy he could enjoy covering himself with something as fine as this. It was a protective disguise, a curious twist, and he wondered if Carol's assumption of brittle assurance welled from the same uncertainty.

He took a long, hot shower. Putting on the nightshirt he surveyed himself in the pier glass. Martha ought to see him now. He was a figure to dull any suspicion of infidelity. It was impossible to imagine an illicit romance coming to flower with a man in this shroudlike thing with ruffles at the wrist and a hem flapping about bony ankles. If a girl didn't go into hysterical laughter at the sight she must have the feeling of crawling into bed with her grandmother. It was a wonder that this single article of nightclothing hadn't put an abrupt halt to the propagation of the species. It could well have destroyed the human race. That it had survived was a small miracle.

V

ALTHOUGH he would have denied it, Mark Hillyard was worried about his daughter. It was a selfish concern. She seemed to have so little to do. It didn't seem right that a young girl should spend so much time with an old man or herself.

He watched her covertly now across the breakfast table as she idly turned the pages of a Richmond paper. He had a feeling that one of these mornings she was going to ball up the sheets, throw them at him and announce she was leaving. He didn't know what he would or could do if that happened. He'd have to let her go. It wasn't something a man could argue about. She had a right to a life of her own. It wasn't natural a girl should want it this way. Irritably he wondered why she had made no friends. The only person she had shown any interest in was John Harkness and, if he wasn't too old for her, he was married to a pretty woman of his own. The best that could happen to Sister would be a rock on a blanket or in the back seat of a car. That wasn't good enough. He was comforted a little by the idea Sister wouldn't settle for that. He wasn't sure just why he believed this but he did. It would be a cheap compromise. Anyhow, it had been three months since Harkness had come over with the horse. He had telephoned once to ask about the filly. Sister had been out and he gave her the message when she returned. She only nodded and, as far as Mark knew, never called back.

In the hope she would be entertained, he had invented an excuse to go to New York and asked her to come with him. She took New York as she did everything else, with little display of interest. They had gone to a few Broadway shows together, eaten in the speakeasies where the food seemed to be better than any place else. She had bought herself a lot of clothes and things for Julia, and had some of the girls she had gone to school with for lunch and a matinee. It wasn't, he admitted, that she was sullen or a pouty kind of a girl who didn't know what to do with herself. When they had walked down Fifth Avenue in the sharp, metallic air of November, her eyes had been bright, her cheeks colored by the nipping wind. She had linked her arm with his, laughed at some of the things he said. People turned to look after her when they passed and he was filled with a wondering pride that this girl was his daughter. She made him go to a tailor and he dressed for dinner every night, grumbling and snorting but enjoying it when she stood before him and deftly squared the black bow of his tie.

Then, one afternoon, she stood at the windows in the living room of the Plaza suite overlooking Central Park. Wind and a cold rain slashed at the trees, stripped now of leaves.

"Let's go home, old man." She turned to where he sat reading a paper.

She called him that frequently. Old man. There was affection in the tone and he understood it had nothing to do with age.

"I bought everything I saw I wanted. We've seen the shows, liquored ourselves up in French speakeasies, drunk the absinthe specials in Tony's basement. Now, you all, carry me back to ol' Virginia."

She looked up now from the outspread pages of the Richmond paper and smiled at him for a second before her attention went back to the news. The white-coated colored man who served their breakfast on the south terrace came to her with a list from the kitchen. She glanced over it, took a pencil from him and made a correction or two, and gave it back with a nod.

She ran this big place, he thought, without any effort. How the hell did a girl her age know what to do? In the beginning Julia had made twittering and ineffectual attempts to cope with the establishment but she had no idea of management or discipline. The servants learned quickly Miz Julia was no one to fear. The disintegration was gradual. The maids began to forget small things. The food was indifferently served and badly prepared although the kitchen help sat down to a lavish table. The gardener, his assistant and the yardboys spent lazy, happy hours in the sun, snipping their clippers into the air to make a sound but never touching a hedge. Carol said nothing to Mark or Julia but went to the kitchen as the seat of domestic confusion.

Fifteen or more persons were seated about a long table on which there were hams, a huge turkey, potatoes, greens and peas all served on the manor china and with the household silver and linen. She stood in the doorway and stared at them. There was a shuffling, uncertain movement and then one by one they stood up, feeling the chill and eying her apprehensively.

"I don't know you or you or you or you." She snapped the words at unfamiliar faces. "Get off of the place and don't come back." She waited until the subdued guests sidled toward the back entrance. The household servants darted their eyes at each other but no one questioned the slender, angry instrument of authority. "Cora Ann." She selected the cook. "Do you like this job? Do you want to keep it?"

Cora Ann murmured an eagerly worried assent that became a small chorus. They dropped their eyes but cut a look up now and then with sudden hope.

"You all know better." The words were a tipped lash of scorn and impatience. "You've worked in good homes before. I wouldn't have a stable run the way this house has been going. Now, you'll do your jobs or get out. I don't intend to speak to any one of you again about this. If I do it will only be to pay you your wages and let you go."

That was all it had taken. They actually seemed grateful that someone had stepped in to bring order out of the confusion. Now they came to Miz Cahrl with their troubles, their questions. She paid the bills and the salaries from the account which Mark had made jointly at the Court House bank. The mechanics of the household were smooth and effortless. Neither Mark nor Julia knew of the scene in the kitchen but they were aware of the change. Mark kept his approval to himself. Sister, he thought, wouldn't expect to be complimented but he knew she knew he knew. That was the way it was between them.

He studied her now as she frowned over something in the paper. He had taken a membership in the country club, but as far as he knew, she had never gone to the place. There were golf clubs and tennis racquets in the closets of her room. He guessed she'd learned to play those games at that girls' school. She never used them. He wondered why.

"You said something once about a man named Jim Haney." Her words cut across his gloomy thoughts. "Where is he?"

"We got offices in Houston. We got a whole buildin', really. Jim moves around a lot for me. Here and there."

"I think you ought to have him come down here." She lit a cigarette.

"What for, Sister?" The request surprised him.

"So I'll know him." Her eyes were level. "If you died tomorrow I wouldn't have the slightest idea about anything."

"I ain't goin' to die tomorrow nor the day after." He was undisturbed.

"Maybe not, but just the same, this is a hell of a way to leave things." She was incisive but not angry.

"The Guaranty Trust, in New York, an' my lawyers along with Jim know about everything. You just ask them what you want to know when the time comes."

"I don't want to ask anyone. I want to know myself. Call this Haney or send him a wire. Tell him to come on down and spend some time."

"A woman ain't worth a goddamn where business is concerned. Things are all wrapped up for you fine does somethin' happen to me." He dismissed her with a wave of his cigar.

"I don't want them wrapped up. I want to look inside and see what's there now. You send for Haney, Mark." She said this almost absently but there was an unmistakable command in the tone.

He stared at her as her attention went back to the newspaper. What the hell kind of a girl was this one, anyhow?

"Sister," he returned to what had been in his mind before her interruption of his thoughts, "why don't you give a party here? There are a lot of young people around. I see them all the time when I go into Court House; boys and girls your age."

"Are you going to send for Jim Haney?" Her eyes lifted and held his.

"All right, by God!" His voice raised with baffled annoyance. "I'll send for Jim if that's what you want. I'll send for him an' you can dance a jig on my grave that ain't even dug yet." He managed to be angry and injured at the same time.

She laughed at him and then, sliding from her chair, crossed to his and sat on the arm, leaning with the affection of a cat against him, the fingers of one hand scratching his head.

"What the hell kind of a young girl are you, anyhow?" He was not soothed. "I'm gettin' old." There was a hypocritical self-pity in the statement. "This here place ought to be a home an' that means you should have friends, fellas to sit on the stoop when they come courtin', girls to come around an' talk about whatever girls talk about. Things ain't changed so much since I was young. I know how they ought to be an' you ain't doin' it. The only time I seen a little fire in your eye was over that Harkness man an' if he wants you at all it'd only be for one thing."

"Is there anything wrong with that?" The fingers halted their movement on his head abruptly.

"He's married, that's what's wrong." He was outraged.

"This is a hell of a time for you to be getting moral, Mark Hillyard."

"It's different for a man." The exasperation welled.

"Who said so? A man?"

"Now, Sister, you know good an' well what I mean." He had never been able to cope with her directness. "What about them young people—relatives or somethin', weren't they—that Harkness had come to see you?" He was anxious to get off of an uncomfortable tangent.

"They are away at school."

A week or so after John Harkness had delivered Black Dancer a car rolled up the long driveway and halted at the door. A young man and a girl sat for a moment, their heads bent toward each other, their conversation whisperedly earnest. Now and then they both glanced at the house and once the man made a move as though to drive away. The girl reached foward and turned off the ignition key. Then, hand in hand, they marched up the steps. Carol, who had watched their performance with an amused surprise, came to the front door just as they reached the porch.

"Hello." She knew without being told that this visit was being made at the prompting of John Harkness.

"I'm Angela Warrington." The girl smiled tentatively. Her voice had the softly pleasant cadence of the region. An accent flowed gently through the words. "This is my brother Bootsie."

The Warrington twins were an astonishingly handsome pair. Tall, blond and deeply tanned from swimming and tennis, their features were identical. They were twenty-two and, at the moment, obviously uncertain just what the amenities of the situation demanded of them. This was a duty call but since they were both healthy, friendly animals they were prepared to make of it whatever Carol indicated.

"I'm Carol Hillyard, of course." She gave them her hand and smiled inwardly as Bootsie Warrington managed an awkwardly courtly bow over it. "It's nice of you to come over. Let's go down by the pool where it's cooler." On the way to where a cluster of striped umbrellas shaded deck chairs, she turned to Warrington. "Is your name really Bootsie?"

Boothby Warrington flushed. He was a huge youth with curly hair so blond it was almost white against the tanned skin. He wore gray flannel slacks, tennis shoes, a yellow sweater and walked with the heavy grace of a St. Bernard. He rubbed at his face with embarrassment.

"Well, ma'am"—from experience he knew this drawling locuting had a stimulating effect upon all Northern girls—"my papa an' mama just got carried away at christening time. They named me Boothby and then forgot it. I've been Bootsie ever since and that ain't a happy name to carry around." Carol was certain the *ain't* was deliberate and part of the character Warrington created in the presence of impressionable girls. "It kept me fighting through grade school. Now I'm used to it." His smile was engagingly confidential.

They had iced tea in the garden. Carol wasn't sure whether she should offer anything stronger, finally decided against it. They tried desperately to make small talk and reach a common plane. Angela hopefully offered a few names of girls from New York she had known, seeming to feel one mutual acquaintance would end the constraint. Boothby, who was a sophomore at the University, lounged with an indolent grace in the chair and stared admiringly at Carol. They exhausted the weather, the last dance at the country club, which Carol hadn't attended. The moments of silence grew longer and dragged agonizingly.

"John Harkness shouldn't have done this, should he?" Carol was suddenly frankly sympathetic. "I'd hate it if someone asked me to go and see someone I didn't know."

"Cousin John said we'd like you." Boothby stretched out his long legs, crossed the ankles and twisted his feet in the air, peering at the result with a rapt fascination. "He said you might even like us." The laugh was softly appreciative. "Anyhow, we were dyin' to see this place. Everybody is, I guess."

"Bootsie!" Angela was mortified.

"Well, we were." He was indifferent. "Everybody is. What's wrong with that?"

"Bootsie thinks he's real good-looking and can say anything," Angela explained.

"Well," Carol was solemnly judicial, "I guess Bootsie *is* real good-looking." She made it sound as though Warrington wasn't there.

He nodded a pleasant agreement. An obvious fact had been stated. "Virginia has many natural wonders—the caves at Luray, the stone bridge, Bootsie Warrington who has survived his name." He studied them for a moment. "It's just too bad all three of us are fair." He made the word sound as though it had an *h* in it. "I always look better 'longside a black-haired girl." He sighed.

"Bootsie is quaint." Angela tested the adjective and liked it. "He's real quaint for sure."

Warrington chewed an icecube with the sound of a dog crumbling a bone. "It would give me real pleasure, Miss Hillyard, to call upon you another time without my sister."

"Do you wear a Confederate cap around the campus at the University?" Carol's question was innocent.

He dropped his feet to the ground and sat up with surprise. "All Northern girls have a sharp tongue." He spoke sadly.

Carol laughed at his stricken face. She liked him. The caricature of himself was deliberate. He enjoyed drawing it, broadly and without being offensive. He was a naturally amiable young man whose remarkable success with girls had, miraculously enough, only given him an added, easy charm. He liked being Bootsie Warrington, liked most persons and took it for granted they would like him.

64

The constraint between them evaporated gradually and without conscious effort. School for the Warringtons opened in a few weeks. Boothby was going back to Charlottesville and Angela wanted a modeling career in New York. She had enrolled in a training school. They left with vague suggestions they get together again.

Carol walked to the car with them and after holding the door for Angela, Boothby turned to her.

"It is only fair, Miss Hillyard, that you know the Warringtons are impoverished gentry. My sister here is reduced to baring her body for photographers while I must strive for a career. After a lot of thought I have decided upon marrying a wealthy girl. And child," he eyed her happily, "you just seem to be rolling in it. At the earliest opportunity I shall call upon your father and request the honor of paying court to you and his money."

"Boothby Warrington." Angela forgot her soothing tone and shrilled.

"We Warringtons are nothing if not honest." He ignored his sister.

"I'll tell you what." Carol nodded. "You come around during Christmas vacation. Mark is usually in a giving-away mood at that time."

"Ma'am, we have a date." He studied her fondly. "You are young but it is in the nature of things that you grow older." He bowed with exaggerated gallantry and a quick grin.

"Maybe," Mark was saying now, "you should have gone to school down here in Virginia. No sense in havin' your friends four or five hundred miles away."

She stood up. "I've been thinking I might go back to school. Not to any place like Miss Farmington's. There's something called The Wharton School of Business, at the University of Pennsylvania. I'm not sure whether they take girls."

If she had suggested entering a whorehouse he couldn't have been more astonished. "For God's sake, Sister, whoever heard of a girl goin' to a business school? What would you want to do that for?"

"There are a lot of things I'd like to know. Maybe I could learn them there."

He was completely baffled. "Sister," he was in earnest, "I don't know what to make of you. I get a feelin' you maybe ain't normal. The Hillyards have had some real characters among them but I don't think none carried it as far as you're about to. A girl as pretty as you goin' to a business school." He snorted his outrage. "Couldn't you just go along an' do the usual things like runnin' away with a drummer or gettin' yourself into trouble with a man? I could understand that. I got a real broad view of the human frailties. But a business school." He was sadly mystified. "Why, a girl like you should be havin' herself a lot of fripperies." He hadn't the slightest idea what the word meant but it sounded frivolous, expensive and feminine. He slumped in his chair and gazed at her dismally.

She bent and kissed his forehead quickly. "All right. I'll go out and get some fripperies this afternoon. I'll get maybe a dozen or so in assorted sizes and colors." She left him there staring bleakly at the river.

From a corner of the empty bar BillJo Adams watched the blond girl as she dropped a quarter in the jukebox and pressed the selector keys. Light from the machine's base created a shadow box and the slender outlines of her long, exciting legs were plainly drawn beneath the sheer skirt.

Although he had never spoken to her, BillJo knew who she was. Sooner or later he struck up an acquaintance of sorts with most of his customers. Her name was Carol Hillyard and she lived over by the river in that big place her old man had built. She had been in The Cottage half a dozen times or so, always ordering a rum and coke with a sprig of mint in it. She drank one or two, played a few records, minded her business and left as quietly as she came. She never had a man or another girl with her and BillJo thought this was funny, because she didn't look like one of those lonesome drinkers. He didn't have her figured out. She wasn't looking for a pickup. A couple of times men had tried it. When they spoke to her she turned slowly, staring at them over the top of her glass with an expression of innocent wonder that they were capable of speech. This always worked. The words of invitation trailed off uncertainly and the man would move away, almost hurriedly, to another section of the bar where he pretended an intense study of the drink before him. She was young, but most of the young kids were drinking these days. If they were afraid to be seen in The Cottage one of the boys came to the back door and bought a pint, taking it with him to the car. BillJo figured if they were old enough to be out and driving around they were old enough to drink. The whole business was illegal anyhow and a buck was a buck. You took it when you could.

The Cottage was set back from the highway in a grove of fine old oaks. It was a single-storied house of white clapboard with green trim about heavily curtained windows. Thick ivy was massed at the entrance, giving an air of prim respectability to the place. Only the unusual number of cars parked in the darkness beneath the tress at night marked it as not being the simple dwelling it seemed.

BillJo had come to Court House by way of devious and muddied channels. Georgia born, from Valdosta near the Florida line, he had hopped bells in a Savannah hotel, hustled girls for the guests and supplied them with corn moonshine distilled in the piny flat woods by a couple of Cracker brothers. BillJo made a good thing of this, collecting two ways in tips from the men and a percentage from the girls. The 'shine cost him a dollar a pint which he sold for three. He hoarded his money, spending only what was absolutely necessary. A pint of corn to the giant Negro chef in the kitchen gave him the privilege of snatching a furtive meal there. He collected and saved the long cigarette butts from the trays in the rooms when he was called, and had his girls from the flat-faced little whores who were dependent upon his good will. He was as shrewdly cunning as a raccoon, vain of his dark good looks inherited from a Mexican mother with a strain of Negro in her, and as rapacious as a weasel in a chicken yard.

When he had saved what he thought to be enough money he left the hotel, bought a secondhand touring car and drifted down around Sapelo Sound with its twisting, sheltered waterways. For a couple of weeks he hung around the backwater docks with a room in a boardinghouse built on piles in the mud tidal flats. The place stank with the dead, salty odor of salt muck and hot marsh grass but the blowsy fisherman's widow who ran it took Billjo to her sweaty bosom and creaking bed. Now he no longer paid board, and helped himself to cigarettes behind the counter, the whisky stored in the depths of a bait barge and the widow.

At night, every two or three days, the small boats threaded in through the Sound with their cargoes of whisky and rum brought up and in from Bimini and Cat Key by the big rumrunners who made their rendezvous in the treacherous channels between Sapolo Island and Doboy Sound. With the widow properly submissive BillJo convinced her the small retail trade she was doing was a waste of time. He had a car. All she had to do was put up the money for a load of whisky as it came in "hams"—a dozen bottles wrapped in burlap sacking—from the boats. He would pack it in his car, run it inland to Waycross, tripling her investment. Throbbing with her autumnal passion and greed the woman became BillJo's partner. They loaded the hams in the touring car, after reinforcing the springs. She kissed him with lingering moistness and he drove away.

That was the last the widow ever saw of her money, the whisky or her lover. A little tipsily she would would sometimes tell the story of his perfidy, ending the tale with a shake of her head and BillJo's description: "A sure-enough sweet-back sonofabitch who screwed me goin' an' comin'."

BillJo prospered. He made contacts in St. Augustine and around New Smyrna, in Florida. He bought another car and hired two local boys cheaply as drivers. Sometimes they ran the stuff as far north as New Jersey but there was a profitable market closer at hand, in the Carolinas and Virginia, if the residents could be weaned from their congenital love for white corn, warm as mother's milk as it came from the still's worm. One night, on the road to Roanoke, BillJo slowed and then halted at a red-lighted construction sign. Four men moved out from both sides of the road with shotguns. They jerked BillJo and his relief driver from the car, took his whisky and then beat them both with hysterical, laughing pleasure.

BillJo said to hell with that. He had a lot of money now. What he wanted was a nice, comfortable, profitable place where he could make the right connections and operate safely and in semirespectability. He roamed about Virginia until he came to Court House. The chief of police was an amiable, underpaid and worldly man. He saw no reason why BillJo shouldn't open a nice place on the edge of town. The chief would drop past now and then to see that everything was in order, but since this came under the heading of extra duty, he would expect Mr. Adams to arrange a weekly compensation. He'd also take care of the sheriff if Mr. Adams would set aside a reasonable amount for a fund which the sheriff was building up for his old age. "We can't have, though," the chief warned, "no chippies brought in to hang around your place. The local talent has a hard enough time makin' ends meet as it is, what with the girls from respectable families givin' it away for free."

BillJo was agreeable. He'd serve liquor and maybe food. He was a man of fine instincts himself.

He found The Cottage for sale, bought it for cash and turned it over to the painters and carpenters. At the back he built a garage apartment for himself and had an interior decorator from Richmond furnish it. He liked to think of The Cottage as his club to which members of the county's best families came. He had a good bartender, a capable chef. There was never any real trouble in the place. Now and then he had to put up with a drunk, but usually it was a salesman or someone from out of town and BillJo's bartender hustled the troublemaker out with a deft clutch at collar and crotch.

Sometimes though, when he stood at the bar looking at one of the girls or maybe a young married woman from Court House, he was possessed by a feeling of envious unrest. He had almost everything a man could want. He was twenty-seven, good-looking, healthy and with an easy way with women. He subscribed to *Vanity Fair*, read Woollcott as a bible of faraway places, and all the articles on men's fashions. His shoes were handcrafted and his clothes tailored in New York. It was a small conceit that he liked to imagine himself a fascinating, mysteriously important figure in the underworld. Now and then, when he'd had a few drinks, he became whisperingly confidential, talking with a sinister, corner-of-the-mouth hoarseness of Al, the Dutchman; Bugs Moran; Larry Fay; Texas—meaning, of course, Guinan; the Detroit or Chicago mob. BillJo was frustrated rather than envious. It didn't make him bitter but only ambitious.

The first families of Court House were among his regular patrons. They were politely friendly when they came in. Now and then he would move with a studied casualness to a table and order a round of drinks. No one ever asked him to sit down though. They looked up, smiled their greeting, called him BillJo or sometimes even Mr. Adams. It wasn't anything he could really put his finger on, but without effort they somehow made the distinction between bootlegger and patron clear. A couple of times he had voiced the opinion he ought to get out more and find some exercise. Golf maybe would be the thing. They were interested, politely attentive, but no one ever suggested putting him up for membership in the country club.

These things didn't rankle as they might have. BillJo didn't become bitter or pretend a swaggering indifference to the invisible but definite line of demarcation. By God, he told himself, I don't blame them! If I was in their place I'd be hard to get also.

He had girls from the wrong part of the town who came to his apartment with excited giggles, but then he'd see someone like the

Hillyard girl and experience a restless dissatisfaction that made him feel so sick in his stomach he wanted to vomit. Sometimes during the winter months, as a form of release, he would go to Miami or Cuba. There he stayed at the most expensive hotels, gambled at the tables or the tracks, wore handsomely tailored clothes and threw his money around with the careless gesture of an easy spender. He was Mr. Adams. A liberal tipper who never hedged on a bet or tried to cash a check. The women were easier here and a cut above what he had to take in Court House. The relief he had from these trips was never more than temporary and he returned to The Cottage more dissatisfied than ever. He prowled about this cage of his own fashioning like a captive animal born to this confinement and looking for an escape into an alien world in which he probably could not survive.

The Hillyard girl, as he watched now, turned away from the jukebox and came back to her stool. On the bar her drink was frosting in its glass. A sprig of mint, hoary with powdered sugar, was a Christmas ornament above the ice. She pushed it away from tickling her nose when she lifted the drink and glanced at BillJo as though he weren't there. There was no arrogance in the look. He just wasn't there, didn't exist.

He moved up along the bar. "I'm BillJo Adams, Miss Hillyard."

"I know." The tip of her tongue rested on an icecube, her eyes slanted upward.

"Could I buy you a drink?"

"I have one, thanks." The words were not curtly or ungraciously spoken. They merely state a fact.

He hesitated. There was something about her, despite the deliberate monotone of her voice, the air of complete detachment, that mysteriously encouraged him. He felt a small edge of excitement. BillJo had a sharp, feral instinct about women. It had never betrayed him. It was something he felt but could not explain. Sometimes no more than the way a girl sat or moved or looked up when spoken to. But it was there, as definite as a scent or an animal's mating sound. This one was ready but, and this was something new to him, she was ready only on her own terms. A man wouldn't be able to make the conditions or set the time and place. She wasn't to be taken or had for the asking.

"Mind if I sit down?"

"Why?" Her half-smile was veiled. "I mean, why do you want

to sit down beside me—not, why should I mind?" She stirred the ice in her glass with a finger tip.

He didn't know the answer to this. Neither did he know how to retreat from the situation. She saved him.

"Sit down. It's your joint, isn't it?"

He slid onto the stool and as he did, his knee brushed the soft warm of her thigh. He hadn't meant to do that. BillJo was too smart for such a clumsy trick; one of the little broads from town, yes; but not this one. She studied him, aware of the brief contact, wondering if he was a complete fool. She made no attempt to pull away but the immobility was no invitation either. BillJo was aware of this and stored the small grain of information. On the padded seat he hooked his feet firmly on the stool's rung, held his knees together stiffly so the distance separating them was constant. He beckoned to the bartender and ordered himself a bourbon and plain water. She snipped off a mint leaf and licked away its sugar, examining the petal with interest.

They were alone, save for the bartender. The jukebox unwound its music slowly. What was going on was as old as man, as deliberately stylized as the dance of a crane, the brilliant spreading of a peacock's fan, the rearing command of a stallion. She felt it as a strange languor crept through her veins like a drug. What she experienced was not curiosity. It was an earthy, drenching heat. She sucked in her breath and felt her loins constrict in a quick spasm. This was no thing to be said in words between them. She had no idea whether it was this man or a man she wanted. If it was this man she wondered why. Between the fingers of both hands he revolved the glass slowly on the bar and the tendons were ridged beneath the skin. His face was set in a mask. The bartender was at the far end, reading a newspaper, and she thought it incredible he did not feel the explosive tension or hear the primal cry as it screamed through the room. She was stripped naked and panting.

"Not now, today." Her words were barely audible.

The glass between the fingers turned more slowly. BillJo didn't look up, he didn't answer. He didn't ask why.

She didn't know why she had said that or why this man so abruptly and mysteriously compelled her. It was something for which she was not prepared, either by experience or imagining. What she felt was a curious exhaustion rather than excitement; as though what was to happen had already taken place. He was a stranger. They had exchanged no more than a dozen words. He had touched her briefly and without assurance. For him she felt no gentle longing, no tenderness, only a need, and the desire was frightening in its searing intensity. What she saw behind her closed eyes shocked and fascinated her. It was a fury, a tangle of locked bodies with sweat, blood, and words yelled in obscenity; of torn bedclothing and pillows ripped apart as rutting animals might leave a threshed and beaten trail through the heavy underbrush. In her there was no precedent for this all but slavering hunger that had come without warning. It could be, for all she knew, unique. There was in her no desire to captivate, binding a man to her with the tenuous cords of affection and respect. There was the need only to be taken, drained and left gasping, sprawled and weary.

She summoned her will and stood up, her legs without strength. "I'll be back, sometime; maybe not tonight. I don't know." The words were a hollow whisper.

He gave no indication of hearing her. In this moment he felt no triumph, no elation. He understood dimly there had been no victory for him. He made no move to turn and face her.

Behind him she did not hesitate or make a temporizing gesture that would tell him not to let her go. He heard the rap of her heels on the floor; felt, rather than saw, a bar of the afternoon's sunlight as it fell through the opening door. Then, the room was quiet again.

The bartender, who had looked up from his paper as she left, came forward to sweep up her half-filled glass. He glanced at BillJo.

"Miss Hillyard forgot to pay for her drink." He ran a towel over the damp circle where it had rested.

An odd smile, ironic and resigned, hovered for a second about BillJo Adams' mouth. "I'll pick up the tab," he said.

From outside came the sound of a starter whining and then the explosive burst of a motor as it was stamped into life. BillJo listened until it receded. Then he swung from the stool and walked out of the bar.

He stood for a minute or more within the mottled shade of an oak. His shirt was damp, sticky with perspiration which had stained the unlighted cigarette between his fingers. He took a deep breath and started around the cottage for his apartment. He was riveted by the screech of tires as a car slewed recklessly from the highway to The Cottage.

72

"Get in, BillJo." Her hands were tight, the knuckles blanched, as they held to the top of the steering wheel's rim. "Get in."

He sat, head partly bowed, eyes that did not see staring fixedly at the unfired cigarette which he clung to as a talisman. She spun the car heedlessly across the lawn, digging ugly furrows into the green, roared it back into the drive and on to the highway. He lifted his head to watch the speedometer's black arrow as it bounced upward and then crept along through 70, 75, 80. The wind screamed across the nickeled top of the windshield. A car coming from the opposite direction was a blurred spot for a second. He was indifferent to the danger. There was a numb certainty that this was the way it had to be, a thing of violence.

A short, corduroy bridge loosely spanned a drainage ditch on the right. She must have seen it from a long way off, for by the time they reached it she had braked the car to an easy roll. She turned expertly, bumping across the logs, and picked up the deep, sandy ruts of a wagon track through the flat, unkempt land. Where the woods thickened she skidded the car across the ridges of the trace and let it plow through the scrub. Thorned and wiry branches clawed long streaks from the enamel with a rasping sound. Within a small clearing, ringed by the twisted growth, she stopped the car and let the motor run.

For a moment she sat there, breathing heavily as though she had been pressed to great physical exertion. Then she faced him and her lips were wet and parted.

She tore at him, her crimson-tipped fingers clawing his shirt open, ripping it across his chest, and the buttons snapped off with the sound of corn popping.

He shouted as her nails opened bloody tracks over his ribs, and dragged her from the car to the hot, sandy earth.

They spoke no words. The sounds were snarled almost, or raised to a keening whimper as they spent an unsuspected violence upon each other. In this agony of soul and body there was a release from the dark corners where they both had unknowingly hidden themselves since childhood.

When it was over, BillJo lay face down in the loamy soil and the dirt rose in tiny, spurting geysers beneath his nostrils where the the breath whistled. A strange peace and quiet was upon him.

Her face was turned to the sky, one arm held across her eyes as she clung to this retreat. Her clothing was ripped, her hair a

Medusa's tangle of twigs, leaves and pieces of bark, but her features were in complete repose, an ivory carving of serenity.

They did not speak and neither did he offer an assisting hand when he stood above her as she rose. This was no coarse oversight or deliberate contempt. He was, somehow, sharply tuned to her mood. There was no solicitude between them but neither was there callous indifference. What they felt but did not put into words was an unfamiliar elation. There was the accord and understanding of zealots who have walked barefooted over a bed of coals, experiencing and surviving the torture. And, reasonably enough, at this moment neither was sure he or she would want to repeat the performance.

In the car he lit and offered a cigarette. She took it without a change of expression or thanks and drew deeply, sending the smoke out in one long, steady, tight jet. She ran a hand upward from the nape of her neck, dislodging a small filtering of sand. For the first time she smiled and then ruefully. Beneath the torn blouse she now wore nothing. The controlling bandeau had been ripped and thrown away. She glanced down at the obvious rents and shrugged, making no futile effort to pleat them together. She stared ahead for a moment and then backed the car out to turn around.

At The Cottage she drove to the rear garage apartment and without invitation got out and trotted up the steps, waiting only until he had unlocked the door.

While she was in the bathroom he poured a drinking glass half full of bourbon and took a full, grateful swallow. He heard her leave the bath, hesitate and then go to his bedroom. He offered no advice as to where she would find a comb, brush or whatever else she needed. He tasted the whisky again, rolling it caressingly in his mouth.

When she came back her hair was in place. The leaves and twigs brushed from skirt and blouse. Her legs were bare, the torn stockings stripped off and left in a corner. She smiled absently at him, as commuters who are accustomed to seeing each other each morning on the station platform but who are not friends might nod.

From his hand she took the remaining liquor, drank it slowly, reflectively, and lit a cigarette. Then she walked out and down the steps.

VI

JIM HANEY glanced down the long, narrow length of the table and studied Mark Hillyard's attempt to create a picture of glowering ferocity.

"Tell her what she wants to know." The old man stabbed at the contents of his plate, swirling his fork into mashed potatoes and meat. "Give her an accountin' right down to the last paper clip we own. Stay here a month if you have to. There ain't goin' to be any peace in this by-God place until you do."

Carol met Haney's eyes and grinned impudently. They both knew Mark too well to be fooled by this display of simulated outrage. He was making a transparent effort to hide a secret approval behind a screen of shouted words and baffled snorting.

"I don't want to know about paper clips." She separated a piece of lamb from the slice before her. "Just explain to me how we operate. What, exactly, is the Hillyard Corporation?"

Haney leaned comfortably back in his chair. This girl delighted him. "It's pretty involved, Carol." He was not patronizing. She might be, as Mark repeatedly pointed out, only nineteen or so but there was an unswerving drive, a purpose, a determination, an unyielding will which he had to respect. She refused to be diverted by Mark's indulgent ridicule or his airy assumption that the whole business of her insistent inquiry belonged in the mysterious realm of female complaints. "I don't," he concluded honestly, "know exactly where to start."

"She's dancin' a rigadoon on my grave." The old man's eyes lighted with pleased surprise. "How the hell did I ever know that word? Rigadoon." He repeated it with satisfaction. "Yes, sir! That's what she's doin'. Kickin' up her heels before the undertakers have patted down the last spadeful of ground. It ain't decent an' it sure don't comfort a man to have an unnatural daughter." He pointed his knife at Haney. "When she knows as much about things as you an' I, you'd better start lookin' for another job. She's likely to turn out like them female spiders that eat the males when they've done their turn. That's a hell of a reward for doin' your level best, ain't it now?" He considered this dourly. "You take any normal girl now." He pretended Carol wasn't at the table. "She'd be buyin' herself diamonds, a yacht maybe, or one of them Italian counts for a husband an' not givin' a damn where the money come from. Not that one, though. Not Sister. She's got to open the lid an' look inside."

"Do you have a family, Mr. Haney?" Carol ignored her father. "I mean, are there people you want to be with at Christmas?"

"No."

"Then stay here, spend it with Mark and me. Every morning you and I will have an hour's class. You can start from the beginning."

Haney nodded. The idea of the holidays here pleased him. It would be a pleasant interlude and this girl excited his interest. He looked at Hillyard and saw the old man's eyelid drop almost imperceptibly with approval.

"I'd like that." He smiled at her. "It's been a long time since I've felt part of a family."

Jim Haney bulked hugely in the chair. He had the hands and shoulders of a longshoreman and the face of a dissipated choirboy.

76

His rust-colored hair was graying but the cheeks were pinkly flushed with health and Irish whisky. He and Mark Hillyard had known each other for a lifetime, their paths diverging in youth and then mysteriously crossing and recrossing in such unlikely places as Tampico, Nome, Alberta and Dallas. Haney had put himself through law school, working at night to make his expenses. A year as a clerk with an Indianapolis firm convinced him he was no man for inside work. An ambition drove him as it did Mark Hillyard but he drifted with odd jobs, propecting, wildcatting, always searching for the big opportunity. waiting for the improbable break. He had been in a field outside of Houston when the news of Mark Hillyard's strike raced through the state and later tracked him down in Galveston in a noisy bawdyhouse which he had taken over on a week's basis for himself and his crew.

"You can use me." Haney had not asked for a job.

Hillyard had his feet on a table, a bottle in one hand and a girl on his lap. A crap game was in muttered progress on the kitchen floor. He thrust the bottle at Haney and pushed the girl from his knee.

"What can you do?" There was no friendliness in Hillyard's question, no recognition of a lifetime's friendship.

"A hell of a lot of things you can't." Haney all but drained the bottle.

Mark had peered at him with an expression of cunning suspicion. Finally he nodded and pulled the girl back to him. "You're in. Give me back my bottle an' get one of your own. There's a dozen cases in the kitchen."

There had never been more of an agreement between them. What Haney was to do and how he was to do it developed slowly. It was a happy combination. They complemented each other. On the path to great wealth Mark Hillyard struck out with the conquering stride of a confident freebooter. He had the reckless energy and fierce cupidity of a pirate combined with the cold shrewdness of a gambler. He reached for everything with an unmoral disregard for the consequences. Money was glittering power and he snatched for it as a robber crab will drag any shining thing into its hole. Behind him, quietly, methodically and unassumingly, Jim Haney worked. He shored up the conquests with contracts, agreements, small cartels and mergers, building a foundation for Hillyard's gleaming pyramid. As the money poured in he diverted the stream into a hundred different channels. He had an instinct that led him to temporarily insolvent but potentially sound enterprises. He bought here and there, calculated risk and profit to the penny. Hillyard was the flailing thresher who stripped the wheat from the stalk. Haney turned it into flour and loaves. Backed by a capable law firm and tax experts, he set up a vast complex of holding companies and inter-locking directorates. Mark Hillyard never questioned his judgment. When, as sometimes happened, a venture failed, they wrote it off without comment.

Haney set his own salary and drew for himself an annual bonus. He allocated stock to himself when he felt he deserved it, telling Mark what he was doing but never asking his consent. Time, a native curiosity and intelligence, the refining influence of money, had polished Jim Haney. As a guiding hand on the many Hillyard enterprises, he traveled constantly across the United States, into Mexico and South America and Europe. His association with lawyers, scientists, corporate heads, professional men and experts in widely varied fields had given him an urbanity and easy social grace which Mark Hillyard would have scorned. He had time to read extensively, picked up a small knowledge of music and art. Where Mark stubbornly remained the uncouth and woolly specula-tor, Jim achieved a sophisticated assurance, a quiet voice and pleasant humor. He had been astonished, at first, and then charmed by this place which Hillyard had created here in Virginia. It was a creation in which he would have liked to have had a hand. He marveled a little at Mark's compliance with the decorators and authorities who had worked for him. That he hadn't interfered or intruded was apparent in each small detail of the great house. He looked forward to the visit for several reasons.

Mark grunted and pushed back his chair, swinging half around to cross his knees and light a cigar. Carol, almost too primly and with downcast eyes, picked at the food on her plate.

"You don't fool me none, Sister," the old man rasped. "I don't get taken in by that Quaker-girl-at-meetin' look. I knew a card sharp in Kansas who had the same expression when he checked a pat hand at the openin'. Ring for some whisky."

She touched the small silver bell at her hand and the servingman came to bring a decanter of aged rye. Mark poured a large drink and motioned the whisky toward Haney, who shook his head.

Mark tested the beaded, oily liquor with satisfaction. "I don't

78

know as we ever spent a Christmas together, Jim." He was in a mellow humor for a moment. "But," he chuckled, "if Sister is goin' to run things, don't be surprised if Sandy Claus comes down the chimney carryin' the corporate books."

What might have been dull hours of attempting to explain the complexities of the Hillyard enterprises to Carol became, to Haney's surprised interest, encounters with a keenly inquisitive mind.

They had no stiff or formal periods. Sometimes they drove in her car through the afternoon's pale winter sunlight down country roads where the gray cabins stood like cardboard cutouts against stark branches. Other mornings they sat long over their coffee before a fireplace, talking. If Mark was in the room he pretended not to hear or listen. Once, however, he had interrupted Haney: "By God, I didn't know that myself."

Usually, though, Mark left them alone. They walked across bare fields or by the river and a couple of times had lunch in the non-alcoholic taproom of the inn at Court House.

"What I'm trying to give you, Sister"—he had begun calling her that, also—"is mostly background from the time I came in. There wasn't much before that except confusion. Mark never knew how much he had or where it was. If you really want all the details of operation down to the last paper clip, as Mark says, you ought to go into the offices for a while."

"I don't want that and Mark knows it." She shook her head. "But also I don't like the idea of other people knowing more about my business than I do. It isn't a question of wanting to run or manage anything. You seem to do that very well. Mark," she was grave, "isn't as strong as he pretends. Maybe you've noticed."

Haney nodded. The old man seemed to be withering as if in some unseasonal frost. It had shocked him.

"So," Carol continued matter-of-factly, "all of this may drop into my lap at any time. That's why I want to know." She paused. "Mark once said we owned some newspapers but that they didn't make any money. Why?"

"They were and are good for our purpose. There is a pretty involved tax structure in all this."

"That isn't much of a reason for owning anything—or is it?"

He watched the mobility of her features. "What drives you, Sister?" The question was abrupt.

79

She looked up and smiled. "I don't know. Who put the spurs to you or Mark? Maybe it's the same rider." Her expression changed quickly. It was determined now. "Don't act as though it is something indecent or a shameful form of perversion."

"It's a little unusual. You have to admit that. A girl of your age. . . ." He left the sentence unfinished.

"How old do I have to be before I can begin to think for myself? Mark is only half serious when he bellows protests. But I have a feeling with you that it's serious. You really think I'm queer. After all, I'm not walking around naked in the market place."

"You take a little knowing, Sister," he admitted wryly. "I have to keep readjusting my thinking. I wasn't prepared for you. Usually a girl or a woman tries to take out her frustrations in a career. I can't picture you as frustrated. But I should have remembered you're a Hillyard. They don't come in standard sizes, ready to wear, do they?"

"Tell me about the newspapers." She returned to the subject. "Not why we own them. I understand that. But why aren't they first rate?"

"No one has tried to make them first rate. We don't want them successful."

"That's a hell of a way to run anything. If you print a paper you take on an obligation. At least, that is the way it seems to me. If you have a voice you should care how it is used and who listens. Just to run sheets of paper through a press is irresponsible. Too many fools may read and believe what you say."

"For the first time," he smiled quietly, "I detect an evangelical note in you."

"I don't know about that but I do know that when I thump a tambourine on a corner it is going to be because I have something to say. It may be true or false, but people will stop to listen." She leaned forward, her lips slightly parted with excitement. "Could you get me a job on a newspaper, Jim?"

There was no mistaking her earnestness. He didn't laugh. Somehow, he wasn't even surprised.

"I don't want to go to work on one of ours." She diverted an obvious reply. "I'd like a job on a good paper. To find out how a successful one is run. To know why one is a voice and another a whisper. There must be a job somewhere, where I could start."

Haney did not reply immediately and when he did it was not to answer her question.

"This is a big place in which to leave an old man alone. Are you sure you want to do that, Sister?"

"I don't think Mark honestly expects me to stay. We're too much alike. Oh, I guess he'd like it but he doesn't really believe it will happen. I don't have much choice. It's get out now or stay, marry and raise a family. I'm not ready for that. I'm not sure I ever will be. Mark may shout and howl at first, he does that about everything he hasn't thought of. It's the habit of being contrary. These are good years for me. I want to use them. I," she smiled, "have an itch, also. It makes me want to scratch and not sit on the steps, a colonial belle waiting for her lover to ride home from the wars."

"We have a lot of connections." Haney spoke slowly. "You understand, if I can get you a job it won't be because a paper needs you. They'll take you on as a favor to me, us, because I asked it. You start with a handicap."

"I'll work at whatever job they give me. I'll learn to do it well and earn my salary."

"I'm sure of that. Where do you want to go?"

"Wherever the best papers are published. New York?"

"I guess that's a matter of journalistic opinion. New York. San Francisco, maybe. Chicago, no. Washington, perhaps. Take your choice."

"New York." She hunched forward in the chair, eager. "After Christmas?"

He nodded. "I'll go up with you." He was soberly thoughtful. "Don't surprise Mark with this. Tell him now. Get it over with. Give him a chance to get used to the idea."

"I'll tell him." She stood up and gave him her hand. "Thanks, Jim."

As though he suspected that time alone with her would result in something unpleasant, Mark pretended an elaborate occupation with innumerable, mysterious problems. He locked himself in his "office"; hurried outside at odd times to consult with the head gardener over nonexistent projects; drove into Court House and stayed there for the better part of a day. She finally cornered him in his bedroom.

"It won't work." She eyed him mockingly. "You know I want

81

to talk with you. I'm going to New York. I want to work on a newspaper for a while." She expected a tirade of objection.

"I'll miss you, Sister." He didn't look at her but peered into a mirror, stretching out the corner of his mouth with a finger, examining his teeth carefully. "Couldn't you find a paper nearer home? Set up one in Court House?"

"That wouldn't do and you know it."

He pulled at his nose, scratched his ear, bent to one side and another, studying his reflection in the glass with squinting interest. He wouldn't turn to face her.

"You do what you got to do, Sister. I always did. I ain't got the right to tell you to stay an' sit by the fire with an old man."

"You cut that out." She almost shouted, because he was touching her with this deliberately pathetic maneuver of studied resignation. "You're a damned old fraud. You went helling around for years when I was a youngster. Half the time you didn't even remember where you left me."

"I never figured you to be bitter about that, Sister." The pathos was so blatant, so counterfeit. She could have sworn he managed to squeeze a tear from his eye. "I did what a man should, the best he knew how for a poor, motherless child. I got her a lot of the world's goods so's she'd be secure." He glanced at her hopefully.

"You're a ham. You're the worst damned actor I ever saw. You ought to have concealed violins to play 'Hearts and Flowers' when you talk that way."

"Didn't work, hey?" He was suddenly cheerful. "I guess it's a wore-out trick. I used to do pretty well with it. When I was a young fella I learned the best way to get a woman was just to put it in her hand an' cry."

She moved her head incredulously. "You're a sneaky, foul-talking old man with the conscience of a hungry fox."

He chuckled, complimented. "I guess I never figured you'd be satisfied to sit around here. New York ain't too far away an' I got Julia. Yes, by God, I've sure got Julia! You wouldn't want to take her off my hands, would you?" He waited hopefully and then shook his head. "No, I guess not." He moved and touched her cheek with one hand. It was a rare gesture of open affection. "I've had the best of it, Sister." He spoke slowly. "Don't worry about me. I've already done everything I want to do." He studied her for

82

a moment. "Don't wait too long, Sister. What I mean is, don't get so busy you forget you're a woman until it's too late. The female really don't change much inside no matter how much she gets emancipated. Inside she keeps wantin' the same thing—a warm cave, a piece of fire an' a man to bring her meat to cook. That there is fundamental an' a woman without it just becomes a piece."

She reached up to kiss him, clinging for a moment. It surprised them both. They were rarely demonstrative with each other. She felt his grizzled, leathery cheek against hers and then he made the first move to let her go.

"Maybe," he tried to cover his embarrassment, "I'll take Julia on one of them world cruises. I could even get lucky an' marry her off." He considered the idea with relish and winked at her.

The frenzy had worn itself out. They approached each other warily now. It was the studied caution of boxers, each certain the other was seeking an advantage, determined not to be surprised by an unexpected feint.

It was BillJo who displayed the first concern over her incautious visits to the apartment. He put her car in the garage and closed the door. When she was ready to leave, he insisted on going out first to see who was in The Cottage or parked in the yard. She accepted these precautions with a certain puzzled amusement.

"I thought you'd like it." She stretched indolently on the couch. He had told her she was a fool to time her meetings with him here in the late afternoons when customers could be expected. "I had an idea it gave you a kick."

"You mean because the princess comes down from the hill to screw the peasant?"

"I deserved that."

"You're damned right you did." He was angry but controlled. "I just don't have the proper gratitude, I expect."

She watched as he made himself a drink without offering her one, knowing she infuriated him and wondering why it gave her a twisted satisfaction to see him writhe. This headlong excursion into a consuming fire sometimes frightened her. An unsuspected capacity for sheer physical gratification with this man was unnerving.

Why BillJo Adams? She had no ready explanation. He was common, all but illiterate. Away from the bar in The Cottage, where he had acquired the small, routine social graces demanded of a tavernkeeper, he was ordinary and unsure of himself. The brass always showed through the thin plating of gentility. His mind ranged no farther than the sporting pages. They never tried to talk of anything beyond the commonplace. Their relationship, she thought with disgust, was that of a boar and sow; nothing more.

Because he so frequently revolted her she was, inexplicably, reassured. This was a freak encounter. It was a small perversion which, in all likelihood, would not reoccur. What she felt for him was unique in her limited experience. Certainly she had not been moved this way by John Harkness or any of the boys she had met while at school. She was no nymphomaniac, a quick and easy bang for anyone who came along. At times, with him, the idea she might be was frightening. This experience had alerted her to the danger of being possessed by her body. To use it was one thing. To have it use and sublimate her was another. That was a weakness she would not tolerate in herself. The question of morality never entered her mind. She had, unknowingly, been hungry for a strange and unfamiliar food. BillJo Adams had innocently supplied it. When she left him it would be to put behind her this unnatural appetite. She would have other men but they would never know her as had this one. It surprised her a little that she felt no regret over leaving him. But, and this puzzled her, she experienced no relief as though escaping from an intolerable situation.

"I'm going to New York."

"Good." He lit a cigarette and quickly blew out the flame as it began to tremble. "That's a hell of a fine idea."

"Aren't you going to miss me?" She mocked him.

"I wish to Christ I'd never seen you."

"Why?" She sat up quickly, interested by this small indication of vulnerability. "Why did you say that?"

"Because you're not human. I saw a picture once of a thing they call the Iron Maiden. Outside it looked like a woman. They put a man in her and there was nothin' but spikes to stab his guts."

"You know," she watched him speculatively, "I think we must really hate each other. If so, this is the queerest affair on record."

"I don't hate you." He was shaking. "All my life I had an idea about someone like you. It's class. I even learned from you that's a cheap word. If you have it you don't use it. You don't have to.

84

People know it like they can tell good whisky from rotgut. It don't need a label or a fancy bottle. I don't know how you got it; not from that old man of yours. From what I hear he's as common as me. But it's there an' it's a rock. I ain't goin' to beat my brains out against it. You never give an inch. I'm a stud for you."

"Why don't you let it go at that? Why do you want more?"

"Because it makes me sick to my stomach. So sick I want to puke." He grabbed her wrist, pulling her from the couch. "It's like bein' thirsty an' drinkin' what looks like water but ain't. There isn't anything you've got that I want except you. I'm not after your money. I got plenty of my own. You don't mean anything in this town where family counts for so goddamned much. But you've got a confidence; like you were born to have what you wanted. You walk in a kind of a pride even when I dirty you. That's what I want an' can't get over. It's like that first day when you drove back here an' said: 'Get in, BillJo.' I did, too, by God. I got in the car an' sat there. You drove me to the woods an' I serviced you. I've been doin' it ever since. For the first time I know, maybe, what a whore feels like. It ain't pretty. It's a real hell of a feelin'."

"You're hurting my wrist."

He dropped it but without apology. She studied the marks of his fingers on her flesh and felt a tingle of excitement.

"Why are you goin' to New York?" He made an effort to control his heavy breathing. "How long you goin' to stay?"

"I don't know. I mean, I don't know how long. Fix me a drink." She took the cigarette from his fingers and walked to a window, staring outside, watching a squirrel as it raced across the yard. "I'm going to get a job."

"I could come up sometime." He paused and after an interval she heard an icecube drop into a glass. "I go to New York three or four times a year." The statement was a question.

She shook her head and then turned to face him. "I don't think so. I think it ends where it started. Here." She took the drink he had made and smiled, almost wistfully. "I haven't any idea how it is going to be with another man. It may be better. It may not be so good. But it won't be the same, if that is any satisfaction to you."

"It ain't—isn't. I get sick all over again thinkin' about you with another man."

He was pleading now but the spectacle, instead of arousing compassion or understanding, crystallized a growing revulsion. She didn't want to see him squirm. It suddenly made her ashamed of him and herself. She put down the drink and almost ran from the room while he stood and cursed her with a deadly, unemotional monotone that was frightening in its flat obscenity.

VII

THE January snow whirled in gusty loops up Broadway from the Battery, spinning across City Hall Park and driving the loungers, pigeons and hot-chestnut vendors to shelter. Only those who must be were abroad and they walked into the cold wind with lowered heads and overcoats flapping.

The storm whipped over the dingy building on the corner of Chambers Street, piling in serrated ridges along the windowsills. Inside the rooms were warm and brightly lighted and the suspended bowls trembled faintly as the presses ran out the Home Edition.

In the sparsely furnished waiting room, with its yellow walls, unmatched chairs and couch, Carol stood up as a shirt-sleeved man came from an adjoining room. Past his shoulders she had a glimpse of figures bent over typewriters and beyond them the horseshoe-shaped copy desk where men scribbled with pencils or leaned back, staring at the ceiling as though to find the sought-for words written there.

"Miss Hillyard?"

She nodded, smiled and extended her hand.

"I'm Chris Chandler." His hand was impersonal. "I had a note about you."

"Thanks for seeing me." She waited.

Chandler appraised her quickly. The mink coat she wore represented a couple of years' salary. He did not resent this. For one reason or another it tickled his sense of humor. He indicated the couch and when she was seated, took a place beside her.

"I want a job." She smiled. "But of course you already know that. I would liked to have come another way, without intercession from above. But then," her quick expression of amusement caught his fancy, "you wouldn't have seen me, would you?"

"We usually see everyone, if only by proxy. The low man on the rewrite is detailed to come out and say: 'Mr. Chandler, the city editor, is busy just now. May I help you?'"

"He doesn't hand out jobs, though, does he?"

"Almost never."

"Then I'm glad we didn't waste his time. Is it all right if I smoke?"

"In here, yes." He tore a match from a paper tab and lit it for her. "In the city room, no. It is believed to cloud the thinking there and lend a dissolute air to the place." He said this without a change of expression. "We don't have any reporters who keep pints of whisky in their desks either, and no one calls me Sport or Boss. So much for the movies." His glance traveled over her lizardskin shoes to her crossed knees. "Just what is it you can do on a paper?"

"I could sweep out, if necessary. I can run errands or copy. I can, also, write a simple declarative sentence and get names and addresses right."

"*Cum laude. Cum magnum laude* from the Columbia School of Journalism would recommend you no more highly than that."

"I'm not sure," she was momentarily doubtful, "my nose exactly twitches for news. It's supposed to, isn't it?"

"That, Miss Hillyard, is an occupational tic. You acquire it, or so they say. Frankly, I've never seen it. In any event, you wouldn't be expected to display it at first. The AP and City News will twitch

88

for you. You rewrite what they write." He leaned back, stretched his long legs and grinned companionably at her.

"That seems a little silly. Don't the AP and City News write well?"

"They are rewritten only to avoid a monotonous uniformity in all the city's papers." He looked her over again. "I expect you will lend a certain tone to the shop. We rarely, if ever, have the hired hands come to work in mink coats."

She blew the ash from her cigarette. "I could get a plaid mackinaw and a pair of Boy Scout shoes. I could even report with a blanket wrapped around my shoulders, if that will help you achieve the norm. Don't be a snob, Mr. Chandler."

He nodded approvingly. "How old are you, Miss Hillyard?"

"It's elastic. I can be twenty, twenty-one or two. What's a good age for starting on a paper?"

"There is none. Does it occur to you this is an unorthodox conversation between prospective employer and employee?"

"You started it."

"So I did. It was a dull morning until you came in. I assume you can use a typewriter? Despite the leisurely atmosphere here we do not write our copy with quills and dust the ink with sand. It only seems that way sometimes."

"I can't remember why, but I took a course in typing and shorthand in school. It was offered at Miss Parkinson's with the same misgivings a series of lectures on harlotry would be included in the curriculum."

He looked at his watch. "I usually have a late breakfast at this time. Would you like some coffee?"

"Yes, thank you." She dropped her cigarette into a tray.

When he came back with his coat on they walked down the short flight of steps and across Broadway to Schrafft's. He indicated a table at one side, near the window.

"Is it usual for the city editor and the hirelings to have breakfast together?"

He took a swallow of the strong black coffee that was put before them immediately and lit a cigarette. "This is an oddly formal informal paper. I started as a copy boy fifteen years ago. Once out of those hustling ranks I was never called anything else but Mr. Chandler by the city desk, the managing editor and, even, the publisher. First names are known and used only by the cashier who makes out the weekly checks. However, outside there is an easy relationship such as this. No one thinks it strange."

The waitress brought ham, scrambled eggs, marmalade and muffins for him and another pot of coffee for her. He ate hungrily and without apology. She wondered if his attitude of casual banter was usual or displayed for her benefit alone.

"Why do you want to go to work on a newspaper, Miss Hillyard?"

Old Mark wouldn't have done it any better. "I own three or four. I want to know how a good one is run."

"I see." There was no break in the motion as he cut through the ham slice, no change of tone or expression. "The ones you own, then, aren't any good?"

"I don't know enough to have a real standard of comparison. They probably could be better." He had been too decent to her, she thought, to leave things as they were. "I said what I did, Mr. Chandler, knowing exactly the way it sounded. But," she was earnest, "I wanted you to know I wasn't a wide-eyed debutante looking for a rumored thrill on a paper or expecting to be titillated by contact with the working class. I have a serious reason. I want to learn." She paused. "I could say I'm sorry about the mink coat but I'm not. It's cold outside."

"You can grow real old learning this trade." He buttered a muffin slowly. "You're right. It is cold and none of my business if you want to wear a winding sheet." He finished the muffin and lit a cigarette. "This is a craft you learn by instinct. There isn't anything mysterious about it. A good rule is to ask yourself what you would like to read in your paper if you were paying for one at a stand. What knits a paper and its staff together is quite another thing. It is a mutual respect between desk and man. The staff learns in a hurry when the advertising department flows into the editorial. When that happens he loses respect for his paper although he is realist enough to know few persons can resist the pressure of a dollar. When the daughter of a department store owner is caught in a hotel with a married man, he shouldn't have to wonder how his paper is going to handle the story. It has to be printed, of course, but it can be written with liberal quotes from the family physician who states that the poor girl was a victim of amnesia and had no idea where she was or what she was doing. In that way it is possible to preserve a certain integrity and the department

90

store's big advertising account. You can print it straight, however. That's the best way if the man behind the desk or in the publisher's chair has the guts." He picked up the checks and helped her into her coat.

Outside, they stood for a moment within the doorway watching the snow and the ghost-ship passage of a bus.

"Do you want to check in Monday morning at eight o'clock? We usually start a new man out on the lobster trick, from three in the morning until eleven, but not when the new man is a girl."

"Would you have dinner with me tonight?" she asked impulsively. "After Monday I don't imagine that would be possible."

"Oh, I don't know." He stared at the clouds tearing themselves apart against the Woolworth Building's tower. "Despite the Hollywood legend, city editors rarely have the opportunity of dining with an heiress. In your words, the idea titillates me. What time?"

"Any time that suits you." She pulled the collar up about her face.

"I usually check out after the final edition goes in. That's around four-thirty. I'll kill some time at the A.C. for a while. How is seven?"

"Fine." She gave him her hand. "Thank you. I'm sorry if I was fresh but not really."

"It has added a certain fillip to my morning. What's the address?"

She gave him the number on lower Fifth Avenue near the Washington Square arch.

He whistled sharply at a cruising cab and put her in. "I assume you don't have a car and chauffeur waiting?"

Her face, hooded within the sleek fur of an upturned collar, was vividly disturbing. Her eyes studied him with a bright curiosity.

"You have a nasty habit of being patronizing, Mr. Chandler. I allow myself this and similar comments until eight o'clock Monday morning. After that I expect the rod and scourge."

"I voice only the natural envy of the masses, Miss Hillyard." He closed the door and stood at the curb until the car pulled away.

She gave the driver the address and leaned back in the seat. On the thick carpeting of snow the cab rolled silently. The morning had grown lemon-colored as the sun thrust against scudding clouds. She was now a part of this dirty, overcrowded city; committed to it for a while, at least. More than that she had become a small working piece on a newspaper of great tradition. If there were things to be learned she could study them here.

She and Jim Haney had come up from Richmond together after New Year's. He had used the vague excuse of business to see that she was settled and comfortable. The interview with Chandler was the result of a telephone call made to the publisher. Jim, apparently, had lines out in many directions. If Mark had been sorry to see her go he gave no outward sign.

"Jim'll set up an account in New York for you, Sister, an' leave word you can draw whatever you want. I've about decided to take Julia to South America. It's summertime down there now an' them hot-blooded Latins are probably hotter. Maybe she'll make a catch. Likely enough I'll see you in New York." He touched her chin with his fingers. "Take good care of yourself now."

The holidays in Virginia had been unexpectedly festive. Even Mark had yielded to the mood, plodding about the place, whistling Christmas carols with the almost tuneless monotony of a dirge, needlessly superintending the stringing of lights and the placing of wreaths. With one of the yardboys they had gone into the woods for holly and mistletoe, piling it crisp and sparkling in the back of the car and selecting a huge conical fir to be cut for the tree.

Boothby Warrington was home from Charlottesville for the vacation and he drove over to ask her to the Yule Dance at the country club. She had gone with reservations and was pleasantly surprised by the warm, friendly curiosity that made her feel welcome. Out of it grew invitations to cocktail parties and supper gatherings in Court House and early morning rides across fields which sparkled and snapped with frost. For the first time she had the feeling this was home, a place where she belonged.

Bootsie was a daily caller. They walked and rode or he lounged comfortably at her side before the fireplace, consuming almost incredible amounts of Mark's special rye whisky in hot water, stirred with a cinnamon stick. He was as insinuatingly friendly as a setter, asking only to be liked, patted on the head and allowed a place at her side. There was a cheerful, unspoiled ingenuousness about him. The booming laughter which went with the huge frame bounced from the walls and echoed throughout the house. He moved with the deceptively heavy grace of a good-natured sloth. He liked everyone and just took it for granted everyone would like him. He delighted the servants and his effortless courtesy even thawed Mark's native hostility for handsome men.

He was exaggeratedly alarmed by the news that Carol was going to New York.

"That's a town just filled with Yankee fortune hunters." He brooded over the traps which might lie in the path of her innocent footsteps. "I sure hope none of them gets to you before I do." He reached over to take her hand. "I'm kind of counting on you to rescue me from a future of genteel poverty. I've even spoken to my daddy and mama about it. They are agreed that a wedding with you an' your money is a real solution. I'm savin' myself for you, ma'am. I sure enough am." He thrust his nose into a steaming glass and inhaled the vaporous aroma with a gusty sigh.

Watching, listening to an artless chatter, Carol was suddenly struck by the notion that he probably meant exactly what he said. There was no affectation, no guile in Bootsie. The undercurrent of seriousness beneath his words was not meant to be undetected. He was offering what seemed a reasonable and fair exchange. To her surprise she discovered it wasn't offensive.

He was sprawled in the chair with the jointless ease of a rag doll. "You look up Angela when you get there." He sucked the toddy through curled cinnamon bark. "I'll write her to keep an eye on you. She'll have ol' Bootsie's interests at heart. You can count on that. If you get serious about another man I'll come a-runnin' in my old tennis sneakers to snatch you away. In the meantime I'll do my best at the University. I'll be true to you, true and trusting. After you think about it long enough you'll come to see how hard it would be for either of us to do better."

"I'll lock away this proposal, if that's what it is, with my most cherished romantic memories." She grinned.

"You just do that, child." He unwound himself from the chair. "Remember, true hearts are more than coronets. After all, you Yankees cut quite a swath through Virginia. It is only right some reparation should be made. With you on my arm the Warringtons would consider all debts canceled. This could be a real opportunity. A union between us could bind up the wounds of a nation."

"The appeal to my patriotism really gets me." She nodded gravely. "You're a pretty slick character."

"I also have a most sunny disposition which flowers in the warm sun of indolence. You would find in me a helpmeet of charm and social accomplishments. Between us we could produce numberless fair-haired progeny to warm your old father's flinty heart and be a comfort to us as well."

She watched with frank interest as he went to a table, took a fistful of English walnuts from a bowl and cracked them all at once with the closing of a hand. He had an undeniable grace and charm with a baby's complexion and blandly inquisitive blue eyes. After BillJo Adams he was a fresh wind. When he kissed her, an act which he took for granted she wanted performed, it was with a surprising gentleness, almost concern. He was human and male enough but he seemed to want to lead her quietly. She found herself responding, not with fierce, consuming ecstasy, but with the pleasant sensation of security. No demon rode her.

She hadn't seen BillJo since their last meeting in his apartment and he made no effort to call her. It was an episode closed, all but erased. There was now a sinister grotesqueness about the affair that gave it a distant aspect of swarming horror. She had put him behind her without regret. He had served a purpose better than he could know. He had stirred a volcanic fury. It was a thing to watch for. Never again would it take her by surprise.

One night, driving with Bootsie, he had suggested stopping at The Cottage for a drink. Before she could refuse he had changed his mind.

"Your papa's whisky is better and free, too."

She wondered if gossip had been tossed about in Court House and then decided it hadn't. She would have been aware of it through the people she had met with Bootsie.

"You know," she looked up at him now as he crunched the walnuts between his teeth, "I just might marry you after all." The statement surprised her but not him.

"This here now thing," he drawled, "is bigger than us both."

"Sometimes you sound like the Three Black Crows or Amos and Andy."

He nodded complacently, regarding her fondly. She understood he deliberately broadened the normally soft and unobtrusive accent for her benefit and because it amused him. He had a trick of making the word "hair" come out as in two syllables to sound something like "hi-yah." She tested the combination.

"Ah want some a-yah en mah hi-yah."

He cocked his head and listened critically. "That isn't just it.

94

Northerners never seem to get it right. It's 'eye-yah en mah hi-yah.' "

"Air in my hair." She translated and laughed at the flatness of the intonation. "You have something there, Bootsie."

"Yes, ma'am. I know it." He was pleased and emphatic. "That there thing works like Spanish fly on Yankee girls. Could I get it in bottles to sell I wouldn't have to come marrying your papa's money. You could come marrying mine."

Riding now through the streets of this alien city she thought of Bootsie with a pleasant indulgence. At another time, another place. Maybe. He and John Harkness had a common, anachronistic elegance of quiet manner and confidence. The appeal, in both cases, had been the same.

The cab drew up before the canopied entrance and a doorman moved out from the lee to open and hold her door. She paid the driver and hurried inside.

The apartment had been Haney's suggestion. She had thought first of a hotel until she was settled.

"You own the building," he told her. "At least the Hillyard Enterprises does and that's the same thing. We keep an apartment there for business use but you'd better take it. There is a Norwegian couple to take care of the place. She is the cook and he's sort of a butler-houseman. They'll look after you and you'll be a lot more comfortable than in a hotel. There are charge accounts at all the stores and stock of pre-prohibition liquor and wines."

"Every aid to the working girl?" She had been amused.

"Why not?" He was serious. "I never subscribed to the theory that life in a hall bedroom was an ennobling or necessary experience."

The apartment turned out to be half the top floor of the building. A planted balcony overlooked Washington Square Park, the dingy maze of Greenwich Village and the North River. On the walls of the spacious living room were two original Corot landscapes and a Sisley. A small study-library and the four bedrooms were faultlessly decorated. In a drawer of a desk she found a tooled leather book with three pages of names and telephone numbers of what could only be call girls. She thought the Hillyard Enterprises did very well for itself and business associates. The Norwegian couple had the fresh, healthy appearance of figures on a skiing poster and were quietly competent.

Haney, apparently, had briefed everyone from the building superintendent to the cleaning women, and she moved quickly into a comfortable feeling of permanence.

Chandler arrived promptly at seven o'clock. She went to the door herself to let him in.

He whipped a snow-splattered hat against a leg and glanced quizzically about the foyer.

"No French maid?"

"Norwegian houseman and you stop this nonsense. You know better. I refuse to be intimidated in my own home. Put your things in the closet there."

He was not embarrassed by her obvious annoyance.

Leading him into the living room, she looked up to ask: "What did you do at the Athletic Club—lift weights or throw your own around?"

"I shrank my head in a steam bath in an effort to achieve the proper humility."

"It didn't work. What will you drink?"

"Anything but a cocktail."

There was a wheeled cabinet at one side of the fireplace. He sniffed the bourbon appreciatively and at her request helped himself. She had a rye with plain water.

From one end of the couch he stared at the fire. Wood instead of the usual gas logs burned and crackled with the fresh scent of good oak.

"After I went back to the office I looked you up in the clips. Mark Hillyard is your father, of course."

She nodded, wondering a little at his frankness in admitting the curiosity.

"He has a genius for keeping himself out of the news, hasn't he? We didn't have much on him. He burrows in an anonymity which is rare in these publicity conscious days. Where is he now?"

"Back home, in Virginia. You didn't have to go searching the files. I would have told you anything you wanted to know. That would come under the heading of information to be included in the application for a job."

"You already have the job." He tasted the bourbon with an expression of dreamy contentment.

"And you resent it, the way I went about getting in?"

He shook his head. "No. You wanted a job. There wasn't a

chance of your getting one if you came through the usual channels. When you have influence use it. I do every day."

"Are you young to be a city editor?"

"I'm thirty-seven. That's neither too young nor too old. I've been lucky. I had some good teachers on the way up." He smiled at her. "You're really serious about this, aren't you? I keep wondering why. Oh, I know the world is filled with young and eager who want to be newspapermen. A myth persists about the calling. In general it is underpaid and routinely dull. No romantic fancy drives you though, does it?"

"No. I'm not caught up in the legend. At least, I don't think so. Help yourself to more bourbon." She waited until he came back and sat down again. "It never occurred to me I would step outside the conventional ring. The pattern was set. I could get married, raise children, interest myself in the social activities open to women who have no financial problems. My husband would neither have to have money of his own nor work at making it. Mark had already taken care of that. Frankly, it sounded pretty dull but I didn't know what to do about it."

He lit a cigarette. "What set you off on this kick?"

"It isn't a kick." She was tightly angry. "I'll damn well prove it to you." She relaxed. "I suppose that's something I will have to contend with; not only from you but from everyone else." She took a deep breath. "I could name a dozen women offhand who run department stores, beauty salon chains, cosmetic companies, fashion magazines. Only an idiot would suggest they are off on a kick; irresponsible flutter-heads playing with big, shiny toys. Since I can't believe you are an idiot I can only assume you are deliberately trying to infuriate me." She glared at him.

He was undisturbed. "Why newspapers? Hillyard Enterprises flows in many directions."

"I honestly don't know." She smiled. "One day Mark said something about some newspapers we owned. I was surprised at first and then I was a little shocked when I found out they were bought only for tax purposes. I don't really understand that. It's something to do with writing off a loss on one thing against the excess profits on another. I thought, and I told him, that wasn't much of a reason for owning newspapers or anything else. It is more than a waste of manpower but I can't think of anything more deadening than working on a paper that is deliberately unsuccessful. One of these days, after I've learned what I can, I'm going to run them right."

"What do you really expect to learn here?"

"Not how to run a newspaper." She smiled quickly. "But maybe what makes a good one. A little of that must filter down even upon the head of low man on the rewrite desk. So, to reassure you, I'm not expecting to be taken by the hand. I want to work, learn my job and watch."

The man, Peters, came in to announce dinner and Chandler finished his bourbon and rose with her.

"One thing about this paper." They walked to the dining room. "You will eventually do a little of everything except sweep out."

As with everything else in the apartment the dinner was perfectly planned, cooked and served. Chandler flashed her an appreciative glance of commendation. They talked with easy unrestraint. There was no feeling of strangers meeting for a brief moment. A small companionship had built itself without effort. That, she thought, was probably what he had meant by a formal informal paper.

"There are some fights up at the Garden. Would you like to drop in for a while?"

"I've never been to a fight. I think I'd like to see one." They had coffee in the living room and he refused a brandy. "You don't drink much, do you?"

"Sometimes, but I reserve them for vacations. That fiction dies hard also, doesn't it? The classic figure of a drunken reporter. I've often wondered how it started. I never knew a good man in any job who was a rummy. What made anyone believe a reporter could cover a story or write it lushed to the gills? It just isn't possible."

While he waited for her he roamed about the room, studying the paintings, the small, exquisite Chinese porcelains. Despite the perfection of detail it was a comfortable room, escaping a stiff formalization. That, he mused a little wonderingly, was why it was perfect.

Outside it had stopped snowing and here, where there was little traffic, the fall lay with heavy, unblemished chilled beauty and in silence. A block away, at the Brevoort, there was a cab stand. He glanced down at her slipper-clad feet.

"Wait here. I'll walk down."

From behind them the doorman moved to the curb and shrilled a blast on his whistle. A taxi moved out quickly and toward them.

Chandler grinned. "Sorry. This takes a little getting used to."

"You're a liar." She said it calmly. "You knew damn well he was there. This is a bucolic pose struck for my benefit. I am no longer amused. It is supposed to make me self-conscious. Well, it doesn't. You keep it up and I'll get a car and chauffeur to drive me to work every morning and call for me at night. You do not overawe me with this simple-man-of-the-masses act."

He was surprised by her vehemence. Then he nodded. "I'm sorry. I mean it. It was clumsy humor, a bad joke stretched too far; a cover-up because I am the one who is impressed and don't want to admit it."

"The peasant smock doesn't become you." She was not completely mollified. "Stop trying it on. I'm not working for you yet and when I am I'm still going to live as it pleases me."

He told the doorman they were going to the Garden and took the seat beside her. She kept her face turned to the window, ignoring his presence.

"If I'm impressed," he spoke slowly, "it's not by Mark Hillyard's money, a mink coat, Fifth Avenue apartments and servants. It's you. I have the feeling you are not only a little outside my experience but also, anyone else's. And that," he concluded, "is as much of an apology as you are going to get."

"It's more than I expected." She turned and slid a hand beneath his arm. Her smile was cockily impertinent. "Let's forget it."

At the fights and later, as they waited in line for a cab, she was astonished by the number of persons who knew Chandler and greeted him with obvious friendliness. The cops outside the entrance, the loungers and hangers-on, taxi drivers and newsboys called his name or lifted a hand in hello. They rode across town to Reubens, at Fifty-ninth Street. The Negro doorman swept an exaggerated bow and flashed a brilliant smile.

"Good evenin', Mr. Chandler, an' ma'am."

"How are you, Jack?"

Clerks behind the delicatessen counter, the headwaiter and patrons in the booths spoke or waved.

When they were seated and had ordered, she voiced a mounting curiosity.

"You make this seem like a country town. Does everyone know you and why?"

"After you've lived here for a while you'll make the same discovery everyone else has. You settle in an apartment, draw a circle around a couple of blocks and that becomes your village. You know the officer on the beat, the man at the newsstand, owner of the delicatessen, clerk in the chain grocery store, operator of the speakeasy. My village has just been a little larger. I've been around a long time, filling in on sports, writing a night club column for a while, covering districts and headquarters. You run into a lot of people that way and they remember you."

Enormous sandwiches were put before them with pots of coffee. She divided one into manageable segments. While they ate there were frequent interruptions as prize fighters, a Hollywood actress, columnists from other papers, producers and promoters stopped at the table to exchange a few words with Chandler. They did this, she felt, because they genuinely liked him and not only because he was the city editor of an important paper.

When they were again alone, she glanced at him with a speculative smile. "They all seem to like you."

"Is that a question?" He laughed. "I made friends, did favors when I could because, generally, I like people. Now that I'm behind a desk a lot of good will comes back in one way or another."

"Were you a good reporter?"

He lit a cigarette and studied the curling match before blowing out its flame. "Yes. I worked hard at it because it was the only thing I ever wanted to be. There is no real secret about it."

"Is there a formula? I mean, what do they teach in schools of journalism?"

"Everything they can but, as with every other school, you run into the imponderables. You can teach a man to make fine, clean lines on a drawing board but you can't teach him to project these into a beautiful building. That spark, the imagination, comes from within the student himself. There may be a general pattern to follow. I'm not sure." He smiled faintly. "If I owned a paper I would have carved over the door: 'Abandon all your sensibilities ye who enter here.' There should be no such word as privacy in a reporter's vocabulary. When a child is run down by a truck in a crowded street, the mother cannot be left alone to rock in her screaming agony. She must be talked with and photographed, preferably holding the dead child in her arms. The stricken driver must be made to repeat his version of the accident although he retches on each word. Without those things you have only a couple of lines of type. You must remember that most persons derive a small, secret satisfaction from the misfortunes of others. So, if you run a success-ful paper you must give them every detail. They want to gloat a little. Enough is never enough. The average man is inarticulate when questioned by a reporter. He must be badgered, hammered at, and even have the words put into his mouth until he really believes he said them. We have district men who barely got through high school. On the phone you will find them almost illiterate. They are not supposed to write. You do that. They are invaluable because nothing is sacred. Their hide is thick. They will pursue and ask questions a finer-tempered person would shy from. They are con-vinced the press cards they carry dissolve all barriers and bear an authority not exceeded by the great seal of the United States Government. No paper could survive without them." He beckoned a waiter.

"Adolph said no check, Mr. Chandler." The man started to pull back the table.

"He knows better than that."

The man glanced at the headwaiter and then shrugged. He wrote out a check and accepted the money reluctantly.

"Do you always pay a check?" She asked the question on the way downtown in a cab. "I always heard newspapermen were the world's greatest free-loaders."

"Not on this paper. The exception is the night club columnist. It is a rule and a good one to remember when you are running your own. Not that your reporters will actually be able to pump your columns full of free publicity. They can't, but it is better they feel an obligation to no one except the paper."

She made no comment on his easy acceptance of the fact that she would run a paper someday, but it did not escape her. If he believed it, then it was not impossible.

He kept the cab waiting as he took her to the apartment elevator, refusing the invitation to come up for a drink.

"It's been nice—being with you, I mean." She gave him her hand. "I didn't think to ask if having dinner with me would be inconvenient or if you were married and wouldn't like to bring your wife."

"If it had been, I would have said so. And I'm not married. By the time I could afford a wife I wasn't sure I wanted one. Good night." He released her hand. "I'll see you Monday morning."

He stood, waiting until the doors closed silently upon the picture she made within the car's frame, and then turned away.

The legacy she represented was nothing new. They came hopefully down from the publisher's office with a note or after a telephone call. They were the sons and daughters of big advertisers, politicians or important industrialists. Usually he found a place for them in the city room. They rarely stayed long, quitting with embarrassed apologies after a few weeks or months when they discovered the work was neither glamorous nor exciting. He wondered a little about this one, however. There was something there, a small radiance, an independence that came not alone from the security of great wealth. She would, he mused without surprise, do exactly what she said she was going to do. He only wondered why.

VIII

THE days pleated themselves into a bright accordion of weeks and months with the city becoming, as Chandler had said, a familiar village in which she took her place with an easy assurance.

Beyond the small world, spinning in its own orbit, there were vast and unbelievably squalid reaches into which she had ventured on her own time and with a frequent, reckless lack of ordinary caution. There was the cold, cadaverlike decay of the lower East Side. The sullen, daytime face of Harlem that broke open like a poisonous, night-blooming flower with the darkness. There was the subdued roar of the North River docks and the oddly contrasting Old World air that seemed to hover over the Battery, Coenties Slip, Jeanette Park and the East River piers. She played no part, pretended to be nothing but what she was, but she didn't wear a mink coat. Her shoes were low-heeled and meant for walking and her clothing good but unobtrusive. She was stunned sometimes by the poverty and wretchedness in this, the greatest of all cities in the richest of all countries, but she felt no particular compassion. This disturbed her a little. She wondered why misery did not stir her to pity. It didn't. If she felt anything it was only to report it, accurately and dispassionately. A drunken, witch-haired harridan staggering out of an abandoned warehouse beneath the arches of the Brooklyn Bridge aroused no sympathy. She knew only curiosity and wondered why and how. By what strange paths had she come to this place?

On the paper now she no longer felt strange or uncertain. Looking back to the first days and weeks she could realize the effortless friendliness and tact of the men and women with whom she had come in contact. Her name was Carol Hillyard. She was new on the paper, nothing more. A few may have wondered how, without experience, she had found a place, but the question was never asked. Newspaper work, she thought, was singularly free from the petty strivings, the pushing ambitions and intramural intrigues that seemed to bedevil most occupations. No one had a greedy eye on the job of the man next to him.

It was, as Chandler had told her, a formal informal paper. Sometime during the first week the managing editor had left his unpartitioned desk in a corner to walk over to ask how she was getting along. He was a tall, soft-spoken man of inherently gracious manner, and a legend in the world of newspapers. He smiled and asked her if everything was going all right. He meant it, too. She understood, somehow, the action hadn't been prompted by the fact that she came to the city room through the publisher's office. He made the gesture because he meant it. It was his nature to do this.

She had moved haltingly through those first weeks. Her nervous errors were small but many. She rewrote single paragraphs from City News and Standard News, striving with a tight concentration to make them different and trying too hard. Usually what she wrote ended on a spike on the city desk. The first time she saw Chandler's assistant do this with the precious lines she was miserably mortified.

Once, on his way back from the late breakfast, Chandler stopped at her desk. "Take it easy." He smiled reassuringly but impersonally.

"This is a dry run. You're expected to be nervous at first. You'll get the feel of it."

There were two other girls in the city room. One, Jo Hart, on rewrite, and another who seemed to float in and out mysteriously on special assignments. Jo—she later learned her name was just that and not Josephine—was her own age, but she went about her work with a professional competence that made Carol admiringly envious. Now and then they met in the hall where the staff drifted out to smoke. Jo was casually friendly but not inquisitive.

"How do you like it?" she asked one morning.

"When I know what I'm doing, I'll like it better."

"I eat in a speakeasy over on Park Row. We'll go to lunch together if you like."

This had been the beginning of a friendship, a little guarded at first on both sides for reasons which neither could have explained.

"I'm not a girl's girl," Jo had explained. "I'd much rather eat with a man, but not here or for an hour's lunch. You just looked lonely. I was, also, when I first came."

Now, with a few months behind her, Carol was surer of herself and what she was doing. She learned to recognize the voices of the district men and their manner of delivering a story. She acquired a facility, limited but apparent, in giving the small items a little freshness. No one told her how to do this, she simply repeated Chandler's advice and wrote what she would have liked to read.

Gradually she lost her awe for a verbatim report and began lacing the essential facts with touches of her own. She discovered she had a sense of humor, a feeling for the ridiculous. Once, after rewriting a City News story on a frog-jumping contest up in Central Park, she had ripped the page from the typewriter and balled it up. It was a dull, factual account and nothing more. She rewrote it in dialogue between the weary frogs themselves who wondered who the hell Mark Twain was that they had to leap about every year this way. It came out pretty funny and she was rewarded by seeing a faint smile on Chandler's face as he read it over and marked it for a two-column head. If she had won the Pulitzer Prize she couldn't have been more elated. In the privacy of the apartment that night she read and reread the seemingly immortal lines with gratified astonishment that they were hers.

It was, as Chandler had told her, a paper on which you learned eventually to do a little of everything. The older men from rewrite frequently sat in on the city desk when Chandler or one of the regular assistants was away. A general assignment man would suddenly find himself writing for the editorial page during the vacation periods. A Protestant would be sent to cover Catholic ordinations, and a Jew went to Communion Breakfasts. A ship news reporter would cover a beauty contest in Palisades Park or someone from the drama department report a prize fight. The result was a singularly well-rounded staff.

New as she was to it all, Carol began to have feeling this one was unlike any other paper in the city; perhaps even in the country. It was noted for its small wage scale and yet it drew some of the best talent. Men worked on it with the same sense of pride a doctor might interne at Johns Hopkins or the Mayo Clinic. He felt he had the best and wanted only to make it better if that was possible. Because what she wanted to learn was, she felt, beyond the mechanics of putting a newspaper together, she tried to analyze and understand the unique accord that existed and was reflected in the columns of print.

It was a paper, she began to realize, where members of the staff voluntarily went outside the paid-for hours in search of stories to lighten the pages of general news. No one waited for the desk to hand out feature assignments. It was possible to go to Chandler and say, "I think there may be something in this" and to outline the idea. Chandler would listen carefully and if he agreed, nod his head saying, "Take a crack at it, why don't you." No one received anything extra on his paycheck for this. If he was given a by-line, that was enough; and if he wasn't, he was somehow satisfied just to see the story used. The result was a subtle atmosphere of good men working together at a job they loved. If the suggested story didn't pan out, Chandler never questioned the time spent outside the office or how it had been used. He assumed his staff knew its business.

Little by little Chandler began easing her out of the city room. He did this as he did with everyone at first, testing and assaying the potentials. He wanted to know as quickly as possible what the individual was capable of. What she was given at first were the business luncheons, the civic gatherings and women's clubs. These were routine. She knew it. The speeches were mimeographed and available in advance. Now and then, though, it was possible to pick up small, personal touches to lighten the copy. After a dozen or more of these she was struck by the notion that a really ingenious person could eat very well in this city for nothing. There were few breakfasts but almost unlimited luncheons and dinners held every day and night in the different hotels.

She had been surprised at first that no one ever questioned her right to attend or asked for credentials. At the entrance to the banquet rooms it was necessary only to mention her name and that of the paper and be shown immediately to the press table. There, the publicity director brought the addresses, and the waiter promptly set before her the inevitable chicken à la king or broiled, the frilled lamb chops or *filet mignon*.

The idea grew, but she hesitated to discuss it with Chandler. The whole thing was so simple. Anyone with a decent dress or a suit of clothes could, apparently, walk in and with a few words be shown to a press table and a meal. On her own time, in the evenings and on her days off, she began testing the plan of dining out for nothing. From the calendar of daily events in the paper she would select a banquet or a luncheon. At the door she would say: I'm from the *Times*, the *World*, the *Journal*, the *Telegram*, the *American*, or any paper that came to mind. Not once was she asked for a press card. The publicity chairman was delighted. If there was no press table, one was made for her. The whole thing was ridiculously easy. Anyone could do it. When the material was assembled and documented, she wrote the story and left it on Chandler's desk one morning when he was at breakfast.

She kept glancing over when he came back, exasperated by the fact that he read proofs, made notations on the assignment sheet, answered his phone and did, in fact, everything but what he was supposed to do. Finally, with relief, she saw him pick up her copy, lean back in his chair and begin to read. When he had finished he put it on the desk. She felt a small nausea at his indifference. It was the first thing she had ever tried on her own. He might at least have shown some interest.

Late in the afternoon a copy boy came to her. "Mr. Chandler wants to see you."

At his desk he motioned to a chair and then picked up the copy. "This is a pretty funny idea, but I'm not going to use it."

"Why?" The question came automatically without a thought for its impertinence.

Her face must have been stubbornly set. He smiled understandingly.

"Not," he was softly patient, "because you didn't handle it well. You did. But it would give too many persons ideas. They would figure if you could get away with it, so could they. You've opened up a whole new field for the grifters and the moochers who already know most of the tricks. This is one I don't think they have thought of. I don't think we ought to give it to them. Do you understand now?"

"I suppose so." She was doubtful and disappointed.

He spiked the copy and she actually winced. "That was a stab right through my heart." She managed a weak grin.

"It was a good try. You wrote it well." It was as close, she understood, as he ever came to a compliment.

She was in the hall, finishing a cigarette with Jo Hart, when he left for the day, hat down over his face, a late edition sticking from an overcoat pocket. His nod of good-by was impersonal and included them both.

Jo dropped her butt into the large, sand-filled urn. "When I first came on the paper," she confided as he disappeared down a turn of the staircase, "I had the real gimmies for Chandler. I was almost rolling on the floor like a cat in heat, mewling 'Here 'tis.' He didn't go for it. I wonder if he has a sex life or if he takes the sports final to bed with him."

"I guess he's human enough."

"You too?" Jo's glance was shrewd.

"I don't know." There was no embarrassment in her reply. "I haven't thought much about it."

"The hell you haven't." It was a flat expression of disbelief.

Carol shrugged it off. "Maybe." She changed the subject. "We're both off at five. How about coming to my place for a drink?" This was the first time she had asked anyone from the paper to the apartment. "We can eat in if you like."

"Suits me. I don't have a date. Wish I had. Other women dull my wit and glands. See you." She went back inside to her desk.

This was the clean-up time of the day. Small items might be called in, but the bulk of the final edition was set.

She walked down the long hall to the clubroom overlooking the small park and the graying, colonial simplicity of City Hall. The poker game, starting every afternoon after Chandler left, was a huddle of quiet concentration. She stood for a moment watching, and a couple of the men looked up without expression. There was no hostility or recognition in the glances. They were impersonal, as though she were possessed of a strange sexlessness, a neuter gender. She wasn't accustomed to having men look at her that way. It was disturbing, baffling.

On the way uptown in a cab she spoke of this to Jo. "It gives you a funny feeling not to be noticed. It's something you expect and when it doesn't happen, you have to wonder why."

Jo was indifferent. "Most of them are male enough outside the plant after a few drinks. Besides, they were playing cards. A man once told me that a poker game and a good leak were women's only real competitors. Do you always take a cab?"

"Usually. If you can get in the subway you have to fight your way out at Fourteenth Street and then walk down or take a bus."

At the apartment entrance when the doorman touched his cap and greeted her by name she could sense a faint, ironic surprise in Jo. The airy indifference with which she regarded the subdued elegance of the lobby was exaggerated, the pose too obvious. It made her uncomfortable and then angry when she realized she was on the point of explaining the building. I'm behaving, she told herself, as though I ought to be ashamed of living here instead of in a Village walk-up. Why should I apologize to anyone?

She let herself into the apartment and saw Jo Hart's eyebrows quirk themselves as they walked into the terraced living room.

"My! What a cozy little place." Jo's sarcasm was undisguised.

There was no need for Peters. She always had a drink when she came home. There was ice in the bucket on the cart and everything she wanted at hand. Perversely she rang for him. It was a small gesture of defiant irritation. Why should she care what Jo Hart thought?

"What will you drink?"

"Scotch over some ice, no water." She watched with bemused appreciation as the man fixed drinks for them both. When he left the room, she flopped indolently into a chair and whistled softly. "Now I'm beginning to understand the wild mink from Russek's, the dresses and suits from Patou and Bendel which need no label, the pearls that never heard of Tecla."

"Do you?" There was an edge to Carol's question which she didn't attempt to sheathe.

Jo sat up suddenly and grinned disarmingly. "No I don't. Whoever keeps you is doing a great job of it. What I don't understand is why you want to chip away your fingernails on a typewriter all day long. This is good Scotch." She sprawled her legs in awkward comfort.

For a moment Carol was on the point of explaining things and then she said to hell with it. Why should I? Maybe it's even better if she and everyone in the office think a man is taking care of me. It gives me—she laughed to herself—the earthy touch.

"Feel like eating here?"

Jo lit a cigarette. "Larks' tongues?"

"Under glass."

Jo cocked a raffish eye. "I'm sorry, honey." The apology was honest. "That was the green-eyed cat in me. It, this, is none of my damn business. It just caught me a little off base, that's all. Want to talk shop or gas about men?"

"You'd get too nosy; about the man, I mean." She decided to keep Jo's speculations on this track. It was a simple explanation for everything.

"You're damn right I would. Does he have a brother? This"— she flapped a limp hand to include the apartment—"is better than a backstairs maid's dream of Hollywood. Isn't it," she added with a touch of awe, "wonderful what that little thing will get you if it is worked right?"

Things were better after that and a couple of drinks helped. Jo Hart was a naturally gregarious girl without complexes or frustrations. She had broken in on a small New Jersey paper and when she came to New York had sheeted herself in a brittle cover of flippant sophistication. She had done this because she was young enough to imagine it was necessary, the proper complement of a newspaperwoman. Now it had become a habit.

"I wondered some about your clothes." She trickled Scotch into her mouth without spilling a drop. "I even ran a hot, greedy hand over the mink in the coatroom. When I got my job on the paper I was one for tailored suits and low-heeled shoes. I wanted to look as much like a man as possible. I must have. It sure didn't get me one, and it made me pretty unhappy. Then I got sexy and wise to myself. I made a big play for Chandler but had to settle for a man on the *Times*, the conservative type."

"Do you see him? I mean, all the time?"

"Mostly." Jo finished the drink. "This is getting to be real dormitory confession stuff, isn't it?" She straightened up. "Should I fix myself another drink or do we ring for Jeeves?"

"Mix it yourself and to hell with you." She waited until Jo came back. "Is it serious, you and *The New York Times?*"

"I don't know. I've never been able to tell. I guess, maybe, I'm not too susceptible. He's kind of like one of those Chinese ivory back-scratchers. You like what it does but don't feel any real affection for it." She sipped her drink. "This is good likker. You could get real boozy on it. I get twitchy when I drink."

"I've never been really drunk." Carol leaned back comfortably. This was the easy, casual talk with another girl she had missed. "I don't mind what I do as long as I know I'm doing it. Why don't you spend the night?" The invitation was made impulsively and she realized that without knowing it she had been lonely in the city.

"You wouldn't happen to be queer, would you?" Jo looked at her.

"No."

"Well," Jo sighed and the philosophy was inspired by the Scotch, "what's the use of my staying? I'll have a drink or two and a piece of cold lark's tongue. Then maybe I'll call the *Times* and find out what's new. Some other time, we'll have a slumber party. You know, with half a dozen guys."

In an apartment just off Gramercy Park, Chris Chandler was stretched out on a couch, an untidy pile of the late editions of all the afternoon papers beside him on the floor. He had gone through the columns only half aware of what he was reading. The face of the Hillyard girl persisted in overlaying the print. He wondered why he thought of her in that term and not as Carol or Carol Hillyard. It was, he decided, some sort of obscure defense against her intrusion as a personality. The Hillyard girl was neutral.

He twisted up from the relaxed position and went to the kitchen. On the way he paused to stare meditatively at the telephone. There was no reason why he should call her and every argument against it. Assuring himself it was only an act of idle curiosity, he picked up the directory and riffled through the leaves. There was a page or more of Hillyards but no Carol. There wouldn't be, he thought. A new book wasn't due for several months. He did find Hillyard Enterprises. The address was the correct one. He put the book back on the stand but left it open. The idea that she was an "enterprise" somehow tickled his fancy.

From a cabinet above the stove he took an unopened bottle of Scotch. In these days of prohibition good liquor was one of the unadmitted emoluments of his job. The paper's ship news reporter had a wide acquaintance among the customs men detailed to the transatlantic piers. Stewards of the French, Cunard and Hamburg-American lines, in return for unsealed liquor stores, let the inspectors take what they wanted and sold the old and uncut whiskies to their friends at ship's prices. It was a pleasant arrangement which hurt no one. He pulled the cork and sniffed the fine, peat-smoke aroma. It was almost too good not to be shared. Hillyard Enterprises. That was a hell of a way for a pretty girl to be listed.

Drink in hand he walked back to the living room and the windows overlooking the fenced-in park. There was a village air about the district despite the fact that multistoried apartments were rearing themselves above the older houses. It was one of the few sanctuaries left in the city and the park gates opened only to the residents who had keys. In a few more months summer would transform its stripped, winter bleakness into a square of pleasant greenery and dotted clumps of flowers.

He scooped up the untidy litter of papers, pausing to look over again the front page of the *Journal*. At heart he was a "Hearst man." There was a vigorous, rowdy character to the *American* and its afternoon sister, the *Journal*. They somehow kept alive the tradition of free-for-all reporting. They were sensational in character and make-up and laced into a story with the enthusiasm of a bully-boy in a dockside brawl. He had often thought he would have liked to work for Hearst. That he was city editor of a paper as conservative as his own frequently surprised him.

He finished his drink. Tomorrow was Saturday and he didn't go in. Nothing ever seemed to happen on Saturday afternoons. The fights, the murders, the fires, invariably saved themselves for the night and were covered by the Sunday-morning sheets. There were two days now during which he didn't have to be on call. He could spend them as he pleased. Where and with whom? A girl, of course. He was kidding himself by pretending to be vague on her identity, mentally fumbling through a list of names. The Hillyard girl. Where? He knew that also. Somewhere down on Long Island. Southampton, boarded up against the winter gales. Montauk, where the island thrust boldly into tumbling, gray seas. There would be a few places open with logs flaming in the fireplaces and the cold wind sheeting against the windows.

Peters' accented voice answered the call. He asked for her, giving his name, and in the interval almost hung up, regretting the decision and vaguely uneasy.

"Hello."

The word was an exclamation. There was no question in her tone. He knew, somehow, there wouldn't be.

"Would you have dinner with me?" This was the quick plunge.

"I'd like to." There was a pause and then the question came. "What made you call me just now, at this moment, when I was thinking of you?"

"Not because I knew that. It would have been easier if I had. I've been stalking this telephone for the past couple of hours."

"You make up your mind quicker behind the desk."

He smiled and some of his embarrassment was gone. "The decisions there are not quite as important." He paused, wanting to be certain his next words were properly casual and open to a couple of interpretations. "I had an idea of taking the car and driving down around Montauk, coming back Sunday night." She could make of that what she would. It was an invitation and it wasn't.

"I see." The two words came slowly, thoughtfully, as she made up her mind. "You know, of course, I'm supposed to work tomorrow." There was no question here either. The ball was tossed for him to catch.

"I can leave word for Harper that you're on an assignment."

"That isn't like you, is it?"

"No. It isn't. I'm not sure I can explain it or want to try. All I do know is that tomorrow's edition isn't particularly important at the moment."

"What shall I pack?" Her voice was soft.

"It will be cold down there. Take something tweedy for tramping over the moors. They are sand dunes, of course, and the beach, but not bad substitutes."

A small bubble of laughter floated over the wire. "Sensible shoes for a frivolous assignation. Tweeds instead of black lace and chiffon. Whatever in the world do you have in mind, Mr. Chandler?"

He was uncomfortable, made so by the knowledge he must have sounded stuffy.

"I always thought Montauk was boarded and locked away for the winter?" She relented a little.

"There's an old inn down there that's open. It has a big, stone fireplace, pegged floors and ceiling beams made with the timbers of wrecked ships."

"Kenneth Roberts stuff? No bathrooms, probably, and warming pans beneath the homespun sheets?"

"They've made a few concessions to the eccentricities of tourists from the city. They haven't spoiled anything, though."

"I don't know." He understood she was being deliberately bemused. "How an invitation to dinner can evolve into talk of beds and warming pans. How did we ever get on this subject or didn't you really intend to feed me from the beginning? Was it all a ruse?"

"I never had much talent for intrigue. Simple things simply stated."

"About this rustic inn of yours. I think you ought to know I despise hot buttered rum. We won't have to be that colonial, will we?"

"No buttered rum. No coonskin caps. No linsey-woolsey stuff. When will you be ready?"

"By the time you get here."

He replaced the receiver slowly, lifted it again and made a call. Harper would be in at three. The Saturday edition was almost a morning paper, hitting the stands around ten o'clock. He left word with the switchboard. Carol Hillyard was on a special assignment. You're damn right she is, he thought. If Harper was shorthanded he could pull someone else in on rewrite.

He hung up, feeling certain the man on the board knew exactly why Carol Hillyard wouldn't be in. It was ridiculous, of course. No one could know. He went back to the kitchen and poured himself a small drink. Never before had he permitted his private life to intrude on the paper. This made him feel cheaply conniving, offending his sense of order. He thought of what someone had once said about Hollywood: "There is nothing lower than a director who will screw an extra girl." Even though he knew there was no basis of fact for his feelings—Carol Hillyard was no extra girl—he was bothered by what he had done. It would have been better to let Carol call in at eight o'clock and report sick. He knew that numberless small affairs were carried on throughout the paper; department heads with their secretaries or assistants. A couple of times, at the office Christmas parties, when everyone was overly stimulated by too much to drink and the holiday spirit, he had taken one of the girls from classified or another section home and to bed. These had been casual, one-night joustings, understood as such by both parties. There were no carry-overs. None was expected. It was Christmas, wasn't it? This was different. He wanted to find an excuse for it and couldn't.

Aside from an almost too-studied greeting, with the offer and refusal of a drink in her apartment, neither spoke again until they were across the Queensboro Bridge and out on Northern Boulevard. She leaned back against the seat, her head tilted. The flickering of light and shadows played across her face, giving her features a curious mobility in repose.

"I wonder," she mused aloud, "why this doesn't seem to be an extraordinary thing to be doing. A lot was taken for granted, wasn't it?"

"No. It's hard to explain. I wasn't sure you would want to come, but I somehow was pretty sure you wouldn't be offended."

"I'm not very good at throwing my hands up in horror." She glanced at him and smiled. "Just the same, I'm puzzled over how you knew."

"I didn't. There were no signposts. Someone had to make the first move. I was sure of that."

"It could have been I."

"Yes." He nodded, eyes on the traffic. "It could have been. It might well have been you. It's better this way, though."

"Did you leave word for Harper?" Her expression was composed but a small, provoking current ran through the words. "I imagine," he could feel the laughter, "that was the hardest part, more difficult than the proposition to me."

"It wasn't a proposition." He was on the defensive.

"The hell it wasn't," she contradicted without heat.

"I suppose it was. I didn't think of it as one. Invitation sounds better."

"Invitation is a creepy euphemism; like saying sleep with a girl when that is the last thing the man has in mind. Do you know"— she sat up and lit a cigarette—"I detect a Puritan strain in you. I'm afraid you're noble. I have an idea your conscience bothers you. That you honestly believe you are taking advantage of our relative positions; the poor shopgirl and the evil, beaver-hatted employer, twirling his mustache and saying: Come my pretty or lose your job. Submit or be fired."

"That's ridiculous." He was angry because she was so intuitively skirting near the truth.

"Let me reassure you." She took a deep draw of the cigarette and exhaled slowly. "I am not coming fearfully. It is quite possible that one of these days you will be working for me."

He risked the traffic to stare wonderingly at her. By God, she meant it! This was no defensive posture. She made the statement with complete self-possession. It was a matter-of-fact appraisal and not absurd. Oddly enough, and this made him wonder, there was no bite, no sting in what she had said.

He made a solemn gesture of tugging at a forelock. "Yes, ma'am. I'll keep that in mind and do my very best to be satisfactory. I hadn't really thought of this as an opportunity for me."

"Neither did I." The implication was unmistakable. The tone, though, pleasantly conversational, the glance accompanying it one of limpid innocence. "Now. Let's forget it, shall we?" She slid across the seat until their shoulders touched.

They had dinner at Port Washington in an old frame house that sagged a little with the weight of a century or more upon it and overlooked the Sound. Cocktails were brought in thick china cups which, somehow, spoiled their flavor but not the effect. Later, with the steamed clams and broiled lobster, a white wine was smuggled beneath their table. It came wrapped in brown paper as though they had brought it with them.

"When I'm running a paper, this is the sort of thing I'll yell about." She touched the wine with a finger. "Hypocrisy, a nation wallowing smugly in it. I don't necessarily mean prohibition. The whole business of dismissing something unpleasant by pretending it isn't there. That goes for our slums, the legislators who drink wet and vote dry, the pleasant myth of democracy in a country where a large segment of the population has been disenfranchised because of its color. I'm going to holler my head off, Chris. I'm going to take a big club and lay about me."

"As you grow older your capacity for sustained indignation will fade." He smiled tolerantly.

"You're wrong. I'm going to be a shrewish old woman. A real bitch. I'll ride a broomstick to the office. I'm going to knock some heads together or off. You once said something about a motto for your paper. I'm going to have one. It will be: Get it; print it."

"You can skin your knuckles thumping on a tub."

"You don't believe me, do you?" She was intensely serious. "You still think this is some sort of a joke, a whim. That I'll work for a year or so and then go back home, using it all as a conversation piece: When I worked on a paper in New York." She took a deep breath. "I don't know how much money Mark has stacked up but I'll spend it all just for the pleasure of kicking some sacred cows in the udders." She grinned suddenly and with a disarming delight. "That's a creepy euphemism, also, isn't it? I mean tits. Kick 'em in the tits. That sounds better than teeth. Besides, its harder to kick someone in the teeth."

He laughed with honest pleasure. "That's a fine motto for a paper." He wondered if this enthusiasm would survive the complexities of running a paper, the politics and the business office. No longer did he question the ambition. She would do it. "I'd put that right on page one so no one would be in doubt as to your policies."

Back in the coupé, the radio playing softly and the dash light making the compartment seem warm and intimate, they rode in silence for a while. It was not strained. They had no need to talk for talk's sake as strangers might. She broke it finally.

"How far is it to Montauk?"

"It's a long drive. We could stop at Riverhead if you'd rather."

"No, let's get there. We're still too close to the city. I'm going to take a nap. Wake me up when the fun begins."

It was almost two o'clock when they pulled up before the old inn. A single light burned downstairs and the place had a deserted and eerie look beneath wide-spreading oak trees. When he shut the motor off they could hear the ocean, a muffled roar that was continuous and seemed to have no part with the breaking of individual waves.

A sleepy man in a faded flannel robe finally answered Chandler's persistent knocking. He merely grunted at the sight of them and the bags, retreating to a counter and taking a key from a slot.

"Two rooms, if you please." She made the request softly and with a disarming smile.

The landlord grunted again. He had long ago ceased to be surprised by tourists. He'd never figured for a minute they were man and wife anyhow. Married people had more sense than to leave a warm apartment in the city for a whirl they could just as well have in their own bed.

"Upstairs, to the right an' at the end of the hall. Register in the morning." He yawned. "Too damned late to read or write. No regular time for breakfast. Fix you up with somethin' when you're ready. Good night." He padded away with the uncertain shuffle of a sleepwalker in a hurry.

Alone in his room Chris opened a bag, took out a robe, slippers and pajamas. He wasn't surprised. Nothing she would ever do would surprise him. He undressed. "Behold!" he intoned to his reflection in a bureau mirror. "The bridegroom cometh."

The boards, outside a small, oval-shaped hooked rug, were cold and the wind whistled in sudden gusts and seeped through the window frames. It was, he thought wryly, a fair night for bundling. He pulled back the bedspread and covers, testing cold sheets with his hand. He was bent over when he heard the door open and close. She was still dressed.

"I'm not being coy. Do you understand?" She was actually asking for understanding. "It's just that I don't like sharing a room or waking up in the morning in a rumpled bed, feeling a little frowsy myself, beside a man who needs a shave and will make the same sounds I do in the bathroom. I don't think it has to go that far no matter how right it is. There should be a small corner of privacy." With a strange gesture of reassuring him, she put out her hand.

He took it. "You didn't have to explain."

She studied him with grave approval. "I know I don't. That's one of the reasons I came with you. I have a feeling we can understand each other without a lot of exploratory fencing. I want to go to bed with you, but I also want to wake up alone and in my own room. Will you come?"

"Would you like a drink?"

"Bring the jug with you. We'll do it quietly so as not to disturb the sleeping colonials. Give me about fifteen minutes."

He watched her as she turned and left the room. Then he took a bottle from his bag and had a straight swallow from the neck. I'll probably need this slight edge, he thought.

Standing at the window, staring out into the night which seemed to be gathering itself in violence, he smoked a cigarette. He wondered, for the first time, about the men she had known. With him they must have shared this astonishment, the realization she could not be taken or tricked by emotion or desire. Always she stood outside herself and watched. It gave a man a feeling of apprehension.

He glanced at the watch on his wrist. With the uneasy sensation of answering a summons he picked up the bottle and walked out of the room, across the hall to knock upon her door.

IX

WHAT had happened could not be true, since everyone in a position to know had said it was unthinkable in this greatest of countries in the best of all possible worlds.

But the lines of jobless grew until they stretched across the nation. The fruit of loom and mill, factory and hearth gathered dust in warehouses and shelves. Crops rotted in the fields because the prices they brought were not worth the harvesting.

It had started on an October day in 1929 with the voice of doom speaking through cabalistic signs on the yellow paper tape as it unrolled from the tickers in Wall Street. Now, in its second year, the country no longer fought back. It watched with a numb wonder and the words of cheer from the White House were empty of meaning.

Below the apartment houses on Riverside Drive at 72nd Street a coolie village of unbelievable squalor sprouted. The hovels were fashioned of cardboard and tar paper, roofed with flattened tin cans. They steamed beneath the leaden heat of July and there was the stench of decay and hopelessness. Gray-faced men sat daylong on the rocks, staring vacantly at the Hudson River and the deceptively lush greenery of the New Jersey side. They banded together in beaten apathy. There was no fury in them and they did not roam, as might have been expected, as a scavenger pack through the homes along the Drive and tree-shaded West End Avenue. They simply squatted and waited. A few tried to keep themselves clean, washing in the shallows where oil made an iridescent slick on the water. They made an attempt to shave, heating the water in coffee cans over small fires and scraping painfully with old blades in rusting safety razors. Each morning they went out to look for work that was not to be found. Others had long ago given up. They were possessed of the fatalism of savages who, realizing they are dying, wait in beaten patience. Those who lived in the apartment houses and who could look down upon the spectacle drew the blinds so they would not have to see, and the police looked the other way, pretending what was there did not exist.

On the windows of restaurants there appeared signs. ALL YOU CAN EAT FOR 15¢. The trouble was few had fifteen cents. They had holes in their shoes and their trousers were raveled at the cuffs. They had shirts with frayed collars, and a haunted look.

A desert's stifling heat was a pall upon the city. It burned with relentless rage within the densely packed streets of Harlem and the lower East Side, driving families to the scorched parks where they lay dull-eyed and panting. The emergency relief shelters were empty ovens. Those who could afford the subway fare went to the beaches, Coney Island and Rockaway, to sleep a fevered night.

A small dole, free meals ladled out by perspiring social workers, the columns of shuffling men seeking any sort of a job, were no longer phenomena but a way of life. Those who were thrown into it were not the city's habitually unemployed, the unemployable. They were clerks and laborers, lawyers and small merchants, artists and architects, actors, writers, mechanics and masons, carpenters and plumbers. Once they had been the country's bone and muscle. The pulse of a nation faltered.

Misery was no longer news but evocative of a macabre humor. Songs were written about it. "Brother Can You Spare a Dime?" Cartoons were drawn of top-hatted, frock-coated and striped-trousered men selling apples from a box on street corners.

Those who still had jobs ran to them, hurrying out of the subways as though fearful their places of employment had vanished during the night. Those who put down a nickel or a dime for an apple did so hurriedly, unable to meet the vendor's eye. They snatched up the fruit and turned away quickly as if they were risking contamination from the plague afflicting him. Good men lost their capacity for anger. A sleeping sickness took its place.

The city's newspapers grew slimmer as the pages of advertising were dropped. Reporters and men on the desks counted their years of service as they might a rosary, hoping to find the bead of seniority that would save them. The staffs were pared and shaved again with the vague assurance of jobs "when things pick up."

For the first time in her life Carol Hillyard felt the stirring of pity. It was an unusual awakening. She had never felt a kinship with the mass of humanity swirling about her in this city. This was no Bourbon pose. A bond simply did not exist. Now she looked about her and was outraged by what she saw. To be hungry. To go to bed with an empty stomach and to awaken in the morning and face another day. That was something which happened to the conditioned swarms in India, China, when the floods came and crops failed. It didn't happen here, to the people you saw on the streets. It couldn't be true in a nation that had told the world of its radios, its automobiles, its washing machines and shiny bathrooms. Yet there it was and a skeletal specter of fear stared through the windows of thousands and thousands of homes.

Concern for the man or woman who sat beside her on the subway was so new it confused her. Talking with them, she began to understand how naked and vulnerable they were; how tenuous their hold on security; how fragile the bridge they walked from week to week, payday to payday. She found also, in talking with the jobless, examples of unexpected generosity. Landlords did not press or threaten. What was the use? They were all caught in a gigantic squeeze. He fought for himself and them with the banks who held the mortgages. You help me and I'll help someone else. We'll cling to each other and form a dike against this wave of terror. Small merchants extended credit far beyond the point their regular customers could decently expect. Families helped each other, sharing their small resources of shelter. The milkman left a bill but didn't ring the bell. It was not all nobility, of course. Greed and arrogance walked openly. There were unnecessary foreclosures, bankruptcies and forced sales; a callous turning-away from a plea for understanding.

All these things she saw, heard and wrote about and was ashamed of her ignorance. Save for those dim years when, as a child, Mark Hillyard was reaching to test the strength of his destiny, she had never known anything but comfort. Money was a token, a counter, small metal things to be used in a game of Jacks. It had no particular significance, since she had never had to earn it. It was there. A way of life. I am, she told herself angrily, intelligent enough to have known those things. The complacent arrogance of those who walked with the invisible shield of money, and she among them, filled her with shame and the unreasoning passion of a convert to do something about it. Where and What? They were twin doors which had to be unlocked. Who had the key? She didn't know and neither, apparently, did anyone else.

She wrote with a blazing anger that frequently disregarded logic, and Chandler, who sensed the conflict within her, spiked the copy.

"You can't," he told her patiently, "take on the world. You are immoderate, intemperate. You are personalizing this instead of being objective."

"How can you be objective about misery?" she flared, knowing he was right.

She had been on the paper almost two years now and during that time had worked harder than she had ever thought possible. She had moved steadily, gaining confidence and skill in her work. There was no mystery to it. Her apprenticeship had been brief, the mechanics easily grasped. She had learned what thousands of other newspapermen had learned, but she learned it quickly. She had an instinct and no more thought to question it than does a medical student who makes his first incision with a sure hand where others fumbled and were uncertain. One child takes a pencil and draws while another makes meaningless lines. Notes rise clear and true from one throat; they croak in another. If she had ever thought to state an obvious talent it would have been in those terms. She used what she had, an instinct.

Her relationship with Chris Chandler halted at the entrance doors on Broadway. Neither would admit it to the city room. They were impersonal and friendly, nothing more. Here she respected his wisdom but felt no awe. For his part he saw her as a reporter, a name on the day's assignment sheet. If, as he sometimes did, he glanced at her, it was with a small wonder at the competence her flashing beauty held. He did not regard her as a woman, a girl capable of surprising tenderness and passion, of gaiety and laughter, of silence without constraint.

She and the city were no longer strangers. She had covered every facet of it. Never once had Chandler held off because she was a girl. The overnight copy he found on his desk in the morning sometimes was only what he expected. It was there because during the long, silent hours when downtown Manhattan was hushed she had come up the back way, through the empty composing room, turned a light on over her desk and written until the lobster trick came straggling in at three o'clock. That was the job, and he sent her where she could best serve.

She had a knack of making people talk and of translating their words and emotions into sharp, vivid copy. There were a few others like her. Mike Berger, on the *Times*, Gene Fowler, Nunnally Johnson, Stanley Walker. People liked her on sight and this was more than half the job of getting in where others failed. She had built a wide and varied acquaintance ranging the island. Sometimes she rode the paper's delivery trucks, talking and smoking with the drivers, watching the bundles heaved to the sidewalk stands and small stores. She drank beer in the Twelfth Avenue speakeasies with union stewards from the hiring halls and chewed a piece of pepper sausage with a Polish longshoreman on a North River pierhead. She moved to a first-name basis in the magistrates courts and counted ward politicians, precinct sergeants and detectives, clerks in the Municipal Building and officials in City Hall among her contacts.

Jim Haney, in and out of New York half a dozen times a year, introduced her to a higher echelon. Haney channeled the Hillyard Enterprises through innumerable sources. Although he usually stayed at the St. Regis or Plaza, he used the apartment, with her permission, for small, informal dinners and cocktail parties. When it was possible, she took over the role of hostess for him. On an afternoon or evening there were legislators from Albany, congressmen from Washington, judges, industrialists, bankers, advertising men, industrial representatives from Europe, South America and Mexico standing about drinking, talking. She moved among them with the assurance of a beautiful and talented girl. A little sex, subtle flattery, an attentive and sympathetic ear, opened many doors and minds to her. She began to play upon a complex organ for the benefit of the paper.

Now, in the second year of its depression, she was caught up in the murmuring agony of a great city. She wrote of the times, and what they were doing to a people, with an awakened understanding. She stood with the jobless outside the dingy employment offices along Sixth Avenue. She ate from tin plates at the public kitchens and sat with silent men in litter-strewn parks. She wondered, idly at first and then with a quickening interest, what had become of the women. Where were they? The career girls, fashion designers, models, secretaries, the minor executives and on down the list to waitresses, manicurists, stenographers, shopgirls, what had happened to them? They did not shape up with the men waiting for jobs. Rarely did she find one in the bread lines. A world of girls and women who had formed a working part of this city had vanished.

She talked it over with Chandler. "What's become of them? There must have been thousands and thousands of women without ties or means of support outside their jobs which they no longer have. Why don't they crowd the missions looking for a place to sleep? How do they eat? All you see are the men."

"Why don't you find out?" He studied her, feeling the electric current of her curiosity. She was good, this one was. He envied her. "Find out what's happened to them. How they are living. I sure don't know. I never really thought about it."

For weeks she hunted the city's jobless girls. They were there all right. She sat with them on the smooth benches of employment agencies. She talked over cups of coffee in the Automat and shared the want ad sections of different papers. She discovered they did not wear the cowed and bewildered faces of the men. This, in part, was because they did not have the male responsibility of wife and children. They were not haunted by the terror of eviction notices with furniture piled upon the sidewalk, of a baby without milk or shelter, of a wife who expected a husband to protect her against these things. That was what whipped the men. But there was more. There was an unsuspected feminine tenacity and an instinct for preservation. They were neatly dressed, their fingers self-manicured,

125

their hair waved, their lipstick bright. They were out of work but they kept the desperation from their faces. Also, they were untroubled by standards established by the men. It took a long time before an actor would take a job washing dishes in a cafeteria. A show girl put on an apron and worked at the steam table in a restaurant with the bright insouciance she once wore on the runway of *The Follies*. An architect hopefully waited for someone to put him at a drawing board. An executive secretary rolled up her sleeves and did someone's housework. An engineer wanted a job commensurate with his ability. A laboratory technician would wash a dog, polish a car, take her pittance with a quick and unashamed grin.

Listening to their stories, Carol felt an astonished pride in her sex. She learned, also, that most of the single girls had a little money put aside. Entertainment, during the good years, had been provided by the eager and questing male. The attractive ones rarely had to spend money for anything but their clothing and lodgings. Out of work they had this small security to hold back the frost of unemployment. They banded together, not in the shuffling, dejected herds of the male, but in rooms and small apartments made bright by their chatter and hopes. They displayed a surprising generosity toward each other. Sharing a room, a small flat in threes and fours, they would lend each other a little of the best until, well dressed and confident appearing, one could look for a job. A great many, of course, had left New York and gone back to their Kansas, Ohio, Pennsylvania, Florida and Georgia homes to live with their parents.

She worked with little rest, talking with hundreds of girls and women. She stood with them in the women's courts, sat in the Village tearooms. Together they scanned employment office bulletins, walked a dog in the park for fifty cents, picked corn on Long Island farms. Then she wrote, full and well.

It was a warm, human story filled with understanding and pride. It bounced from her fingers when she hit the typewriter keys and from its unhurried flow she knew it was good. This rhythm was a thing to be felt in the hands rather than in the brain.

The paper ran it as a series, holding it on page one under a three-column head with the by-line: Carol Hillyard. It had bright flashes of color, unexpected humor and pathos. It was a revealing and compassionate study written with understanding and enthusiasm.

For the first time in many weeks she was relaxed. She and Chandler had driven up toward Yonkers for dinner at an old and famous restaurant where an outdoor terrace caught a summer night's breeze from the Hudson.

"It's been a long time." She smiled and reached over to put her hand on his. "I've missed you."

A waiter brought ice-cold martinis in frosted glasses. The restaurant ignored prohibition. It was an establishment of such venerable tradition that a federal agent would have rather arrested his grandmother than raid it.

"We did a good job, didn't we?" She bit through the pearl onion on the end of a toothpick.

"You did. It was a damn fine piece of reporting. I'm proud of you. So is everyone on the paper. It could be a Pulitzer Prize, you know that." He lit her cigarette and watched the copper tone of the flame in her eyes. "A lot more than digging for facts went into it. There was an extrasensory feeling that brought it alive. A long time ago you asked me what they taught in the schools of journalism. What you have no one can teach. I owe you an apology for ever doubting it."

She flushed, feeling absurdly pleased. Chandler wasn't free with compliments. A reporter knew by the play he gave a story whether he liked it.

"I think I'd like another drink." She finished hers. "I'd like to get a little tight and then go home and make love in a fine alcoholic mist. I feel as though a plug had been pulled and everything drained out of me. I need replenishing, Mr. Chandler."

In many ways theirs had been an odd relationship. It was contradictory, a paradox; intimate, and at the same time casual. There had been pleasure and understanding in the association but somewhere, just short of love as each imagined it, it halted. There was an invisible barrier.

Once, as she lay within his arm sharing a cigarette, they skirted the question of love cautiously. It was a word neither had ever used to the other. They held back without quite knowing why.

"Maybe it's my fault, Chris." She spoke quietly in the darkness. "This thing called love. It's a subordination and most often on the part of the woman. By nature, by desire and instinct she yields. I can't do that. I don't want to try. I like being with you but this thing which sends a girl dewy-eyed to the altar repels me a little. It calls for a certain renunciation, a retreat to the cave. If I ever marry it will be a man who has a charming weakness. I won't have to fight him. He will need me and not I him."

"Why would you want to marry at all then?" The cigarette's coal was a bloody eye in the darkness.

He could feel her shrug. "I'm not sure I do. If I do, it is a mating instinct, an atavism, a form of self-protection in the stability of a home and children. A woman alone becomes an object of curiosity, a little bit of a freak in her middle age."

They had never discussed marriage or a permanent relationship before, each a little wary of the other. They met after working hours at a speakeasy, a restaurant or at his or her apartment. They went to the fights, the ball games, the theatre and the movies. Neither saw any reason why the relationship should be a secret thing because she was a subordinate employee on the paper of which he was city editor. That Chandler and Hillyard went together was an accepted fact. Their friends were drawn from their own or other metropolitan papers, but their interests ranged, reaching into many pursuits. The list of acquaintances was long and catholic.

When they had dinner at his apartment, it was usually sent in from a nearby restaurant, fitted into metal warming boxes heated by a flaming can of Sterno and brought by an Italian boy who wanted to be a bullfighter.

Chandler could laugh to himself now over his first experience with her when, unconsciously, he had waited for her to slip easily into a temporary role of domesticity. He had quite honestly expected her to want the part. Usually the girls who came to his place did. They were, in his words, always a little "nesty," working happily in the small kitchen preparing a meal, setting a table and looking about for candles to light it softly. They had a couple of drinks. He was relaxed comfortably in a deep chair and she sat on the arm, leaning against him.

"I thought maybe we'd eat in. There are a couple of steaks in the icebox and a bottle of good Burgundy breathing on the cabinet there."

"Mmmm." She purred the assent, scratching at the back of her head with fingernails.

They had another drink. She went to the bathroom, came back and lit a cigarette. For a moment she stood at the window, gazing out at the park. He was getting hungry. She picked up one of the evening papers, whacked a couple of pillows on the couch and stretched out with a comfortable sigh. He eyed her with a small astonishment.

"Aren't you hungry?"

She looked up, across the top of the paper. "Starving! What about you?"

"I had breakfast-lunch at ten thirty in the morning." It was a reminder.

"I should think you would be hungry then." She folded back a page and gave it her attention.

He rubbed at the corner of his mouth with a knuckle and watched her. The top of her head was visible over the paper. He was as conscious of the passing minutes as though they were being ticked off by a clock. The only sound was the rustling of a page. Then he grinned. She meant it, by God. She was waiting for him to fix dinner.

"How about going to Barbetta's?" This was a surrender, he understood that even as he spoke and made the suggestion.

She swung up off the couch. There was a mild surprise in her expression.

"I thought you wanted steak?" She folded the paper and put it on a table.

"I just said there were a couple of steaks in the icebox." This was an obvious retreat. He knew she knew it. He was damned, though, if he was going to fix dinner.

"Barbetta's sounds fine to me." She picked up her bag.

In the cab she slid her hand beneath his arm and lifted her eyes to his.

"It was a good try, Buster."

That was all she said and with it she established the pattern.

At her apartment dinner was served by Peters when they ate there. She offered no excuses for not being traditionally feminine. Sometimes, late at night, when they wanted a sandwich or a snack they went to the kitchen together, each searching the icebox for what he or she wanted, finding and taking it out. She ate on the counter, perching herself there, watching with bright interest while he made his own sandwich, swinging a leg idly, chewing on a chicken drumstick or nibbling at a piece of cheese. This was a small, guarded truce which each observed while pretending it didn't exist.

Now, on the restaurant's terrace, while the waiter brought their dinner, frogs' legs for her, thick lamb chops for him, a bottle of chilled rosé, he saw the happiness reflected in her face and felt an almost overwhelming love for this girl. She was not for him beyond what they had. She was probably not for any man completely and without reservations. Another man might accept them. He knew he couldn't.

"What's going to happen to the paper, Chris?"

"I don't know. There are rumors, of course. Everyone passes them back and forth. I guess it depends on how much money they can afford or want to lose to keep it going."

As the depression had lengthened she waited unhappily for the day when Chandler would have to tell her she couldn't be kept on. Good men, reporters with years of service to the paper, were being let out. Salaries had been cut and cut again and still the revenue shrank. She went about her job with a feeling of guilt. She didn't need the salary. What she was getting might keep someone with a family in a job. She had to wonder if she was being kept on simply because she had come to the city room through the publisher's office. Finally she had gone, not to Chandler, but to the managing editor.

The chair beside his desk was always there for anyone on the staff who wanted to talk with him. There was no protocol, no channels to be observed. He nodded with a pleasant reserved smile.

"Sit down, Miss Hillyard."

"I want to keep my job." She went immediately to the core.

"I want you to keep it. This has been a bad time when I have had to let good men go."

She knew that each dismissal had hurt him. Chandler had told her that the man was paying several salaries from his own pocket to men who had been released. They were his own form of severance pay for long service.

"I know you will understand." She hesitated. "I don't need the money. I'll work for nothing if that will let someone who does need a job stay on."

His smile was tired, unhappy. "I have made this paper my life, Miss Hillyard. Very little goes on of which I am not aware. I know who you are, of course, but not exactly why you are here. That, however, is your affair. Mr. Chandler and I have reduced the staff with the greatest reluctance. It has been a heartbreaking task. We have had to weigh the men and their talents without too much regard for sentiment. Believe me when I say that you have been kept on, not because you came from Mr. Anderson's office, but for the reason that you do your job a little better than any of the men we let go could do it."

"I want to believe that." She felt a rush of affection for this man she knew so slightly.

"You are intelligent enough to know it. So, even though I understand you do not depend on what you are paid, we still couldn't let you work for nothing. You are a fine newspaperman, Miss Hillyard."

"Thank you, sir." She stood up. "I feel better."

"Hang on to that sensation. It is becoming increasingly rare these days." He rose as she left his desk, an unconscious courtesy which was so much a part of a wise and gentle man.

She never learned from Chris whether their conversation had been repeated to him.

Taking a frog's leg in her fingers now she bit into it with hungry pleasure. Chris was intent upon his chops.

"How long can this thing go on, Chris?"

He shook his head. "I've never been through a depression before, not one that really affected me. I don't know. It seems to be a long, empty tunnel. I suppose it ends on the other side of the mountain, wherever that is. A new man, a new spirit, a renaissance of some sort makes the breakthrough."

"They wouldn't really fold the paper for good, would they?" The idea was impossible. This paper was New York, as much a part of the city's tradition as the Battery.

"I guess it depends on how much of a beating they can or want to take. A lot of papers have gone under all over the country."

"My father, Mark, will be here tomorrow. I'd like to have him meet you."

"I've always heard he hates reporters."

"No. Just what they do. He says a man is a sucker to get his name or picture in a paper; it lets people who want to make a touch know where he is."

"I'd like to know what Mark Hillyard thinks about all this."

"Uh-uh." She shook her head. "You won't get it from me. I won't quote him for you. To tell the truth I'd be afraid to know what he thinks. I don't think it's very pretty. I have an idea he believes people are getting what they deserve. Anyhow, come and have dinner with us tomorrow night. You can find out for yourself."

He nodded and she smiled a little to herself, anticipating the impact of Mark Hillyard on Chris Chandler. As she ate, a small idea was kindled and took fire. It would be a thing to talk over with Mark and Haney.

X

LEGS spraddled, feet thrust into the carpet's deep pile, Mark Hillyard leaned forward as though bending into a hurricane and glared at his daughter.

He was being confronted by a will as unyielding as his own, and it infuriated him to discover she wouldn't fight according to his rules. Instead of yelling back at him when he shouted, she laughed. It was pretty damn sneaky.

"I ain't goin' to buy no newspaper, not here nor no where else." The repeated declaration already had an empty sound to his ears and he understood it fell without emphasis on hers. "A girl your age should be married an' in a family way. I piled us up a hell of a lot of goods. A man who does that has a right to expect to leave some kin behind to think kindly of him when he's gone. He needs grandchildren, a grandson named Mark Hillyard Whatshisname to carry on like a monument or something." This was logic and sentiment, irrefutable.

She regarded him dispassionately. "I expect you've whelped enough bastards around the country to have one of them, at least, named Mark Hillyard by now. Doesn't that satisfy you?" She poured a fine trickle of brandy into the small cup of black coffee.

With a gesture Mark appealed to Jim Haney. "You hear the way she talks?" He wanted a recruit on his side. Finding no encouragement in Haney's expression, he turned again to Carol. "No, it don't satisfy me none at all. I want a legitimate grandson though God knows I'm gettin' more an' more doubtful of his mother who uses words like bastard an' drinks French brandy. A girl who started out with a fine an' gentle upbringing." His voice rumbled out unhappily.

"Ha!" she snorted, and winked at Haney.

"A girl that's had a father's lovin' care since she was a pulin' baby." This was a new gambit. He ventured cautiously into unabashed soul quivering.

"You're a goddamned old hypocrite." She made an affectionate compliment of the charge.

"You see?" He wheeled triumphantly on Haney who smoked calmly in a chair at the far side of the room. "What was to be a nice girl talks like a drunken rigger." He waited for a nod of agreement from Haney.

"Let's get back to business, old man." She glanced up at him with a tiny smile. "I want you to buy the paper if it can be bought."

She had thrown this at him after dinner when Chris had left and the three of them were alone. It was something she had been thinking about ever since she heard the first of the rumors that the paper might fold up.

"We already got three an' to keep 'em goin' I'm carryin' us all right up over the hill to a poorhouse. Every minute of the day an' night I'm schemin' an' lookin' for a sucker to unload 'em on."

"I don't care what you do with those. Maybe I do," she amended. "Maybe we'll keep them all. If they were good enough to save you money, they're worth taking a loss on for a while longer. That isn't important right now. If this one is for sale, I want it."

"Now, Sister." The tone was wheedling. He spoke with sympa-

thetic patience to a slightly backward child. "This country is restin'
in the bottom of a wet paper sack. No tellin' when it'll give way.
The thing to do is wait until it spills out. That'll be the time to
get some real goods. General Motors, Anaconda Copper, General
Electric, factories, real estate, oil companies. It ain't a good time
for newspapers. Radio stations maybe—that there is a comin' thing."
With a shift of mood he turned to Haney. "You look about for
some radio stations, Jim."

"You're going to buy this paper, Mark." She was undisturbed
and not diverted by his oral gymnastics. "I know more about Hillyard Enterprises than you think. You can take the scratch and
never feel the needle." She added a little more brandy to her coffee.

He snatched a bottle of rye from the cart and took a swallow,
washing it around in his mouth, giving himself time to figure out
a new approach. He corked the bottle and replaced it. He was going
to be patient and understanding.

"Sister." The expression on his face was one of concern. "Are
you sure you got all your woman glands? Them things that make
you come around an' behave like a regular female who wants a
home, a husband an' a family to give a man some grandchildren?
Is there somethin' missin' in you, Sister?" He suggested this with
a benign hopefulness. "If there is you can sure enough tell your
old father. I ain't a person without understanding. We could maybe
have the doctors do somethin' about it, like they transplant stuff."

"My glands are fine. They all work just dandy. Why don't you
sit down? You know you're going to do what I want you to do
in the end."

"Like hell I will," he shouted.

"Like hell you won't." She refused to raise her voice.

For a moment he was uncertain. They were meeting head-on the
way a couple of rams butted into each other. He wasn't sure how
long he could stand the buffeting. He tried an evasive tactic.

"Sister." He came to the couch, took a place beside her and
gathered one hand in his two, caressing it fondly. This was the
sympathetic friend, the old family doctor to soothe and make well.
"This here is probably no more than female trouble. It upsets a
woman, makes her restless till she don't know her own mind. They
got stuff for it like Lydia Pinkham, an' I recollect a Swamp Root
tonic girls used to take. You try some of that." He was encouraging. The case wasn't hopeless. "Then you come back to Virginia

with me. Marry a boy of good family an' get your functions goin' again." He was patient and encouraging.

"I want this paper, Mark." She lit a cigarette and blew softly on the match.

He made a grave popping sound with tongue against the roof of his plate. He wasn't thinking about the paper as a property Hillyard Enterprises could absorb without effort. It was a thing that kept Sister here. He was lonely in that damn big house.

"I'll tell you what." This was a concession. "We'll have a survey made." He liked the vagueness of the suggestion. It implied action without actually committing him to anything. "We got a whole firm of accountants." He warmed to the idea. It was a nice, comfortable trap. "They got nothin' much to do right now. Let 'em make a survey. Then we'll see. They can send us word to Virginia." He watched her with sly optimism.

"We don't need a survey. The paper is losing money. Most of them are. That is the only reason it might be bought. I want Jim to make some inquiries and I want an honest report. A yes or a no."

"That fellow who was here for supper. Chandler." He spoke the name of a vagrant, an itinerant tinker. "He probably put you up to this to save his job." He knew this wasn't true but it was a diversion. "Not that I blame a fellow for tryin' to take advantage of a girl." He was rewarded by the anger snapping in her eyes. "It's a natural thing to do. No man can be held at fault when he tries to diddle a girl out of something. She expects it in a way. It's a girl's lot to have it put to her without complaint." This was a pious admission of man's baseness. "A man wants to hang on to his job these days. He'd do most anything. Who's to blame him? I expect he'd marry you for your money if it was said to him right." This was a furtive exploration. He didn't want a newspaperman for a son-in-law.

"Without my glands?" She laughed and stood up. "I'm going to bed." She spoke to Haney. "Will you start on this tomorrow? You must have confidential sources of information."

Mark didn't like to be left out this way. "It ain't really in me to deny you anything you want, Sister." He was weakening but with a purpose. "Say we were to buy it? Would you come home then an' be a comfort to an old man in his last years?"

"If you don't do it," she was unmoved, "I'll wait until you're dead. You can't carry your goods along in an extra casket."

He snapped up. "You oughtn't to talk like that, Sister. When a man gets on in years he don't like to think his relatives are nudging him toward the grave. He don't like to be reminded ashes is ashes an' dust is dust." He regarded her uneasily.

This was an unexpected chink. She pried at it. "When you're dead all your money isn't going to do you any good. There'll be nothing to tell who Mark Hillyard was. I'll just have a hole dug in a vacant lot and cart you off to it. I'll put a stick in the ground with an old tin can on top of it. People will pass by and ask: 'I wonder who that old bastard was that no one cared enough about to bury decently?' That'll be the monument you're always talking about. And if I ever do have children, I'll send them out with little buckets and shovels to play in the sandpile Grandpa made." She patted his cheek affectionately. "Good night. Good night, Jim."

He sucked at his teeth, watching her as she crossed the room. It had been a good argument, made no less satisfactory by the knowledge he wasn't going to win. It had made an evening pass pleasantly. He waited until she reached the door.

"Sister?" he called. She halted and turned. "Sister," the tone was hopeful, "you goin' to leave the label on that old tin can? Don't get no spinach one. I never could abide the stuff." He wrinkled his nose and winked at her. She smiled back and blew a kiss with her finger tips.

Old Mark waited until he was certain she was beyond hearing. "That one's a cutter, ain't she?" He poured himself a drink, lit a cigar and settled in relaxed comfort. "I don't know," he reflected dreamily, "as I'd ever be satisfied to have a boy around after Sister. I was goin' to let her buy that paper all the time."

"I thought you were." Haney studied the man. "When are you going to get that medical check, Mark?"

"I'll get it, I'll get it." He was irritated to be reminded of his health. "There ain't nothin' wrong with me except a slow wearin' down." He was made uneasy by Haney's quiet study. "Maybe I ain't been up to taw lately but it's nothin' more than a man ought to expect."

"I'll be satisfied after the doctors give you a check." Haney was grave.

"All right, all right." The words were snapped impatiently. "But I sure God don't know what doctors can do. At my age, an' after

137

what I been through, it's like patchin' up an old automobile tire. You fix it here an' it blows out there. What good is that?"

"You can get a few more miles out of it that way." Haney pretended to make a small joke.

"Let's get back to this paper of Sister's." The purchase was an accomplished fact in Mark's mind. "I already looked into it some. I started the day she went to work on it. I wanted to know what she was gettin' into. It's always had the best of the afternoon circulation. It's the paper people take home with them; the good, solid, steady workin' middle-class core. They share it with the upper brackets, bankers, brokers, professional men. It's a good, conservative paper an' reassures people that God's up there in His heaven an' all's right with the world. They like to sleep on that even if it ain't true. It got the real top layer of the advertisin' cream. When things pick up it'll stand on its own an' make money. Until then we can afford to carry it. You know," he mused, "I got a feelin' for old things an' solid respectability. Like that place in Virginia. This here paper goes back more'n two hundred years. It used to be printed by hand on a single sheet an' sold for half a penny. That's the kind of thing I like to own."

Nothing Mark had said surprised Haney. The old man liked to pretend he was in his dotage, a bumbling, vague character who wasn't quite sure what was happening around him. When his adversaries were made unwary, he whirled and nipped them on their behinds. If a paper was important enough for Sister to go to work on, he would want to know all about it. Right now he probably had the facts stored away in his mind. The circulation figures, the advertising lineage averaged over the past twenty years, the salaries of everyone. He would have gathered this data beforehand. No survey was necessary. It had already been made.

"I'd like to make a deal with Sister." Mark sipped his whisky meditatively. "That's what I was tryin' to do all evenin'. If she'd given me a chance to dicker some, I would have pulled it off. But, by God, that Sister don't move over an inch. She's stompin' an' gougin' all the time with that quiet smile on her face. A man's got to look after his nuts when Sister's around. She likely to kick 'em right out when he ain't watchin'. I was hopin' for a trade, makin' out like I was doin' what she wanted if she'd come back to Virginia. That there is a big house for a man to be alone in. It gets so, sometimes, I hate to wake up in the mornin' knowin' there ain't no one

138

there but Julia. I was never lonesome before, never had time. That's the real hard part of bein' old. Everything takes so damn much time; to eat, to go to the toilet, even to get to sleep. It ain't much of an arrangement." He finished his drink. "Let's get some sleep. I'm wore out."

In her room Carol sat on the low bench before a dressing table, elbows on the surface, head between her hands. She massaged her scalp with sharp fingernails and there was a weary but triumphant grin on her averted face. Old Mark had given in. She knew he would. What they had gone through was a ritual, a necessary ceremony. To have yielded anything without an argument would have spoiled it for him.

She stood up, stretched with the easy movement of an animal uncurling itself and began to undress. Mark. She never could be sure when he was putting on an act and when he was serious. That he would honestly want grandchildren, to have her go home, marry and surround him with a family was an almost frightening gesture of dependency. It was as contradictory as a domesticated leopard. She loved this old man, the bond was woven tightly between them. It needed no open display. They both knew it existed. She smiled a little ruefully. If that was what he really wanted ... She couldn't bring herself to complete the statement or accept the commitment. If it were possible to breed and leave the litter on his doorstep she would do it.

In negligee she picked up the paper's late edition. In her hand it was no longer just a sheaf of pages. Actually, it had never been that. Working on it she had identified herself with its columns, they had become a part of her daily life. Even when her contributions had been routine and anonymous, the shadow of the paper walked with her. She saw it first on the newsstands, in the hands of men and women on the street. Now, however, she felt a possessive jealousy of ownership. Mark would get it. He would find a way. If there was a weakness in its financial structure he would unerringly search it out. She found herself not caring what methods he used. Beyond the city room the personnel was shadowy figures without substance or names. She had met Roland Anderson, the publisher, only once and had never even seen him in the halls. She had no idea whether he owned the paper or was a joint holder in its stock. Mark would know. If it was necessary to squeeze someone out, he would do it. He would be ruthless, indifferent to who might be hurt. There were a dozen pools from which he would draw his information. He would know exactly how badly Anderson needed money, how precarious the paper's financial situation was. If Mark Hillyard had to fight to get control, it would be the sort of savage contest he enjoyed. She was surprised to realize she shared, for the moment at least, the excitement of conquest. No quarter! It was a ringing phrase. Damnation to my adversaries! She grinned at the extravagance of the words. They were to be shouted from a quarter-deck or a newspaper's masthead.

To feel the weight of it, smell the sweetish odor of its ink, turn its pages, generated a fierce emotion. It was hers or would be. The knowledge didn't frighten her. Never for a moment did she question her ability to run this paper. Not today or tomorrow, perhaps. She wanted a little time in which to learn more and have her opinions crystallize. She had no intention of rushing in and making a fool of herself, having to depend on the experience of others when decisions had to be made. When the words CAROL HILLYARD, *Publisher* went on this paper they would mean exactly what they said. In the meanwhile Jim Haney could set up a holding company for Hillyard Enterprises to take over the operation. Anderson or a figurehead could sit in the publisher's chair until she was ready. With a start she realized Hillyard Enterprises already owned three other papers. They were only names. She had never identified herself with them. Now and then, out of curiosity, she picked up editions at the out-of-town newsstand near the *Times* Building. She read them carefully, studying the make-up, the editorial policies. They were, she felt, without personality. Right or wrong, that was what Hearst had given his papers. No one could mistake them for other than what they were—the reflection of one man. Hearst had started with less than Carol Hillyard had.

She put the paper on a table. She wasn't tired, knew she couldn't sleep now. Stripping off the negligee she went to a closet and selected a light dress. This, she laughed to herself, was the way a youngster behaved on a Christmas morning; unable to resist the temptation to handle the presents before the time of ownership was declared. She wanted to stand alone within the dark and silent halls.

A single light from a frosted ceiling bowl made a pool about the city desk. Chandler, feet propped on an open drawer, smoked thoughtfully and stared through the window at the blank face of a building across the street. He wasn't sure just why he had been impelled to this visit. Never before could he remember coming to the paper at this hour and without a reason.

Leaving the Hillyard apartment after dinner he had walked up-town, across Fourteenth Street and through Union Square. He had no destination, no purpose, and was unwilling to confess an unidentified uneasiness.

Madison Square Park was a deceptive oasis. The leafed trees were motionless, held so by the city's heat. Across from one corner a skeleton of steel was beginning to rise out of the deep pit which once enclosed Madison Square Garden. As a copy boy on the paper he had gone to the fights, the six-day bicycle races on passes from the Sports Department. There Harry K. Thaw had shot and killed the architect Stanford White over a show girl. He sat on a bench, listening to the persistent but muted hum of the city. The sound was constant, rising to shrill and brazen clangor during the day, dropping to the whir of a giant dynamo at night, but never completely absent.

Mark Hillyard hadn't surprised him. In many ways Carol, with small and unconscious flashings of her personality, had given him an image of the father. He had met many Mark Hillyards under different names. They bore a common stamp and heritage, the hawked features of a predator. They had sacked Rome and Carthage, torn continents from the hands of their natives, driven rails from ocean to ocean, and they took great wealth and power as a divine right. The old man displayed himself in such a simple thing as lifting a salt shaker from the table. His fingers closed about it like a prehensile claw and he seemed to tear it from the cloth. There was a violence about him.

He listened as the great clock in the Metropolitan Tower hammered out the hour of midnight. The echo remained for a long time, winnowing in and out of the side streets until it was blended and became a part of the nocturnal whispering.

What was so apparent in Mark Hillyard was subtly reflected in Carol. There was her sudden tilting of the head, an alertness to a sound or nuance apparent to no one else. She sensed a faltering, a concession before it was made. What was unabashedly obvious in Mark was concealed in Carol; masked by a serene beauty, sheathed by immaculate grooming, hidden by a sharp but pleasant intelligence, good manners and training. She was, he suspected, all the more dangerous because of this uncalculated masquerade.

Of all the girls he had known, this one had touched him. In, and with, her he found pride, ecstasy, astonishment and love. The last, perhaps, was a synthesis of the others. To touch and make love to her was to experience the wonder of creation. To walk and laugh with her was to know a free, swinging exhilaration of mind and body. This, he thought, was as close to the definition of love as a man could know it. But with these things he also knew a caution. It was what someone must feel who has made a pet of a tiger, understanding that within its sleek beauty there was the power to destroy. He saw what Martha Harkness had seen. The man-eater. It repelled and fascinated him.

Over dinner Old Mark had adopted an attitude of blunt suspicion. He had many faces but this was the one he chose to wear for Chandler. It had been prompted by Sister's unmistakable radiance when he entered the room. The man's quiet pride and assurance when he took her hand. Mark wanted no part of a son-in-law who was wedded to this city and who would keep Sister here. His impertinent questions kept Chris on the defensive. Where had he come from? Who were his parents? Why was he in New York? How much money had he made as a city editor? At first Chris was lightly amused and then made angry.

"I don't know that is any of your damned business." He had made the reply to Mark's query about his salary.

"The hell it ain't." The old man had been undisturbed. "Any fool could see you're in love with my daughter. She's probably in love with you. I got a right to know what kind of a man Sister's goin' to bed with, now or later." He had slashed at his steak as though it were an enemy.

Carol's glance had caught his and she'd smiled, allowing Mark's assumption of present intimacy to stand without comment or correction.

Mark hadn't been concerned over the prospect that this fellow Chandler might want to marry Sister for her money. Hell! That was as good a way to get it as any other. If he'd ever had the chance, he would have done it himself. What he hadn't liked was Chandler's easy independence. He would stay here, at his job, and in doing so would keep Sister with him. They probably wouldn't take time out to have children. He had glowered and muttered irrelevancies

142

throughout the meal and nodded ungraciously when Chris left early. He had been airily indifferent, even pleased, by Carol's anger when they were alone with Jim Haney.

Chris had left a small pile of cigarette butts below the bench and walked over to Fifth Avenue. He'd caught a taxi and without thinking, given the Chambers Street address. There he had paid the cab and stood looking through the great arch of the Municipal Building. To its right was the tarnished dome of the *World* Building and Park Row. Here, once, the voice of the city had been raised. One by one the newspapers had moved farther uptown. Soon this one alone would remain as a landmark of the era.

From his desk now he glanced at the electric wall clock with the long, slender hand sweeping the minutes away as they gathered. It was a thing he lived by. Its face marked edition time throughout the day. It surprised him to realize he had been sitting here for over an hour.

A watchman paused inquiringly in the double doorway. "Didn't know it was you, Mr. Chandler. Saw the light on."

"It's all right. I'm leaving now. Good night." His feet hit the floor with a thump.

On the way out of the building he stood for a moment in the semidarkness of the composing room. A tubular mercury light burned with a bluish color and a faint, hissing sound. In the shadows the linotype machines were squat figures, and page forms waited on long tables for the men who would be coming in later. The room would gather its own particular momentum with the peculiar odor of hot lead and the rhythmic clatter of machinery. There would be little talk here. Most of the linotypers were deaf-mutes and in this room their affliction was no handicap as they translated men's thoughts and words into print.

At the sound of a step he looked up. Carol stood within a frame of light on the back staircase landing. She hesitated, aware of his presence but not his identity.

"John?" She spoke the watchman's name. "Is that you?"

"Ain't no one here but us linotype machines." He crossed toward her.

"Chris." There was surprise and, he thought, a shade of embarrassment in her tone. "What are you doing here? I thought you had probably picked up a late date." She joined him.

"All my old late dates go to bed early or with someone else these nights."

"That's a nice lie. Won't I do?"

"You'll do just fine, but I don't know how you can explain being out all night to your father."

"I won't try. He suspects a certain amount of hanky-panky anyhow."

Not until they were out on the sidewalk did he ask the obvious question.

"What made you come down here at this time of night?"

"I'm not sure." She corrected herself. "Yes, I am. I'll tell you later. We'll talk about it. I'm hungry."

"So am I. Your old man spoiled my dinner with his inquisition. You'd think I had asked to marry you."

"Why don't you?" There was no smile with the question. She stood looking up at him.

"I'm afraid you might say yes."

A faintly puzzled frown lay like a brief shadow on her face. "You mean that, don't you?"

"Uh-huh."

"Why, Chris?" There was an honest bewilderment in the question.

"It isn't something I'd want to explain in the middle of Chambers Street." He took her arm. "There's a place over on Cherry Street, Catalan's. He stays open all night because he can only sleep in the daytime."

"Wherever you say." There was a reluctant agreement in the words. "But I still want to know why."

"It can wait."

They walked through the tangled cat's cradle of streets toward the East River. Here and there a light burned with a yellow, smoky color. Restless figures turned on pallet-laden fire escapes and dingy curtains were twisted back to allow a small trickle of air to enter dark rooms. This was a barracoon of slums, stacked side by side with small businesses and wholesale food houses. There was an unhealthy stench to the district—sweaty, unwashed bodies, clogged toilets, and a reek of kerosene spray used against roaches and bedbugs.

A single bulb hung nakedly above a canted doorway on Cherry Street. Inside, a huge man, bare of foot and wearing long, soiled woolen underwear, sat in a creaking chair. He beamed a glistening smile at Chandler.

"Sonabitch Krik!" He wave an enormous hand but didn't get up. The accent was part Catalonian, part Brooklynese, and "Krik" was as close as he had ever come to Chris. The "sonabitch" was a term of affection. "She's pretty girl." He admired Carol with an unabashed leer.

"We're hungry." Chris lifted a sleeping cat from a table, balled up the dirty red-and-white checkered cloth and tossed it in a corner. "What's to eat and drink?"

"Sure. Sure." Catalan heaved himself up, scratched at his crotch and then folded his arms across the enormous swelling of his belly. "What you want, hey?"

He didn't wait for an answer but went to a closet and took out a wicker-covered jug of Cuban rum. He bought the rum from the sailors off freighters docking in Brooklyn. With it he brought a couple of old jelly glasses. As a concession to Carol he rinsed them beneath a tap of cold water.

While they drank, he busied himself at a stove with clams in an herb sauce and sautéed chicken. He fortified himself regularly with wine from a goatskin bag.

"Only the fact you must have eaten here before and survived gives me the courage." She watched doubtfully as a duck paddled across the floor. A dog scratched itself with limp thumpings and Catalan lifted it, not unkindly, with his foot from in front of the iron stove. "I guess it's all right. A real healthy germ couldn't live in this place."

They drank the full, rich brown rum slowly, smoking and not talking while they watched Catalan perform his cumbersome magic over the clams and the chicken with saffron rice. He placed the heavy, piled plates before them and went back to his chair. There he rocked contentedly, staring at his stubby toes.

Carol experimented cautiously with the food and then her eyes widened with surprised appreciation.

"It's wonderful if you can forget where it came from. How did you ever find this place?"

"Some of the boys from the *Telegram* dug it up." He ate for a moment. "What brought you down to the plant?"

She broke a half-opened clam apart, dipped the meat into a

fragrant sauce. When her eyes finally met his, they were level, a little challenging.

"I'm going to buy the paper, Chris."

Later, when he thought about this, it was with astonishment that he hadn't been surprised. Now he merely nodded.

"It's something I've been thinking about," she continued slowly. "Tonight, after you left, I had a talk with Mark." She laughed. "It was more than a talk; a toe-to-toe slugging match. Then I was so excited I couldn't sleep. I had to come down and look around. I didn't expect to find you there."

"I didn't know the paper was on the market."

"I'm not sure it is." She separated a piece of chicken from its bone.

"But," there was a faint irony in the tone, "if you want it, it will be?"

There was immediate surprise in her eyes. "Why, yes." This slowly. "I guess that's exactly what I mean. Only, you somehow make it sound a little nasty."

He wondered why he resented her at this moment. The paper had been slowly bleeding to death. This was common knowledge. What she proposed was a transfusion, a business deal. Newspapers had been bought and sold before. A change of holding interest on this one was none of his affair beyond how it might ultimately affect his job. What really annoyed him was her calm assumption of privilege, which made the transaction casual, almost trivial.

"Well?" She had been waiting.

"Well what?" He dribbled some rum into their glasses.

"Well anything." There was a rough edge of impatience in the words.

"I don't know what I'm supposed to say."

"You damn sure aren't expected to behave as though it were an act of rape or that I have done something underhanded, like foreclosing a mortgage on widows and orphans. The paper is in trouble. Hillyard Enterprises can shore up the structure. Would you rather have it fold? I'm damned if I know why I should be apologetic and that's what you're trying to make me feel." She pushed her plate away angrily. "I intend to carry it until this depression is over and turn it into a money-maker. Is there something reprehensible in that?" She took a deep breath.

She was right, of course. His reaction had been petty. He couldn't quite explain it to himself. He was pouting because someone else had something he would have liked to own.

"I guess it's envy." He made the admission honestly. "I've never been close to this kind of money before. It awes me a little to see it in action and realize what it can do. It's like hearing that a private collector had decided to buy the Magna Carta or the Declaration of Independence and slapped his price down on a barrelhead with the assumption he needed nothing more."

"You're going pretty far afield, aren't you? The paper, after all, isn't the original stone tablets of Moses, engraved with a fingernail."

"All right." He leaned back and lifted his hands with a gesture of surrender. "I'm sorry. What are you going to do with it?"

"I'm going to run it the way it deserves to be run." She relented and made no effort to hide her excitement. "Forget this man and woman's-place-is-in-the-home stuff. I should think you would be glad. It means you can bring back the men who have been let out. I expect to lose money. You can stop depending on the wire services and open the paper's own Washington bureau; put correspondents where they belong, in London, Rome, Berlin and Paris." She paused, and undisguised surprise was in her expression. "You'll work for me, won't you, Chris?"

He knew her well enough now to know this was no loose expression of her thoughts. It wasn't a careless stringing-together of words into a question. She had said, and meant, work for *me*.

"I don't see why not. I have to work for someone. City editors' jobs aren't exactly wide open these days. That's my trade."

"You didn't like what I said, did you?" This was an intuitive probe.

"It startled me. I don't think it should, but it did. You couldn't have said it any other way. The possessive plural isn't in your vocabulary."

"You're a sensitive bastard, aren't you? Sensitive and resentful and envious." With an impulsive smile and movement of her hand she robbed the statement of its bite. Her hand lay, palm up, waiting for his to cover it. "At least those are human qualities. I like you best of all when you're just Chris Chandler. Get sore if you want to."

"I'm not sore." He grinned. "I'm like confused."

Her fingers tightened on his. "I'm very much in love with you. I get a mixed-up feeling. It's what you once described as 'nesty.' Only," her eyes clouded, "we'd tear the nest apart between us and never mean to. I'm not the one for egg sitting. Someone would have to do it."

"You know"—his smile was warm and amused—"I'm not very bright. With a little patience, tact and scheming I could probably get you to marry me. I'm as fond of money as anyone. It wouldn't embarrass me in the slightest to marry it. Good tailors, cars, an apartment in the city, a place in Connecticut. I like all of those things. With a little conniving I could maneuver myself into sort of a roving managing editorship with the whole world as my beat. The job of prince consort isn't a bad one."

"That's one of the things I'm curious about. Why haven't you tried for it?"

"I don't know. Not because you're Hillyard Enterprises. I'd be a little leery of you if you didn't have a dime. You have a devouring instinct. I have one for self-preservation."

"You make it sound as though a vampire bat was at your throat." She was only partly amused.

"I sometimes hear the soft velvet whirring of wings and carry a sprig of wolfbane in my pocket."

"You're a fool." Her eyes were soft. "We've been good for each other. It will be even better now."

"I'm not so sure." He deliberately pretended to misunderstand. "I never went to bed with my employer before."

She pushed back her chair and stood up. "This is as good a time as any to start."

They walked through the hot, clinging city. A small wind lifted over the East River and stirred the sooty curtains in tenement windows. Behind them Catalan rocked in his chair. He tilted the spout of the goatskin wine sack and the scarlet stream hit a corner of a closed eye, running in a true course into his open mouth. He sighed and wondered how it must be to be young again and go to bed with a long-legged blond girl of such shining beauty.

XI

ON THE surface, nothing had changed. Edition time
came and went, dictated by the city room clock. Papers spilled
from the folding machines to be bailed and sent rocketing down
a chute to the delivery trucks that spread them over the city to
be read, thrown away, or wrapped about a piece of fish on Fulton
Street.

Although there had been no real need for secrecy, Jim Haney had
worked quietly and behind a screening cover. The transaction was
no brutal squeeze. A fair price for the property was offered and accepted. Roland Anderson, who had inherited the paper, was grateful
and glad to get out. He had no feeling of being victimized or caught
in the middle of a power grab. He experienced only a lightening relief

when the burden was lifted from his shoulders. He had been going broke trying to carry the paper for sentimental reasons. It was a losing struggle. In a few years, he was convinced, no one would read. Everyone would sit at home listening to news on the radio. Still in the laboratory stage they had a thing called television through which you could both hear and see. He was glumly entertained by the fancy that in a few thousand years the world would be reduced to a great pair of buttocks and a single, staring eyeball fixed upon a picture screen. Man would have lost his use of arms and legs. Food would be taken in small capsules through a slit in the faceless face which had no mouth, since there was no longer any need to talk. None of this would have surprised him quite as much as Carol Hillyard.

After the papers had been signed and the corps of lawyers satisfied with each clause and comma, he sat in his chair in the big office upstairs and stared at the familiar scene below. The sale of the paper was not something which could be kept secret, but it had been made to a dummy corporation and the name of Hillyard Enterprises was not mentioned. Anderson knew, of course, as did the managing editor downstairs. The staff, with the exception of Chandler, was ignorant of the actual purchaser's identity. What counted was the fact that jobs were secure again, and men who had been let out returned to their desks and beats.

Anderson couldn't remember ever having seen Carol Hillyard since that first day a couple of years ago when she had come to him with a letter of introduction and explanation from an old friend and president of the National City Trust Company. As a matter of routine he had sent her to Chandler. He wasn't even sure they had given her a job until a year or so later he saw her by-line on a story.

Now a secretary tapped lightly and opened the door, standing just inside to announce Miss Hillyard. When he stood up, she closed the door with the secretive air secretaries adopt.

Anderson regarded Carol with a smile. She reminded him of one of his daughters—trim, self-assured, carefully groomed, well bred and pleasant mannered. She offered her hand and he took it.

"Newspaperwomen have changed, Miss Hillyard. In my day there weren't many. They wore long, tweedy skirts, cotton stockings and sensible shoes. Newspapermen regarded them as freaks which, I suspect, they were. Sit down, won't you?"

She took a chair and lit a cigarette, glancing about the room. The walls were covered with framed copies of the first papers, trophies, awards and mementos of a couple of centuries of publishing history.

"I suppose you have some changes in mind." He tried to make it easy for her by opening the subject himself. "This chair"—he tapped the leather arm rests where he sat—"is going to be a little large for you. I meant that literally, not figuratively."

"I don't intend to try to fill it, Mr. Anderson. Not now, anyhow."

He was, she thought, an exceptionally handsome man with a great shock of silvery white hair. He was big, heavy. A cartoonist's idea of the successful politician with a quick smile and an engaging laugh.

"Most persons," he regarded her with interest, "can't wait to try the driver's seat."

Her smile was one of knowing impudence. "I have an idea the driver's seat is behind a desk in a corner of the city room."

He leaned forward confidentially. "You musn't ever let anyone hear you say that. If it became common knowledge that the managing editor ran the paper, the league of newspaper publishers would dissolve through inertia. They would no longer be invited to banquets, sit on the Mayor's committee or provide a welcoming group for visiting heads of state. In short, a lot of publishers, you among them, would be out of jobs."

"I was hoping you would stay and keep the chair." The suggestion, which might have been an impertinence, was softened by her honesty. "I am going to run this paper someday, but not for a few years. I don't know enough and I have no intention of making a fool of myself. The girl wonder." She shook her head.

He smiled a refusal with the words. Never for a moment did he find anything extravagant in her statement that she intended to direct the policies of the paper. He only wondered a little at her wisdom in not trying to take over now.

"I suggest," the idea as it formed tickled his sense of humor, "you go to Actors Equity. Tell them you want to hire an impressive-appearing character man. Take him from the boards and put him in this seat. That will provide you with a distinguished figurehead which, between you and me, is just about all you need." He opened a silver humidor and took out a cigar. "I was never a newspaperman at heart. That is probably why I have been satisfied with this office. I'm certain you won't be. The suggestion of an actor isn't a bad one. I wish I had thought of it years ago. Now, I'm going to retire, play golf, raise hothouse flowers." His eyes roved musingly about the room. "I'm going to leave this office as it is. Everything in it belongs to the paper and the men who made it, not to me. And that," he smiled again at her, "is as close to an expression of sentiment as I'm going to come. I won't say I can leave here without a certain twinge, but that is only the pain of finally having the tooth out and not the loss of the tooth itself."

After she had left, he sat staring at the bright sunshine in the park. It suddenly occurred to him that there was nothing for him to do. With a grin he rang for his secretary.

"If the new publisher wants me, tell her I have gone to my grand-mother's funeral up at Yankee Stadium."

He took his hat from its rack and went to the elevator, whistling as happily as a copy boy with a pass from Sports and a day off.

The dinner had been Jim Haney's idea. Now, over brandy and coffee, she smiled down the table at Chris, and caught a slightly quizzical expression on the face of Stephen Keith, the managing editor. It had been a pleasant meal and she had listened, for the most part, while the talk ranged over a wide variety of subjects.

"If anybody thinks I'm going to make a speech, I am not." She might as well get it over with. "Jim thought some things ought to be cleared up and this was the best way to do it. Actually, I don't know why there should be confusion in anyone's mind."

Keith touched the ash of his cigar against a tray. A smile lighted his handsome face. "Mr. Chandler may find it a little difficult to send the paper's owner out to cover a fire, Miss Hillyard." His rich voice still carried with it the soft accent of his native Kentucky.

"I hope you don't mean that." She appealed to him, ignoring the appreciative grin on Chandler's face. "I'm not a youngster with a new red wagon who can't wait to coast it down the hill. I work for the paper, for you and Chris—Mr. Chandler. Hillyard Enterprises owns it." She paused and then continued slowly, "That's not exactly honest, is it?" She frowned slightly. "I'm not sure I can be. I'm find-ing this a little difficult." For the moment she was extremely young and uncertain. "How do we go about it?" She directed the question to Keith.

"Well," he was not condescending, "let's start out with a question or two. I assume you don't want my desk or Mr. Chandler's?"

"Of course not." She was impatiently emphatic. "I don't want Mr. Anderson's office either. Not now, maybe never. I want to stay on the staff. I may"—her self-confidence reasserted itself—"pick out a few choice assignments for myself." She winked at Keith. "Also," unconsciously she became brisk and faintly commanding, "I don't think we can continue to stick our heads down the rain barrel and pretend the country isn't in a hell of a fix simply because Mr. Hoover is President and we have always been a Republican paper. If a horse develops heaves in the middle of a stream you had damn better change or go down with him. I don't think we ought to be anyone's paper, Republican or Democrat, except as the situation dictates."

Keith studied her unsmilingly. What he saw pleased him. She had control and a rare wisdom beyond her years. She would change the paper. There was no doubt in his mind of this. But she would do it with tact when possible—this was no impetuous novice. When tact wasn't possible, and he chuckled to himself, she would probably be a hellion and no one's head would rest easy at night.

"This is the wealthiest country in the world"—she was talking to them all now—"and millions are out of work. Mr. Hoover says things will get better. They won't unless someone does something to make them better. Slum-clearance projects with government loans should be started. Federal dams and reforestation with money from the United States Treasury would put men to useful work. I think this paper ought to start yelling for those things and government action."

"That's the Socialism Norman Thomas talks about." Chandler made the statement dryly.

"Then Norman Thomas is making a lot more sense than the Republican Party." She displayed the edge of a temper. "I never thought of myself as a humanitarian. I'm not sure I am now. I guess I just went along with most comfortable persons who understood vaguely that others went to bed hungry, underclothed, badly housed—but they weren't personal problems, they could never touch me and so I didn't give much of a hoot. Maybe Carol Hillyard still doesn't, but I think her paper should. I also think," she accused Haney, "the other papers which Hillyard Enterprises owns should start fighting for some sort of decent order."

"Is that to be our policy, Miss Hillyard?" Keith meant exactly what the question asked. The tone was the same as he would have used in discussing something with Roland Anderson.

"Yes." She snapped the word and then, realizing the emphasis of her tone, relaxed and smiled a little ruefully. "Yes, sir," she added with a small, embarrassed grin.

Keith nodded an agreement without a change of expression. It struck him as not at all incongruous that this young woman should boldly strike out in a new direction for a paper grown stodgy in its conservatism. She did not affront his long experience but neither was she overly impressed. She maneuvered skillfully, intuitively, toward the ends she had in mind, leaving the impression she was seeking the approval of older heads while selecting her own pattern. She had her way without offending anyone. It was a rare gift. There was about her a quality which denied the years. At fifty, he thought, she would seem neither older nor younger than she was at this moment. On general principles he disliked the word genius. Just the same, it couldn't be denied. What had made tough soldiers follow a maid in her teens, named Joan? The analogy struck him as being a little on the extravagant side, but it was proof that age was no insurmountable barrier and men only made fools of themselves when they attempted to equate it with wisdom.

"How much money is Hillyard Enterprises prepared to lose during the next few years?" He directed the question to Haney.

Jim shrugged. "I guess that's up to you and Sister here. We've never fixed a limit. It would be pretty hard to hurt Hillyard Enterprises to the point where we'd yell."

"We'll spend all we need, Mr. Keith." She took the decision in her own hands. "A long time ago Mr. Chandler said something to me." She smiled briefly in his direction. "He said to make a paper what I would like to pick up on a newsstand. I think ours needs a face lifting. Those solid columns of type on page one look as dull as the almanac. I like to look at pictures. I think everyone does. A fresh face may startle some of our old readers, but we'll get new ones. Everyone who buys the *News* or *Mirror* isn't illiterate."

What she proposed was something Stephen Keith had been urging on Anderson for a long time. The publisher's attitude had been one of stubborn refusal to accept the changing times. The voice of God was a somber one.

"We'll remake the paper, Miss Hillyard." He was aware of a growing excitement. She generated her own and passed it on to others. "I want to expand the staff. The paper's news should be written by our own men and not taken from the wire services or syndicated columnists. I'd like to see our Washington bureau re-established and our foreign copy datelined by our own correspondents. This is an important paper or it is nothing."

"That doesn't leave us much choice, does it?" She pushed back her chair and they rose. "I haven't any inclination to be nothing."

They walked in a group to the living room and she tried to catch Chris Chandler's eye, wanting him to stay after the others left. He deliberately avoided looking at her.

"Chris—I'd like an assignment." She used his first name with a purpose.

He understood her better than anyone in the room. She was establishing their future relationship and he wasn't sure he was capable of being both lover and superior, one thing in the bedroom and another in the city room. Right now he wanted to get away and think things over.

"Governor Roosevelt is making sounds like a Presidential candidate. I'd like to go to Albany or Hyde Park and do a couple of stories about him. Up until now we have pretended he wasn't around."

"We have a man in Albany. Haley." The statement was an unmistakable dismissal of her suggestion.

"But he's not doing a very good job on the Governor, is he?" She was exaggeratedly patient.

"If we didn't think so, we wouldn't keep him there." The reply was short. It was even surly. He hadn't wanted to make it that way, but the words seemed to have formed themselves. "If you don't think so, you can call him in."

She recognized the path which both, unwillingly, were putting their feet upon with an unnecessary recklessness. She realized Keith and Haney were embarrassed. The decent, honest thing to do was to acknowledge Chandler's authority here and not strip him naked for others to see. A perversity which she despised goaded. For just a second she looked almost appealingly up into his face. She was saying: Don't let me do this, Chris. With an equal stubbornness he ignored the opportunity.

She was infuriating in her serenity. "Suppose we call Haley in then, Mr. Chandler."

"Is that an order?"

"If you wish to interpret it that way. It could be a suggestion."

"Since this is a business meeting," he would not yield, "I have an idea we ought to keep it that way. I don't see any good reason for sending you to Albany, Miss Hillyard. As long as I am behind the desk, I'll continue to make the assignments. Mr. Keith will have to decide whether Haley is covering for us in Albany. Good night."

He left them there and no one spoke until the sound of a closing door reached them. Keith was regarding her with surprise. A will, even willfulness, he had expected. The capriciousness both startled and made him uneasy. This was the Red Queen calling: "Off with their heads!" There had been no need to force Chandler. She must have known he would react immediately, and not only because there were others in the room. He would have made the same challenge of her assumption if they had been alone and in bed. Emotion had tricked her. He sighed inwardly. Intramural affairs were always dangerous. This one was explosive, supercharged, and could end in disaster. She or Chandler must decide how it was to be between them. She could be his mistress, as she probably was, or his employer. It was inconceivable she could fill the triple role of mistress, employer and employee. The balance required was too delicate. No one could maintain it.

"Good night."

She was staring down the hall at the door's blank face, and he had to repeat the phrase before she was aware of his speaking.

"Oh! Good night, Mr. Keith." She put out her hand with a troubled smile.

Haney remained behind as she walked with Keith. He went to the bar and fixed himself a drink. She came back without a word and stood at the window looking down upon the all-but-empty street. He stirred the ice in his highball. The back she presented was stiff, defiant, yet he had an idea she might be crying softly inside.

"I don't think you can have it this way, Sister." He spoke quietly. "He's too good a man. He won't take it. If you were honest about only wanting to work on the paper, it has to operate all the way down the line. You can't take a whimsical advantage of an authority you say you don't want to exercise right now. Either take Anderson's office and try to run the paper or let it alone. You'll wreck it this way."

"He didn't have to behave as he did." Her voice was small.

"You magnified a situation which had no business to arise. A man in Chandler's position has to be a little edgy. You can't intrude a personal relationship into this. There ought to be a tight door between your bed and the city room."

She turned from the window. "Does it show that obviously?"

"Of course it does. I think you even meant it to show tonight.

156

If you are in love with Chandler, then marry him and get out of the paper. But of course you won't do that."

"I'm not sure he wants to marry me or I him. I think we would only wear against each other like a couple of cutting stones until one ground the other down. I wouldn't want that to happen."

"Then 'get thee to a nunnery,' Sister, or find yourself another man. Come here." He indicated the couch.

After a moment's hesitation she crossed and sat beside him, leaning her head against his shoulder in an attitude of weariness.

"I did some checking on everyone on that paper before we went into the deal. I know as much about the staff as the personnel director. Chandler is a good man, one of the best. In normal times he could find a job on any paper in the country. He's too good to lose. I don't mean he is exactly irreplaceable but I'd hate to see you force him out. We need him. This isn't just a shiny top for you to spin. My suggestion would be for you to let this affair die out or seal it down with marriage and some sort of an understanding between you and your husband." He put his arm about her. "A good rule to remember is never play cards with a man named Doc and never go to bed with someone who is as smart as you are."

She didn't smile at the absurdity. "Sometimes I've thought it was love. You know, the real, old-fashioned kind tied up with bows and forget-me-nots. Other times I've wondered if it is only my hormones a-callin', Caroline."

"Whatever it is you've worked yourself into a bad situation. I have no objection to career women. A lot of them do a damn fine job. I only object when they imagine themselves as Catherine the Great and begin commanding the serfs to bed and expect them to go to the fields in the morning."

She kicked off a shoe and stretched her leg gratefully. She couldn't argue the problem with Haney. It was something she would have to decide for herself.

"I wanted to talk with you about Mark." She sensed his reluctance. "That's the reason I stayed behind."

"What about Mark?" She sat up.

"I had a talk with the doctors at Medical Center, the ones who gave him a check. There isn't much they can do. He's a dead man."

She spun on the couch to face him, her hands on his shoulders, incredulous and concerned.

"Mark?" The word came slowly. "What's wrong with him?"

157

"Leukemia. You know what it is, of course?"

She nodded, stunned. Not Mark. He was the rock, the granite of mountains, imperishable. It was as difficult to believe Mark Hillyard could falter as it was that a giant redwood should fall in a breeze.

"You're sure?"

Haney nodded. "I think you ought to go home, Sister. He's a lonely, dying man. You are all he has but he won't ask for you. He'll even pretend he doesn't want you around."

"Of course I'll go." She was up from the couch and then relaxed. "It isn't just across the street, is it? I'll call him tonight and get a train in the morning. What did the doctors say about time?"

"They wouldn't fix it. Weeks. Months."

She had picked up the telephone, but replaced it. If she spoke to Mark now she would only betray her concern. It would make him angry. He wouldn't want her thoughtfulness because he was dying. She would go to Virginia and arrive without notice. He would like it better that way and understand the reason without having to phrase it.

Haney got up from the couch. "I'll stop by the Pennsylvania Station on my way uptown and pick up reservations for you."

She nodded, feeling a constriction in her throat, afraid to trust her voice.

After Haney left she sat alone, staring at the empty fireplace. A thousand memories crowded her mind. Mark had been a little of everything to her, but most of all her friend—the known quantity which needed no testing, no assay. She could not imagine a world without him. It lay barren and a little frightening.

The news about Mark made the earlier scene with Chris petty. It was a thing to be talked out between them. She picked up the telephone again and called his number. For a few moments she wasn't even aware of the monotonous whine of the unanswered ring. Then it began to beat against her ear. She could imagine the bell shrilling unheeded. He was home and wouldn't answer because he suspected it was she, or—and for the first time the idea of another woman intruded itself—he was with someone else. Slowly she replaced the receiver and the faint click seemed the breaking of a cord.

Within the darkened room the small red cone of the cigarette pulsated at long intervals, giving a brief light to their faces. The girl beside him turned within his arm and trailed a finger over his bare chest.

"This wasn't very nice of you, Chris." There was no real rebuke in the statement. It was made with regret.

"I suppose not." The smoke was harsh in his mouth and he stubbed out the butt.

"It's even a little dirty because you knew I wouldn't say no when you called."

"I'm sorry." His arm tightened about her.

"I thought"—she spoke so softly the words were almost inaudible— "we had something real going for a while. What happened? All of a sudden it was over. I never heard from you. I heard about you but not from you. There's a hell of a difference."

She was right, of course. To call her after this long time, to come to her bed, his mind filled with another girl, was inexcusable. It cheapened them both. He had come running, the way a hurt or frightened child might want the sight and touch of familiar and reassuring hands or face. It was the behavior of an uncertain adolescent.

"Do we have to talk about it?"

She jerked angrily away and sat up. "Yes, by God. We have to talk about it. I'm not the injured or outraged woman but neither am I someone's old pot."

There was, he knew, no point in trying to lie to Jean. She was too smart, had known him too well. With another girl he might have invented and temporized, saying he suddenly wanted to see her again, that he had missed her. He would have to tell Jean about Carol Hillyard or say nothing. He decided it was better to keep quiet.

She studied him for a moment and then the anger subsided. "That's better. I was afraid for a minute you were going to wriggle and hand me some crap about how the memory of my beauty suddenly aroused you." She was deliberately vulgar.

With a turn of her body she twisted up and out of bed, standing naked for a second before she reached for a negligee tossed across a chair. She went to the the bathroom, and when she came back she tossed him a large bath towel.

"Wrap yourself up and let's have a drink. I won't ask any more questions. I'm properly grateful for the service you performed. You're still a good, earthy bang even if you are a bastard."

A street lamp on the corner of Madison Avenue gave them all

the light they needed in her living room. He fixed a drink and lit a cigarette for her and then took a straight bourbon for himself.

She sat in an open window, her face turned resolutely away. The dark mass of hair fell to her shoulders and was touched lightly by a wandering breeze. For a long time he and Jean Tifton had maintained a curious state of casual intimacy which seems possible only in a great city when both persons move in separate orbits. They had their work, their own circles of friends which sometimes merged briefly, activities outside each other which kept the relationship from consuming them. Jean was an assistant fashion editor of a woman's magazine. Her world was peopled by artists, models, designers. She was talented, ambitious, a little brittle and self-sufficient with an income as large as his.

There was a mutual admiration and respect, an attraction which eventually led them to bed. She had never asked for more than she was willing to give and valued her independence quite as much as he did his. What they had achieved was a condition of emotional suspension through which they floated, touching each other but never quite merging. He had never concerned himself over the probability she had other men. She tacitly assumed he knew other girls. When he called her office and apartment she frequently said she had another date. He never felt more than a brief disappointment.

Their friends moved in the concentric circles of the city. They were drawn from newspaper, radio and advertising men, artists and writers, all digging in for a toehold on the stone mountain. They lived in apartments scattered from Greenwich Village to Fifty-ninth Street. The cocktail hour was becoming an institution in the speakeasies. They drank a great deal, talked incessantly and made love as though they all had appointments to keep. They were the quick and eager whose prophets were Cabell, Mencken, Fitzgerald and Nathan, and *The American Mercury* the Koran.

The affair, if it could be called that, moved smoothly and without conscious effort on either side. Love was not a sentiment but something to be made. The relationship slid downhill as easily as it had climbed—a descent without violent jolts or sudden stops and starts. After Carol Hillyard his calls became fewer. Without admitting it, he had avoided the places where they were likely to meet. She had telephoned him a few times, dropped a couple of scribbled notes, and then instinctively known he had found another interest. She had missed but not mourned him. She was busy and successful.

The city was filled with congenial men in brisk competition with each other.

Until tonight she had felt neither anger nor a sense of loss. Now, however, she was annoyed. The impatience was directed at herself. He had made a casual assumption that her bed was empty and waiting. His call, coming at the hour it had, was no invitation to talk or go any place outside her apartment. He had merely asked if he could come over and she had said yes without any feeling of elation or triumph.

She turned from her study of the street with a little smile of resignation.

"I'm dying to ask what happened," she confessed, "but I'm damned if I will. I know who she is, of course. We have a lot of mutual friends. They came a-running with the story of how the boss was disporting himself with a blond hired hand. I just said: Good for her. That's one way to make it."

He laughed inwardly. The boss might have been having a frolic with a hired hand but not the way Jean imagined.

"She owns the paper."

Jean stared unbelievingly at him and then leaned against the window's side with a throaty gurgle of amusement. Her eyes were bright with the tears of laughter.

He grinned sheepishly, feeling a little ridiculous with the situation. The inadequate towel didn't help either. The knot kept slipping. Despite the classical figures of the Greeks, he had always thought a man looked pretty silly, dangling as he did.

She wiped at her eyes and made an effort to compose herself, finding a diversion in the towel.

"For God's sake stop clutching at yourself. You look like a frightened virgin when the blast of air goes up her skirts in the Fun House at Coney Island. Take the damn thing off and put on a pair of shorts or nothing."

He retied the knot and compromised by sitting in a chair within easy reach of the whisky.

"So what happens now?" She cocked her head and regarded him alertly.

"I don't know."

The sky over the East River was the color of a smoked pearl. The casement provided a frame for her dusky beauty. He wondered if it would be possible to lose himself in her. The Ariadne to lead him out of this labyrinth of indecision.

"Have another drink." She motioned toward his empty glass. "We might as well stay up now and you can go to the paper bleary-eyed."

As though the decision had been dormant in his mind all the time, he realized he had no intention of reporting in today. Not this morning, or perhaps any other one. He had a three weeks' vacation due. There would never be a better time to take it. He'd call in and then talk with Keith later. He'd understand.

"I have to go to the office for a little while." She was no longer laughing. "Why don't you stay here, Chris? If that's what you want." The suggestion was made with soft understanding.

He nodded and rose to move beside her at the window. Daylight was cracking through the murky shell, breaking a cloud bank into long, ragged streamers. Down this pleasant side street between Park and Madison avenues there came the wind-bell tinkle of milk bottles set upon stoops and the soggy thump of morning papers being delivered.

"I will if it's all right with you." He felt her shoulder against his ribs.

"If it wasn't all right I wouldn't have suggested it." She was annoyed with herself. If he wanted a cave in which to hide, she should damn well let him find it for himself. "You want some more booze or coffee?"

"Coffee."

"Good." She moved from the seat. "A man in my bed I don't mind. A boozy, melancholy one is something else again."

He stood with her in the kitchen while she put a kettle on to boil and then measured out coffee and fitted the aluminum drip-pot together. The small domestic clatter was somehow reassuring.

"Would you marry me?" He wasn't conscious of wanting to speak the words.

She was half bent at the icebox and turned to look up at him with wonder.

"Not at five o'clock in the morning. Not ever unless you have a better reason for asking than you do now. Get the hell out of the kitchen. Get yourself a shower and a shave. You know where everything is."

He stood in the stall with a full pressure of cold water beating down upon him, driving some of the confusion and indecision from his mind. The image of Carol Hillyard persisted and he couldn't wash it away. Last night, he thought, was only the first, small indication of what would happen. Without realizing it perhaps, she had the acquisitive instincts of Mark Hillyard. She would possess and be satisfied with nothing less than complete, acknowledged ownership. He realized, with a start, that he was actually a little afraid of her.

When he was dressed and went into the front room, Jean had set orange juice and coffee out upon small tables at both ends of the couch.

"I was going to fix some eggs and bacon but I said no. That's going too damn far." Her eyes were shadowed with an abrupt seriousness. "You can forget what you said back there in the kitchen, Christopher."

He drank some of the coffee and lit a cigarette, wondering if he did want to forget it.

XII

MARK'S car and the chauffeur, Josh, had met her at Richmond. She drove now through the fragrant countryside at a speed which made the man turn wondering glances her way and brace himself against the slewing curves into which she swung the heavy car with a tight recklessness.

There were some two hundred and fifty miles to cover. The wheels ate at them steadily. She pushed the car as she did, not through any feeling of urgency but because an impatient anger fired her and speed was a release.

Before leaving New York she had tried to reach Chris at his apartment twice during the night and once near dawn when, if he was coming home at all, he would be in. She didn't know where he had gone but she thought she knew damn well what he had done and why. That he was in bed with a girl, touching her, sharing himself, smoking quietly in the soft darkness of repletion, gave her an empty sensation of nausea. This was jealousy, a stark and ugly thing, and she was unfamiliar with its face; the fury and self-loathing it could arouse. She felt the unreasoning compulsion for physical violence; to break and smash something, kicking at the strewn pieces. For the first time she understood the dark passions which drove men and women to sordid and bloody crimes. The knifings, stranglings, the merciless beatings when a bullet would be too swift, too impersonal. Because this emotion was so new, it was also terrifying. She tried to back away from it and found she was rooted before an evil, grotesque and leering thing which mocked her judgment. No matter what she had said or done, Chris had no right to do this to her. When reason attempted to intrude, she slammed the door of a perverse and illogical rage upon it. I am a woman. She told herself. I feel this way.

The fury died slowly, leaving the hot ashes of resentment. She began to do certain things mechanically because they had to be done. There were bags to be packed. Since she had no idea how long she would be away, trunks might have to be sent later.

At eight o'clock she called the city desk. Stanfield, Chandler's assistant, was sitting in. She told him what was necessary and asked for Chris. When Stanfield said he wasn't coming in, she asked to be transferred to Stephen Keith.

"My father is ill." This was only a preliminary to what she wanted to say, to ask. "I am going down to Virginia on an eleven-o'clock train. I haven't any idea how long I'll be away."

"I'm sorry to hear about your father, Miss Hillyard." Keith was gravely and sympathetically concerned. "I hope it isn't as serious as you think. Please keep in touch with me, will you?"

"Yes. Of course." She was almost rude. "Where is Mr. Chandler?"

There was a silence, just a little longer than might have been expected. "Mr. Chandler had a vacation due. He asked to take it, starting today. There seemed to be no reason why he shouldn't."

The managing editor was discussing an employee with the paper's publisher, nothing more.

"I see." She hesitated. "Thank you. I'll call from Virginia. You know where to reach me, of course." This, they both understood, was for Chandler if he inquired. "Good-by."

She delayed leaving the apartment until the last possible moment, wandering restlessly about the room, waiting for the telephone to ring. He didn't call. He wasn't going to call. Damn him. He was sitting some place with stubborn satisfaction. She tried to tell herself she didn't care. The ashtrays filled with half-smoked butts and her nervous pacing gave a lie to the declaration. Finally she told Peters to have the doorman call a cab.

Jim Haney met her at the gate and walked down the ramp with her to the car. Her compartment had fresh flowers in it, a bottle of Scotch wrapped in gold foil, a couple of current novels. She glanced at them with appreciation and thanked Haney, kissing him lightly on the cheek.

"You let me know how things are going, Sister. I'll be in Chicago, at the Ambassador East, on Friday. If you want to reach me before that I'll be at the Book-Cadillac in Detroit. I'd go with you but there's nothing I can do, and this may be a long period of just waiting. It won't be easy."

The trip had seemed interminable and she wished she had taken a plane. She kept to her compartment, having the meals served there and drinking most of Haney's Scotch until it dawned on her that she was using the liquor as a drug to induce a state of numb indifference....

Slowing down now as they passed through one of the innumerable villages which broke the long road's sweep, she turned to Josh.

"How is Mister Mark?"

"He ain' well, Miz Cahrl. Neva see a man go downhill so fas'. One day he's a-yellin' an' raisin' hell, natural like. The next he take to his bed. What he got thas' wrong?"

She didn't answer. The news that Mark was actually bedridden shocked her. She couldn't imagine his restless energy confined to a room.

Glenallen, Apple Grove, Holladay. They were names on a map, communities which she skidded through with brake and horn, indifferent to traffic signs and outraged shouts. She wanted to get home. In the peace of quiet and familiar surroundings she would unseat the demon which rode her.

They were on the last fifty miles, in well-remembered country now. She eased the driving pressure of her foot upon the accelerator and Josh sighed with audible gratitude. She smiled at him, feeling better.

She'd call Chris. No, damnit. He would call her. This she was sure of. They'd talk, both giving a little and working back to a plane of understanding. Maybe—the idea grew—he could come down and spend his vacation here with her. Nothing really irreparable had happened. It was a matter of both adjusting to a new situation. He had been angry, unreasonably so she felt. Because of this he had gone to bed with some girl. All right. She could understand, forget that. It had been something done under stress and not because he wanted or needed another girl. There was no point in chewing on it, a casual one-night stand without significance beyond the bed.

They stood for a moment in the gauzy sunshine on the worn step of the small stone house of pre-Revolutionary days. A man and woman filled the doorway behind them wearing fixed, professional smiles of approval; their standard expression for newlyweds.

As they started down the narrow graveled path, Jean glanced at him with something close to embarrassed amusement.

"As Jane Ace puts it, 'You could knock me down with a fender.' "

"Me too."

He lit a cigarette and offered it to her. She shook her head and took his arm.

"It's not the worst thing that could happen to us, Chris?" She made the statement into a question. "At least I hope not. You don't suppose the four drinks we had before lunch made our heads ring with the sound of wedding bells?"

"I was a damn sight soberer than the judge back there who read the ceremony."

"I'm glad. I kept thinking I caught the scent of applejack when it should have been orange blossoms. It's a heady perfume."

At the car he held the door for her and then closing it, rested crossed arms and smiled. She reached to put her hand over one of his. It was a gesture of confidence and it touched him. He felt a great tenderness for this girl who was now his wife.

Neither had been quite sure how or why it had happened in just this way. After Jean had left for her office he had sprawled on the couch, reading the morning paper with the day maid working around him with cloth and vacuum. He experienced a sensation of repose, almost of gratitude, for the small sounds of a well-ordered household. He had checked with Keith and Stanfield. If the telephone rang here it would not be for him. He thought he must feel as a salmon does when, after fighting its way upstream, it comes suddenly upon a quiet, deep pool. He was beyond the current now.

Jean had returned at eleven and stood above the couch regarding him with a quizzical brightness. He swung up.

"I thought, maybe, we could go some place for lunch. I'm on vacation."

"We could have it here." She took off her hat with an easy, careless gesture. "Whatever you feel like doing."

He knew what he wanted to do, firmly shutting out the reason. Beyond this room, this girl, he could see nothing but confusion.

"I feel like getting married." He reached for her hands.

She came to him just a little reluctantly, the question in her eyes. Finally, she nodded.

"All right, Chris. I'm not going to ask you any questions."

He had kissed her and her fingers touched his cheek inquisitively, as though they reached for an answer to be found there.

She had packed a bag, called her office. They stopped off at his place for the things he would need and then drove north, halting at Rhinebeck for lunch and then taking the ferry across the Hudson to Kingston, where they took out a license and found a marrying judge.

Now and then, on the way up, he caught her studying him. There were things she wanted to ask but she kept them to herself. What they were doing no longer seemed unusual and neither attempted to charge it with a false excitement.

Here, on this quiet street, Jean Tifton Chandler studied her husband now.

"Maybe," she spoke slowly, "I'm a little delayed action over all this. The things I should have said just didn't come to me at the time. If I'm taking you on a bounce from the backboard, I'm a little sorry for us both. I wasn't exactly bowled over. Along with all the propositions there have been a few proposals. It would have been easy enough to get married. I think maybe I always wanted you. It was safer to pretend we were easy, in-and-out-of-bed pals. I guess, underneath, I have a fine, middle-class yearning for respectability and virtue. I like the idea of being your wife, Chris. I hope we'll be decent, gentle, and a little kind with each other. It would hurt me to have it any other way. If there are any reservations in your mind, let's call it off here and now. I'd hate to find out I'd

168

opened the door to a con man who cried: Sanctuary." She drew back. "That's my speech. Did you want to make one?"

He shook his head and leaned to kiss her, softly and with infinite tenderness and gratitude. He and Jean would not senselessly tear at each other. Between them they could adjust and find a warm and comfortable pattern for their lives.

An early fall was walking down the mountains to the Catskills' folded valleys. High on the rounded summits, in thinner, colder air, the leaves were beginning their transformation and the pageant of color moved slowly to the base. In small fields, straw-tinged shocks of corn and pumpkins spoke of a coming winter. Thin vines of gun-metal smoke grew from rock chimneys.

Jean leaned back, the soft wind whipping at her cheeks. "Where are we going?"

"There's a place up near Margaretville. It's a working farm but they take a few summer boarders. At this time of year we'll have it to ourselves."

"Are we going to be hardy and tramp over hills?"

"That's for Boy Scouts. In the evening we'll drink a little apple-jack. You can sit on the floor in front of the fire and I'll scratch your ears."

"Mmmm. That sounds good. I have the domestic instincts of a cat. Give me a warm corner, feed and treat me well. That's all I ask. You will, won't you, Chris?"

She swayed a little to rest her head against his shoulder and thought what a good thing this could be for them both.

If Old Mark was surprised to see her, he refused to show it. He was propped in his bed. Newspapers were strewn on the floor. He was lighting a cigar when she cautiously opened the door and peeked in.

"I thought you was Julia. She's always doin' that, like I was a baby in an incubator. By God, you've been away a long time, Sister. Come on in."

She went to his side, bent and kissed him gently. "How are you, Mark?"

"That's a damn fool question to ask. How the hell would you be, tucked into a bed, denied whisky, tobacco and the other comforts of man?" He waved the cigar. "I got a stock of these hid away. Liquor, too."

She offered no explanation for her unexpected arrival and he didn't ask for one. The reason was understood. There was no need to talk it over. His eyes followed her with bright pleasure as she crossed to pull back the curtains.

"You look good, Sister. I've missed you."

She turned with a smile. Nothing in her manner or expression betrayed her shock. He was thin, wasted, a dried and dead branch clinging stubbornly to the tree.

"I thought it was time I took a vacation and came home for a while."

They let it go at that but the understanding was between them. He was grateful for her coming. He understood she knew he was dying. It wasn't anything to talk about.

"You got here in the nick of time. A couple of weeks more and I'd starved to death. How the hell they ever come to the conclusion I'm goin' to live happy on Jello-O an' Cream of Wheat is one of the mysteries of medical science. You get things in order around here, Sister."

Later in the afternoon she had a talk with Aunt Julia. The woman, because it was her nature, wanted a scene of tears and hand wringing. Carol shut her off without sympathy.

"Mark is dying, Aunt Julia. We all know it. If you want to weep and cover your head, you'll have to do it some place else. I won't have it. Do you understand? I want this damned tiptoeing around stopped. It gives me the creeps and God knows what it does to Mark. Who is taking care of him?"

Julia sniffled. She had no will to argue with this determined and angry girl. She was Mark all over again and that was a double cross, too heavy for any woman to bear. Carol repeated the question.

"Dr. Warren. He's new in Court House. The other doctor said he'd be damned if he'd have anything more to do with a sonofabitch like that." She covered her mouth with a hand, horrified by the words. "He said it. I didn't."

She drove into Court House, found the office and gave her name to the young nurse who acted as a receptionist.

Earle Warren was surprised. It hardly seemed possible an old wolf could produce this remarkably beautiful girl. He stood behind his desk until she was seated.

"Tell me about my father, Dr. Warren."

He reached into a cabinet for a file. "This is the report from the doctors in New York."

She shook her head. "I don't want them read to me. Is he in pain?"

"No, Miss Hillyard. It's a wasting away, the disintegration of flesh and bone. There isn't a lot to be done. I give him some intravenous shots and chant a little mumbo jumbo at the bedside. Actually there is no specific treatment for leukemia."

"Is there any reason then why he can't have what he wants?"

Earle Warren shook his head with an amused reminiscence. "No, I guess not. Of course he demands some unusual things for a man his age. The last request was for a young girl to sleep with him at night. It seems the bed gets cold."

"If that's what he wants, we'll get one for him."

Watching her, listening to the assurance in her voice, Warren never for a moment doubted she would do it, ordering a girl as dispassionately as she would call in a nurse.

"Does he know how sick he is?"

Warren nodded. "I didn't have to tell him. He knows."

She stood up. "He wants steak, fried potatoes, cigars and whisky. Is there any real reason why he shouldn't have them?"

He walked with her to the door. "I didn't leave any diet instructions. If he isn't getting what he asks for it's because Miss Julia has an abiding faith in calf's-foot jelly as a cure-all for everything from a sore throat to cancer. He can have what he can eat or thinks he wants to eat. I stop in once a day as a matter of routine and to run up the bill. I have had very few Mark Hillyards in my practice so far." He understood she wouldn't be offended by the statement.

She wasn't. "I don't blame you. He'd do the same thing in your place."

Outside, she stood for a moment, feeling the warm sun, aware of the subdued tempo. No one was in a hurry. She nodded to vaguely familiar faces as they passed. Actually, she knew surprisingly few persons in the town the Hillyards called home.

In the middle of the block, where she had parked the car, Bootsie Warrington was half draped over a front fender in an attitude of idle waiting. He smiled his pleasure at her approach and unwound himself with an easy grace.

"Bootsie." She covered the last few steps quickly. It surprised her a little to realize how glad she was to see him. "How are you?"

"I'm just fine, child. I was down the street a-piece when you went in that there doctor's office. I didn't figure a yell would be polite, so I just waited."

He reared above her despite the fact he stood in the characteristically limp slouch, and the grin of honest pleasure enveloped her as did the hand taking hers.

"I'm glad you did."

Staring up at him, she was conscious once again of his ingratiatingly lazy charm. He was a fine handsome animal, she thought, who managed to wear slacks, sweater and tennis shoes with an air most men couldn't achieve with the finest tailoring. Bootsie threw himself against no currents. He stood and let them swirl about him as a man might dangle his feet in the shallows of a turbulent river. Nothing, she thought enviously, disturbed him. Everything would come out all right because he was Bootsie Warrington.

"Could I buy you a coke or a piece of dime store candy? You know, ma'am, I've been wonderin' when you were comin' back to ol' Bootsie. I been a long time waitin'."

"You can stop dropping your g's and turning on that counterfeit Rebel talk."

He took her arm possessively and guided her to the car, bending to regard her sorrowfully.

"I forgot." He was perplexed. "It doesn't seem to get to you like other Northern girls. If I can't buy you a coke or a licorice whip to chew on, let's go to your house an' drink some of your papa's whisky. Your papa and I are pretty good friends now. I go to see him 'most every day."

"You what?" She halted and looked at him with astonishment.

"I've been co'tin' you by proxy. Your papa, sick as he is, has not been insensible to my virtues. We get along just fine."

While she was trying to adjust herself to this statement he put her in the car, walked around and climbed in behind the wheel. He twisted his long legs in an effort to find a comfortable position.

"I usually hang one foot out over the side of my Ford," he explained ingenuously. "The native girls think it's kinda cute. I don't suppose you would, though."

"No." She held back a smile. "No, I wouldn't."

He started the car. "I guess New York does things to people, like ruining their naturalness. I've even heard they wear tennis sneakers up there only when they play tennis." He waved to four girls in a convertible who turned to stare after them.

She lit a cigarette, studying him while pretending not to. She had made no attempt to get in touch with Angela Warrington in New York. Actually, she had forgotten Bootsie. She still couldn't quite believe his statement that he had been visiting Mark daily.

"What in the world do you and Mark talk about?" She settled back, willing to accept the fact he could drive with one finger and his attention on everything but the road.

"We talk some about you." He reached over and patted her hand reassuringly. "I told your papa right out I'd like to marry you. He wanted to know straight if I was after your money and I said yes. After that we got real friendly. I guess it's a novelty for him to see an honest, shining face like mine."

"You're crazy." Even as she made the statement she was certain he was telling the truth. "I don't believe it."

"You can ask him. Of course, I told him money wasn't everything." Bootsie chuckled. "You know what he said to that?"

"No." She didn't believe he was making this up. "What did he say?"

"He said I was a goddamned fool. He said one girl was like another, only a lot are poor and a few are rich. Only an idiot would marry a poor one when he could get a rich one. I had to agree with him. That's how we get on so well. He thinks I'm a little too easygoing and wouldn't be able to stand up to you. But I guess he figures that's my lookout. He'd really like to have me for the father of your children. You ask him. He'll tell you."

She thought with quiet amusement that a record of the conversations between Mark Hillyard and Bootsie would be a collector's item.

"What have you been doing? Were you graduated from the University. Do you work?"

"I was last in line when they handed out the diplomas, but that was only because they called the names alphabetically. I got through all right. I looked around for a career but this is a lean time. I don't reckon it has been harder for a gentleman to get along in Virginia since the carpetbaggers were here. I do a little golf instructing at the country club. So you see"—he nodded with an engaging simplicity—"it's up to you."

Bootsie made the drive to the house one of continual social exchange. He waved and called the names of persons they passed: a Negro driving a flat-bed wagon on canted wheels; a man leaning over a fence talking with a friend; a boy dangling a line into a ditch where a few bream swam and occasionally nibbled at the bait. Bootsie knew everyone and they all responded with broad smiles of appreciation as though his casual greeting were an accolade. She was a little astonished to realize how relaxed she was in his company. There were no complexities about Bootsie.

"I want to drive over to Harkness sometime next week. I had Black Dancer sent back when I went to New York. I'd like to bring her home while I'm here. Would you go with me?"

He nodded. "Cousin John has been having a hard time along with everyone else. From what I hear he is about to lose Harkness. That would really hit him. This depression is a thing, isn't it?"

The depression of the cities seemed an alien monster in this pleasant countryside. She found it hard to believe it existed or could strike at those who lived here. Yet common sense told her it must. The nation had been geared to a great industrial complex. When that broke down, the fracture reached into every corner.

"Like everyone else," Bootsie screwed up his features into an expression of seriousness, "Cousin John has been trying to hang on and keep his pride at the same time. That's a real hard thing to do. After we're married I expect we ought to give Cousin John a hand. You'd be kin then and he could take it without feeling shame."

To her astonishment she discovered Bootsie's complete assurance wasn't offensive. He simply repeated what he had in mind until the statement achieved a certain validity through repetition.

Mark was awake when they went to his room. Bootsie regarded him with a bright interest, his head cocked inquisitively to one side.

"How you, Mr. Hillyard, sir?" He smiled and took a seat in the open window, blocking it completely. "I brought your daughter home."

"He's after your money, Sister," Mark growled, but there was no resentment in him, no real warning in the words. He even seemed to take a puzzled interest in Bootsie. "He came right out and told me so."

"Yes, sir, Mr. Hillyard." Bootsie nodded emphatically. "I told Carol, too. A man and a woman shouldn't enter into the holy state without having everything clear between them. Of course"—he turned a fond smile on Carol—"she's got a lot to recommend her besides what you're going to leave. When you add it all up, Miss Carol here is a catch. There's no doubt about that. I'm a real lucky man." He divided a warm and friendly innocence between them.

Bootsie contradicted everything Mark Hillyard had always regarded as desirable qualities in a man. If he had been put to naming an unsatisfactory candidate for a son-in-law, it would have been Bootsie Warrington. There was no drive, no toughness. He was indifferent to or oblivious of the standards by which one male usually measures another. But, Mark admitted to himself, he was a fine healthy stud. He'd pin Sister to a bed and keep her there until she was with child. Mark was confident once this happened, Sister would begin behaving the way a normal woman should. Too much of Mark Hillyard had gone into this place in Virginia. It was an expression of stability. He wanted the roots to go deep into the soil. It couldn't be allowed to rot away as had the original in Mississippi until it became a gutted shell, filled with bats and the ghosts of dreams. Mark knew as much about the Warrington family as they themselves did. The blood was good, the stock sound. This big fellow could pass it on through Sister. The only thing that bothered him was whether Warrington would be able to stand up to Sister. She'd break him if he crossed her. But, and Mark was relieved by this knowledge, Bootsie wouldn't be likely to cross anyone unless he had to. He had no inclination to be aggressive.

Carol pretended to ignore the confidential exchange between Mark and Bootsie. By a mysterious process known only to themselves the pair had achieved a unity of purpose. She couldn't imagine a more unlikely fusion but it was there.

"I saw Doctor Warren." She sat on the edge of the bed. "He told me you could have anything you wanted, including a girl to warm the sheets. I'll send out a call."

"Don't get me no skinny one." Mark was emphatic and then he chuckled complacently. "I'd give a sound dollar if you could have seen Earle's face when I told him what I wanted. He thinks I'm a character. Maybe I am." He mused with satisfaction on this. "There was another doctor. He didn't have a sense of humor. All the damn fool wanted to do was keep me alive, as though that was enough to satisfy me." He turned on the pillows to stare past her at Bootsie. "Don't you have no ambition at all?" He almost yelled the accusing question.

"No, sir." Bootsie scratched a tanned ankle thoughtfully. "I guess what I have really couldn't be called ambition the way you'd define it. What I'd like to do after you're gone, passed away as they say, is to move my things over to this big place and take it easy for the rest of my life. I don't want you to think I'm in a hurry about your passing over. I'm not prodding you." He smiled reassuringly.

"I never knew a fellow like you." Mark made the statement with something close to grudging admiration. Listening to him Carol was amazed by the fact Mark didn't seem to resent Bootsie's casual reference to his dying. "I thought, at first," Mark continued, "you were the damnedest fool I ever listened to. I must be sicker than I know. By God, you're beginning to make a little sense to me."

"Yes, sir." Bootsie wasn't flattered. "I was certain you'd come around to it. You've got a lot of common sense, Mr. Hillyard. Sooner or later that'd make you see the light. You'd just have to ask yourself: Why should a man who is going to marry my daughter want to go to work and get ahead? How much farther ahead could he get than putting his hands into the Hillyard till? A man could work a lifetime and not even get close to that much money. So why should I try? I've a lot of faith in your good judgment."

"You're both insane." Carol lit a cigarette calmly.

Old Mark shook his head. "What he says adds up, Sister," he defended Bootsie. "He's not the idiot he pretends to be."

"No, sir," Bootsie agreed artlessly. "That would just hardly seem possible. It's sort of a protective coloring, like a chameleon, and lets me move about." He regarded Mark fondly. "I grow on people. Take you, for instance. In the beginning, if I had come right out and said I wanted to marry Carol, you would have run me off the place with a whip. Now, you're beginning to recognize certain qualities. I'm going to toss your money around like it was lint flying from a cotton gin. We're going to stock this place with fine horses and children. The Warringtons have always been real prolific breeders. Yes, sir. We'll set up a dynasty here after you've passed beyond the vale—whatever that is. You can count on it."

Carol rose. "If you two have finished whacking up the brood mare, let's have a drink. I've had a long trip and a hard day."

Old Mark pinched his nose between two fingers, hiding a frosty smile as he studied Bootsie Warrington. He'd sure like to be around to see how it all turned out.

XIII

SHE was dressed now and moving almost fretfully about the room, waiting for one of the girls to bring up Mark's lunch and the salad ordered for herself. There was something a little frightening about the old man's intense preoccupation with the idea of food. It was, she imagined, a form of rebellion against the thing which stalked him. He demanded huge meals and then fell asleep when they were put before him, the way a drowsy child might nod over its bottle.

She had been home for eight days and little of the time had been spent away from the house. Instead of making the trip to Harkness she had telephoned John. Black Dancer was brought over in a trailer. A ride in the morning had been her only recreation. The rest of the time was devoted to Mark. She had been reluctant to admit what he profanely accepted. This was a death watch. Oddly enough, he didn't seem frightened. He was angry. He cursed the specter and would not be cowed by its presence. It was just one hell of a thing to happen to Mark Hillyard.

On a desk at the side of her room was a stack of newspapers. They lay untouched, cased in their brown mailing covers. What they contained no longer seemed important. Mark absorbed her time, thoughts and energy. Things happening beyond these walls were without meaning.

This, she admitted, was not wholly true. Chris Chandler mattered. She caught herself thinking about him continually and was, by turns, furious and miserably unhappy. There had been no call, no letter. He knew where she was, or could have known if he had cared enough to inquire. Once, as she lay sleepless at three o'clock in the morning, she had reached for the telephone. She listened as the impersonal voices of the operators put together the circuit from Court House to Richmond to New York. The steady pulse of the unanswered ring was not broken, as she somehow knew it wouldn't be. Half-ashamed of her weakness she found herself making excuses for him. Who would spend a vacation in a city apartment? Why should she expect him to be there? This was a desperate form of sophistry. He damn well should have let her know where he was.

What, in the beginning, had been little more than impatience—a completely feminine supercilious tolerance for a childishly stubborn male—was crystallizing now into cold anger. She wanted him to be lonely and hurt as she was. She knew he wasn't and the thought sickened her. If this is love, you can have it. She sought desperately to reject the idea. Who would willingly be a captive to this thing which drained you of strength and reason? Carol Hillyard, apparently. She yearned for it with a disgusting eagerness; an adolescent, trembling beneath a boy's touch and raising docile eyes to beg for more. It was degrading. It was a thief making off with your self-respect. It was a torture that made you humbly beg for more. If I ever get over this, she told herself. This was the trembling rummy, the quivering wreck who tried to exorcise the DTs by solemnly chanting never again while he waited outside for the bar to open. She kicked savagely at a chair.

For something to do she began opening the newspapers, slitting the jackets with vicious strokes of a fingernail and then carrying them to a chaise longue. Stretching out, she lit a cigarette. There were papers from Richmond, Washington, and her own in New York. The news was stale, heard as it was made, almost, on the radio. Keith, she saw, was already changing the familiar make-up. Page one was broken by pictures and three-column heads where single columns of solid type had been traditional. Already the paper looked fresher, brighter, easier to read.

She picked up a Washington paper, running through it idly. Later, she was always to wonder at the curious presentiment she had felt as her eyes moved down a syndicated Broadway column. It was written in a monkeylike, chattering style of hysterical excitement to make the trivial seem important. There was nothing here to make her pause. She had no interest in the people mentioned and yet, she continued to read with a strange sensation of dread. She came upon it as she was somehow certain she would: a two-line mention of Chris Chandler's marriage at Kingston, N. Y., to Jean Tifton.

Nausea clotted in her throat and for a moment she was certain she was going to be sick. The sensation was that of being kicked violently in the stomach. She pushed the paper away and held tightly to herself, staring at the ceiling. She experienced shock beyond words, beyond outrage. She thrust a knuckled fist against her mouth, honestly thinking she might scream.

Who, she asked herself numbly, was this girl Jean Tifton? Where had she come from? Chris had never mentioned her name. She was either someone completely new or belonging to the years past. Chris had no capacity for intrigue. He would never have tried to carry on two love affairs simultaneously.

"You fool," she whispered aloud. "I could have given you so much. Why have you done this to me?"

She stood up and discovered she was shaking. This gesture of senseless defiance he had made—it was if he had said, I'll show you. There was no excuse to be made for him now. He knew what he was doing and how it would hurt and humiliate her. He wasn't in love with this girl. He couldn't be. She walked up and down the room, seeking a release from the torment through movement.

Slowly the fury subsided, draining her of emotion. It was a thing learned and not to be forgotten. Never again would she be fool enough to allow herself to be tender. It was a trap; a thing with those carnivorous flowers that opened their petals to unwary insects.

Her animal-like pacing became more deliberate. Her eyes were cold agates of calculated anger. It was a senseless thing he had done; a feeble defiance which would deceive neither of them. It was a display of pique unworthy of him, of any man. Never then or later did she admit the real reason that made Chris Chandler do what he had done. Spite was easier to believe.

She strode to the bedside table and the telephone. Her expression was composed, the outstretched hand without a tremor of hesitation. She placed the call to New York in level, measured tones.

When she had Keith her voice was impersonal. Hearing the man's familiar and gentle tone recalled every detail of the city room; of Chris at his desk, the spasmodic clatter of typewriters, the slap of leather cylinders as they dropped from pneumatic tubes with proofs from the composing room. The brief exchange of inane pleasantries was almost unendurable. She answered the necessary questions about Mark and herself with cold patience. She would not be tricked by what she felt.

"Do you know where Mr. Chandler is?" The question was crisp.

The brief silence at the other end of the wire was revealing. She could feel Stephen Keith's reluctance, for now he would know why she had called.

"Yes, Miss Hillyard. He is just outside Margaretville, a little place in the Catskills."

"Then you will please get in touch with him, Mr. Keith. Mr. Chandler is no longer working for the paper. You will tell him so and use your judgment in the matter of severance pay commensurate with his service."

It was out now, irrevocably done. She could not call back a single word. For a moment she thought she was going to vomit and swallowed rapidly, bending her head listlessly.

She thought she detected the small sound of a weary sigh as Keith delayed his reply to the order.

"You understand what I have said, Mr. Keith?" She blew upon her anger, keeping it hot, fighting against a feeling of shame.

"It would be difficult to misunderstand you, Miss Hillyard." The rebuke was there, gentle but unmistakable. "I hate to lose Mr. Chandler. He will be hard to replace."

"I don't think so." The contradiction was sharp. "There are a lot of good men out of work. In the meanwhile, move someone up on the desk. We can make a final decision later, after I come back."

Listening to the unmistakable command, Stephen Keith realized nothing could be gained by attempting to discuss this with her. It was no question of Chandler's ability. This was personal and bitter. This was naked, ugly power heedlessly exercised. This was no rational weighing of a situation. Outrage and vindictiveness had usurped reason.

"Are you still there, Mr. Keith?" The question crackled and sparked.

"Yes, Miss Hillyard." The lean shoulders, stooped slightly from many years of desk work, drooped dejectedly. He was a man of gentle mood. Never had he discharged anyone in anger. "You wouldn't like to think this over for a few days, would you?"

He was giving her an escape, a chance to delay. She refused it.

"There is nothing to think over, Mr. Keith. I would like to have the matter taken care of at once." She softened just a little. "I'm sorry if I have been rude. Good-by."

Keith put down the receiver regretfully. Why Chris Chandler had done what he had was unimportant now. He must have weighed the possible consequences. To argue with Carol Hillyard over the telephone about a personal matter would achieve nothing. Ultimately it would place him in the position of having to resign. It was that or accept her willful decision and carry out the orders of an imperious and bitter girl smarting beneath the humiliation of being rejected. She would leave no question unanswered as to who owned and ran this paper. Unhappily he glanced over the room. This was his life. Into it he had poured a fierce loyalty, pride, and an intimate association which transcended the job of managing editor. To leave it would be to walk with ghosts throughout the remaining years.

He thumbed through the back pages of a desk calendar to where he had penciled Chandler's rural telephone number. It was a thing to have done with if it must be done. He gave one of the girls on the switchboard the number reluctantly.

A pearl-gray scarf of mist lay over the mountains and trailed through the valleys. Crows hunted in the empty fields and the stream below the farm ran sluggishly as though clabbered by the air's new chill. In the living room of the house Jean Chandler sat cross-legged on the floor before the fireplace, contentedly munching an apple. The fruit broke beneath her teeth with a crisp, autumnal sound, and the heat from twisting flames came out in little waves.

Through the open door leading to the low, whitewashed kitchen she could hear Chris at the telephone and wondered why the office was bothering him on his vacation. She smiled with a softly radiant happiness. This ten days or so had been a good time for them both; a time of understanding, of sharing a strange and compelling quiet assurance that filled their lives and was reflected in everything they said or did. Somehow, a small miracle had been achieved through the ritual of a few words and the placing of a platinum band on her finger. It was an enriching experience to belong to someone and yet, not be possessed. In many ways what they were doing had been done many times before. Over the broken years they had known each other she had awakened to find Chris beside her. They had talked, shared a breakfast table, walked, drunk and made love. So none of this was new. She wondered why it was different. It was not a thing to be named and called marriage, but something to be felt and almost shyly touched. It was the sensation of returning home, to familiar things, and closing the door with the feeling of security and confidence.

She sighed happily. It was good to have known each other intimately before this happened. There had been no awkwardness, no uncertainty, no cautious exploration of personalities or adjustments. She was as familiar with his quirks, his likes and prejudices as he with hers. I am, she told herself, a little smug over this. I want to stop people and tell them about it. She laughed quietly and her teeth nibbled squirrel-like about the apple core.

She looked up inquiringly at the sound of Chris returning and the smile vanished quickly. His step was heavy, deliberate and thoughtful. She knew what had happened. Without saying anything to him, she had expected it. There was no need for her to know Carol Hillyard. A woman would do what a woman would. Chris must have been incredibly naïve not to have anticipated it. He stood above her, gazing steadily at the fire. She didn't ask the obvious question.

"I've just been fired." There was no flippancy, no false and transparent bravado. He was hurt and incredulous. "That was Keith."

"I've always thought it was a particularly loathsome word. Fired." She took a cigarette from her shirt pocket and lit it, not wanting to watch his face. "It has always seemed to strip people of dignity when one person can say to another, You're fired. No matter what you've done or how well you've done it. Get out. You're fired because I say so. I hurl the lightning."

He didn't smile as she half-hoped he would. "Let's take a walk." He reached for a pullover on the back of a chair and handed it to her. "I'd like to kick through a few leaves."

"Sure you wouldn't rather do it alone?"

He shook his head, extending a hand and pulling her up from the hooked rug. For a moment they faced each other, not knowing what to say. Then impulsively she made the gesture of kissing a finger tip and pressing it to his lips.

"I'm glad it's over and out in the open." She put the jacket on. "I don't really see how you thought it would be otherwise. No one jilts the boss, brother. Just no one."

They moved together down the slope from the house to where the mountain stream split its crystal surface against the rocks. It ran with a chuckling, musical sound over a log dam and fell into a deep pool where the trout lay. He picked up a few small stones and tossed them aimlessly at tree and stump.

"Hit her once for me." She encouraged him with a grin. "Chunk it hard."

He was as embarrassed as though he had been caught in a childish act, and dropped the remaining pebbles to the ground.

"This is a hell of a depression, isn't it?" He forced a wanly reluctant smile.

"What did Keith say?" She understood the close, unexpressed bond existing between Chris and the managing editor.

"What the hell could he say?" The smoldering anger flared and trapped him. "I'm sorry. I didn't mean to take it out on you."

"Yell if you like." She was sympathetic. "Come home and beat the wife, kick the kids around." She grinned. "What the hell else are they good for?"

"I still don't believe it." He shook his head stubbornly.

"Then you ought to be editing Uncle Piggly Wiggly stories instead of a newspaper. No one can be that innocent, bud. What did you think she would do? Send us a wedding present?"

"My job on the paper shouldn't be something to be booted around like a personal football."

"Then you should have kept it impersonal." She was just a little impatient. "Bed fever is hard to control. There is no real cure for it."

They walked in silence for a few minutes. She understood he was trying to adjust himself to an entirely new situation.

"It must be a shock for a bride to discover her husband is on the dole."

"Now, you listen to me." The tone was sharper than she had meant it to be. "I didn't marry you because you had a job. I have a damn good one of my own. I'm also smart enough to realize there aren't a lot of city editors' jobs open. You are not going to walk out of one office and into another right away. Neither are you going to brood over this. We're all right. We're solvent and have each other. Come to think of it, I have a lot more than I ever had before, Chandler. At least I won't have to wonder if you're knocking the publisher off in her office between editions."

He smiled quietly, feeling better. "I'd like to go back to the city, though. If it's all right with you. Just sitting here when I ought to be doing something would spoil it for us both. I'd be restless and you'd know it."

"It's all right with me. Want to go now?"

"I think so." He took her arm.

In the room they packed their bags unhurriedly. Before they put the bottle away they had a couple of drinks of good Scotch and felt better.

"By the way." She looked up. "Do you realize we have two apartments on our hands? Yours and mine. We'll have to get rid of one. I don't care which. I'm the whither-thou-goest type."

"It'll probably be easier for me to move than you."

He paid their bill, glancing out of the window to where she sat waiting in the car. She appeared so serenely confident that the sight of her made him feel better. He had been a good reporter. He could be again. The adjustment was no more than a lot of men had made. He'd start making the rounds tomorrow. The idea didn't depress him. He even began to experience a sensation close to relief. In the back of his mind he had been wondering what he would do when Carol Hillyard came back to the paper.

The maid had rapped several times on the door before she was aware of the sound.

"Come in." The tone was weary, indifferent.

The girl stood hesitantly on the threshold. "I was fixin' to take Mr. Mark's lunch to him or did you want to do it, Miz Cahrl?" The question was voiced hopefully.

"I'll take care of it."

184

She turned slowly away from the telephone. An almost desperate loneliness possessed her and it was not something to be driven away by the presence of other persons. She didn't want to see or talk with Mark or anyone now. The idea of having to sit and watch him eat, making small conversation, pushed her close to hysteria. She didn't think she could stand it.

The rolling cart with its warming compartment, heated with a can of Sterno, was in the hall. The maid wheeled it down the corridor and to Mark's room. She smiled with furtive gratitude and hurried away. The old man in that room terrified her.

From the door Carol could see him, bolstered in his usual position against the bank of pillows. He seemed to be asleep.

"Mark?" she called softly, hoping he wouldn't hear. "Mark. Are you awake?"

She waited, noting the small movement of his breathing. He was sleeping, wandering through the semicoma which came upon him so often. There was nothing to be done. Dr. Warren had told her this was probably the way it would end. The long, deep sleep without pain. She closed the door. They could cook fresh chicken for him later if he still wanted it. Absently she picked at the salad with her fingers.

She wanted to get out of the house, away by herself. She hurried down the stairs and to her car.

It was pleasant driving. There was an unexpected warmth in the sun. High in the sky and to the east a flight of ducks drove southward. Early fall was a pleasant time here. The winters were mild and no one made preparations against it as they did in northern countrysides. The harvest was in. Fields could be turned again. Now was a lazy period of standing against a wall or gathering on the narrow porches of country stores to talk of crops, dogs, and the shooting to come.

She drove slowly through the back roads, letting the turns and ruts take her where they would. She was calmer now, secretly regretting what she had done but convinced Chris had left her no alternative. From the day the Hillyard Enterprises had assumed ownership of the paper she was aware of his attitude of tolerant amusement. He didn't believe her capable of running a paper. Eventually they would have had it out. Without realizing it, he was prepared to treat her with a quizzical humor.

She halted the car and crossed her arms on the wheel, leaning forward upon them. None of this was true. She was trying to rationalize and find an excuse for herself. Chris had tried to adjust himself to the situation. She had forced the issue, bringing it to a point of no return that night in the apartment in front of Keith and Haney. He had taken the justified position that he was the city editor. She could be publisher or reporter but she couldn't be both. Those were the inescapable facts and she knew it. Chris Chandler had not been fired because there had been a conflict of authority. He had been discharged because he had left her for another woman. It was that simple, that difficult to admit. Now was the time of regret. She was ashamed of what she had done. It was a cheap gesture. The shrill vindictiveness of a back-alley slut. But it was a thing done and not to be called back or set right with a reinstatement and a few words of shamefaced apology.

At a crossroads filling station she stopped for gas and put in a telephone call to the house. Neeny, one of the girls, told her Mark had awakened, yelled for his lunch and her. He was in a bad temper because she had left.

She hung up, saying she wasn't sure when she was coming home and to tell Mr. Mark that. She wasn't worried. His petulant anger was a good sign. As long as he held to it he was all right.

At a small general store she stopped and bought a box of crackers, a wedge of leathery yellow cheese and, after a little whispered conversation, a pint of corn whisky and a bottle of Coca-Cola. Indifferent to the silent curiosity of the men who sat in canted chairs and on the rickety steps, silently communicating with each other, she took a place at the end of the porch. With her back against a two-by-four pillar she drank some of the moonshine, chasing it down with the coke, and ate hungrily of the cheese and crackers. With a half-smile she offered the remaining liquor to one of the men, who accepted with a grave nod of thanks, drank from the bottle and passed it down the line. She fed the rest of the cheese to a tawny hound and went back to the car. The men watched her with quiet interest. She laughed to herself. No one had spoken a word. No one had asked who she was or why she was there. That was the way she had wanted it to be. They were probably talking it over now, and later it would provide conversation at home.

It was dusk when she finally came out on the main highway. She was some fifty miles from Court House. Small lights in scattered farmhouses began to prick tiny holes in the darkness.

There was a gradual acceleration of the car as though, of its own volition, it began to keep pace with her mind. She knew where she was going and suspected the reason without admitting it fully. An excitement and a demanding sense of urgency pushed her.

The time she had been away had not changed the outward appearance of The Cottage. It still appeared to be what it was not. She parked beneath one of the leaf-heavy trees out of the driveway. There were lights in BillJo's apartment above the garage. She started for it and then changed her mind, almost hurrying to the entrance.

Two men on stools were hunched over their drinks. They turned at the sound of the door opening and studied her with alert hopefulness as she walked past and slid into the seat of a booth at the back of the room.

The bartender was new since she had last been here. He left his place a little reluctantly and with an expression on his face that told her she could just as well have sat at the bar and made the service easier.

She ordered a drink and as he started back called to him.

"Is BillJo around?"

He glanced at a clock. "He don't usually come down until around seven." He made a quick and shrewd appraisal and his tone changed slightly. "You want me to call him?"

"Never mind." She lit a cigarette, leaning back against the cushion, feeling a little as though she had been running and was short of breath. "Make that a double Scotch."

It was the first time she could recall ever really wanting, almost feeling the need of, a drink. She took it straight with a water chaser, tapping the glass, signaling the bartender for a refill. While pretending no interest, he couldn't hide completely a faintly puzzled speculation as he put the second drink before her.

She began to feel the whisky almost immediately. It started as a warm ball in her stomach and spread itself as a soothing poultice. She took the third drink with a little water and smiled briefly at the bartender when he brought it, feeling an easy companionship with the familiar room. With an almost amused detachment she began to tabulate the effects of the liquor. First it smoothed out the tight knots of tension and made once-important things unimportant. Then it made the body seem weightless and imparted a new clarity to mind and vision. It was easy to understand, she mused, the compulsion of an alcoholic. Who wouldn't reach for forgetfulness when it was so close at hand? She became aware of the fact that the two men no longer turned covert glances in her direction. One even smiled an invitation and she ignored it. It diverted her to watch them in their silent contest. They each now made a pointed effort to be unaware of the other's presence. She suspected that before her entrance they had been casually friendly. Now they were all but stiff-legged and bristling as they sniffed a pickup with a girl who was quite obviously getting herself tight and in the mood for easy conquest. A low growl of warning all but rumbled in their throats.

The bartender, without her ordering it, came with another drink and took an unnecessarily long time in picking up the empty glasses and turning out an ashtray. She studied him with a cold insolence and he coughed, embarrassed and uncertain. He all but backed away from the booth.

Idly, she tried to make herself wonder why she had come here instead of going home. None of the reasons she gave herself was satisfactory. The truth was difficult to admit. She was ashamed of something done, and felt the need for self-immolation. BillJo Adams was to be the wrack and, she made the vulgar pun to herself with surprise, the screw. I must be tight. She stood off and surveyed herself with astonishment. It wasn't bad. BillJo the wrack and the screw. She was unaware that her laughter was audible and caused one of the men to wink at the bartender. The other studied her glumly, knowing the time for them all had passed. A dame who laughed like that to herself was only looking for trouble.

BillJo came briskly through a side door, immaculately tailored as usual, crisp and self-assured. He nodded pleasantly to the two customers and went behind the bar, halting at the register. The bartender whispered something but BillJo gave no indication he heard. He methodically checked the figures on the tape against cash in the drawer. Took some bills and folded them into a money clip. Back to the room, he mixed himself a drink.

Glass in hand he walked toward her. She saw his step break with surprise as he recognized the lone occupant of the dim booth. Then, he came on and slid into the opposite seat.

"Hello, Carol." The eyes were flat and without expression. "I heard you were back in town."

"Order me a drink, BillJo."

"You're half-loaded already." He regarded her with questioning surprise and then called over his shoulder to the bartender. "You on a booze kick now?" He leaned back, puzzled.

There was the scraping sound of a stool being shoved back. One of the men tossed a bill on the bar and left with disappointed reluctance. The bartender brought her fresh drink and moved softly away.

"What brought this on?" There was no friendly concern in BillJo's question.

"Do you care?" She eyed him over the glass. Her hand was completely steady and there was no uncertainty of movement or voice. "Just felt like having a drink."

"Why here?"

"It was handy." She lit a cigarette.

He shook his head. "I don't believe it. You want something; your back scratched, maybe."

She controlled her surprise. He was smart and perceptive where women were concerned. This she had recognized before. She took a deep swallow of the drink and shuddered. It had begun to be a little nauseating.

"You're acute, BillJo. That's spelled a-c-u-t-e and doesn't mean like you're a cute thing." She wanted to see him angry.

He refused the challenge. "I know what it means." He reached over, took her cigarette and lit one of his own from it. "I'm even beginning to know why you're here."

"So?"

"Up in the hills of Tennessee there are people who eat dirt. They go on a ball with the stuff. Really eat it because they like the taste. They get a craving for it every now and then. Know what I mean, Miss Hillyard?"

She made an unconscious gesture of touching a cheek with the back of her hand as though he had spat in her face.

"Go on home, Miss Hillyard." There was a soft menace in the command. "Do your penance some place else. This isn't my day for climbing on a cross to help you out."

The immediate reaction was incredulous anger. This cheap bootlegger was walking away from her as though she had been soliciting on a street corner. She could feel the blood drain from her face, leaving it a plaster cast. Her breath was a deep, shuddering gasp. Then, the anger left her. She stared at him. How could he know the reason behind the reason for her being here; that getting drunk and maybe going to bed with him would be a distorted form of expiation?

"I'm sorry, BillJo." She whispered the words.

"I think, maybe, that's the first honest thing you ever said to me." He was almost gentle. "Who was he? What'd he do to you, Carol?"

She shook her head and smiled wanly. "You've got it wrong. It's the other way around."

"I guess I'm not as a-cute as you thought." He mispronounced it deliberately. "I just never would have figured you to be sorry for anything you did." He called to the bartender, ordering coffee for them both, and then pushed their glasses to one end of the table. "This stuff is no good for that. All you get out of it is a crying jag. That'd only make your nose red and spoil the joint for my customers."

She was miraculously sober now and drank the coffee with sugar and cream because she wanted it and not because it was supposed to be a specific. She relaxed.

"Did you really mean it, BillJo?" She was femininely curious. "You wouldn't have gone to bed with me?"

"I've been through the meat grinder with you once. That's enough for any man in his right mind. It wasn't your fault. I just couldn't wait to stick my hand in the chopper. But I'm a little older, a little smarter, and know better now."

"I might even get to like you, BillJo." She reflected on this as though it were a completely novel idea and one which had never occurred to her before. "It's possible."

"No." He wasn't interested in the notion. "You're just reaching around for something, someone; an anchor, maybe. In the end you'd find out you felt as you always did and that hasn't anything to do with liking someone."

She refilled her cup from the silver pot. How could he know of the small fear, the feeling of desolation, of standing alone on a horizonless plain?

"You could end up a real lonely and unhappy woman, Carol. I'll tell you why." He leaned forward on his elbows. "It's because you're going to scare off the men who fight in your class and at your weight. First thing you know you won't be able to get a match."

"An allegory from BillJo Adams?" The sarcasm was meant to conceal an uneasiness.

Her exaggerated surprise didn't irritate him. He actually smiled. "I don't know what that means but if it's like a story to make a story, then I guess it's an allegory. That's a nice word. I'll remember it." He was thoughtfully silent for a moment. "If I were you I'd settle for a good, reliable sparring partner who'd let you be flashy in the ring and just stick with you because it was his nature. In the end you'd have someone to talk with around the training camp at night after everyone else had gone, if you know what I mean."

"I still say you're acute, BillJo. Your mother must have been a gypsy. I just might take your advice. After all, it wouldn't have to be a title match, would it?" She laughed with a sudden good humor. "You've got me doing it. We're beginning to sound like a column on the sports page."

She stood up, opened her bag, fumbling for car keys and wallet.

He rose. "Never mind the tab. I got used to taking care of it with you."

"I wasn't thinking of paying it." The smile was honest. The statement friendly. "I wanted some phone change. Is there a booth in the joint?"

"Up front—but if it's private, use the one in my office."

He took her to a room off the bar, turned on the lights and indicated the desk and telephone. Then he closed the door behind him.

She sat on a corner of the desk, lit a cigarette. Her heel tapped with the steady beat of a metronome. She wondered if she was still a little tight. What a few hours before had been a fantastically impossible situation was now shaping itself into a reasonable, almost logical and recognizable form. She was astonished to find it so.

She lifted the receiver and asked the operator for a number. She did it calmly and without hesitation.

The voice was warm-soft and pleasantly curious. It was a reflection of the man.

"Bootsie. This is Carol."

"Well, yes ma'am. I guess I'd know that right away." If it was possible for a tone to lounge indolently, his did. "You know, this is getting to be a little more like it. You calling me, I mean. Makes me think of the fraternity house with the phone a-ringing."

"What are you doing, Bootsie?" Her eyes smiled.

"You mean that literally or is it just a figure of speech like?"

"Just a figure of speech like."

191

"Well then, I'm not doing anything you couldn't interrupt. Like what do you have in mind?"

She took a deep silent breath. The pause was almost imperceptible.

"Like getting married," she said quietly.

The low, soft whistle of astonishment rippled through the wire. When he spoke, the surprise was gone.

"I've had the town clerk and the Reverend Willcote alerted for the past week. They thought Bootsie was crazy but I just had a feeling charm and right would prevail. I knew you'd get the call. How did it come, like a whispered voice or a trumpet blast?"

"Like a bootlegger's allegory."

"God A'mighty." He was impressed. "This here now Cupid takes on a strange form, don't he? I know it's *doesn't* but *don't* gives my speech flavor. It's an old-timey dialect I picked up at the University."

"Get into your tennis sneakers and I'll come by to pick you up."

"My, but you Yankee girls are impetuous." There was admiration in the statement. "This here is going to be a great day for The Commonwealth to say nothing of a large and insolvent clan of Warringtons. You just have no idea how many relatives you are going to get. They're going to come tumbling out of the woods and a-whoopin' to the pantry."

"You sound like Jeeter Lester in *Tobacco Road*."

"Yes, ma'am. I was meaning to." When he spoke again the caricature had been erased from his voice. "Besides Nature taking its course, have you any real reason for doing this?"

"Uh-huh." She was emphatic. "I want someone to talk with around the training camp at night."

She hung up before he could reply, carefully mashing her unfinished cigarette into a tray. It was done but it could be called back. She shook her head. No. It was done.

On the way out she pushed a five-dollar bill across to the bartender. BillJo had left. She went outside and stood in the velvet darkness. She wondered a little at herself and what had happened. Strangely enough, she felt no surprise. That was the really astonishing thing about a completely unpredictable situation. Maybe Bootsie had been right all along.

XIV

THE first storm of the equinox swept inland from the boiling shoals of Hatteras and across the Virginia capes to lay wind, rain and black scuds of clouds along the ridge where they buried Mark Hillyard.

Carol was alone above the ugly gash in the earth. Behind her Bootsie, Jim Haney and Aunt Julia stood apart. Two men with shovels waited, glancing now and then at the sky and wanting to get on with the job before the rains fell. After a moment she made a small, indecisive gesture with her hand and turned away.

They let her go, understanding she wanted no company and that the walk to the house was one which she had to take by herself.

If there were tears, she kept them inside her. If there was sorrow, it was hidden. Her face was expressionless. Much of what she was lay behind her in that grave, but only the wind whimpered and made soft lament.

The old man had died without knowing his daughter was married to Boothby Warrington. He had gone in a continuation of the sleep into which he had fallen during the afternoon. She felt no regret at not having been in the house when he died. Mark would have been profanely angry if he had realized anyone was keeping a silent watch at his bedside. There was no dignity in death. A man became a pitiful and helpless thing as the last of the skein unwound. He would not have wanted anyone to see him.

They had been married in the parsonage with Dr. Willcote's wife and a servant for witnesses. Standing with Bootsie she had made the responses, glancing up at the big man who was to be her husband with a feeling of shyness completely foreign. To have and to hold. To cherish. They were solemn words. Part of her stood here, in a softly lit colonial parlor, listening to a gentle man as he read the service. Another Carol Hillyard, or so it seemed, stood outside in the darkness to peek through the window with astonishment over what was happening to her twin.

When Dr. Willcote closed the book and there was a small flutter of congratulations, she wondered what it was she felt. Not the radiance of a bride, certainly. Neither was she completely unmoved. She was of no particular religious persuasion or convictions. Save for the years spent in school when church on Sunday, if not compulsory, was generally accepted as the thing to do, she had never attended services. Why then did the words repeated from this mystical book strike a small and muted chord?

They covered the few miles back to the big house in silence and this, also, struck her as being odd. Bootsie had the great gift of laughter and a gusty, irresistible good humor with small tolerance for gravity. He was subdued now, and studying him in the dim light from the dash she felt the giggle of a schoolgirl bubbling in her throat. He sensed the suppressed laughter and managed an uncertain grin. Impulsively she moved closer and worked a hand beneath his arm.

"You're a pretty glum bridegroom."

He nodded. "This here now thing we've done is a real serious matter. I've got to get myself used to it. Going to bed with a girl is one thing. Going to bed with all the Saints a-looking on is another. It depresses me to have so much company."

It actually startled her to realize that in a couple of hours she and Bootsie would be in bed. It was something she hadn't really thought about one way or another. They had necked around in the car before she went to New York, but Bootsie had made that kind of love with the playful mauling of a bear cub. She couldn't help but wonder how it was going to be.

"We'll open some champagne. I'm damned if I'm going to bed with you on our hands and knees as though we were making a pilgrimage to Mecca."

"Oh, that part's going to be all right. You've never seen me with my tennis sneakers off."

"I'm glad to know you take them off." This was a better note.

Bootsie, also, recognized it. He dropped easily back into the character he had created for himself. He lifted an arm, hung it casually over her shoulder.

"Let me tell you there ain't nothin' better than being able to wiggle your stark-naked toes while it's going on."

They had gone hand in hand to Mark's room with the good feeling of honestly liking each other. She no longer questioned what had been done. It was going to work out all right for them both.

The lights were on in the old man's room and he was, apparently, asleep.

"Old man?" she called softly. "Are you awake?"

They moved quietly to his bed and it was Bootsie who bent suddenly to take the gnarled wrist and search with an inexpert finger for the pulse. He straightened up, an unashamed misery in his eyes.

"I'll go and call Earle Warren. I guess that's what you're supposed to do."

There was a telephone beside the bed but he ignored it, using the excuse to leave her alone and closing the door when he left.

She sat on the edge of the bed. Death did not repel her. She touched the leathery cheek and was not shocked by its cold and waxy surface. There had been a great and unexpressed love between them. If either was vulnerable it was because of the other. She bent and pressed her cheek to his face.

"I'm sorry about that fried chicken and the drink we didn't have, old man. I'm real sorry."

When Bootsie came back she was controlled, but turned with a sudden and revealing fury on Aunt Julia when the woman came to weep and shudder, twisting her hands and moaning over her brother's body. She almost shoved her from the room and then stood defiant and panting until Bootsie pulled her to him with an encircling arm.

She went through the things which had to be done, reaching Jim Haney in Beaumont. There were no relatives to be notified and she wouldn't have tried to reach them if there had been. This was a personal matter. She rejected the idea of a cemetery. There was no statute prohibiting the burial on Mark's own land. She had selected the plot on a mound humping itself from the ridge and overlooking the river.

Walking back toward the house now she halted. This was a little ridiculous. She was deliberately allowing herself to be dramatized as grief-stricken. She felt regret. She would miss him and not he her. She waited until the others came up and then dropped into a place between Jim and Bootsie.

There had been few legal formalities to go through. The lawyers had come and gone, the will admitted to probate, but everything was in order. The death of Mark Hillyard had caused a brief uneasiness on the seismograph that was Wall Street. Hillyard Enterprises were too deeply bedded to be rocked by the death of one man. The stock recovered and the tiny ripples of uncertainty swept up again into the larger stream. The current ran as evenly as before.

It did not really occur to her that she was now mistress of one of the world's great fortunes. It was not a thing to be counted or stacked into awe-inspiring piles. It was there. It seemed always to have been there, neither actually Mark's nor hers but to be used by them without a feeling of ownership.

She had a lengthy session with Jim Haney in Old Mark's "office" the day after his arrival. Both accepted the fact that things would go on as before.

"What about you, Sister?"

She sat on the arm of the deep, leather chair worn slick by Mark Hillyard. In this cluttered room she could feel the old man's presence. He had had no patience with filing cabinets. Wire hooks were hung about the walls and on them were strung letters, papers, memoranda, according to his own system. The desk was an untidy litter of pamphlets, geological reports, marketing surveys and almanacs. No one but he would have known why they had been saved.

"What about me?" She gave the question back to Haney.

"Are you going to stay here? Do you want to keep the house or put it on the market?"

"This is Mark's home. Of course I'll keep it. We may not use it often. I have a paper to run. This time I'm going to run it. There'll be no confusing compromise. I may not do it from the publisher's office but I'll do it."

He whistled with soft reflection. "Warrington's a good man; good for you, I think. I'm not sure you're going to be good for him. Somehow I don't see him living in New York and that is where you'll be."

She resented this intrusion into her private life. "Bootsie and I are going to get along just fine. I understand him."

"I'd like to believe he understands you, Sister. Why did you get married?"

"I wanted to see how it felt legal-like." She knuckled his head, shutting the door on this bland inquisition. "Bootsie and I will work things out together." She stood up and walked across the room. "I have the feeling we're on the edge of a great social revolution if Roosevelt is elected. I want to be close to it. I wonder if we could pick up a paper in Washington?"

"With cash you can pick up almost anything these days. What about the ones in Cincinnati, San Francisco and Charlotte?"

"I'll sell them if a buyer comes along. I won't just shut them down, though, and toss a lot of men out of work."

He nodded with a resigned grunt. "You're going to have to bear with me for a few minutes, Sister. If you think I'm intruding, say so. I'd like to have some idea of how the financial setup between you and Mr. Warrington is to be handled."

"I don't know, Jim." She was sincerely vague. "I haven't really thought about it."

"Then it's time you did. As far as I can see, you have a husband with no particular talent other than being agreeable. What does he intend to do or, more to the point, what do you intend him to do?"

"Nothing." The surprise was unaffected. "Bootsie has a unique charm—the ability to do absolutely nothing and make it seem a delightful and industrious occupation. I want him just the way he is."

"You'll make a bum of him." Haney was close to being angry.

"I should imagine it would be extremely difficult to be a bum with two or three hundred million dollars. The chances of being picked up on a vagrancy charge are remote."

"Goddamn it"—he was angry now—"a man just can't do nothing."

"Why not?" The question was sweetly voiced but had a solid wall of determination behind it. "Few men have a talent for doing nothing. Bootsie has. I like him the way he is." She was silent for a moment. "Bootsie has always wanted to breed horses. It's probably a better hobby than cultivating women and no more expensive. Maybe you're right. He should have an avocation. I wish you'd look into the John Harkness estate. We might buy into it or all of it— whatever looks like the best deal to you. Bootsie and John get along fine together. They were born a couple of hundred years too late. They have the instincts of colonial, landed aristocracy. It's worth preserving, the way the Rockefellers are doing with Williamsburg. Harkness is a good, working stud farm and probably in need of money. See about it, will you?" The unconscious command was there.

Haney persisted. None of this completely satisfied him.

"When you go to New York, what is going to happen? Will Mr. Warrington stay here?"

"I don't know. There's no reason why Bootsie shouldn't divide his time between New York and Court House. After all, breeding horses doesn't mean you have to shovel manure or mix the feed. The real job, I suspect, is efficiently handled by the stallion and the mare."

"This is the damnedest marriage I ever heard of." Haney was defeated.

"You're probably right, Uncle Jim. I wouldn't be at all surprised if that about sums it up, but it satisfies me. It fills a need. It blocks an empty cavern that frightened me."

"One more thing." Haney was resigned. "Tell me about money. Do you want to settle an amount on Mr. Warrington? Are the checking accounts to be held jointly or does he come and ask you for a quarter when he needs it?"

"Let's go ask Bootsie." She took his arm. "We'll have a couple of drinks, some lunch and talk things over."

From the south terrace, overlooking the swimming pool, they watched Bootsie as he ambled up from the stables with a Gordon setter pup frolicking and nipping at his heels in an ecstasy of affection. The dog, his golf clubs, some clothes and the vintage Ford were all he had brought to the house.

Watching him as he crossed to where they waited, Carol's eyes softened. There was a wonderful, lumbering gentleness in this man. He could no more imagine a world of ill will than the puppy would expect to be kicked. What she felt for him was difficult to define. He radiated an assuasive aura. Nothing disturbed him. He was an unruffled, sun-drenched pool into which no stone could be cast to mar the placid surface.

"Are the magnates magnating?" He opened a bottle of ginger ale, ignoring the whisky and soda, dropping gracefully into a chair and eying them with a quizzical interest. "You look mighty serious, Mr. Haney."

"Jim is in an executive humor." She fixed herself a drink. "The *i*'s are to be dotted, the *t*'s crossed. He's upset and wants to know what you're going to use for money."

Bootsie's eyes widened with surprise. "Why, I'm going to use yours, child. Your papa and I had a lot of talks about it." He swallowed most of the ginger ale with noisy pleasure.

Haney was openly puzzled by the naïve statement. In his experience men who wanted something did not declare themselves so openly. He searched for a devious motive.

"Jim," Carol was enjoying the situation, "Jim wants to know if some sort of a settlement, a lump sum, should be put in your name so everyone would know where he or she stood."

Bootsie scratched at his head. "I don't know about you all but I'm standing hip deep in the Hillyard clover patch." He scented the crispness in the air of early fall. "I'm going to order me a couple of Purdy guns from Abercrombie & Fitch. They cost about a thousand dollars. I've always wanted a pair but never figured to make it until you came along. I've got to teach you to shoot. Oh"—the thought occurred to him suddenly—"I gave the stableboy, Clete, my old Ford. When I get around to it I'm going to order a yellow Cadillac a block long, or maybe a Rolls Royce. I don't think there has ever been a Rolls in Court House. It'll cause quite a commotion."

Watching, listening, Jim Haney began to suspect that this seemingly guileless man was kidding them both. No one, he thought, could be so completely unaffected. He was either a person of unbelievable craftiness or one of almost frightening innocence. What

199

he said so openly was that the Hillyard money was there and a good thing to have. He refused to be impressed by it. But, and this really puzzled Haney, if he didn't mean that how could you figure him? If he wasn't as artless as he appeared to be, then what was he?

"Jim," there was deliberate mischief in Carol's words, "is worried about your pride. He thinks you ought to pay the bills, order the servants around. He wants you to be dominant and masculine, the manor's lord."

"I'm masculine enough, I guess." Bootsie winked at her and crushed an icecube between his teeth. "I don't know about this business of putting a shoulder to the wheel. It's liable to throw my golf swing off. My pride isn't going to be tainted by your money, child. It doesn't worry me a bit that the grocery store is going to find out you pay the bills."

Haney decided to be rude because he was impatient. "What I'm trying to find out, Mr. Warrington, is what you expect to do when you want or need money. Do you ask me or Sister? Is that how you want it?"

Bootsie eyed him steadily and then decided that the question, unpleasant as it had been phrased, was, perhaps, an honest one.

"I guess that wouldn't be too good an arrangement, Mr. Haney. I'll tell you what." He brightened. "Why don't you just put a little spigot on one of the Hillyard kegs and mark it 'Bootsie.' Whenever I want a dram or two, I'll turn it on." He regarded Haney with a smiling confidence. A solution had been found.

Impulsively Carol rose, went to his chair and kissed him. He dragged her into his lap.

"Bootsie"—she rubbed her head into his neck—"don't you ever change. If you do, I'll leave you." She looked up at the baffled Haney. "Fix up anything you like. If it isn't enough, Bootsie will let you know."

"You know"—Bootsie was uninterested in the solution; he turned Carol on his lap to study her appreciatively—"I promised your papa I'd impregnate you, so don't talk about leaving me. You're going to be busy."

"Like hell I am." She all but jumped from his lap as though this contact was dangerous. "You raise some dogs and horses. I have too much to do to think about a family right now."

He pulled her back, gently but with unmistakable determination.

There was no laughter in him. Watching, Haney glimpsed a will he hadn't suspected. It interested and worried him. It could be very good for Sister or bad for them both.

"I promised your papa," Bootsie repeated. "It's one promise I intend to keep. We discussed your fine pelvic cavity and general physical condition and decided you were a true bearer of children. Mother Nature's mother, so to speak. Your papa is looking for me to keep my word and that's just what I intend to do."

Her short laugh was without conviction. For a moment she regarded him skeptically, seeking a hidden humor. It wasn't there. Bootsie meant it. She pulled away and stood up.

"It's time for lunch. I'll see about it." It was an unconvincing excuse to get away.

She hurried determinedly across the terrace, glancing back once with an expression of apprehension as though she almost expected to be caught up, thrown over a shoulder and carried to a bedroom.

Bootsie watched her go with a lazy interest and then uncoiled himself and stood up.

"I guess that surprised her, a little. It's not often you can catch Carol off balance. She doesn't like to admit it, Mr. Haney, but she hasn't quite got me figured out either."

Walking with him to the open French doors Jim mentally shook his head. The man was almost anything but what he appeared to be. The speech and manner were all openly contrived because Boothby Warrington had long ago discovered they served an agreeable purpose.

"I still don't think we have settled anything." Haney made the objection without force. Bootsie had disarmed him. "We could make you a vice-president of Hillyard Enterprises at whatever salary you'll need." He offered the suggestion with a hopeful desperation.

Bootsie was sympathetic but not inclined to be co-operative. He shortened his stride to match Haney's and his forehead wrinkled with massive thought.

"I'd like to help everyone, Mr. Haney." He was unhappy with the complexities of the problem. "But I sure don't know how I can say in advance what I'm going to need. One year I might decide to buy a private railroad car or an airplane. The next year I might not need nothing more than a few fishhooks or some shotgun shells. No, sir, I wouldn't like to get wedged into a situation like that. You'll have to think of something else. Besides, I don't want to be a vice-president. Why, I wouldn't be Vice-President of the United States, let alone the Hillyard Enterprises."

"Damn it, Mr. Warrington!" Haney exploded. Everything this man said was both incredibly outrageous, and somehow, sensible. "We just can't give you unlimited access to everything."

For an instant Bootsie's eyes were cold blue crystals. "Why not, Mr. Haney? Are you afraid I'll run off with the safe some night?"

That was the way it had sounded. That, Haney reflected, was what he had meant. He halted and stared at Bootsie. He chuckled and the sound exploded into laughter.

"Yes, by God!" He made the admission but there was no insult in it or intended. "That's exactly what I am afraid of. But the more I think about it the more remote the possibility becomes. Why should you run off with the safe when you already have the combination?"

That was the way they left it. Later, when he had time to think over the outlandish conversation, Jim concluded it had been Bootsie's intention from the beginning—to leave it vague and unsettled. So, and this made him stop and wonder, Warrington had achieved his purpose while apparently having none. It was something to remember.

When they reached the house now, Carol turned and stood looking back down the ridge to where the two laborers were turning the loosely piled dirt into the grave. A wrought-iron fence had been ordered to enclose the plot. It would mark off the section for all time. There was no more to be done.

They made an uncomfortably awkward group. Aunt Julia waited, a little apart as a stranger might. She had never understood her brother and Carol was his image. Haney glanced at his watch.

"Is there anything I can do for you, Sister?"

She shook her head. "I think the best thing for everyone would be to get away from here for a while." She turned to Julia. "You may stay, of course, Aunt Julia." The statement was abrupt but not unkindly meant. "This is your home for as long as you want it."

"No. No. I think I'll go to Covington for a visit. I, we, have some cousins there. It'll be nice." She ventured a timid smile. "Maybe I'll do what Mark once said—go and live with the Hottentots in Africa for a while."

Carol looked at Bootsie and he smiled at her, understanding that for the moment she wanted him to lift the weight of decision and carry it for her.

"If your papa was here and one of us out there, I expect he'd go into the house and have a drink." He reached for her hand. "So, let's do it. Then you and I'll throw a few things in an old croaker sack and go some place."

Her fingers tightened appreciatively in his. For the moment she wanted to have no part in decisions. Let the plans and destination be Bootsie's. As they walked up the steps together the first of the rain began to fall and the heavy drops made small craters in the soft, raw earth above Mark Hillyard.

XV

BY CHANCE, as so much had happened to them, they came to this small, scrub-covered island of sand and coral. It lay awash in a tropical sea of unbelievable coloring and bore the improbable name of Spanish Wells.

A road of grass-tufted sandy ruts straggled between a short row of frame houses with their stout hurricane shutters, and lines of polished conch shells drew the borders from yard to yard. The Spaniards had long since departed and left no trace. Those who lived on this link in the broken chain of the Bahamian Out Islands were the descendants of the original Eleutheran Adventurers who had sailed from England to colonize this new world. All but a few families bore the same name and only the men who fished the sea around them ventured as far away as Nassau. A small frame hotel, anchored on the highest point of the island, provided accommodations for the casual sports fishermen from Miami.

They had been here for two weeks now, the cruiser they had chartered in Nassau swinging at its mooring while her captain and the Bahamian boy, who served as crew, steward and cook, waited patiently and talked softly of the unpredictable whims of tourists who would pay for a charter and then allow the craft to lie at anchor while they stayed ashore. They were indifferent to the dazzling white of narrow beaches in a heat-drenched noon; the purples, blues, greens and misty pinks of the water reflecting the bottom; the flames of sunrise which swept across the horizon at daybreak as though they would consume the world; the hush of twilight and the majesty of isolation.

The Bahamas had been Bootsie's idea and she had accepted it with neither reservations nor enthusiasm. As with all things he did he seemed to make no effort, and yet everything moved and meshed smoothly into place from the compartment on the southbound train, the small suite on the overnight ship from Miami, the rooms at the Royal Victoria in Nassau, to the cruiser and this little hotel at Spanish Wells. Studying him idly at times she marveled at the effortlessness with which things were done. He had a genius for seeming to do nothing and accomplishing what he wanted through a lazy, irresistible charm that worked its magic on everyone.

She also was not immune to this drawling sorcery. What she felt for him was no sweeping tide of emotion. In her at night sometimes a small voice still cried the name of Chris Chandler. She tried to lock her mind against him and not to wonder where or how he was, and yet he would come in the darkness and lie between her and the man she had married. She did not know she frequently whimpered softly in her sleep and Bootsie, hearing the sound, would lie awake staring at the ceiling until morning, puzzled by the unidentified presence of this man who made Carol Hillyard Warrington twist uneasily and cry a muted anguish. Frequently he took her in his arms and she would nestle there with a grateful sigh. He could never be sure she knew who held her. These were things which were unvoiced between them. In Bootsie she found a calm, the eye of a hurricane. He was an imperturbable rock before which turbulent waters divided and swept harmlessly past.

With Mark's death, the lingering memory of Chris Chandler and what she had done in spiteful fury to haunt her, she had driven herself with a quiet frenzy in an effort to find an escape. In Nassau she drank too much, harrying them both to fill the empty hours. There was in her a need for movement, to be going some place or doing something. It didn't matter what. To sit and read or lie in a chair beside the palm and bougainvillea-laced pool of the hotel was an unendurable torment. She gathered strangers about her for impromptu cocktail parties. The few bargain-hunting tourists who came on the twice-weekly boat from Miami or the cruise ships happily allowed her to pick up the dinner and bar checks and wondered a little at the burning intensity. She dragged them through the grog shops along Bay Street and made nightly pilgrimages "over the hill" to the lamplit native district. There they drank rum with lime and water, listened to mulatto girls in tight dresses of vivid scarlet and shining yellow sing to the music of tinny pianos while men sat cross-legged on the ground and beat with soft and compelling rhythm on small, fat round drums until the police came to close the dives with courteous authority.

The days and nights became a cage of hysteria. She would awake in the morning dull-eyed and drained, without interest in the day or what it would bring. She began taking a drink before her coffee and then it became necessary to sustain the jolting effect throughout the day. By a mysterious form of telepathic communication the congenital sycophants, the habitual cadgers and free-loaders formed in smiling, buzzing swarms to surround her table or chair beside the pool or a corner of the bar. Without effort she collected a retinue, a small court willing to go any place, do anything at any time, for as long as she signed the chits. They were indifferent to insult or slight and jockeyed with each other for positions of favor at her side. In her sober moments she was repelled by their obvious, small greeds and prostrations. She was disgusted with them and herself and then drank more in an effort to find a dark corner in which to crouch. Her nerves grew tightly strung until the slightest unexpected sound caused her to jump. To relieve this she achieved an alcoholic semistupor which frequently sent her to bed in the middle of the day but brought no real relief. The experience was new and terrifying and seemed to spin in a relentless cycle from which there was no escape. Never before had she taken a drink in an effort to run from herself.

Bootsie made no comment. He was patient but mystified. He was polite to the casual, pickup acquaintances, amenable to the shrieking midnight excursions when Carol would hire a native orchestra and carriages to take them to remote sections of the beach and keep a party going until sunup. This was drinking as he had never known it. Drinking without laughter or real gaiety. There was a wormy quality about it, the senseless writhing of fat maggots. Each ship from Miami brought new faces to take the places of those who were leaving. The beauty of the island was ignored. The peace destroyed. Time became an endless tunnel through which they raced frantically.

One morning, as she sat on the low bench before her dressing table staring with dull eyes at her reflection, he moved to stand behind her. His hands rested gently on her shoulders and there was sympathy if not real understanding in his manner.

"This here is nothing but skid row with a checkbook, Carol."

The undeniable parallel actually shocked her. She had created a plush-lined sewer for them both. There were lines of exhaustion in her face. Her hair was a mat of straw, without life or luster. She felt as though there was not strength enough in her legs to support her. She reached back a hand and thrust the fingers through his and nodded unhappily.

"I don't know what's happened to me." She made the admission in a scared whisper. "I never did a thing like this before." Even as she confessed, she caught herself thinking how just one drink would blunt the raw edges of her nerves. "It isn't any fun, Bootsie. I can't remember when it stopped being fun. It's become sort of a sullen preoccupation and it scares the hell out of me. I'm sick. I didn't know it could happen so fast. Right now I'm wondering about a drink and that's an awful thing to say. It's worse, I guess, than dope because it's easier to get and no one really takes a drunk seriously. A drunk is comical. People laugh."

He all but lifted her from the seat, turning her until she was in his arms, facing him. She was humble and almost pathetic. The admission of helplessness had been difficult to make. He kissed her as he might a hurt child.

"I have a project going." He was quietly reassuring. "The maid is coming in to pack your things. We're going to get away from here by ourselves."

"It isn't the place, Bootsie. Maybe it would have happened anywhere."

"I know." He was troubled. "It's a thing you cry about at night. I don't want it explained to me. I have a feeling it's something you'll have to work out by yourself, but you won't do it in this squirrel cage. Give yourself a chance."

The chance he offered was a cabin cruiser, thirty-eight feet over-all. She lay at her dock, the white hull, mahogany decks and brass-work glinting in the sunshine. He had arranged the charter two days before and she was stocked, provisioned and ready to cast off. As she stepped aboard from the short gangway, Carol wondered again, as she often did, about Bootsie's ability to do things without ever seeming to do them.

For two weeks they cruised the Out Islands without destination. Time ceased to have a meaning. They awoke to the stunning beauty of morning in waters so clear the small fish made bright streaks of color on the deep bottom. This was solitude without loneliness, a world without sound until they made it. The quiet peace of the days sometimes caused them to speak in whispers for fear of breaking the spell.

They dove over the side for their morning bath; caught their own fish for breakfast. They found island shores where it seemed no man had walked before and the slender towers of palms, with their clustered nuts, bent in graceful affection to each other. Sometimes they took pallets and slept on deck with the stars hanging just above their faces from invisible threads, and the tiny slap of small waves against the hull made a running lullaby of liquid music. They would talk with a quiet effortlessness, her head pillowed on his shoulder, or make love with primitive abandon as though they were the man and woman of Creation and were alone in a new world.

She discovered with a warm pride that Bootsie had taken her on no drying-out cruise. There was a locker stocked with liquor but neither felt the need for a drink. The time in Nassau receded like a spell of delirium. She found it nauseated her to think about it.

They loafed at half-speed through an island world of unbelievable enchantment, making a landfall at night and finding shelter within a cove or island's lee. The cruiser carried a ship-to-shore telephone and a radio which brought in the programs from Miami stations. They rarely bothered to listen. They saw no newspapers, read no magazines. Bootsie had bought a couple of dozen books in a Nassau store and they sometimes read for a few minutes before going to sleep. This was an isolation which seemed to contradict the century. It was a world within a world. Everything they needed or wanted was at hand.

The captain-owner of the craft was a Scot of grave courtesy and an inexhaustible fund of knowledge about these islands. The Bahamian boy, six foot three of polished ebony, had a great, rich laughter and a way in the evening on the foredeck with a battered guitar. The sea was his element, these islands the only land he had ever known. He told them that in the small schools the boys were taught the rudiments of navigation along with the lessons in reading and writing. When he was at the wheel he rarely bothered to check the compass but marked the coloring of the water which mysteriously told him where he was. They moved effortlessly through crystal days and and the whispering of great, empty nights.

The islands had a uniform pattern but sudden breaks in the shore-line or an abrupt humping of coral gave them an individuality as romantic as their names. Eleuthera, Big and Little Andros, Rum Cay, Cat Island. On the charts they traced their course and such settlements as Old Bight, Clarencetown and Rolleville on Great Exuma.

Hand in hand they went ashore to the tiny villages and bought fresh fruits, a few chickens and vegetables from the natives, the descendants of slaves who had been brought here and abandoned. The islands had once been the scene of a tremendous social upheaval. With the outbreak of the American Revolution some seven thousand Royalist families had been removed from the hostile colonies. They had come to the Bahamas in British ships of war, bringing with them their household goods, their cattle, their slaves, carriages and silver. Here they had attempted to recreate the colonial life of Virginia, South Carolina, Georgia. Great plantations were laid out, enormous manor houses built. The land wore itself away and the ventures failed. Disheartened, the adventurers returned to England, leaving the plantations to the slaves who must fend for themselves. The shells remained, broken segments of walls and half-chimneys, a ghostly grandeur sleeping beneath the weight of vines and time. Here in the silence the lizards played, the wild pigs of once-domesti-cated swine tore through the underbrush, and the Negroes, whose ancestors had been the Hausas and Fullahs from Africa, walked with a stately dignity. The women wore their hair in tight curls which stuck out at right angles from their heads.

Spanish Wells was to have been their last stop on the return to Nassau. They had intended to do no more than put in for the night, breaking the cruise with a meal ashore, a bath in a tub, a bed which did not rock if ever so gently. Instead, they had stayed two weeks.

From their bedroom window they looked down upon a small schoolhouse of colonial design. In the beginning the paint must have been a bright pink. It had weathered now to a dusty rose color. Beyond was the curving beach where the ocean made its pools of color. A low frame building housed the government office and the wireless which connected the island with the world beyond.

The days and nights were without variety, and yet they both found them satisfying. With a guide who answered to the impossible name of Cow they fished from a little outboard boat. They lay on the beach tanning themselves to the color of light iodine. Sometimes, in the evenings, they would stroll down the sandy road to stand in front of one of the four churches which served a population of no more than four hundred. They made friends with a missionary couple, young, bespectacled and intensely serious Britishers who had a regular circuit through the neighboring islands to which they carried the word to all black congregations. The wife, tall, angular, storklike, wore heavy cotton stockings. The husband, always with a worn Bible in his hand, stalked with the coattails of his blue serge suit whipping about scrawny hips. They were, Carol thought, characters out of Conrad or Maugham, and she felt a little sorry for them both until she discovered the fervor filled their lives more completely than her own.

Now, after two weeks here, she began to feel the first restlessness she had known since leaving Nassau. She had been idle too long. Tremendous things were happening back in the cities and towns. She wanted to be a part of them. It was no longer enough to laze away this endless succession of days and nights.

A radio in the sparsely furnished parlor of the hotel linked them with the Florida mainland. For the past few evenings Carol had found herself irresistibly drawn to it for the hour between six and seven when the news broadcasts were on. A new voice was being heard throughout the land. It crackled across the distance. Its vitality was unmistakable, its confidence overwhelming. She discovered she was being caught up in the spellbinding.

One evening as she sat in front of the couch, on the floor, resting her back against Bootsie's knees, she listened to Franklin Delano Roosevelt.

"I believe the individual should have full liberty of action." The words winged across time and space, cutting through ingrown custom with the incisiveness of a surgeon's knife. "But," the diction was crisp and assured, "I do not believe in that sacred word *individualism*. A few powerful interests should not be permitted to make industrial cannon fodder of the lives of half the population of the United States."

No such declaration had ever been made by a politician before. A man stood on the Mount and spoke to the people. They heard him in the shanties along Riverside Drive, in the caves of Central Park, on the prairies, in the mountains and the forests. The response was electrifying, and almost a little frightening. A great shadow of the nameless people rose against the wall of depression.

She looked about her. The members of the family owning the hotel sat in straight-backed chairs listening. Their faces were expressionless but they were alertly interested. They were British subjects, self-exiled on this spit of sand. Their knowledge of the United States and the rest of the world was vague, limited to the few tourists who came their way. Most of them had never seen a motion picture. Yet, she marveled, they were silent and solemn, caught up in the hypnotic cadence of the speech. When it was finished they sat quietly, unwilling to leave, to break the spell.

She half turned to look up at Bootsie and he grinned understandingly.

"That fellow gets to you, doesn't he?" His hand smoothed her hair. "I'm not just sure what economic cannon fodder is but I guess a lot of people do."

"I want to go home, Bootsie." She all but jumped up, feeling alive and excited. "I want to go to New York and see what my paper is doing. We're going to back that man."

"Well," he was unhurried, "he'll just have to get along without your help until tomorrow. We'll leave in the morning, and if the weather is good, make the run from Nassau to Miami in the cruiser or wait for the regular ship."

"Let's go now. Tonight. Maybe we could fly from Nassau to Miami. I think there's some sort of service. We could find out, anyhow. I want to start."

There was no trouble in leaving. All of their things were on the cruiser. It was only a matter of telling the captain they had decided to return to Nassau at once. The trip itself was no problem.

On the way out of the narrow cut which provided a harbor for Spanish Wells she stood forward as though to urge the boat to additional knots. Her eyes were shining and a new vitality, an animation she hadn't experienced in weeks, brought everything into sharp focus. She was no longer content to be carried by the unseen currents. They were to be channeled and controlled to serve a purpose. Not since the first day she had walked into the paper had she been so sure of herself, her destiny and her ability to fashion it to her own design. She turned and looked back at Bootsie, who stood in the after cockpit. Her hand raised itself in a salute as though she were somehow leaving him behind.

As she walked into the familiar room her eyes instinctively sought the city desk. Unconfessed was the hope that Keith had ignored her order and the slouched figure of Chris Chandler would be at the side near the window. He wasn't, of course, and she was illogically angry, as though Chris were somehow being stubborn and should have made allowances for a woman's anger.

She thought she detected just the faintest break in the rhythm in the room. It was as though a copy carrier halted for a second before thumping in a box, fingers on typewriter keys paused, a boy on the way to the composing room broke his step to stand motionless and faces turned her way with silent expectancy for the briefest moment. Then the interrupted continuity repaired itself and the even flow of action moved as before. It was, she concluded, a small trick of the imagination but she couldn't be sure. Someone in the financial section may have heard a rumor, tracked it down through the complexities of Hillyard Enterprises and come, eventually, to the startling fact that she was the paper's new owner.

She nodded casually, replying to a lifted hand, a tentative smile of welcome, a quick hello that might greet anyone returning from a vacation. There was, though, in the words and gestures the faintest hint of a cautious reserve. She was even a little embarrassed and to conceal it she stopped beside Jo Hart's chair.

"Hi, slave!"

Jo turned from her machine, stared speculatively at her for a fraction of time that was unmistakable. Jo was wondering, as probably everyone else in the room was thinking: What about this bitch who fires a good man like Chris Chandler because he got tired of sleeping with her? How do you handle her? Do you pretend you don't know and burrow into safety through professed ignorance?

Jo decided to play dumb. "Hi!" She stuck out a hand. "When did you get back?"

"This morning." She shoved a stack of copy paper to one side and sat on a corner of the desk. "How have you been?"

"I've been like working my ass off." Jo kept her tone and words impersonal. "You look like the original nut-brown maid. Are you that color all over?"

"Almost." This was the wary sort of fencing with which she had little patience. "Is something bugging you, Jo?"

There was melting innocence in the eyes. "No. Why should it?"

She decided to have the thing out in the open and done with. It was ridiculous to allow herself to be made uncomfortable.

"I have a feeling everyone in the room is behaving as if I were doing a Frank Buck, walking in with whip and chair, firing off blank cartridges to cow the cats. So I own the paper. That doesn't make me a sinister character. I'm damned if I am going to apologize or explain it to everyone. Someone has to own it. It could have folded, you know, and everyone would be sitting on their cold behinds on the curb." She felt better. "I'm also going to run it the way I see fit."

"Good for you." There was no sarcasm in the statement. The grin accompanying it honest and friendly once more. "That's damn well what I would do."

"What time are you going to lunch?"

"Twelve-thirty or thereabouts."

"I'll be around. Let's go together."

Jo pretended to hesitate. "I don't know that I ever had lunch with a publisher before."

"You go to hell." She slid from her perch. "At least you won't get a groping hand on your knee beneath the table."

Jo smiled. "It's been a long time since I've been groped good, by a girl I mean. Come to think of it, I haven't had any real good groping of any kind. See you."

On her way to the corner where Stephen Keith sat she nodded pleasantly to Ray Stanfield, who was in Chandler's place on the desk. It was something she would have to get used to, not seeing Chris there. She wondered unhappily if he had found a job and knew she couldn't ask Keith about him. Maybe Jo Hart would drop something at lunch.

Keith had seen her when she first entered the room and had watched as she stopped to talk with Jo Hart. He had these few minutes in which to study her. He speculated on whether this small display of fraternity with a member of the staff was a calculated move to integrate herself with the city room, pretending she had only been away on vacation and nothing had really changed. He decided it wasn't. She would indulge in no false self-effacement. He stood up as she came to his chair and offered his hand.

"It's good to see you back, Miss Hillyard." He waited until she was seated. "I had your cable from Nassau, but since the time was so short I decided to wait until we could talk things over."

"I like the looks of the paper, Mr. Keith. It's easier to read, easier to see on the newsstand."

"I like it myself. We've picked up our circulation. Mr. Barnes, the business manager, has some figures for you." He paused. The rest was up to her.

"I want to throw everything we have into the support of Governor Roosevelt."

"The switch will startle a lot of people. If there is such a thing as a rock-bound Republican paper this one has been just that. For years we haven't even liked Santa Claus because he was too democratic. That's in secret, of course." He smile faintly.

"I don't have any particular politics yet but I do have a feeling about Roosevelt. Could you have dinner with me?" She caught herself. "I mean us. I'm married."

Keith betrayed no surprise at the announcement. He nodded his acceptance of the invitation.

"How is Mr. Stanfield working out on the desk?" It was as close as she dared come to the subject of Chris Chandler.

"He's a good, reliable man. Not too original. He doesn't have Mr. Chandler's flair or imagination." It was a statement of fact, impersonal.

She lit a cigarette and halted abruptly in the act of drawing on it. She caught his eye and winked deliberately.

"The old man must be pinching his nose in horror if he can smell this smoke over the odor of brimstone." She drew deeply. "It was a silly rule. I wonder why he made it?"

"He thought it was a time waster and an offensive stink."

"Well, let's rescind the order. Put a notice on the bulletin board." There was a quick flash of quiet laughter. "I'm really impressing myself. I'm not accustomed to giving orders here."

"You'll get used to it. I know of no habit more easily acquired than that of authority." He leaned back, regarding her with interest. "How are we going to handle things from now on, Miss Hillyard?"

It was the obvious question. She nodded her acknowledgment of its validity. He wanted to know and so did everyone else on the paper.

"I made a mistake, Mr. Keith." She was completely serious but not apologetic. "I thought I could own a paper and pretend I was just a hired hand. It can't work that way. I have to be one thing or the other. So, I am going to be the publisher if I have to sit upstairs in Mr. Anderson's old office."

Keith reached, almost too casually, for a galley on the desk and handed it to her. It was a proof of the paper's masthead. A single line leaped out at her.

CAROL HILLYARD, *Publisher.*

"I had this set and pulled." Keith was watching her intently.

For a long time she stared at it and then lifted her eyes to meet his. They were serious.

"I think," she said slowly, "for the first time I really believe it. I, we," she amended, "own some other papers. I'd like to talk with you about them sometime. But I never had any real feeling of ownership, of responsibility. I think that is bad. I want to correct it. This"—she touched the galley—"this is different. It almost scares me a little. I wouldn't say that to anyone but you." She handed him back the galley. "Run it, Mr. Keith." She caught herself. "The name is Warrington now. Have it reset as CAROL HILLYARD WAR-RINGTON."

She put out her cigarette and watched as he took a copy pencil and made the correction.

"I'm going to lean on you for a while, Mr. Keith." There was no counterfeit modesty in the statement. "I want the benefit of your experience and judgment. I respect them. But," and the qualification left no unanswered questions between them, "when our opinions conflict and contradict each other, I'm afraid mine will have to be the ones that stand up. I don't know any other way to do it."

"That seems reasonable enough, Miss Hillyard." He caught himself. "Do you prefer Mrs. Warrington?"

"Not in the office."

He nodded. "I don't know how you could run a paper any other way. After all, if I don't like it I can always quit." The statement, they both understood, was not made lightly.

"Exactly." The agreement was without compromise. They accepted each other. She waited, the pause was deliberate. When she spoke again, a pleasant smile of friendliness went with the words. "I hope we never reach that point, Mr. Keith. I can't imagine the paper without you."

"How do you want to handle our switch to Governor Roosevelt?"

"On the front page." The answer was decisive. "I'd like to see an editorial, stating our position and reasons. Of course," she laughed, "I'm not sure whether anyone in 'the cave' back there can bring himself to write anything good about a Democrat. We may have to send outside."

"I'll write it myself, unless"—the rare twinkle was there—"unless you want to try it?"

She shook her head. "No. I'm a convert and filled with a Messianic faith. I have the conviction he may make the greatest President since Lincoln and that if he doesn't do the job, he may well be this country's last President." She paused and then continued with enthusiasm, "I'd like our best man assigned to stay with him right through election day."

"You're a good man, Miss Hillyard."

She stared at him for a moment. "Yes," she spoke the word slowly, "I am a good man." It was an unaffected declaration of confidence. "Why not? It's a job I can do, one I'd like to do." She looked at him gravely. "Thank you for thinking of me."

"It will be interesting to see your coverage. I think maybe this man Roosevelt is at the door of a great social revolution. I only wonder if the country is ready to have it opened."

She was serious. "I've been outside, on the streets. I've seen the lines of the jobless, the beaten and the weary as they shuffle forward for a bowl of soup and a chunk of bread. I've asked myself why they don't pick up clubs, stones, anything, and storm through the avenues, looting and rioting. I don't know why. Maybe it's the faith they have that someone is going to come along and do something about it. By the way, how are we doing—the paper, I mean?"

"We're just about breaking even. That is a lot better than we were doing before."

"Spend what you need. If Jim Haney hollers, let me know. I'd like to see all of our departments beefed up. I'd like to see sports with men of the caliber of Villa, Cannon, Woodward, Rice. Top feature men and a lot more comics, two or three pages. People read funny papers as a form of escape. I've watched them." She stood up.

"What time do you expect me for dinner?" He left his chair.

"Around seven. It's the same apartment."

On her way out she stopped at Jo Hart's desk again. "I'll meet you at the gin mill. Twelve-thirty."

"Sure, boss." Jo knuckled her forehead with a gesture of servility. "How could I refuse?"

She walked from the room, distinctly aware now that all activity was suspended and that a watchful silence followed her through the door and out into the hall.

XVI

SUPINE on the length of the oversized couch, his legs and feet dangling over the end, Bootsie gazed up at her with an expression of innocent wonder. He dropped a grape into his mouth and chewed contentedly.

She stood above him, her feet planted in an attitude of defiance, anger and confusion, and thrust an accusing finger at his face.

"You and your damned romantic beaches," she all but shouted. "Your faraway places and that travel folder stuff. A boat's deck in the tropical moonlight with the scent of island flowers and the Trade Winds blowing and all that other crap you cozened me with."

"That's real bad syntax." He reproved her gently. "But I get what you mean. They sure helped." He thought to himself he had never seen a woman so mad before. "I figured they would."

"I'm pregnant, damn you, Boothby Warrington." She did yell her frustration this time. "It's your fault. You're a sneaky, conniving sonofabitch."

Undisturbed, he reached back over his shoulder and lifted another bunch of grapes from the bowl on an end table, dangled them above his mouth and ate his way upward through them.

"Did you hear what I said?" She was furious, made more so by his unconcern.

"I sure did and I guess the doorman down on Fifth Avenue did, too. About it being my fault—it'd be pretty unreasonable not to expect it to be, considering we were on our honeymoon."

"That's a disgusting, middle-class word. It's sickening."

He winked gravely at her. "It's a real convenient word. How would it sound if someone said: The newly married couple left on a two weeks' screw. You sure wouldn't print it that way in your paper."

She snatched the fruit from his hand and threw it to spatter against a wall. He shook his head reprovingly.

"I've been had." She made the declaration wonderingly. "I've been had by a soft-talking lint-head. I've been put to like some wide-eyed farmer's daughter by the slick, traveling salesman." She was almost short of breath and panting.

He was unperturbed. "At least you're married. That do make it nice, don't it?"

"Stop trying to sound like Old Black Joe." She paced the length of the room and then whirled on him. "You're sneaky. I'll say it again. You took advantage of me on one of those damn Bahama beaches when you knew I couldn't take any precautions, when I was in the mood not to care what happened."

"I sure did." He was equally complacent. "I figured to keep my promise to your papa."

She sank into a chair, glaring at him. "Well, I'll tell you something, Buster! I'm not going to have a child. I don't want to be anyone's mother."

"Oh, you'll have it all right." He was unruffled, even agreeable, but there was an undercurrent of firmness in his words. "You're going to have it if I have to lock you in a room for the next seven months or so."

She sagged dejectedly and tried a new approach. "Not now, Bootsie. I have so much to do. I can't take the time to have a baby."

She had been in Des Moines with the corps of reporters assigned to the Roosevelt campaign and had awakened several mornings with a slight nausea. Also, she was late, but she had always had spells of irregularity and wasn't particularly concerned. An uneasiness persisted, though, and she finally looked up a doctor. What had been only a vague fear now became a fact. Her rebellion was immediate and she had returned to New York for an examination by her own physician. The damn fool had congratulated her.

"I'm going to get rid of it." She made the statement and was shocked by it. A small panic of indecision began to make itself felt. "Do you hear what I say?" She asked the question of him but it was made more to reassure herself.

Bootsie swung his legs around and stood up. "I don't know how it's going to be with us, Carol. This was kind of a funny marriage to begin with. There were some things you could have told me. A few I had to guess at. We have a lot to give each other but it is going to take a little effort on both sides. It isn't just going to happen. We have to work at it or let it go to hell with a fast bang. I'll tell you something else. You need me. I'm sort of a gyroscope thing that keeps you from flying off and breaking yourself into pieces." He made the statement without complacency.

Staring miserably at the floor she experienced an empty, lost sensation. She was trapped, led into a high pit by her own recklessness. She didn't want this child. There was in her no misty yearning for motherhood. The idea was revolting. She saw herself as a fat cow, heavy with calf.

"I have too much to do." She made the statement dully, and somehow the words were not convincing.

What she had seen and heard on the swing with Roosevelt's party convinced her that the country, even the world, had moved toward a great social and economic revolution. The actual reporting of the campaign had amounted to little. Almost anyone could have done the job competently, although British, Canadian and American papers had sent their best political writers to cover the tour. After a while they were reduced to filing stories on what the candidate ate for lunch, what he whispered to Louis Howe as they stood on the train's rear platform, a small joke made to a whistle-stop crowd. The important speeches were written and mimeographed in advance. A copy boy could have taken them to Western Union. Despite the monotonous routine the press corps, even those from opposition papers, felt the confident vitality of this man who kept hammering away at the theme: Things do not have to be as they are. What they all saw and began to recognize as true was the spectacle of the patrician, the purple-robed aristocrat, casting his lot with the common man. It was a time charged with the lightning of change, and the excitement reproduced itself. She wanted to be a part of it. More than that, she had a voice and wanted to use it.

She had a casual acquaintance with several of the New York and Washington correspondents, but she made no effort to ingratiate herself. She did her job in a businesslike fashion, asked no favors and gave none. After the first week most of the men forgot their initial suspicion and prejudice and the fact that she was the owner and publisher of a competing paper. They dropped into a chair next to her sometimes, shared a drink, a cigarette and casual gossip and opinions. They found in her an attractive woman of quick humor, beautiful legs and a sure instinct for her craft. She was completely feminine and traded on this fact when it would serve her purpose. It frequently did.

She contemplated the next few months with brooding resentment. There was no room in her life for a baby. The very idea of a mewling little animal suckling her as though she were a sow was nauseating. It violated her freedom. The knowledge that she was to be big of belly, bovine of temperament, awkward of movement, made her want to scream a protest and filled her with an un-maternal loathing and self-pity.

Yet, and she stared at the carpet's design, she knew with the helpless sensation of desperation she would not be able to bring herself to have this unwanted embryo aborted. The principle involved was one which she could not state to herself. It certainly had nothing to do with religion or fear. The idea of the operation re-pelled her. It was, she thought miserably, murder. There was no other word for it.

"This is just one hell of a note." She spoke aloud, not looking at him. "Worse than that, it's my own damn fault. I should have known better than to take a chance with you. You've been trying to catch me ever since we were married."

"You just weren't exactly carried off and raped, as I recall." He no longer smiled but studied her wonderingly. "Anyhow, I can't see that any real and permanent damage has been done. It may be a little inconvenient. That's about all."

This angered her more than anything he had said. It made her resentment and rebellion seem trivial objections instead of valid. The paper and her part in it were tolerantly relegated to the status of a passing hobby. Some women took up charity work. Others knitted, painted on china, raised dogs or took a distant interest in Chinese flood victims. She owned a newspaper. Eventually, he told her, she would tire of it and go back to Virginia. There they would find their easy rut and settle in it. In the meanwhile he was being patient.

She rose from the chair, calmer now. The first, unfettered impulse for escape had quieted itself. She was stuck. It was a situation she could have avoided by exercising a small amount of normal judgment. Well, she told herself, you make a mistake and you pay for it. You put it behind you.

She walked to the window and stood looking down at the light flow of traffic on the avenue. Without thinking, she pressed the palms of her hands to her abdomen as though to find the child's outlines already there. She was flat, hard and virginal still. She would finish out the campaign tour and then make her plans with the doctor. Everything that could be done to cushion the shock, to relieve the embarrassing time of a female in the period of gestation, would be arranged in advance. They would plot the time and she would shut her mind to everything but having this thing done and over with. Although she was still furious with Bootsie for his use of the word, she would make it what he said it was: a minor inconvenience. She turned from the window to find him studying her contemplatively.

"All right." She shrugged but did not smile. "I'm going to have the baby. Not for you or because of any of the idiotic things you and Mark decided between yourselves. I'm going to have it because I can't accept the obvious way of avoiding it. I don't know why."

He came to her across the room, taking her arms in his hands. She made an impatient movement as though to twist away and his fingers tightened. She stared at him with surprise. He was hurting her and he knew it.

"I didn't figure you meant what you said." He was soothingly understanding. "I guess most girls feel the same way when they get the news. It'll be a good thing for you, Carol. A good thing for us all."

"Uh-uh." She pulled from his hands. "I think it is a hell of a thing. I'm going to have a child I don't want. I can't see how that is going to be good for anyone."

"You're just scared." He was sympathetic.

"I'm not scared, damn you. I'm normal and with all my functions, as Mark used to say. When this baby is weaned I'm going to drop it in your lap. I'm going to leave the bundle on your doorstep. I'm saying this now because I want you to know what is going to happen."

"You'll change your mind. Nature'll sort of take over."

"Stop talking like a drooling idiot or I'll throw something at you."

Bootsie grinned and scratched at his ear. "You know," he spoke in a tone of pleasant reverie, "I had a setter bitch once. We bred her well and she liked it fine while it was going on. Later, when she got big and too heavy for shooting, I had to leave her home. She used to look at me with those big brown eyes like she was asking: What have you done to me? She was pretty miserable, but when she had the litter she changed. She wouldn't move without those pups. They used to tumble over and around her and she couldn't get enough of them. That's how it is, I guess." He had solved the problem of motherhood for all time.

She could only stare at him. He meant it. The analogy didn't strike him as being outrageous or preposterous. It was meant to soothe and comfort her. She wanted to scream. Instead, she shook her head incredulously.

"You have a boy, this first one." He made the request with gentle consideration. "It's good to start a family with a boy. After that a couple of pretty little girl-children."

She snorted. "I'm going to wear a diaphragm on a silver chain around my neck like a gypsy's amulet. Buster, you don't catch me again." She glanced at her watch. "I'm taking a plane out of Newark for Cleveland this afternoon."

Bootsie refused to be impressed. "This here Roosevelt, if he gets elected in November, ought to make you an ambassador or something. You've been throwing a lot of weight his way, haven't you?"

She was honestly surprised. "I didn't know you ever read anything but *Field and Stream* or the sporting page." The statement wasn't made unkindly.

223

"I read your paper. I read yours and a lot of others. It seems to me Roosevelt has you all running in big, wide circles. I pick up one and a fellow writing just proves Roosevelt is one of those Communists. Then I get another and I'm damned if he doesn't show how Roosevelt is aiming at what they call a Fascist state. What do you think he is?"

"A great man. Maybe the greatest in a long time."

He walked with her to her bedroom where her bag was packed and lying open for any last-minute additions. She looked about and then closed the lid.

"Want me to drive you over to Newark?"

"If you like." She turned. It occurred to her that she hadn't the slightest idea what Bootsie did with his time, where he went, whom he knew, how he filled the days and nights. "What do you do with yourself, Bootsie?"

He leaned against the door and studied her with a small light of amusement in his eyes. "I wondered if you ever thought about that. I sure don't have much time with my wife."

"I have a job to do. I'm trying to do it." The reply was curt, just a little impatient.

He nodded, unimpressed. "That's the way with New York. It's just filled with busy people. They're running even when they sit down. I get tired just watching them. They're scared, too—scared of their jobs, the people they work for, the man just ahead of them, the man behind."

"Whatever you do, is it enough?" She was curious now.

"I play some squash at the University Club. I mosey around through the museums, have lunch with Angela or some of her friends. She's got a lot of odd-balls on her list, men and women."

"I should think you'd go crazy with nothing to do."

"It gets dull, sometimes." He made the admission cheerfully. "But then, I'm just sort of shuffling my feet here until you get enough of this newspaper business and come back home with me." He paused. "While you're away this time I'm going down to Virginia. Mr. Haney was in town last week. We're putting together a deal with Cousin John."

She was surprised. Nothing had been said about Jim's being in town until now. Also, she had all but forgotten she had once spoken to Haney about Harkness.

"What sort of a deal?" She looked again at her watch as she

spoke, and with this gesture the question was automatically relegated to something unimportant. "We ought to be leaving if you're driving me to Newark."

Peters came in to take her bag. Bootsie waited until the man had left.

"You honestly don't give a damn, do you?"

She glanced at him, surprised. "About what?"

"About anything but what interests you."

"Don't be childish." She picked up her gloves. "If you, John and Haney are getting together on Harkness that's fine. It's something you always wanted to do. I'm glad it is working out."

He shook his head wonderingly. She wasn't even curious about the investment: its size, their plans. They were making conversation the way a couple of strangers might exchange casual generalities.

They walked out together, rode down the elevator and went to the car parked in a NO PARKING zone in front of the apartment house. Not until they were in Jersey City did they speak. His attention was on the traffic, hers on the afternoon papers bought from a boy on a corner when they had stopped for a red light.

He lit a cigarette.

"Me, too." She murmured the request without glancing from the paper.

He gave her his and lit another for himself, watching her preoccupation with an oddly baffled expression. She folded the paper, pushed it down on the seat between them and opened another.

"What scared you, Carol?"

"Mmmm?" She wasn't listening.

"Put that damn paper down for a minute." His words exploded and she started with surprise.

"What?" She was astonished by his vehemence. "What is it?"

"I asked what scared you. What frightened you into getting married the way we did? Something had you on the run then. You don't really want to be married to anyone. So, I keep wondering why."

"Does it matter?" A quick, soft smile robbed the question of the sting it might have carried. For a second she placed her hand on his atop the steering wheel. "I'm sorry. That wasn't much of an answer. You've been good for me, Bootsie. It's hard to explain why. Can't we let it go at that? I'm grateful."

He gave up trying to reach her. To pursue the unanswered ques-

225

tions would be a mawkish form of sentimentality. It would also make him appear a little ridiculous.

"All right. I'm the old rugged cross. Cling to me when the tempest strikes." He grinned at her.

"Don't you get bored, Bootsie?" The query was honestly voiced.

"No. I guess I'm real easy to amuse. I just sit on top of the big sandpile that's the Hillyard Enterprises and wriggle my toes in it."

They were in the dingy mazes of Newark now. She glanced up once and thought this must be one of the most unattractive cities in the world, surrounded by marsh, heavy with smoke and the choking odor of chemicals. Even the people appeared a little sooty. Already its airport was obsolescent. There ought to be a better site. Somewhere out on Long Island to serve Manhattan. It might be something for the paper to drive for. A modern air terminal laid out in the open country of the island would anticipate a need and provide a lot of jobs. A good crusade always whipped up reader interest. She made a mental note to call Keith from Cleveland in the morning and suggest it to him, and didn't even hear Bootsie's reply.

Chris Chandler stood at the bar of the speakeasy next to the Tribune Building. It was one of the few all-male retreats in the city; a pleasant room of dark paneling, deep leather chairs, soft lights and good whisky. Its trade was drawn almost exclusively from metropolitan newspapermen and it was a commonly held belief that the *Tribune* encouraged its existence because the city desk always knew where to find the absent members of its staff.

It had been months since he had been here. Months during which he had tried to find a job and failed. It wasn't a place an unemployed reporter or city editor would seek out. Too many friends and acquaintances passed through the door. Seeing him there, knowing he was out of work, would make them uncomfortable and easy conversation impossible. You couldn't offer to buy a drink for a man without a job for fear it would sound like charity. You wouldn't want to accept one either, wondering if he could afford it. His presence would have created an uneasy tension as though he carried with him a fever that could spread by contact.

He slid his glass toward the bartender, Fritz. When the Scotch was mixed with a little plain water he drank it with the slow enjoyment of a man whose world was again secure. He had a job. No longer was he the outcast, the alien. He was a part of the city once more. He could look up and nod to someone he knew without feeling the question in their eyes, without wondering if he appeared eager or hopeful. He took a deep breath and thought how good it was to be alive.

Unless he had gone through it, no man could know the corrosive effect of being unemployed. It ate at your soul like an acid. It dissolved pride and your confidence. It made you avoid those you liked and seek out the silent company of the shabby men who sat in the parks, staring with dull eyes at nothing. You went to movies, the dingy hideaways on Forty-second Street, and sat through pictures you didn't see or you stayed at home, waiting for the telephone to ring and the instrument became a small, black monster of torture. These were the things you did after you had made the rounds of the papers in New York, Brooklyn, Jersey City; the weeklies out on Long Island and up in Westchester. The men he knew in the city were honest. They hadn't tried to avoid him or be evasive. With minor variations they had all said the same thing.

"Jeez. Chris, I wish there was something. I couldn't even hire a copy boy right now. You know how things are."

No one asked why he had left the paper. City editors were not usually let out unless there was a reason but the question was never asked. He couldn't have answered it anyhow.

He and Jean had arrived at an understanding. She knew he was hurt. A false cheeriness, the pretense that everything was fine, a whistling unconcern over what had happened, would only have aggravated the situation. It wasn't a question of money. He had saved some and she had her job. They didn't have to worry about the rent. What concerned them both was the creeping desperation which numbed a man until he began to wonder if there was a place for him in the world and if he would ever find it.

When she came home she never asked what he had done. They would have a drink or two and talk without conscious effort of whatever came into their minds. The real change in their lives was that they deliberately avoided their friends, the restaurants and speakeasies where they might encounter them.

"I don't want anyone to feel sorry for me. At least," Chris told her, "I don't want to put them in the position where they would have to hide it or pretend they didn't know. You'll just have to get along with my company for a while."

"That's fine with me." She nodded. "As long as you don't begin to feel ashamed. It isn't anything you could help. You're a good man, Chris Chandler."

They walked the city's streets in the fine, crisp evenings of the fall. They ate in the small Italian restaurants on the upper West Side or the Armenian places on Lexington Avenue around Twenty-sixth Street. They dropped into the Trans-Lux newsreel theatre or sat in the comfortable loges of Loew's Lexington to watch a Garbo picture. Sometimes on weekends they drove up to West Point, watched the Sunday afternoon parade and had dinner at a fine old roadhouse near Garrison. Without thinking about it they wove a sturdy fabric of companionship.

The telephone rang one morning before Jean had left for the office. He was shaving with the bathroom door open and could hear the faintly surprised note in her voice when she answered the ring.

"Chris. Joe Garnett's on the phone."

With the lather still on his face, razor in hand, he went into the bedroom and picked up the extension, wondering what Garnett wanted so early in the day. They were old friends but for one reason or another rarely saw each other. Joe had been an editor on Hearst's *American Weekly*. He remembered vaguely that he had left to take a job with one of the broadcasting chains. Automatically he moved from one orbit to another in the city's life. His friends and habits changed. Their paths no longer crossed or even ran parallel.

They went through the small ritual of asking each other how things were, the commonplace greetings without which no telephone conversation can take place. Then Garnett broke it off.

"How about having lunch with me? That French speakeasy on Forty-eighth Street where we used to go.

"It'll be fine with me." Chris still wondered what Garnett had on his mind. "One o'clock?"

He hung up and stood staring at the telephone. It wasn't just a casual invitation to get together. He looked up to see Jean standing in the doorway.

"Joe wants me to have lunch with him. I wonder why?"

"Because you're old friends, I guess." She was careful to avoid any suggestion it might be more than that. "Give him my regards." She blew a kiss from her finger tips. "If you feel like it meet me at Tony's around five-thirty and we'll have a drink." This meant that if something good happened as a result of Garnett's call they could celebrate. They both understood. If it was just a luncheon get-together, then they wouldn't have magnified its importance and there would be no disappointment. "Bye!"

He went back to the bathroom and resumed shaving. If Joe knew of something, then it would be in radio and he knew nothing about the medium other than that you turned a switch and voices came out of a little box. He had spent a lot of time listening to it these past months.

Radio. He had a newspaperman's immediate prejudice. This was a new and blatant form of communication. It shouted at you with exhortations to buy this or that while larding the commercials with frantic entertainment. He examined a small nick on his chin. He felt about it, he thought, the way actors of the New York theatre regarded Hollywood. It wasn't quite decent. It was shrill, brassy, young and superconfident. It was knocking over the established icons of news dissemination, shrinking the world.

He poured some witch hazel into a hand and rubbed it over his face. What he felt, he decided, was the suspicion of every newspaperman for this interloper that had invaded his field. Entertainment was one thing; the broadcasting of news was another. Radio had no facilities for the gathering of news. The stations simply lifted the current items from morning and afternoon papers. The reporting of events was made by announcers who were the products of some elocution school, or unsuccessful actors who hadn't been able to get a job any place else. The business offices of the newspapers screamed their outrage at this open thievery. Not only did radio steal its news but it frequently found a fat sponsor to pay them for it. The newspapers and press associations gathered the news and paid for its transmission. Radio took it without cost to itself and made a handsome profit. Every newspaperman he knew resented the broadcasters as doing a whore's work. The sounds were those made by an idiot parrot. He wondered again what Joe Garrett had in mind.

Walking up Fifth Avenue in the heady sunshine of late October, he stopped at a newsstand at the corner of Forty-second Street and from long habit bought the home edition of the paper. He glanced over page one with professional interest. No longer did it resemble the paper he had known. She had changed it completely.

He stood out of the pedestrian traffic, near the entrance of a United Cigar Store, and turned the sheets between his fingers. Un-

229

consciously a smile touched his mouth. He was wondering what the members of the Union League Club thought about this paper. Once it had been their afternoon Bible and spoke to them with unruffled dignity. Now it yelled. It had a driving, restless energy and made unimportant things seem important through sheer emphasis.

Where the old paper had been aloofly conservative in the reporting of the city's divorces, adulteries, murders and scandals, this one shouted gleefully and laid them out for everyone to see with pictures, diagrams and a brisk and airy style of reporting. It was as though a slightly tipsy dowager had staggered out of the Plaza to kick up her heels and swish her skirts in a can-can on Fifty-ninth Street. The performance, though, drew an audience. He could see that the advertising lineage was up. He knew the circulation had jumped. That was what Carol Hillyard had said she would do and she had done it.

There were pages of comics, puzzles, a half a dozen contests running at the same time. Broadway gossip, borrowed unabashedly from the style Winchell had created, was set in two columns on the split-page. There was a column of breezy social chit-chat, a Washington column filled with the unlegislative activities of the legislators. The amusement section ran to three and four pages. It was a newspaper of spinning cyclorama and it gave the impression of having been put together by men in a frenzy. It was astonishing and provocative and, he thought, if it had lost a lot of its old readers it must have gathered many more to take their places. He wondered what Stephen Keith thought about it. The sensation, he imagined, must be that of staggering in an uncontrollable whirlwind. He dropped the paper in a trash basket and walked on up Fifth Avenue.

The entrance to the speakeasy was through the grilled-iron door in one of the brownstone houses which stretched up and down the midtown streets in identical style. As with so many of these places, Pierre's, André's, Jean, Louis, the food and the personnel were authentically French. Half of that nation, he thought, must be riding this tide of prohibition. While he waited for an answer to his ring he wondered idly what they had done before the Great Experiment.

The small, square dining room with its curtained windows at sidewalk level was filled. He saw Joe at a corner table, a martini before him. He waved from the entrance and dropped his hat on the prong of a rack.

"Long time." Garnett stood up to shake hands. "How are you?"

"I'm fine, Joe. You look great." He took a chair and ordered a vermouth.

They eyed each other for a moment with an easy, bantering smile. Garnett, Chris thought, radiated this vitality of a new industry that knew it couldn't help but succeed. He was tailored, smooth and sure of himself.

They made small, "do-you-remember" talk throughout the meal and Chris had the feeling Garnett was weighing and estimating. No mention was made of his not being with the paper. He knew it wouldn't be.

The brandy, which came with the coffee, was true and served in a bottle, left on the table. You paid for it by the inch; a small strip of ruled paper showed the amount consumed.

"I seem to remember you speak German." Joe lit a cigarette and poured a little of the liquor into his demitasse.

"My mother was German, married my father in Cologne. Why?"

"Just wondering. Anything else?"

"Some French and a passing acquaintance with English. What's on your mind?"

"I have an idea how you feel about radio. If it isn't a pimp, it's a pimp's sister. I used to feel the same way, thought I ought to cover my face and whimper: Unclean! Unclean! when I ran into anyone I knew." He chuckled. "The money got to me first and then I really became interested in what it could do. I'm a vice-president now in what they call 'Special Events.' That covers a lot of things from on-the-spot broadcasting of a fire to setting up a transatlantic interview with Winston Churchill." He rested elbows on the table. "I'm not trying to give you a sales pitch." He seemed a little embarrassed.

"Go ahead." Chris smiled. "I haven't anything else to do. The brandy's good and you're paying for it."

"Do you realize what this thing can do if it is set up properly? It could cover a revolution in South America, a war in Europe. It can carry a running account of what is happening while it is happening into the homes of a hundred million persons. Hell! It can bring the sound of the guns and the bombs to the living room as they go off. Before it does that, though, it has to break with established practices. It has to stop taking a free ride from the newspapers, the AP, INS, UP. It has to quit being a pilot fish and learn to swim by itself."

"So"—Chris was not unaware of a faint interest and excitement—

"what do you want from me and why does it make any difference if I can speak German?"

"I have finally wangled permission to try something. It took a lot of talk, a lot of persuading, but I have the appropriation. I want to set up a European Bureau. I want a good man to head it. You."

"I don't know anything about radio." The objection was mechanical.

"I'm not talking about radio—the Hoffman Hour, The Happiness Boys, Amos and Andy, Rudy Vallee, George Shackley and The Moonbeam Maids. I'm talking about news. News the way it was never reported before. News that comes from London, Paris, Berlin, Cairo and Peking as it is happening. If there's a riot in Calcutta I want to bring the screams, the sound of clubs on heads, a running account of what is going on through America's loud-speakers. If there's a flood in China I want our audience to hear the water. That's the kind of radio I'm talking about."

It was impossible not to be swept up by Garnett's enthusiasm. What he outlined was a new, incalculable force in journalism. It was as revolutionary as the transmission of news through a transatlantic cable against a four- or six-week delay in dispatches carried by a ship. The scope of the idea was so great that Chris found his mind racing ahead through the problems, the advantages. He merely nodded, though, to indicate he understood Joe's concept.

"We'll start first with the European Bureau," Garnett continued. "Set it up in Berlin. Things are going to happen in Germany. I can feel it. The lid may blow off. I want a city editor who knows and can anticipate news and is able to handle men. That's you. We'll meet whatever salary you were getting on the paper and give you an almost unlimited expense account and a completely free hand. You'll have the facilities and the backing of a multimillion-dollar corporation. I want you to put together a staff—not these goddamned mincing, ham actor announcers with their carefully articulated vowels but trained reporters. Instead of writing and filing their copy by cable or wireless they'll speak it directly to every radio set in the United States. We'll gather our own news, Chris. We'll ask no favors of foreign correspondents on the scene. We'll match them good reporter for good reporter. I want men who won't have to take their interviews and observations through an interpreter. Our correspondent in Rome will have to speak Italian, the one in Paris, fluent French. We'll do it right or we won't do it at all." He drained

232

the brandy in his glass and reached for the bottle. "Do you realize what it means?"

"I'm beginning to." Chris smiled. "It's the difference between the linotype machine and the hand press."

"Exactly. It's instantaneous transmission. Where a time differential makes this impracticable we'll make a recording of what is happening, a phonograph record, and play it back at a time suitable for the United States. Right now the Federal Communications Act prohibits the use of transcriptions. We're working on it. We'll have it changed. Well"—he leaned back—"do you want it?"

"I want it." Chris kept his tone even. "It's a great opportunity. Thanks."

"When can you leave for Europe?"

This was a small jolt, the abruptness of the question. He would have to leave Jean. He knew, though, she would understand. A man's work took him where it would. He dribbled a little brandy into a spoon, stirring it into his coffee.

"Today. Tomorrow. Next week. Whenever you say."

Joe grinned as though they shared an exciting secret. "We've already booked passage for you on the North German-Lloyd for Hamburg. Saturday. Come over to the plant in the morning. I'll have a contract ready, a letter of credit. We've set it up with the State Department so you can pick up a passport in five minutes downtown. There is a room at the Adlon Hotel, in Berlin, waiting for you. After that you're on your own. Get us good men, Chris. You may have to steal them away from their jobs with the wire services. Hang a carrot of Yankee dollars on a stick. We're sending an engineer with you for the technical end. That's about it."

They shook hands across the table, filled the small brandy glasses and drank a silent, eye-winking toast to the venture.

They parted outside the speakeasy and Chris stood watching Garnett until he turned the corner at Fifth Avenue. The sun was brighter, the air with a flavor of good, dry wine. He wanted to yell at the sky. Instead he walked with a free, swinging stride across town, turning down Broadway to feel the pulse of the surging artery. He was a part of the city, of the world again.

He finished his drink and laughed softly while the bartender, Fritz, darted a puzzled look his way. Then he sorted out a nickel from the change in his pocket and went to a telephone booth to call Jean.

XVII

THESE, now, were the years of tremendous upheaval. The first one hundred days of Roosevelt were long since past. Banks had closed and cautiously reopened while a thousand projects fanned out from Washington to sweep at the depression. The gates of the Treasury were thrown open and a golden tide rushed into the dry gulches of a dust-blown economy.

New words: The Brain Trust. The New Deal. The Blue Eagle. The C.C.C. The N.R.A. and A.A.A. Boondoggling. Leaf-sweeping crept into the vocabulary. New names: Howe. Farley. Rosenman. Moley. Berle. Tugwell made news. Prohibition had been repealed. The country was off the gold standard but Fort Knox bulged. Dollars crept back for deposit and were guaranteed by a Federal Deposit

Insurance Act. Almost four billion dollars had been appropriated for the relief of the twenty million unemployed through a vast program of public works.

Slowly, cautiously, a conservative minority crept from their storm cellars to stare with the dazed expression of Rip Van Winkles at the sky. They weren't sure what had happened. Here and there a voice was raised in protest. It was gloomily predicted that when the public debt reached fifty billion dollars the nation would be teetering on the abyss of bankruptcy.

That Man in the White House cocked the long cigarette holder at a jaunty angle and talked to the people with a paternal indulgence by radio in Fireside Chats.

Peter Arno drew a cartoon for *The New Yorker*. A group of bejeweled dowagers with their top-hatted and paunched escorts called an invitation to friends at an open window. "We're on our way to the Trans-Lux to hiss Roosevelt."

The year was 1935 and the prophets of gloom were at work. Mark Sullivan wrote that Roosevelt would be "a one-term President."

In Germany an unpredictable man with a comic's mustache spun from the ashes of the Reichstag fire like a hysterical genie. No one paid much attention to his rantings. There was also another funny fellow, an Italian journalist by the name of Mussolini. Vaudeville comedians imitated his pouter-pigeon stance, the upthrust chin, the bull-like rantings.

Gray-faced children were no longer working in the North Carolina spinning mills in twelve-hour shifts for a few cents a day.

No one knew exactly what had happened but it was generally agreed that nothing could be worse than what the country had experienced.

The nation's newspapers balanced themselves on a picket fence of indecision. They were cautious with their criticism of The Messiah, but here and there in the editorial sections doubts were voiced. It was possible the country trooped in an abandoned procession behind a reckless Pied Piper. Huey Long said so. Father Coughlin thundered from a pulpit in a Detroit suburb. Gerald L. K. Smith also said it. No one, save a few, paid much attention.

That Man talked to the people; not with them but to them. He soothed and reassured. "The only thing we have to fear is fear itself." It sounded good but the holders of great wealth strained angrily beneath the strictures of a planned economy. The United States was the home of the free and the land of the brave. Dole was a foreign word. The true, red-blooded American didn't want charity or made work. He wanted to stand on his two feet; sockless, perhaps, or with holes in his shoes, while a haggard wife explained to the children there wasn't anything to eat because they were all individuals and wouldn't take the food stamps to the store or cash the relief checks.

Carol Hillyard Warrington walked down Vine Street, in Cincinnati. She had just fired the managing editor of her paper here because the man had permitted editorial suggestions that someone ought to take a closer look at what was happening while That Man dabbled his feet in the waters of Socialism. This was a city of the Tafts, the Longworths, and a large German population filled with thrift, independence and solid virtues. The paper's stand had found a receptive audience.

The interview had been brief. She had strode into Cosgrove's office and said, "You're fired. Get out. Sue for the balance of your contract but get the hell out of this office. You knew what the policy of this paper was. You understood my personal feelings. You chose to disregard them. You're through." She had turned and walked from the room.

At the city desk she stopped. A huge, untidy man with shoulders outspanning the width of his chair, a shock of henna-red hair and an impudent grin, rose.

"You're flying like the spume of an angry sea and twice as beautiful, Mrs. Warrington."

She sat on the corner of his desk and lit a cigarette. "Stop with the phony Irish blather. I'm in no mood for it, O'Shea. Cosgrove is fired. You're it from now on. When you check out, come over to the Sinton Hotel. I want to talk with you." She examined the big frame and added absently, "Stay for dinner."

Walking from the city room she knew each head, every pair of eyes, swiveled to follow her. She had been a familiar figure here during the past year. In and out of town on flying trips which took her from San Francisco to Charlotte, New York and Dallas. Of the newspapers which Mark had bought, the only one she let go was the one in Charlotte. Into the others she had poured money and a furious energy. She had spent millions beating life into them. Her raids on the staffs of other papers were becoming legendary. When she wanted a man she took him, doubling his salary as the incentive. She shifted her staffs as a general moved his troops, to places where

236

they would be most effective. Her small wars for circulation blazed and crackled on every front. She pumped the adrenaline of her personality into the columns of type and the papers reflected what she thought and felt.

The Warrington chain, small as it was compared to Hearst or Scripps-Howard, raised an unmistakable voice. They were the girded champion of the forgotten man; the noisy torchbearer for Roosevelt's policies. Nothing That Man did was or could be wrong. The papers were vital and electric, scandalmongering, curious and prying. They flailed out at everything which offended the opinions of their publisher. When issues were needed they created them, tearing into state and local administrations wherever laxity or political chicanery revealed itself. They all looked alike, from make-up to content, and made a frank appeal to the majority who wanted its news predigested and in capsule form, easy to read and understand. They were violently pro-Roosevelt and rabidly international in concept. THE WORLD IS OUR BUSINESS was a standing line at the top of the editorial page. What happens in Tibet eventually affects Cedar Rapids. The famous warning against foreign entanglements was no longer valid. We cannot escape them, for the world is kin. This was the theme Carol Hillyard Warrington hammered at the papers' readers. For those who took little interest in such things and would rather not be concerned with thinking, even when it was done for them by someone else, there were columns from Hollywood, pages of sports, limericks to finish, puzzles to be solved, free trips to the Zoo and here, in Cincinnati, a nursery service for working mothers and excursions on a great stern-wheeled riverboat down the muddy Ohio. The circulation figures multiplied themselves. She had made her papers successful.

On her way to the Sinton she paused to look over the city's famous Fountain Square. It was solidly Germanic in its execution, a heavy reflection of the good burghers who had settled here and, at one time, filled the city with outdoor beer gardens and tootling German bands. She thought the paper might start a drive for additional planting of flowers and bright shrubs to give color to the Square. Always there must be something to strop the edge of local interest. That was the way old readers were held and new ones added. Right now the paper was engaged in finger pointing and a posture of moral indignation over the whorehouses and cribs along George and Longworth streets; prodding the police into reluctant action while filling its pages with eye-tickling photographs of half-naked girls being loaded into paddy wagons. This was a hypocritical pose of virtue which Carol and everyone on the paper recognized. No one really cared what went on, whether the girls worked on sidewalk cots in broad daylight. The anti-vice crusade made lively reading and that was all that mattered. After the poor drabs had been harassed to the point where reader interest became indifference, a new crusade had been planned. A series had been prepared on the gambling houses and brothels across the river in Covington, Kentucky. Only a river separated Blue Grass vice from Ohio virtue. One sensational exposé must follow another. That was the way circulation was held and increased and the paper maintained its lead over such a prosy companion as *The Enquirer*.

She went through the lobby without stopping at the desk. Mail and telegrams were delivered immediately to the suite which Hillyard Enterprises maintained on a year-round basis. The rooms had been completely redecorated and furnished. They were intimate and personal, reflecting her tastes, and she felt as much at home here as any place.

She glanced through the mail and as a matter of habit fixed herself a drink. In the act of tilting the bottle over icecubes she paused, wondering exactly when she had found it necessary to turn to alcohol in the middle of the day for relaxation.

The resin-colored liquid spilled slowly into the glass. It was a large drink and yet it never occurred to her that this had become a fixed ritual. She would have ridiculed the suggestion that she drank. Two, perhaps three drinks blunted the sawtoothed edges of her nerves. With them she could find herself unwinding. She thought better and made her decisions easily and without reservations.

Carrying the glass to the draped windows she stood looking down into the noisy street. If Cincinnati had a distinctive sound, she thought, it was the bells of its streetcars. The tracks laced the city from those which carried the Zoo-Eden cars to the incline to the Highland Avenue and interurban service. In an age of rapid transit they seemed curiously outmoded and almost quaint, but their clanging was an unmistakable part of the city.

She took a long swallow. A pause in the day's occupation, she smiled to herself, known as the children's hour. That was it. She had begun drinking a little more during the time of her pregnancy. It was an attempt to block from her mind the inexorable process of Nature. She had been in continual rebellion and had then achieved an almost sullen stoicism. When the physical evidence of the child became unmistakable she had shut herself away from everyone she knew except Bootsie, who couldn't be avoided. She found a couple of touches of bourbon relieved the monotony of waiting.

"I don't know as I ever heard of a corn-fed child before—not in liquid form, anyhow." Bootsie's protest had been mild, almost curious.

"Mind your own damn business." Even as she had replied she realized this wasn't at all like her.

"It sort of is my business." He watched her with a faintly puzzled interest.

A scene had followed. She was angry with herself and him. Her voice became shrill and she despised herself for the display of emotional weakness even as she shouted her resentment over the inconvenience of having a baby. Bootsie had listened and regarded her with the polite wonder he would have displayed in the presence of a hysterical stranger. She had been tricked. Led into the trap of motherhood. The accusations were incoherent but no less violent and she finally dropped to a couch and cried.

This Bootsie could understand. It was feminine and womanly to cry. His mothers and aunts had always cried when they were upset. He sat beside her, taking her hand. She jerked it away. He held to the serene confidence that once the child had been born, Carol would change. When she held it in her arms, things would be different. She was not an unnatural, an abnormal, girl. The maternal instinct must lie somewhere below this turbulent surface. Her tears halted as abruptly as they came. She was in control of herself again and put the untouched drink aside because she refused to admit she wanted it.

"How about driving out to Long Island? We could go down along the North Shore, around St. James, and walk through the woods?" He made the suggestion hopefully.

"To hell with that. If you or the doctor think I am going to parade around looking like a baby blimp, you're both crazy. I'm going to stay right here in the apartment until it is born or, at least, until it is time to go to the hospital. The child is perfectly fine where it is. Why should it be any better off for my jolting it around with a walk? It is active enough right now for us both. I'm sorry I yelled at you." She meant it but she also meant she regretted the spectacle of Carol Hillyard losing control of herself. She was ashamed of this rather than of what she had said.

The child had been born in the high tower of the Wickersham Hospital. During the period of waiting until they took her to the delivery room she refused to cry out. She bit upon a towel and strained with white-faced, silent agony. Bootsie waited beside her until she jerked her head toward the door with a speechless command. Even through her pain she felt this was a preposterous spectacle and an ordeal to be endured alone. What good were all the expensive refinements of civilization if a woman must twist and writhe like the lowest animal?

Within the hospital there was a quiet and pleasant bar. The doctor took Bootsie down and introduced him to the bartender, a man grown wise in the ways of handling expectant fathers. He mixed a drink and was politely concerned

"At what corner of the bar, Mr. Warrington, would you like to have your confinement?"

Bootsie had suspected it was an old, well-tried and never failing pleasantry, but it made him feel better.

Standing now at the window she found herself thinking of that day, some two and a half years past, and of how, at last, a great sense of peace had enveloped her. It was done, damn it. It was the great trick of Nature, she thought, that the actual sensation of terrible pain could not be remembered. All you could say was that it had hurt, but not how or to what degree. The sensation receded into a dim memory. That was the way Nature tricked you. If a woman could recall the torment, feel it again, she would go through the business of childbearing only once and that might well be the end of all things.

She glanced at her watch, curious at the train of memory leading her back to that day. She finished her drink and lit a cigarette, seating herself on the ledge of the open window. She could recall Bootsie, standing at her bedside, and almost laughed now as she had come near to laughing then. He was waiting anxiously for the sacred glow of motherhood to envelop her in a shining, mystical aura. She felt nothing but relief. When the nurse brought in the swaddled infant and insisted with professional brightness upon placing it within the cradle of her arm, she glanced at the puckered face with interest but with little feeling it was a part of her. A seed had been dropped carelessly and without plan. This was the result. She neither rejected nor accepted the idea of motherhood. It was all too strange; something which had happened to someone she knew.

Now that it was over she could revert to the plane of easy friendship with Bootsie. She wanted to laugh at the silly expression of wonder and pride on his face; his awkward, finger-poking attempts to cement a reality between the baby and himself. He even made a ridiculous gurgling sound in an effort to evoke a response from the sleeping infant.

She was no longer angry, ill-humored or desperate. A few months had been blocked from her life. She could again take it up as before.

"What do you want to call her, Bootsie?"

Neither thought it strange that the question of naming the daughter should be one for him to decide. She had asked the question with a purpose. It was his child. He and Mark had wanted it. Mark was no longer around but the taking over of the responsibility was Bootsie's and might as well start now. He missed the question's implication.

"I always like Anne, spelled with an *e* at the end, but not said like Ann-e." He bent for a closer look at the hooded bundle. "I sure like the sound of Carol, too. Carol-Anne would be a right pretty name."

In such a fashion had Carol-Anne Warrington been christened.

What Carol regarded as the ultimate miracle of childbearing was not the baby but the rugged elasticity of her own body. The ordeal which, she was certain, was without parallel save by crucifixion had left no visible mark. Within a couple of weeks she could again look at herself, studying her naked reflection in the mirror, and approve of what she saw. The flanks were slim, legs slender and perfectly sculptured as before; the belly flat. What she had felt was a pendulous grossness had vanished. Because this seemed so incredible, she began testing herself in various ways. Alone, she drove down Long Island to Smithtown, renting a hunter from a stable there. She rode across the country with spirit soaring and in flying pride. Her muscles responded as they should, the reflexes sure, the seat firm and the hands without indecision. She deliberately went to dinners, receptions and cocktail parties to learn whether motherhood had dulled the automatic interest in men's eyes that she had come to accept as natural. It hadn't. She gave away her wardrobe and refitted herself for the sheer pleasure of seeing herself extravagantly groomed and hearing the delighted murmurings of saleswomen and designers over her sleek appearance. She was as provocatively sensual with Bootsie as an accomplished whore because she felt the need of knowing a man's humble desperation. The power was intoxicating.

Carol-Anne had been a formula baby from the beginning. Nothing could persuade Carol to have it any other way. Bootsie was completely bewildered. He had been reared in a tradition. A mother fulfilled certain natural functions. One of these was to take her child to breast. He was seriously convinced that a stream of life flowing from Borden's or Sheffield Farms somehow carried with it a mechanical pollution. To him and to the doctor, Carol shook her head. The latter felt that breast feeding would be good for them both.

"You are rich and full, Mrs. Warrington. There is no reason why you shouldn't feed your child."

"You are an idiot." She made the statement calmly. "That is for wolves in a cave. You get your little pump or whatever it is you use. I have no intention of being treated like a fresh cow. I will not be suckled, if that is the disgusting word for what happens. I want a nurse who knows her business and a good formula for Carol-Anne. I am not the cooing, belly-button tickling type of mother. I don't want to know anything about diapers, bathing, powder-dusting or feeding time. Carol-Anne seems to be a fine, healthy little animal. She will be as carefully tended and reared as the offspring of blooded stock. I do not have the time for it so we will find someone who has. She is a foal, a puppy, a kitten, with only the most elementary desires at the moment. All she asks is to be fed, kept dry and warm and be allowed to sleep. That is the work of a groom or a nurse and certainly doesn't require much intelligence to perform."

That was the way she felt and after a few minutes of embarrassed and uncertain conversation, the doctor left. Bootsie stared at her as though he had married a female who devoured her young because they bored her.

Of these things and of a mother who sometimes looked in the nursery, the young Carol-Anne was happily unaware. She grew healthy, strong, straight of limb and happily uncomplicated by too much attention.

On the anniversary of the child's first birthday, Carol was in London. She was writing a weekly column from Europe. In Nuremberg she had watched the great tide of hysterical adulation lift a nondescript-appearing man in an old trench coat to the position of a national deity. In Berlin she had talked with American Ambassador Dodd, filed an interview with a fanatic by the name of Julius Streicher and had a pleasant but completely baffling talk with Sir John Simon, the British Foreign Minister. Now Simon, Laval and Flandin were meeting in London. She cabled a story that France and Great Britain were agreeing on a deal to free Germany from the armament restrictions of the Versailles Treaty. In New York, Stephen Keith read the copy. He had no idea what her sources of information were. It didn't seem possible that Great Britain and France were bending a knee before the rantings of a brown-shirted madman. But he trusted Carol and carried the story, as he would have even if she had not been the paper's owner, on the front page.

In her rooms at the Savoy she was having a drink with Larry Coe, the paper's London correspondent. He was an old hand, wise in the ways of maneuvering through the narrow corridors of British officialdom. His contacts had been invaluable to her and she was grateful. They talked of giving him a couple of assistants and she made a mental note to give him an increase in salary.

On the way to freshen her drink she turned on the short wave radio. It hummed and bubbled for a moment and then the words were clear.

"This is Chris Chandler in Berlin."

She was immobile, listening to the voice rather than the words, and marveling a little at the magic of memory to move her after this long time and stir emotions she had thought were safely buried.

"Today"—the report was even, unemotional—"Adolph Hitler scratched out the military provisions of the Versailles Treaty and ordered universal military service and the conscription of thirty-six army divisions."

"For God's sake!" Coe's exclamation broke into the statement.

She shook her head for silence, fully aware of what Chris was saying and of the incredible implications of the report. She had known, of course, he was in Germany. The press and radio corps in Berlin was a growing but still small family. Everyone knew everyone else. She hadn't seen him at the Adlon or The Taverne where the correspondents gathered to eat, drink, smoke and talk. While she had been in Berlin he was somewhere in the Saar. She had made inquiries, casually.

"This is Berlin. Tonight." He signed off with the familiar words.

The set whined with the high sound of static and then bubbled inarticulately. She continued to stand, staring into the empty cavern of the speaker with the curious feeling that she could reach out and touch him. She was reluctant to turn away and break the spell.

"Chandler is doing one hell of a job." Coe's statement held a grudging but impersonal admiration. "Radio never went after news the way he does. They beat the hell out of the press associations time after time."

She nodded without comment and realized that her fingers had been so tightly closed upon the glass that they were painfully cramped.

She had sailed from Southampton the following day on the *Berengaria*. It hadn't been her plan and in the privacy of her cabin she admitted to herself that she was running away from a situation which could strip her of dignity and pride. Every instinct compelled her to a return to Berlin and to Chris Chandler.

She had remembered Carol-Anne's birthday. A month before, in Paris, she had bought a small, bright toy. As an afterthought she purchased two more and had one each sent to New York, Court House and Harkness. One of them would certainly reach her. She didn't think it at all unusual that she didn't know where her husband and child were. They were all right: if they hadn't been she would have heard. She was interested in Carol-Anne, her health and the fact she was well taken care of. But she was not at all concerned over her happiness. She was happy because she was fed regularly and changed when wet. At the age of one, life was that simple. To be unhappy you had to have a basis for comparison. That came with the years.

She had felt only a momentary curiosity when the ship docked in New York and Bootsie wasn't on the pier to meet her. Then, she confessed to herself, she wasn't at all sure she had let him know she was returning.

From the apartment she had talked with Keith for half an hour on the telephone. Then she had a bath, changed to a negligee, had a couple of drinks and told Peters what she wanted for dinner. After that she put in a call for Court House.

They had talked as friendly acquaintances who now and then ran into each other.

"How are you?" It seemed a ridiculous question to ask. Bootsie was always all right.

"I'm fine, Carol." He was pleasantly reserved. "How are you?"

"I got in this morning. I couldn't remember whether I had cabled you. I sent Carol-Anne a present. Did it arrive?"

"All three of them, eventually. She says to thank you. Three times. I mean, that's what she would say if she could talk yet."

"I have a few things to do." She realized she was making conversation. He was forcing her to it. It made her feel a little ridiculous. "As soon as I'm finished I thought I'd come down for a rest."

"That'll be fine. Let me know. I'll meet you in Richmond."

She waited for him to say more. He didn't. There was a faint buzzing on the line which told her the connection was still open. He was sitting there, leaving it up to her. Oddly enough she caught herself wishing he would say he was glad she was back or that he wanted to see her, or even say something about Carol-Anne, a new tooth or a word spoken or learned. She wanted to be part of something warm and reassuringly secure. Before she could speak again she heard the click as the receiver in Virginia was placed upon its hook.

Now, here in the hotel in Cincinnati, she was remembering she hadn't gone to Virginia that week or the week after, and that she had a daughter who was almost three years old and who wouldn't know her if she walked into the room.

O'Shea leaned back in the chair and carefully bit off the end of a cigar. The waiter halted in the act of clearing the table to light it for him. He nodded his thanks, sharp eyes studying Carol Warrington. She disturbed and puzzled him. There was between them an unspoken thing and it made him uneasy. In her manner of asking him to dinner there had been a summons rather than an invitation. This, in itself, he would not have questioned. She was his employer. But, and this was the unsettling trick, she constantly made him aware of her as a woman.

He had come from the paper to the hotel without an apology for being late or not changing for dinner. He appeared she thought, deliberately untidy, a rumpled bed. She suspected the pose but was not offended. She wondered a little at her propensity for vulgar men. BillJo Adams had been one. There had been others since. It was, she thought, because she could walk away from them without regret or wanting to look back. She caught herself thinking of something Chris had once told her. He had known a girl who would only make love while fully clothed. It was a protective device beneath which she hid herself. Dressed, she could pretend it was an act of rape. She was being taken against her will. It wasn't her fault. So, she thought, it was with her and such men as BillJo and O'Shea. They had nothing in common and so the interlude was without importance; as impersonal as washing one's hand or going to the bathroom.

"You've been a good man on the city desk, O'Shea. Find me one as capable to replace you. You know why Cosgrove was let out. Don't repeat the mistake. The only opinions the paper has are my own."

"I'll do my best, Mrs. Warrington."

The open interest of his gaze gave a lie to the faintly obsequious tone. He was talking to her as an employee but his mind was working over her as a woman. She could almost feel him weighing the opportunity, the incalculable advantage to him of being her lover if only for one passing night. The small, crafty mechanics repelled her.

She stood up, unsmiling, and with an unmistakable gesture of dismissal. After a moment he rose. He was astonished and wondering where he had made a mistake.

"Good night, O'Shea." She didn't offer her hand.

On the way down in the elevator he tried to figure out what had happened. He had been so sure of himself and of her. What the hell had he done or said to make her change? She had suddenly looked at him as though he was dirt. A real tough, hard-to-figure-out bitch. Maybe, and he cheered himself with the thought, he was lucky at that. He might have laid her and found himself out of a job in the morning. She was capable of it.

In a deep tub of hot water Carol scrubbed herself furiously as though to wash away the exposure to contamination.

XVIII

UNDERFOOT the grass was slick with the glistening rime of frost and when trod upon crackled like dry twigs snapping. From the stubbled fields an occasional brace of quail drummed out of cover in a panic as the horses moved upon them, and the clear air had the clean, sweet taste of newly pressed cider.

They rode at an easy trot and Bootsie glanced down at the small figure. Carol-Anne, feeling the eyes of her father, looked up with a quick smile of love and confidence. Of all the time of day, she thought, this was the best when they rode together in the early mornings, alone in a world securely theirs. Because she knew he was watching, she straightened her back, holding the pony between strong, young knees with a sure seat. Her hands were gentle but firm as they should be.

On the scattered trees the few remaining leaves were bits of hammered copper or the green-gold of bronze. Here and there were small tobacco barns, an empty pen or a Negro's cabin in lonely silence. Only now and then did a thread of gun-metal smoke spinning out of a stone chimney break the spell of quiet hibernation.

Before them a crooked line of fence, its rails ax-hewn, straggled with a vagrant lack of direction across the field's north end to disappear with the sloping curve of a low ridge. At one spot the top bar had been taken away, leaving a section lower than the rest. Bootsie understood they hadn't come this way by chance.

He saw the tip of his daughter's tongue as it peeked between her lips. It was a characteristic gesture of excitement; a small unconscious trick of hers which betrayed mischief and a hopeful indecision. She was, he knew, measuring this gap in the fence, its height and the ground before and beyond. It was a survey made many times before. She looked up at him but he pretended a musing interest in the triangular inking of a flight of southbound ducks high in the sky. When he turned to glance at her again she was intent upon the distance separating them from the fence. He watched the set of the shoulders beneath a soft tweed jacket and the gathering of the youthful muscles in her jodhpur-clad legs. He knew she was going to take the fence now without asking permission; could almost feel the tense determination of the stripling body. Then her crop flicked and she was gone.

He checked his animal and watched, a great pride struggling with concern. The fence appeared an insurmountable barrier for one so small. Mentally he checked the exact spot where the pony must go up. She rode so well, was so much a part of her mount, that they seemed as one. Then she was up, leaning easily forward as they cleared the bar, straightening with the pony's sure footing and racing stride as they came down. She let it run for a few yards and then brought it around in a wide circle and stood waiting until he came through an open gate in the fence.

"I did it." She fairly bounced in the saddle, her breath coming in short bursts of excitement. "I did it. The big one, too. Let me tell Uncle John I did it, please?"

This fence, or the gap in it, had been a challenge for months. Every morning as they rode together she made a point of bringing them back along a course which would take them to the field's north end. She had asked only once if she might take the pony over this section.

"Not yet, honey. It's too high."

She hadn't argued or pleaded. This wasn't in her nature. He had said no. From that point she must either accept his authority or disobey. They both understood this. He knew, though, that she brought him back to the spot time after time for the purpose of giving him an opportunity to change his mind. Always she frowned when they came to the rails, calculating the run, the height, the footing beyond. Back at Harkness, over her breakfast, she would talk seriously of "my fence," giving it a stubborn personality and discussing it with her oatmeal, a hot muffin, a small mound of jam. These things and not her elders were the audience. The blob of butter became a thinking, rational person and she addressed it gravely: "He says it's too high. I don't think so, do you?" This was a mysterious and intimate form of conversation with the dishes which, apparently, made suitable reply audible only to her. She would talk over the problem with frowning concentration while devouring her audience hungrily.

Studying her now, Bootsie was curious. "Why didn't you ask me if you could take the jump this morning?"

"Because I was afraid you'd say no again." There was candor but not impertinence in the reply. "I knew I could do it. I've known I could ever since I was a child."

He nodded a solemn understanding. "That's a real long time to be studying over something. You're almost six now, aren't you?"

"Six is pretty old when you're young." The small bun of straw-colored hair had shaken loose and hung at the nape of her neck below the low-crowned derby. She reached back to thrust at it impatiently. "I wish I didn't have to wear a hat. Why do I?"

They were trotting back toward the distant outbuildings of Harkness where the sun was picking up and lighting the gilded weathervanes.

"You don't, really. You could ride in a bathing suit with a rubber cap on your head if that's the way you want to do it. Only, and I guess you'll have to figure this out for yourself, a lady doesn't ride that way."

He could see her mind working over this. Finally, she half nodded. The explanation seemed to satisfy her.

249

They walked back from the stables, her hand reaching up to take his, her small legs trying to imitate the masculine stride.

Although she couldn't have phrased it, this was a fine, emotionally rich world in which they lived. Harkness was as much home to her as the big house on the river outside Court House. The love of her father, the tender affection of John and Martha Harkness, were spun about her like a warm cocoon. There were only a few restrictions beneath which she chafed. Going to school, being driven there each morning and called for in the afternoon, was one of them. Bedtime, when everyone else could sit around the big fireplace downstairs talking of horses, dogs, the shooting and the Warren County Hunt, was another. Against these things, though, was a freedom and a life unknown to the girls her age at school. Also, there was certainly no one in the world quite so wonderful as the big man who was her father. Other girls played with dolls and make-believe houses, were primly concerned with their clothes and manners. She had the rich, earthy wonderland of the stables, the dark laughter of grooms and exercise boys. She had seen the miracle of birth and a wet foal teetering on unsteady legs from a bed of clean straw. She had watched the rearing demands of a stallion upon a mare without knowing why this made her breath catch and her heart almost stop beating. She had seen the sculptured beauty of a dog at point when only the nervous ripple of its coat betrayed the excitement. She knew how quail left the ground, one wheeling sharply to lure the hunter while the rest of the flock skimmed out in a different direction with a flashing, brown-speckled beauty of movement. It was a world into which she bounced from her bed in the early morning with the wriggling enthusiasm of a puppy for play.

She was gravely uncommunicative when other girls talked of their mothers; no longer defending against the charge she didn't have one. She had a mother, of course. Everyone knew that. But this mother was unlike any other. Mothers told you when to go to bed, when to get up. To take a bath, change your dress, brush your hair, scrub your teeth, put on clean socks. Her mother, Carol-Anne understood, didn't know about these things. She was a shiningly beautiful visitor from another planet who came to the house on the river from the sky, wheeling down in a silver plane on the private airfield laid out at the south end of the acres. She came and went as the wind, restlessly and without warning.

This was Carol and she was Carol-Anne. The kinship was in the word of *mother* and not in feeling something. Between them there were never any uncomfortable demonstrations. Carol did not fuss over her, there was no clinging embrace of welcome or subdued regret at parting.

Carol-Anne and her father would wait in the car at one side of the landing strip. He usually had the top down so they could watch the sky. First, there would be the tiny, moving dot in the north, then the sound and the shape and the plane would come floating in and land. Out would step this person of crystal brightness.

Bootsie always left the car, walking to meet her halfway. For reasons she couldn't explain, Carol-Anne always waited by the car; not shyly, not defiantly, but only because she had no desire to run and call a greeting. It would have made these glittering arrivals seem commonplace. They always said the same things at first.

"Hello." Carol spoke with a quiet interest.

"Hello." Carol-Anne smiled a reserved pleasure.

They didn't really know each other very well and these simple words were enough at the beginning. Neither wanted to intrude upon the other without a given sign.

While Carol was home the three of them rode together every morning, and for this brief hour or so were mysteriously bound in companionship. Breakfast was a pleasant time of talk and listening; an attempt to share and integrate their lives, to twist the divergent threads into a single cord. But somehow the intimacy, the communion they had known on horseback became elusive, as difficult to hold on to as a pellet of mercury. It trickled away like water in a basin with a faulty plug. No one saw it go. Suddenly it was no longer there. Carol and Bootsie both tried to display an interest in what the other was doing. They succeeded only in creating an illusion as parallel railroad tracks seem to meet and join in the distance. They both made what they thought to be an honest effort, but what they achieved was no more than a fierce concord of their bodies in bed.

When Carol was home they never went to Harkness. Without hearing it said, Carol-Anne sensed that her mother and Martha disliked each other. There seemed to be no reason for this. One never mentioned the other, but the child was aware of the hostility and suspicion. This actually didn't occur to her as being unusual. She knew several children she didn't like at all without being able

251

to say exactly why. Grownups probably felt the same way about each other.

For the first couple of days they were always together. There were noisy matches of croquet on the lawn court. They swam in the heated pool and, if the weather was warm, had lunch beside it in the bronze sunshine. They rode or took long drives in the country with a picnic basket. They sat in the evenings listening to music or Carol would talk of politics, the newspapers, a war which seemed inevitable. Bootsie would try to interest her in what he and John were doing with Harkness. Neither really listened to the other and there were long periods of meditative silence.

Acutely sensitive to her mother's moods, Carol-Anne would feel the restlessness gather until it became a thing to see rather than sense. She would begin with spending half a morning with the telephone and long-distance calls. Then there would be long hours when she worked at a typewriter until the room, once used by Mark as an office, was filled with cigarette smoke and the table littered with papers on which she made notes with a heavy black copy pencil. Finally, a subtle undercurrent of irritation would begin to run beneath her words and manner. She snapped unnecessarily at a servant, was impatient with Carol-Anne's small delays or Bootsie's suggestions for a trip, a party at the house or an afternoon of golf at the country club. She would have three, sometimes four, drinks before dinner and more later while Bootsie watched with silent concern. She seemed unable to sit still, to read or listen, and would rise abruptly from her chair and without a word of explanation take a car and drive off by herself. These were all familiar signs and Carol-Anne knew that one morning she would come downstairs and see her mother's bags packed and waiting in the hall. Now, once again, Carol would be bright, flippantly gay, laughing and apparently filled with a brisk affection for everyone. Over the breakfast table she would make suggestions or plans for them to meet in New York or decide they would go to Europe together and Carol-Anne should go to school in Switzerland. It would be fun to meet in Florida, to fish or lie around in the sun somewhere along the keys or charter a boat and cruise the Bahamas. None of these things ever happened, as Carol-Anne now knew they wouldn't, but it was a game in which she and Bootsie took an animated interest because it made everything simpler.

The actual leave-taking was done in a flurry of excitement with last-minute telephone calls to New York, Washington, and a couple of times, London or Paris. Carol would take Bootsie's kiss, seeming to cling to him for a moment, her cheek against his shoulder, fingers digging into his arms as though she sought a reassurance in his heavy strength. Then she would turn quickly, stoop and take Carol-Anne's slender elbows in her hands and gaze at her as though there were things to say she could not utter. Then she would kiss her quickly, usually on the forehead, and rise almost regretfully and with an unhappy violet shadow in her eyes.

Words of good-by were not spoken. They were always, "I'll see you soon. Take care of yourself. You're going to be a beautiful girl. I'll call from New York." These things were said quickly, self-consciously and in a hurry, as though she were afraid of saying more or staying longer.

They never went to the airstrip with her when she left. One of the boys would drive her to the field where the plane and her pilot were ready and waiting. From the porch or the front lawn Carol-Anne would wait until the silvered wings rose above the trees with an eager whine and then wheeled sharply northward as though it, also, was eager to get away.

Then, for the rest of the day and, perhaps, the evening, Carol-Anne would understand her father didn't want to talk. He would sit in one of the deep, leather chairs staring into the fireplace if it were winter or stand alone in the murmuring darkness outside. There was always a sadness in his eyes at such times. It was the expression of a man who was hurt and bewildered by something he could not understand and who searched desperately for an answer.

At such times Carol-Anne sensed his unhappiness and understood he wanted to be alone. She would go to her room, taking one of her favorite picture books of horses or dogs. Lying, belly down, in the deep-piled rug, she would amuse herself until the nurse, Grannisin, came with supper and to see about her bath and bed. Sometimes, with the light out, her father would come softly into the room and sit on the edge of the bed. She always pretended she was asleep, knowing he didn't want to talk. He would stay for a while and then kiss her gently, make an unnecessary adjustment to the covers and leave quietly.

Usually they went back to Harkness on the day after Carol had left. The river house was kept open with Grannisin and the servants staying behind. This was the best of all times and she was up at daybreak, urging her father out of his room, to breakfast and the car.

Walking back to the house now, Bootsie could feel the excitement in his daughter's small, warm fingers twining with his. She had made her jump. It was something to which she had set her mind. There was, he thought, much in her of Carol Hillyard and maybe, even, old Mark. He caught himself wondering whether this was good or bad.

"I just love everyone this morning." She said it abruptly, her eyes shining.

"That's good, sweetheart. That's a real good way to feel in the morning."

He swept her up, settling her on his shoulders, the booted legs clasped about his neck, but she wriggled and protested until he put her down. The act offended her dignity. It was for a child and not someone who had taken her pony over a high fence that very morning.

Over breakfast every minute detail of the jump had to be told and retold to John and Martha. It was only by threatening to tear down the whole fence that she was finally induced into her coat, took her books and ran calling the news to the boy who was waiting to drive her to school in a station wagon.

When they were alone, the breakfast became a time of silence. Now and then Martha glanced across at Bootsie. There were things on her mind and she waited only for an excuse to talk about them. Finally, she asked the question bluntly.

"Why don't you get a divorce from Carol, Bootsie?"

He had a muffin half buttered. For a second his hands hesitated and then the knife smoothed out the pat. He took a bite and chewed stolidly.

"Well?" Martha persisted, despite her husband's warning glance.

"You mean give up all this butter and jam on my bread?" The question was mildly voiced.

"I never thought you married Carol for her money." She was defending him against himself.

He smiled then, softly, gently. "Thanks, Mart." He continued eating.

"She's ruining your life," Martha persisted. "You don't see anyone, go with anyone. Girls. Women." Her exasperation made her all but inarticulate.

254

"You mean like for fornicating purposes?" He drawled the question with an expression of astonishment.

"All right." She was defiant. "If you want to be dirty that's just what I mean. It isn't natural for a healthy man to live the way you do."

"I've been studying over catching you on a mattress one of these days when John is down at the stables." He contrived a wicked leer.

"At least that would be normal." She flushed but persisted.

"I get along all right, Mart." He refused to take her seriously. "I've been thinking about setting up a little seamstress in the village. Isn't that what the nobs used to do? Or, it occurred to me to take up painting and I could have a couple of naked models running around the place. How'd you like that?"

"I'd like it better than what is happening to you the way things are. She comes down here once, maybe twice, a year or you and Carol-Anne meet her in New York. What sort of a life is that? She doesn't love you, or anyone."

"Mart," John's objection was firm, "why don't you mind your own damn business?" He dropped his napkin on the table and stood up. "Coming, Bootsie?"

Bootsie nodded. He glanced at Martha, reached over to touch her hand. "It's pretty simple, Mart. I love Carol."

Together John and Bootsie walked toward the stables, John packing his pipe, a little embarrassed by Martha's intrusion. He made no attempt to understand the curious relationship between his cousin and Carol. He didn't see how a man could live as Bootsie did. What he had in mind went beyond the normal, physical need of a man. Bootsie could, and probably did, satisfy that when he went to Richmond or New York. He was troubled by the conviction that Bootsie was preoccupied by a problem which actually had no solution. The more he worked at it the more twisted it became. Carol Hillyard Warrington was self-dedicated. That was the real problem and her blind spot. Her capacity for self-containment was so great he would have been astonished by anyone's questioning her right to this single purpose.

"We're doing pretty well here, John." Bootsie put a hand on his cousin's shoulder. "Jim Haney's auditors say we'll better than break even this year."

This was something they hadn't talked much about. Hillyard money had been poured into Harkness. Once, early in their associa-

255

tion, John had been ready to yield to the demands of a different age and abandon the historic acres. On this Bootsie had been surprisingly firm.

"There are only a few things worth saving any more. Harkness, the way of life, what we have here and what Carol-Anne is learning are among them. We'll keep Harkness no matter what it costs Hillyard Enterprises."

They had all but given up the breeding of the hunters and quarter horses for which Harkness had been famous. Instead, they had concentrated on a racing strain. Two of the colts, Discubus and an astonishing filly, Satin Slipper, had won at Belmont, Santa Anita and Aqueduct. They were ready for a try at Lexington. In time, with shrewd purchases and careful breeding, they would have an outstanding racing stable. It was John's moody conviction that away from the tracks the only place one would be able to find a horse in a few years would be the zoo.

Bootsie had worked hard at learning. His interest was genuine and not the passing diversion of a man with unlimited money at his disposal. He was proud of the fact they would make a little profit; not for profit's sake but because he had contributed something. He was, John suspected, vaguely surprised by his own industry.

The sun was warming the land on this morning of early winter, and as they walked to the stables neither heard the rumbling thunder as it gathered an ocean away.

XIX

EVERYONE in a position to observe and listen knew what was happening. But, as with the courtiers and their king with his invisible suit of clothes, no one wanted to be the first to speak.

Step by step, testing each one as he went for a violent reaction, the man Hitler moved upon a continent, a world. He scrapped the Versailles Treaty and nothing happened. He paraded his troops while England and France watched without protesting. He occupied the Rhineland and everyone looked the other way. The German army marched into Austria "to save it from Communist chaos" and Chamberlain told the House of Commons that "nothing could have arrested what has actually happened." The shadow grew into a pattern: all over Europe someone was persecuting the Germans.

And so Hitler's motorized divisions rolled across the Czech frontier to "protect" the Sudetens. Chamberlain returned from Munich and the crowd at the airport sang: "For he's a jolly good fellow."

In Berlin the press correspondents and radio men were told Poland was "threatening the peace of the world" and if Polish aggressiveness continued, Germany would have to "counterattack."

For the first time the British lion loosed a faint rumble of warning but it was too late. The fury of German vengeance was thrown against Poland. England and France fulfilled their treaty obligations, made their official declarations of war and sent a few bombers over to drop propaganda leaflets, but no bombs on the great industrial region of the Rhine. Where German and French troops faced each other loud-speakers, from the German side, assured the French they would not shoot first. In Berlin there was an air of complete unreality. Where, people began to ask, is the war? Who is fighting?

At the Adlon bar Chris Chandler sat with Joe Bates, an American newspaper correspondent who had been given twelve hours in which to leave Germany. Bates had infuriated the top Nazis with a story to the effect that millions and millions of dollars in gold had been secretly deposited in banks in South America by top party officials as a hedge against German defeat or Nazi overthrow.

It had become almost impossible to report the truth from Germany. The propaganda flow was constant and unabashed. The correspondents were expected to repeat it. The theme was repeated over and over. Hitler had only wanted peace. The Poles had threatened the Germans. The terrible bombing of Warsaw had been a "preventative measure." England had really started the war and the Jews were at the bottom of the whole thing.

Chris ordered another drink for them both. "In a way you're lucky," he mused. "I have a feeling nothing honest is going to be reported out of here from now on. Where are you going?"

"Switzerland and then back home for reassignment. I'd like to be sent to Paris. By the way." He put down his glass. "Sigrid Warner told me your old boss is in Geneva. She's raising pure hell because the Nazis won't let her into Germany to report the war."

Chris's expression of moody contemplation didn't change. He knew Bates was waiting for an expression of interest. He wasn't surprised to hear Carol was in Europe. He was a little astonished, though, by her innocent outrage if what Bates said was true. Her papers had excoriated Hitler from the beginning. On their front pages they had carried a two-column box of what amounted to a score. Item by item the Warrington papers had listed Hitler's crimes, his lies, his palpably false excuses for plunging the world into the second great war within a generation. She couldn't honestly believe the Nazis would welcome her to Germany. Yet, he smiled to himself, that was just what she might expect. She believed so completely in what she believed that she would expect others to understand the Carol point of view.

"How is she to work for?" Bates was openly curious.

The question annoyed Chris. He knew there had been a lot of speculation and rumors within the trade as to why he had left an important city desk. He had always covered himself by saying the radio bureau in Germany had been a better opportunity.

"I don't know." He swallowed part of his drink, lit a cigarette and looked directly at Bates. "I never worked for her more than a few weeks. Her people seem satisfied."

The tone was abrupt. Bates recognized it for what it was meant to be. He was unembarrassed, glanced at his watch and stood up.

"I'd better get going before the Gestapo sends an escort. Take care of yourself. It's a pretty confused war except for the Poles. No one else seems to want to fight."

"I expect they'll get around to it."

They shook hands and Chris watched until Bates left the room. Then he hunched himself on the seat and stared into his glass. After all this time he still could not think of her or hear her name without the sensation of hurt, a dull knife twisting somewhere inside. The faces of most persons he had known receded into time and became blurred and difficult to remember. Not Carol's. Every detail, each small mannerism and sound was acid etched on that thing called heart. Love was a lonely cry that echoed and re-echoed without end.

From his pocket he took a sheaf of copy paper. It was his regular five-minute broadcast to the United States and had been passed by the censor. This amused him a little, for in it he had included the news that German forces were massing in the Baltic ports. "It is generally agreed," he had written, "that if England sends it naval forces into Scandinavian waters to halt the marine traffic between Narvik and Germany, the Reich will defend Norway's territorial integrity with the full power of its forces." In other words the High Command had already decided to invade Norway, using as an excuse the violation of Norway's neutrality by England which must halt, at all costs, the shipment of iron ore to Germany from Narvik. He did not say this but it was clearly implied. The censor had scowled over the item. He tapped a pencil indecisively and then nodded a solemn agreement. He was hypnotized by the phrase "preserve Norway's neutrality." Behind the heavy-lensed glasses Chris thought he could almost see the official's mind working along disciplined lines. This was what the Führer had insisted all along. Germany was coming to the assistance of the oppressed. Norwegians would be saved from a rape by the British. It was logical and the world should know Germany was interested in preserving the integrity of small countries.

During those first days of the war Chris thought the German people moved in a haze of curious self-deception. Nothing was real. The stage was set for a mammouth Wagnerian production. The orchestra was tuning up. Soon the great, crashing chords of the fateful music would sound and they would all walk on stage carrying spears, helmeted and chanting in unison. The city was brilliantly lit at night, a new musical extravaganza was presented at the Metropol and attended on the opening night by Hitler. Goering turned the screaming fury of the *Luftwaffe* on Poland and no shot of retaliation was fired by the French or British. Goebbels' newspapers carried an absurd headline: POLES BOMBARD WARSAW, and the Berliners believed it.

In trying to report what he saw, Chris experienced a curious sense of frustration. He wanted to translate his words into clean, hard type. Instead he spoke them into a microphone at the *Rundfunk* and was never sure they were going to be picked up by New York or London. He felt the need to see the story hammered out into solid columns. Instead he had to be satisfied with throwing them like pebbles into the air, not knowing where they would land.

He refolded the copy for the broadcast and signaled for another drink. In many ways his job was easier, if less rewarding in a personal vein, than that of the wire service correspondents and reporters from the chains or individual newspapers in the United States. The Nazis liked radio. It had worked miracles for them. Through it Hitler had sold the German people the great lie. If it had worked on them it would work on the world. So, many of the petty annoyances, the bureaucratic interferences, the deletions of the censors, the haggling over a word, a comma, a phrase, had not plagued the broadcasters as they did the press. Even so, he knew the real story of what was happening could never be fully reported. Terror was beginning to show its twisted face. Over three hundred thousand Jews had made applications to the American Embassy for visas. The German girls, with generations of solid virtues behind them, were being told at their youth meetings that it was their duty to bear children, even out of wedlock, for the glory of the Reich. The sober, thoughtful bulk of the German people had been overwhelmed by a wave of fanaticism. They were left no middle ground on which to stand. No longer did they attempt to explain the diplomatic acrobatics of the High Command. Russia, the fearful monster, was now an ally. England was the threat. If the British would only behave sensibly there would be no war. Even now Hitler was preparing them for the inevitable. A whispering campaign, difficult to nail down, was already underway. Roosevelt's real name was Rosenfeld. He was a Jew.

Leaning back in his chair he watched as Brock, an American correspondent, sauntered into the bar, looked about the empty room and then walked toward him with a beaming and slyly confident smile. He disliked the man, as did almost every American reporter in Berlin, as a liar, a braggart, and possibly a Nazi-subsidized member of the press corps.

With a great show of cordiality, Brock offered his hand and managed to keep the smug grin on his face when Chris pretended not to see it.

"I hear Bates got kicked out." Brock seemed to find a real satisfaction in the statement. He snapped his tongue over it for emphasis and then leaned forward on the table. "I was talking to Dr. Boehmer. How would you like me to do a broadcast for you? The man Hitler. You know? What time he gets up and to work. What he eats. Who his intimates are. How he takes a walk every afternoon in the Chancellery gardens. What he reads. Let the world know what sort of a man he really is."

"I don't think the world could stand the shock." Chris kept his face expressionless. "I think the world would take off to another planet if it really knew."

"You know, you could cause yourself a lot of trouble talking that way, Chandler." The man made it sound as though he were really concerned. "Not that I'd say anything, of course, but you never know who's listening."

Chris lit a cigarette. He smiled at the man and then shook his head with honest wonder. "I think," he said slowly, "you are one of the few real sons of bitches I have ever known and that covers a lot of territory and years."

Brock giggled. It was a small, almost feminine sound and was as obscene as the fixed expression of amiability on his glistening face.

"I was only trying to help you." Brock stood up. "I'll tell Boehmer what you said." There was a sly malice in the statement. He minced away, his fat buttocks swinging.

Chris finished his drink in a hurry, as though there was a bad taste in his mouth.

It seemed incredible that it was November and a war which was unlike any other in history had smoldered at the edges of the world for three months or so. There had been no military action. England and France seemed to think they could bring Hitler to terms and the German people to their senses through a blockade. Chris didn't think it would work and he had an idea men like Churchill didn't either. Sooner or later it had to explode beyond this artificial vacuum. It was a thing he wanted to shout every time he sat before a microphone. Hitler wouldn't permit France to sit behind the Maginot Line and starve him out. The British remembered only that no one had successfully invaded England since the Norman William. This sort of static warfare wasn't what Goering had in mind.

He paid his check, walked out to buy a paper and then decided he was hungry. For lunch he ordered a piece of cheese, some hot bread and a bottle of Mersault.

The waiter was an old man. He merely stood waiting without comment. After a moment Chris glanced up at him with pleasant curiosity.

"That's a French wine, is it not, sir?" The ignorance was politely assumed. He didn't say he wouldn't bring it or that the hotel cellar didn't stock it. He was gently reminding a foreigner of a state of affairs. "You said Mersault, did you not?"

Chris laughed softly. The war had finally come to Berlin.

"Bring me something from the Rhine."

While he waited he caught himself thinking of New York at this time of year. It was one of the best of the seasons with the air sharp out of polished steel skies. Along Fifth Avenue the shops were beginning to reflect the bright colors of a not too distant Christmas. American girls with their easy stride, the wind snapping skirts about long, swinging legs and whipping pink into cheeks. The football fields with their tiered rows and splashings of crimsons, yellows, blues and browns. The Connecticut countryside, a charcoal drawing on a sheet of blue-white paper. He was homesick. Save for a few days each year in Paris when Jean came over for the annual fashion showing he had spent little time with his wife. He would like to be sitting with her now in a farmhouse before a big fire, drinking a hot toddy and smelling pies and gingerbread in the kitchen. He wanted to walk New York's dirty streets again. To eat cherrystone clams from the pushcart at South Ferry. To stand at the Battery and feel the Atlantic wind as it came tumbling through the Narrows. To see a Moran tug booting a line of barges up the North River. He wanted to eat a steak at Keen's, a frankfurter at Nedicks, a Virginia ham sandwich at the Silver Dollar, and feel the thrusting surge of the crowd in a subway during the rush hour. Hell! He wanted to be home. More than that he wanted to again be at work he really loved. There was no question but that radio was doing a job; different from one ever done before. He had established the bureau and put selected men in key spots. They gathered the news and reported it. It was fast, exacting and sometimes exciting work, but it lacked the solid feel of an edition still warm from the press. He thought of the pastry, made of sugar and egg white, which melted in your mouth and was gone before you really captured the taste. That, to him at least, was radio. It never gave him the feeling of substance. When he reported into the microphone, he sometimes caught himself wondering if anyone was listening.

He finished the last of the pale wine, picked the remaining pieces of cheese up in his fingers, tasting its creamy richness. Then he realized he was waiting and because of this the call, when it came, did not surprise him at all. There had been between them this almost telepathic understanding; a mysterious, wordless communication which, in the beginning, had astonished and then almost frightened him.

"Chris." Across this great distance her voice was clear, unhurried, and as perfectly tailored to her personality as her clothes. "What's going on there? Why can't I get into Germany?"

She made the questions sound completely reasonable. It was a conspiracy to keep her from the circus. She knew perfectly well why she was barred from Germany; why her correspondent had been ousted. But Chris was on the scene and she wanted to hear the answers from him as though he were somehow involved.

"Can you hear me, Chris?" She spoke in rapid, colloquial German to the listening operator, demanding a better connection imperiously. "Chris?"

"I hear you fine, Carol." He rubbed a smile from his mouth. "To coin a phrase, I hear you as though you were in the next room."

"That's better. They kicked my man Sheffield out of Berlin. We haven't had anything but the AP and UP."

He understood that the bizarre nature of this one-sided conversation simply did not occur to her. He was Chris Chandler. She was Carol Hillyard. They had loved and walked together in a communion of their beings. For what had happened she offered no apology, expressed no regret. Her voice was that of a woman speaking to an old friend. She had, he thought musingly, decided to forget the whole thing. It was simpler that way, and besides, there was a war on.

"Don't sit there brooding at the floor or ceiling." She was chiding him for being an obstinate boy. "Answer me."

"I had a drink with Sheffield before he left a couple of weeks ago. He was a good man but you ought to know they wouldn't stand for what he was writing. I understand Knickerbocker is leaving, also."

"Well! Where does that leave us, Chris?"

He took the receiver from his ear and stared at it with honest astonishment. She was making him a part of her immediate problem. She was doing this with no conception of how fantastic it sounded. He felt a grudging admiration for this singleness of purpose.

"Why," he spoke slowly, "I'd say it leaves us just about where it did before." The hell of it was, he told himself, he wasn't angry. "What do you want from me, Carol?"

"I want to know what's happening." She was emphatic. Someone knew something she didn't.

"Why don't you listen to the radio?" He would not deny himself this small satisfaction.

She ignored the gibe. Her tack was as expert as the handling of a racing hull by a skilled yachtsman.

"I finally bought the paper in Washington I've been after."

Manipulating matches and cigarette between the fingers of one hand, he lit the tobacco and drew upon it leisurely. What she had just said was a question and not a statement of fact or a bit of news in which he should be interested. She was making an offer

264

obliquely. Not yet would her pride and will permit her to state it.

"You know,"—his smile was genuine, touched with a wintry sadness—"you're one hell of a girl, Carol."

"I didn't call you from Lausanne to talk about sex." She was silent for the ticking of a couple of seconds. "But thanks for remembering." This was added with a deliberate wistfulness.

There was an interrupting babble of voices as the operators at relay points sought to keep the connection open. While it lasted he thought that from this point on it would be better if he said little and thought less.

"Did you hear what I said about the Washington paper, Chris?" Her voice crystallized through the jumbled sounds.

"Yes. Congratulations. Is that why you called me?"

"You know damn well it isn't, and while we're on the subject, if you hadn't behaved as a piqued debutante none of this would ever have happened. If you had said one word or called me. Why didn't you, Chris?"

"I didn't have a nickel handy." His tone was roughly edged despite his effort to keep it meaningless.

There was a long, tense silence. He could feel the tension stretch the wires tautly between them. Then he heard the sharp intake of her breath. It was a swimmer diving into icy water.

"You can have the Washington paper or the one in New York, Chris. I need you."

This was not said lightly. He understood the effort it had taken her to phrase the small admission. He dropped the cigarette into a tray. She would never believe what this cost him.

"I have a job, Carol." It was said. Done.

"Radio." She made of it a dirty word in five letters. "That's for Nelson Eddy or Joe Penner and you know it."

"Just the same I think I'll stick with what I have." Every instinct told him this was the chance to get back where he belonged—on a paper and in the work for which he had been trained. Just as certainly he knew that if he took it he was lost. "Thanks for thinking of me."

"All right, Chris."

He understood she wasn't conceding a thing. There was no acceptance of a situation in her statement. This was a small impasse, a temporary gap to be bridged at another time.

"Isn't there anything you can do to help me get into Germany, Chris?" She was being appealingly helpless now.

"Your connections are better than mine. Why don't you ask the President to telephone Hitler? That man owes you a couple of favors. After all, you helped elect him."

"Don't be ridiculous." She snapped impatiently but he knew she must be thinking over what he had said. Why should she stop short of asking Roosevelt? "I wonder?" She spoke to herself.

He laughed, gusty, appreciative laughter. "I'll lay odds you will. So long, Carol."

"Now you wait a minute, Chris." This was a command.

He had hung up on her. The sound had been definite and final. The instrument in her hand carried now only the voice of the operator at Liechtenstein asking if the connection had been broken intentionally. She dropped the phone into the nickeled cradle. She was certain he hadn't wanted to refuse her offer. He was sulking in his tent. You know—she didn't speak aloud—I could get you fired from that job. I could call Bill Paley or Aylesworth or whoever is the head of your outfit and have you thrown out on your stubborn, damn ear. Serve you right if I did. These were unspoken words but she thought them.

She picked the phone up again but only called down to have a drink sent up. Talking with him, hearing his voice, she realized she had never really accepted the fact that her relationship with Chris Chandler was over. Sometime, somewhere, they would meet and find each other again. Love didn't fly out the window. Someone only closed the shutters upon it. What had been done could be undone. She had been angry, humiliated because he failed to accept what was obvious. He had run to the first girl who came along. Go to bed with her? Yes. That would have been a normal, logical reaction. But to *marry* her. This was the incomprehensible thing. Between them, she and Chris had compounded the error. It was a mistake but not irreparable.

She walked across the living room of the suite and opened the glass doors upon a balcony. It was cold and she shivered, looking out upon the serene, crystal beauty of Switzerland. At the other end of the lake lay Geneva and the marble pile in which the world had buried the League and much of the hope of mankind. It was a remarkable monument to the dead.

She had come to Lausanne from Paris incredulously shocked by what she had seen and heard in the French capital. She had worked hard, talking with Gamelin and Georges, Petain and Darlan. She drew upon all the resources and influence at her command to open doors at the Quai d'Orsay and wrote with sharp incisiveness of what she saw and heard. She had the prestige of her papers and the advantage of political connections, and used them ruthlessly because she found herself in top-flight competition. A new breed of reporter had broken through the almost solidly masculine ranks. Women like Thompson, Schultz, Tabouis, were writing and men read what they wrote.

She had angered the French because she wrote they were obviously preparing to fight the war of 1914–18 all over again. That was what she had found. More than this, though, she was shocked by the apathy of the French people. They moved and talked like sleepwalkers in a suspended world of unreality. They seemed even without the will to argue among themselves. It was frightening and she wrote it for her papers that way. The fierce Gallic eagerness was gone. In its place there was resignation. She wrote in the heat of indignation and said she didn't think the French Army would fight when challenged. She could and did say these things because she did not have to be impersonal or objective. She could editorialize. She owned the damn papers, didn't she? No one on a desk would dare take a copy pencil to her dispatches. It was a personal, angry form of journalism and Carol Warrington rode her typewriter through the countryside, calling out an alarm.

She left the balcony now at the sound of the door's buzzer and took the drink she had ordered. In the act of lifting it she halted. She had no business to be here, in Switzerland. The war couldn't end where it was like an unfinished game on a checkerboard. If she couldn't get into Germany, she could at least return to France. The French Government wasn't happy with her but she would not be halted at the border. She had an idea that when the German Army moved, it would come again through the lowlands and across Belgium despite Hitler's concern for neutral countries. That was where she or any good reporter should be.

She finished her drink and a smile illuminated her eyes. Let Chris Chandler sit in Berlin. The war could come to Carol Warrington.

She called the porter's desk for transportation and rang for the maid to do her packing. Then she sat down and wrote cables to

267

Washington and New York, changed her mind and put in a telephone call for Stephen Keith. While she waited she absently made a note to let Bootsie know where she was, and then just as absently crumpled the yellow sheet into a ball and tossed it into the wastepaper basket.

XX

THE chronology of Europe's agony was rolled out as from gigantic, mobile presses beneath the clanking tracks of the German armored divisions in their sweep toward the once-shining city of Paris.

In three weeks Hitler had achieved what the Kaiser and Ludendorff could not accomplish in the years between 1914 and November, 1918. His armies stood within thirty-five miles of Paris and no Foch defied them at the Marne.

Moving in the van of the advancing *Panzers*, supplied with a staff, press car and an eager subordinate from the Ministry of Propaganda, Chris thought no war had ever offered such detailed reporting as this one. Every facility was made available to him. The Germans were anxious that the world know of their strength and victories, their extent and devastating effect. He had broadcast from Holland and later, from Antwerp and Brussels. There had been remarkably little censoring of what he wanted to say. From the Nazi point of view it was all good, anyhow. He understood he was contributing to institutional publicity on a global scale, but the facts were indisputable. Never had a great country such as France offered less resistance to an invader. England would have to fight this one alone.

Southward, out of Paris, almost half a million refugees streamed in a blind, unreasoning panic. They jammed the roads until all forward movement ground to a halt. Then, in moments of spasmodic fury, the great, human serpent would writhe forward in a screaming, clawing frenzy in which men and women were beaten senseless for a foot of advancing ground. Children were trampled. Babies were born in fields and ditches and their mothers quietly bled to death.

Back in Paris now, Carol tried to write the story of this incredible flight and found she, almost, no longer believed what she had seen. The exodus certainly had no modern counterpart. The fleeing went on foot, bicycles, motor scooters, in jaunty convertibles and gleaming Renaults or Rolls. They pushed handcarts loaded with their household goods or balanced a bedspring and mattress on a barrow. They carried their infants in arms, on their shoulders or led the older ones by the hand, and they streamed into the road from Orléans to Blois, toward Tours, Samur, Trelaze on the road to Nantes. The wealthy sat back in their limousines, smoking fat cigars, eating from picnic hampers, holding jewel cases in their expensively sheathed laps and impatiently demanded that the chauffeurs blow their horns and clear a passage for them through the trudging mob. Then, the fuel ran out and the big cars stalled. The irresistible force of the column behind pushed them off the road and into the ditches. The dazed occupants screamed senselessly at their drivers, who frequently spat scorn into their faces. Then, still holding on to their furs, their monogrammed cases, fuming spitefully at their escorts, they joined this desperate procession in ridiculously inadequate high heels. The useless cars were senselessly looted by those who followed and then the articles abandoned, and the trail was littered with cigarette lighters pulled from the dash, small vases of cut-glass designed to hold a single bud, Thermos flasks and chrome ashtrays. Overhead the German planes whined and spun in search of the French troops which might have used the road.

Stalking the refugees like silent, predatory cats came hunger, thirst and exhaustion. The peasants hid their livestock and refused a cup of milk, a single egg, and sometimes a tin of water in exchange for eagerly outthrust francs which now had no value. There was no food, no rest, no place in which to hide from the unnamed terror. Men and women dropped as though clubbed and lay face down without movement as the dead shuffle of feet passed them by. They halted sometimes without life in their eyes to stare about them as though awakening from a dream in a strange place. Or they sometimes screamed with a hysterical madness and no one paid any attention to the cries. Fear had dulled all sympathy. Man was no longer man's brother or even kin. They were hostile strangers in a lunatic world. They were not even sure now from what they tried to escape but were driven by a lemming impulse to self-destruction.

On that spring day when the Germans marched into Paris, the city was at its luminous best. It was such a day as comes to that city when the air seems filled with the sound of tinkling wind-bells, and fat, white clouds gathered as though drawn by the majestic cadence of a great harp. Only the treble note of traffic was stilled; the laughter which seems to be present even when no one laughs, the tempo of heels upon sidewalks and the movement of a barge in the Seine, which make up the voice of a city, were absent.

German troops marched with a disciplined precision but their eyes were filled with the wonder of what they had done and were doing. This the Führer had promised them. Paris would echo to the boots of the Third Reich, which would last a thousand years.

These were no battle-stained legions but crisp, fresh troops that knew only the shining pride of victory. This was their city. Hitler had no intention of destroying that which must hereafter be vassal to him. The hobnails rang a steady, swelling paean of triumph. Paris watched them march with wonder, anguish, shame and tears. The Germans were indifferent to both scorn and sorrow, humiliation and fear. They strode as blond Nordic supermen across the face of the earth.

There was that first uncertainty and confusion, but German efficiency brought quick order with directives, requisitions and inflexible pronouncements. When it became apparent the Nazis had no intention of looting, burning, raping and pillaging, the iron shutters were rolled up again. The tables came out on sidewalk cafés, shops were opened. The faltering rhythm of the city was cautiously resumed. The defiant went underground and the little whores appeared with gathering assurance.

In the Crillon Hotel the Germans set up their headquarters. The officers of the Ministry of Propaganda took over all communications. Regulations were posted. Food moved into the markets.

Everywhere there were soldiers. They filled the shops, buying perfume, silk stockings, lingerie—anything that was for sale—with their occupation currency. They filled the cafés, the bordellos, and walked in pairs or groups along the boulevards. They all had cameras and they took thousands and thousands of photographs to be sent home to German families as proof of what they had done.

The young German major studied Carol Warrington with curiosity and open admiration. Sitting on the opposite side of his desk, she returned his gaze with a level, self-possessed stare. On the clean surface of the desk there was a cardboard folder. He tapped it with the manicured nail of an index finger and had the uncomfortable feeling she was laughing at him.

"You have not been a friend of The Third Reich, Miss Warrington." He spoke in precise, stilted English as though afraid of making a mistake.

She reached over and took a cigarette from a silver box on the desk. He reached for a lighter, started to rise and then caught himself. She waited, holding the cigarette between her fingers, and then dropped it indifferently to the floor. He flushed, and to cover his confusion, flipped back the folder and pretended to study it frowningly.

"What is it you really want, Major?" She made her tone one of pleasant inquiry rather than impatience.

"I am deciding your situation here as I have done with the other American correspondents in Paris."

She nodded toward the folder. "Don't tell me you have carried my dossier with you all the way from Berlin on the chance I might be in Paris when you arrived?"

"No." Pride in the German method caused him to unbend slightly. "The information here was transmitted to us from Berlin early this morning. Yesterday, naturally, your name came up in the registrations of the foreign correspondents. You have been very unsympathetic. Why?"

"I didn't know the Nazis expected sympathy."

"I could make things extremely unpleasant for you here, Miss Warrington."

She grinned at him. "It won't do, Major."

He didn't understand the remark or the expression of almost elfin amusement.

"Please?" He inclined his head as though he hadn't heard.

"I mean there's no point in your trying to behave like a character out of an old Von Stroheim movie. You're much too young, too good-looking. Your head isn't bald and you don't wear a monocle. You're lousy in the role. Just be a fine, clean-cut representative of the master race." She winked at him deliberately and his cheeks colored like those of an embarrassed girl. "I suppose you could make things unpleasant for me, but you won't."

"And why not, please?" He was amiably curious.

"Because you don't want to be a Hun or a Boche or any of the beastly things the world has a habit of calling the Germans every quarter of a century or so. You want to be liked, admired and understood."

His mouth actually dropped open for a moment and then he took refuge in being brisk. He pressed a button on the desk and an orderly almost seemed to snap through the door. The major gave him the folder for filing, and when he had saluted and left, he turned again to Carol.

"I have never had an opportunity to talk with an American girl this way."

The statement called for no reply and so she made none, watching him with a small, quizzical smile. He was threatening, she thought, to slip back into the character he had created in his imagination. In a moment he would probably offer her a drink and suggest dinner. This was the traditional role of the conqueror with an attractive woman. He couldn't resist it.

"It seems," he continued, "you are more than a reporter. The papers—you own them?"

She nodded and said nothing.

"You are one of the wealthiest women in America. What are the Hillyard Enterprises, please?"

She wasn't surprised he knew these things. The German passion for detail would have set all this down long ago. She made him repeat the question.

"I am the Hillyard Enterprises." She made the statement without emphasis. "I suppose what puzzles you is why I work at the job of a reporter? I like it. Also, I don't know of anyone who can do what I am doing any better. If I did I'd hire him."

"I see." It was obvious he didn't understand. A European woman of great wealth and beauty wouldn't voluntarily submit herself to such work. He picked up a typewritten sheaf, considered the pages for a moment and then handed them to her. "You may cable this as it is."

"Thank you, Major."

He shook his head. "It is no favor I do you. That is a vivid and frightening story of the refugees from Paris. I am pleased that you do not lie in it. German planes could have bombed and strafed those civilians. They did not do so. We are not the barbarians you have told of in your newspapers."

"I wrote what I saw. There was no machine-gunning from the air. The tragedy was the tragedy of the French themselves."

"What I must say now is unpleasant. The Ministry no longer looks with tolerance upon your presence in France."

"Good." She smiled her immediate pleasure. "The war is over, here. I want to get out and to England."

He regarded her with complete and undisguised astonishment. "As you say, the war is over. Why should you go to England?"

"The war is over here, Major. You haven't even started down the road yet." She stood up and he rose automatically and with an un-answered question in his eyes. "Could you tell me"—her voice was even—"if there is a radio correspondent by the name of Christopher Chandler in Paris? He was with your troops."

"Chandler. Yes. I knew him in Berlin." He took a typewritten list from a drawer, his eyes running down the names. "He is at the Hotel Ambassador. You are friends?"

She smiled softly. "Yes, I guess so."

He walked with her to the door and opened it for her just a little self-consciously. He had an idea he should be stiffly polite and formal but she made it difficult. She didn't seem to realize their relative positions and the importance of his in this captive city.

"Would you..." He stumbled with the question. "Could you have dinner with me?" Embarrassment was in every word.

She controlled a desire to laugh at his eager awkwardness. He had forgotten, for the moment, his Aryan supremacy and was just a nice young German, with a rank beyond his years, confessing a loneliness in this alien and hostile land.

"I'm sorry, Major." She touched his arm almost reassuringly. "I have a date. I think." He was puzzled by the expression. "Date," she added, "is colloquial, American English. It means an appointment, a rendezvous. I hope."

By comparison the house on the Île St. Louis was modern. This only meant that it was a little short of one hundred years old; a newcomer among those which had stood here for a couple of centuries.

On a business trip ten or so years ago Jim Haney had bought it for the Hillyard Enterprises. Since then it had been used by a succession of executives from Mark's many corporations as a headquarters when they were in Paris. It was permanently staffed by a manservant and cook. The concierge had small quarters just within the gate leading to a flagged courtyard. They had remained, undisturbed by the terror-stricken prophecies of what to expect when the Germans came, as had most of the residents on the Île. This was their fortress; the Seine their moat. About them the world, if it must, could convulse itself. They were of it but apart and felt a small, superior scorn for those who lived elsewhere.

What had been fine and good, Haney had retained. What necessarily yielded to modernization—the bathrooms, kitchen, plumbing, lighting—had been accomplished without sacrificing the medieval quality of a sanctuary. Windows, facing the Seine, had been widened and made into casements which could be flung open to the day. A worn staircase, tilting steeply upward from the courtyard's polished cobbles, was left for the sake of balance, but a small elevator was set unobtrusively behind a heavy door of rare Flemish carving.

The exterior of the building remained as it had been, save for a few blended patches where necessary. The interior walls had been replastered in muted tones and Haney had indulged himself in bright splashes of color. He had bought such paintings as pleased his eye and for no other reason. The effect was instinctively right and comfortable.

Here, on the Île, the streets were little more than narrow stone corridors, and the granite quays at the water's edge had accumulated centuries of stain. The trees grew up from the banks and were regularly cropped so they would not close the view from the three- and four-story buildings. These sometimes appeared to lean toward each other in rakish attitudes of conviviality. On nights when there was a half- or a quarter-moon and the myriad chimney pots seemed comical hats, they gave the appearance of boozy vagabonds canting their heads together in bawdy song.

The first time she visited the Île, Carol dismissed it as dirty, dark, damp and uncomfortable; infested with rats, probably, and a variety of characters the Greenwich Villagers used to call bohemians. Later, she discovered the beauty of the black opal nights, the curious sensation of suspension from the familiar Paris. Her astonishment over what Haney had bought gave way to a surprised pleasure and an admiration for his taste and judgment.

Now, standing before the open windows, she was waiting with a small nervousness and uncertainty she was unwilling to confess. She turned away impatiently and poured herself a drink of some fine old cognac Jim had stored away. She took it as a medicine, a sedative. It was the third she had swallowed in the past half-hour and was without effect. This, she told herself, is ridiculous. Why should I be trembling like some eager girl for the arrival of her lover? Yet she knew everything she had done during the early evening had been in preparation for the moment when Chris would walk through the door. Her bath had been a sensual experience, the hot water his hands. Her dress and make-up had been selected and applied with only the thought of the effect upon him. Dinner had been ordered, the wine chosen, with the memory of what he liked. Once, she had halted to stare at herself in a mirror with incredulous astonishment, realizing that for the first time in her life she was deliberately con- triving an effect and attempting to please someone. The ridiculous, syruplike lines about an idiot named Alice Ben-Bolt, who trembled with fear at someone's frown and wept with delight when he gave her a smile, flashed through her mind. All right. That was how she felt. She only wanted him to come into the room and take her with- out a word. No hello. No how are you? Nothing. It would be as it had been and there would be little need, at first, for talk.

She had called the Hotel Ambassador but hadn't asked to speak with him. She left a message. Carol Hillyard had called. Could Mr.

Chandler have dinner with her at eight o'clock? This question and her address. Nothing more.

She hadn't expected a reply and none was made. Now she began to torment herself with the speculation that perhaps the message had not been delivered. But she was impatient with herself. Of course it had. She had impressed its importance on the clerk. It had been given to him. He had read it. What then had Chris Chandler thought or said?

She glanced at her watch. It was only quarter after eight. This was a reasonably polite leeway. This, also, was an evasion. You're being pretty stupid, Carol. Chris's life has been regulated by a clock. Edition time has been marked by the hours of the day. Eight o'clock was eight o'clock and not quarter after or quarter of.

She lit a cigarette from the burning stub between her fingers. The smoke tasted like moldy straw fired. An almost uncontrollable nausea crept into her stomach. I'd like another drink, she told herself. but if I take it and get tight, Chris, if he does come, will know why I did it. I will not let him see me standing here, naked and panting.

At the window again she watched the dark tide of the river. In it the reflection of the lights seemed to float like fluttering, amber petals. She shook herself. There was something hypnotic about the quiet movement.

Chris. Chris. She whispered the name to herself. Of all the men I have known, you were the one I walked with and only wanted to be a woman. Why didn't you recognize that and save us both? There was a time. It could have been done.

She snapped the cigarette into the night and it made a small trail of sparks. This was complete self-delusion. It was a pitiful lie. She was what she was and nothing could have changed the pattern. Chris had said it long ago. Years back in that dirty little hole of a restaurant on Cherry Street. She could remember each word. He had said it lightly although, she understood now, it had not been meant that way. "You have a devouring instinct. I have one for self-preservation."

Alone by the window now she knew he wasn't coming. Angrily she told herself she had known he wouldn't come even as she left the message at the hotel. Even as she had bathed, dressed and ordered dinner for him, she had been pretending. It had been an instinctive wish-fulfillment. She was playing house like an idiot child. Everything she had done after leaving the German headquarters that afternoon had been a frightening exhibition of self-induced hallucination. In her bath she had shut her eyes and he had made love to her. As she dressed he took off her clothes. When she ordered dinner he had sat at the table with her. That was how far she had permitted imagination to trick her.

Behind her there was the sound of a step, but she recognized it as that of the manservant, Paul. He made a pretense of seeing that the ice bucket was full, the ashtrays empty. Discreetly, without voicing it, he was asking about dinner and the expected guest. She ignored his presence and after a moment heard him leave the room.

She poured a large drink of brandy into a highball glass and drank most of it. It hit her stomach with a stiffening jolt as it was meant to do. She was fighting herself quietly and without reckless anger. The telephone was there. The Hotel Ambassador no farther away than her hand's reach.

She bit upon her lip until the sweet taste of blood was in her mouth, and when she finished the cognac, the liquor was fire in the small wound. With complete astonishment she discovered she was cursing silently. The words formed themselves in her mind without fury. They were filth and had no real meaning but created slimy images. There was a perverse satisfaction in shaping them with this detachment. She could even wonder where and at what time she had ever heard them spoken or seen them written on a wall. She was attempting to shock herself by drooling this maniacal sewage, covering herself with it. She wanted to feel dirty and abased. This was the ultimate humiliation, prostrating Carol before Carol.

She drew a long, shuddering breath and fought for control. A really demented person, caged within a cell, must behave to himself in such a manner. The thought frightened her.

When she could face herself she turned and calmly studied her features in a mirror. They should be, she felt, contorted into a hideous mask. Instead, the eyes were clear and serene, the skin softly lighted with a healthy glow.

She went to the telephone, picked it up and waited until the operator answered. Then, she dropped it within the metal prongs without replying.

How close she had come to a complete surrender. If Chris had walked into the room five or ten minutes ago she would have behaved with an idiot's rapturous delight. Take me, Chris. I'll do anything you say. Be anything you want. Let me be your love. That's a word for Carol. I need you. Nothing that has happened has a meaning without you. Tell me you love me. Make the word fresh and shining just by saying it. I'm no different from any other woman. I need to be wanted, cherished, adored. My life is empty without your love. Fill it for me, Chris.

"Good God!" She made the exclamation aloud and the sound of her voice startled her. She wheeled and faced herself accusingly in the mirror. "You would have said something like that, you little fool." Her tone was normally conversational. "If he had asked it, you were ready to go tripping down the garden path in a flowered apron to open the gate when he came home in the evening. If you ever see Chris again, thank him. Do you understand? Get down on your knees and say: Thank you Chris, my darling, for not coming that night."

In the butler's pantry the man, Paul, heard the sound but did not understand the words. No one was there so she must be talking to herself. He shrugged and went on with the work of arranging some flowers in a vase for her bedroom.

Still before the mirror, Carol touched the inside of her lip with a finger tip. It came away slightly stained with crimson. She winked companionably at her twin. Bleed away, you silly bitch. No one but the two of us will ever know how close you came to making a complete fool of yourself. I think, maybe, we ought to get a little tight now in celebration. Not everyone is saved from such a slippery precipice. It's a hell of a thing to do alone, though. Get tight, I mean.

She was about to turn away from the glass and then caught herself with a slight frown. She was still being pretty stupid. Why should she be alone? Let us seek out the enemy and make him ours. What was his name? Ulrich. Major Gerhard Ulrich. It was possible he could be in his office at this time of night. If he wasn't, someone would certainly know where he could be reached or how to get a message to him. The Germans had a genuis for such organizational details.

She lit a cigarette and reached for the telephone.

Rain slapped the heavy glass in the small window and the wind whipped it away into a flying spume. High in the night's uncharted sky the plane climbed for the altitude to take it over the Pyrenees. The motors whined an unceasing complaint and small tongues of flame licked out from the exhausts like excited, bright blue lizards.

As always, when flying, Chris was uncomfortable. He had never been able to relax in a plane. This was no luxury flight of peace-time service. The seats, most of them filled, were worn and barely cushioned. The passengers had brought their own food, and many of them, a bottle of wine or brandy. No pert young stewardess came to tuck a pillow at their backs or set a tray before them. Those aboard were couriers, a few minor officials, a couple of Spanish officers and a civilian Chris recognized as a Gestapo man he had known in Berlin. Although the plane was in Spanish service, the pilot and crew were German.

Chris rubbed his head against the nubbed fabric, scratching it lazily. As much as he disliked flying, this old *Lufthansa* ship was the only way out of France at the moment. The flight was from Paris to Madrid to Lisbon. In Portugal he could get a plane to the Azores and then Bermuda to New York. A break in the rain cleared the window and he looked down into the black pit. They were high and if there were lights below he could not see them. That was Europe these days. The dark continent.

The trip home had been weeks in the making and the result of cables and telephone conversations with Joe Garnett in New York. They both understood that the war, insofar as France was concerned, was over for the time being. It would go on in the Balkans, in Africa, in England and on the seas, but right now the news out of France would be so strictly censored it would not be worth reporting. The big push would be directed against England now that she stood alone, and Chris had wanted to go to London. Joe had turned the request down.

"Don't worry about your job." Garnett's voice spanned the ocean. "You have one with us for as long as you want it. You've been at this pretty hard. Come home for a couple of months, get acquainted with your wife. You're well known over here now as a result of the broadcasts. If you'd like to do it, the bureau can set up a lecture tour. One of those 'Inside Europe' things. The boys who have come back are cleaning up on the circuit. Leave Miller where he is, in Berlin, to fill out for you. London can wait for a while. Anyhow, Ed Murrow is doing such a hell of a job from there right now that I don't see how anyone could top him."

He stretched his legs now in the crowded space and twisted his body at a more comfortable angle. There was a bottle of cognac in his canvas bag. He thought idly about a drink and then decided he didn't really want one.

Jean. Saying the name to himself made him feel good. It was funny but you could go to bed with a girl for years and not really know her as you did when she became your wife. It was hard to define. He wasn't exactly sure why. Atavism, probably. You made a cave and shared it. It belonged to you both and suddenly became something more than simply a place in which to make love.

He had sent a cable but hadn't tried to call her. The flight schedule, once he reached Lisbon, was too uncertain to give her an arrival date. He'd have to take his chances and that might mean hanging around Portugal for a couple of weeks.

Home. He smiled to himself. I'm getting to be a pushover for that word. Somehow, it had achieved a meaning. Always before it had been a sound made with the tongue and lips. Edgar Guest wrote poems about it. Dave Guion made it a place where the buffalo roam and the skies are not cloudy or gray. There must be something to it. So damn many persons were preoccupied with the idea. He wondered why it had taken him so long to get around to the notion.

He and Jean could have it—a house, a couple of dogs, a place in Connecticut with some ground around it. It was something they had never discussed. The country was a place where you went to someone else's house for a weekend. He and Jean had been tuned to the city. They ate, slept, drank, worked and made love to its tempo. Hell! They could even have children. Financially he was better off than he had ever been before. His expense account had covered almost everything in Berlin. His need for money had been small and his checks had all been deposited in the New York bank. He was loaded. He laughed aloud at the notion. Chris Chandler knee-deep in the green stuff.

He was tickled by this fancy and decided he did want a drink. Unzipping the bag, he took out a bottle of Martell. It was getting hard to find in Paris. The Germans certainly had themselves a ball. He didn't think there was a bottle of champagne left in the city. The cognac was good, mellow and warming. He remembered how Jean liked to make a small ritual of burning a lump of sugar in a spoon of brandy and dropping the flaming liquid into a demitasse.

Thinking about Jean he wondered what they would say to each other. Not at the airport but later when they were alone. It struck him that the vocabulary of love was a limited one with which to describe the emotion over which men and women killed each other and empires were rocked. Man should speak of love in great hyperbole. It cried for the sweep of a plumed hat and extravagant phrasing. Instead, when you came right down to it, the whole thing was compressed into a few words. I love you. There were minor variations. I adore you. You're my life. After that you began to repeat yourself. The miracle was, he thought, that the words did not grow trite through repetition. Each man or woman minted them freshly or cut them like bright flowers from his own secret garden as an offering to his love.

It was cold in the cabin. He took his overcoat from the rack and wrapped it about his shoulders. Muffled and warm, he began to think about his future. It wasn't, he decided, something he could talk over with Garnett. Joe was dedicated to radio. It was the winged Mercury carrying messages to all mankind. If he wanted a future he could probably have it with Joe and the broadcasting company. He knew this wouldn't satisfy him. He wanted a paper in his hands; a thing to feel, smell and read. All the words tossed into space and vanishing to reappear through the world's loud-speakers could not take the place of that. There was the controlled excitement of a big story suddenly breaking right on top of a deadline. A fast make-over of page one. A good man on rewrite batting the copy out in short takes to his desk. That had guts and substance. All the jokes about today's newspaper being tomorrow's wrapper for fish couldn't change it.

He reached into his pocket for cigarettes, and with the package, his fingers closed about a slip of paper. He took it out. The words he knew by heart. *Miss Hillyard called. Could you have dinner with her at eight o'clock?*

He told himself there was really nothing he could have done about the invitation. He was scheduled on this flight. This was a petty evasion of the truth and he knew it. He could have telephoned. There had even been time in which to see her for a few minutes at least. He began to feel a little ridiculous. What had he been afraid of? He had run. There was no other word for it. He had fled, figuratively bent over like a panicked virgin clutching her pelvic virtue.

He lit the cigarette and a small, wry expression of amusement hovered about his mouth. He was making a big dramatic thing of this. He was Eliza scampering over the ice pursued by a phantom

Simon Legree. From Lausanne she had offered him the paper in New York or the newly acquired one in Washington. Wasn't that what he wanted? He could have taken the job and their relationship would have been no more and no less personal than he made it. Carol's pride would never permit her to make a fool of herself. He wasn't sure, though, what would have saved Chris Chandler.

He blew softly upon the cigarette's coal and watched the fire consume the paper. What he had with Jean he wanted to hold. It was good, satisfying, warmly decent. It was the love a man and woman needed and did not feed upon itself. Carol was the flame. You never quite forgot its touch and once burned, you stood at a respectful distance. He had an idea men didn't ever fully recover from the Carols of this world but he wasn't sure they could survive with them, either.

He put the cigarette in a battered tray recessed in the seat's arm, and slowly tore the message into small pieces which would defy patching and even memory.

XXI

ON THIS day in September the rain whipped and raced through the still broken streets of Manila. It drove with booming sound into the small, empty caverns of bombed structures, tore at the ragged fronds of palms and sounded like scattered B-B shot on the windows of a military hospital.

In the great bay of Tokyo the Japanese delegation stood in miserable silence until brusquely motioned forward to a table on the deck of the battleship *Missouri*. One by one they put their signatures to the formal articles of capitulation and the world's greatest war was at an end.

At Harkness, in the Virginia Piedmont, the approaching autumn was wrapped in the soft, clinging night with a star-blazoned sky.

A small breeze which had run carelessly from the distant mountains played across the warm earth and tugged with nagging insistence at the starched curtains in the windows of a darkened room.

Unrelated as these things seemed to be, they were part of a design. The pattern, long in the making, was not yet complete, but it was being slowly, inexorably blocked in by the indelible imprint of the years.

On a bed in the Manila hospital Carol Warrington lay and listened to the radio broadcasting an account of the Japanese surrender. She was drawn, hollow-cheeked, yellowed and too bright of eye from the fever of malaria and dysentery, yet she fumed helplessly against this confinement. The great, final chapter of the war was breaking and she didn't even have the strength to go to the bathroom by herself. It was outrageous and unthinkable that this was happening to her.

For almost five years she had followed the blazing orbit of this conflict. It had taken her through the London blitz, across part of Africa, up the long, bitter road from Sicily to Rome and into the Pacific. She had drawn upon unsuspected sources of energy. She had cajoled, flattered, pleaded and used every influence at her command to get her way. For her papers she had written with great compassion and understanding. Her war was a conflict of individuals; the lonely and sometimes frightened men in the line. She went where no woman had gone before, and in this she was not alone. There were other good reporters of her sex. Marguerite Higgins, of the *Herald Tribune*. Martha Gelhorn. They were a breed new to war and they did a job. After they recovered from their first sense of outrage and invasion the men, soldier and correspondent alike, accepted them for what they were. They were good reporters who would ruthlessly beat your pants off on a story if you weren't careful. The world, once so sharply divided between men and women, no longer existed and would not return.

From thousands of miles away she held a tight rein on the policies of her papers. She left good men behind on the city desks and in the chairs of managing editor, but nothing they did escaped her attention. At her orders Jim Haney, wanting now only to retire but staying on because she needed him, picked up half a dozen newspapers in medium-sized cities throughout the country. They, as did the metropolitan dailies she owned, reflected the passionate convictions of Carol Warrington. Her dispatches were syndicated features in them all and her name rode proudly at the masthead. The New York paper served as the fountainhead and from it, through Stephen Keith, flowed the electric current of her personality to each of her other papers. She drove her employees as she did herself and demanded perfection.

She tried to burrow beneath the blankets now as a sudden chill of this damnable fever gripped her. There was no warmth in the bed. A couple of days ago she had looked at herself in a mirror. An old woman with lusterless hair, gaunt and haunted, stared back. She almost dropped the glass. That witch could not be Carol Warrington. The doctor's soothing assurance that the condition was temporary did nothing to break the uneasy spell of having left herself behind somewhere. She had burned with the hot torch of ambition to report this war better than anyone else; to make the voice of her papers loud and clear. What she saw in the mirror was an ugly piece of slag. She shook her head in mute misery at the young doctor's words.

"You'll get over this, Miss Warrington." He seemed cheerfully oblivious of the specter. "The dysentery will clear up, although God knows what variety of amoeba you have running around in your guts. The malaria will reoccur now and then over the years. You'll have to expect that. Don't worry about your hair or skin. The schoolgirl complexion hasn't been lost forever. You're in good shape compared to most of the cases we have here."

Privately, she thought he was an idiotic, lighthearted ass, but nodded listlessly and said nothing.

Lying here, listening to the broadcast, she wanted to yell and curse her sense of frustration. To have come this far and not be in at the kill was the final irony. She crossed wasted arms beneath her head and stared at the ceiling. All right. It was over. The important thing now was to get back to the States. She had newspapers to run, a small empire to consolidate or expand. How the hell was she going to get a priority on a plane out of here? She began sorting out the most influential persons she knew, the wires to pull, the pressure to be exerted. She didn't want the long, slow trip back on a hospital ship. There wasn't time for that. Someone would have to be bumped to make room for Carol Warrington and she didn't give a damn who it was.

She struggled to pull herself into an upright position. The paper in Washington was her first interest now. It needed an aggressive man on the desk. She didn't trust Truman or some of the men he had around him. This could be another Harding administration. Yet, she had an idea her Washington paper should be local in character, a small-town sheet. Everything that happened in Washington should interest it and be reported.

The effort of sitting up wearied her and she slid down again. A few weeks in Virginia would straighten her out. Bootsie and Carol-Anne. My God! She'd be a visitor from another planet. She had seen Bootsie and her daughter only once in all this time. They had met her in New York as she came through on her way to the West Coast and the Pacific. It had been a miserable time of trying to get acquainted and no one behaving quite naturally. No one, she caught herself, except Carol-Anne, who would have nothing to do with the polite charade. She had regarded her mother with a cool, appraising interest, as though trying to make up her mind whether they were going to like each other. The physical resemblance was startling. The same hair, eyes, coloring. They shared these. But, and Carol smiled to herself, Carol-Anne didn't seem to consider her mother's comment on this as a compliment. Searching her memory now for a date, Carol was startled by the realization that Carol-Anne was thirteen. Her mannerisms, the inflection of her speech, were those of Bootsie. When she laughed it was his laughter. This was only natural. There had been no opportunity for her to imitate, unconsciously, her mother. Well, there was a lot of time ahead of them all. They'd get to know each other. She'd go down to Court House from Washington and spend a few weeks resting.

Damn that Chris Chandler! She bit the words off angrily and it never occurred to her how illogical was the sequence of thought. Washington meant the paper for which she had found no time during the past years. The paper meant Chris and no one else. He could give it the character it lacked. He alone would understand what she wanted. Washington was a small town, made up of people from small towns. She would make this paper unique. It would cover the national and international scene but at the same time be a personal journal for those who lived and worked in the Capitol. Nothing local would be too unimportant to print and it would keep a hard, bright light on Congress and the White House. She needed Chris for this particular job and he knew it. Once, she tried to remember how long ago, she had written him from London in care of the broadcasting company. In the letter she made a straightforward offer and made no reference to the time in Paris when they might have sat

287

down and talked everything over. She had fought to keep the letter crisply impersonal. He had never replied. The paths she had followed as the war marched steadily across the Pacific had frequently crossed his but they had not come face to face; although a little effort on his part could have brought about a meeting. She had made an offer. He was too smart not to understand that without saying so she had included herself. Apparently he wanted neither her nor the paper. She didn't really believe this. At least, she didn't want to believe it. This was a time of great confusion and nothing could be seen in its proper perspective. Now the war was over. Everything could be re-evaluated, calmly, dispassionately. Chris was stubborn but he was no fool. A newspaper was his life. She'd talk with Stephen Keith in New York. Her eyes closed wearily.

In the dark bedroom at Harkness, Carol-Anne Warrington pulled the light covering to her chin and sighed rapturously. She was wildly, ecstatically in love with an exercise boy by the name of Davie Morton. He was old, of course, seventeen, and only last year, when she had been twelve, he had been patronizing and called her kid when no one was around. When she was with her father or Uncle John, he spoke her name, Carol-Anne, with a sly, mocking deference that had once caused Bootsie to regard him with a sharp curiosity.

Davie, she thought, didn't give a damn about anything except horses. He was as cocky as a bantam and with the darkly handsome features of a Romany lad. She thought he would look wonderful with a gold ring in his ear. This year he would move up to an apprentice jockey for Harkness, and perhaps ride at Hialeah during the winter meet. Then, in the summer, they would all go to Belmont. In a couple of years, she speculated dreamily, she would marry him. He could bring his things to the big house and they'd all live together.

He was fresh. She laughed softly and wriggled within the covers. That afternoon they had been down at the paddock, hanging on the railed fence and watching the young horses as they raced and challenged each other with playful rearings. His elbow had slid along the bar until it touched her breast. He had pretended he didn't know what he was doing and she gave no sign. But the contact had sent a sudden, trembling shiver through her. Afraid of betraying her excitement, she had dropped to the ground and strolled indifferently back

288

toward the barns while he remained on the fence, staring fixedly at the colts.

She slid her hand up now over the sheer linen nightgown and cupped the hard swelling with a quick, fierce pressure. She was always astonished by the development. One day, or so it seemed, she had been as flat as Davie with nothing but little brown, acornlike nubs there. Then this had happened. Martha Harkness had explained everything to her but it didn't make much sense. It was like a setter bitch coming into heat or a mare in season. She had an idea it ought to be different with people.

She frowned. In a few weeks she was going away to school. That meant leaving her father, Harkness and Davie—everything she loved —and there was no telling what might happen while she was away. Davie was a stinker. He would probably get himself another girl. They hung around him all the time whenever he was in the village. They drank malts and cokes they didn't want just to sit with him at the drugstore fountain. She didn't look forward to Stuart Hall, at Staunton. It was cold there in the winter, with snow and ice piled high and winds freezing the mountains into ugly lumps. Girls schools were silly places anyhow. Maybe, she explored the notion, she and Davie could get married. Maybe, if she let him, he could get her into trouble and then her father would have to let them get married.

She giggled at the idea. The servants would have to call her Mrs. Morton. She put a fist to her mouth and bit softly on the knuckles. Bootsie would run Davie off of Harkness with a whip if he even suspected what she was thinking. It wasn't likely he would let Carol-Anne Warrington marry an apprentice jockey or even a jockey, for that matter.

She sighed, thinking how complex life became after you grew up. All of a sudden the world became a place of fences and boundaries, marking where you could go and what you could do. Her thoughts began to chase each other as erratically as a puppy racing for its tail. Maybe Stuart Hall wouldn't be too bad. There was the military school in Staunton and another at Fork Union. They had parades and dances and on Sunday the cadets came to call. The brothers of some of her friends were there and so she'd probably have a chance to meet a lot of boys. Carol was on her way home. That was a funny thing. She never thought of her as Mother but always as

Carol. Maybe it was because her father never said "your mother." He spoke of her as Carol.

He had a telegram or something from her. It had been telephoned from the Western Union office in the village and after he hung up he sat in the big leather chair, slumping way down as he always did when he was thinking, staring out of the window.

"Carol wants to know if we'd like to meet her in New York. Would you like to go?"

"Did she say she wanted to see us?" Carol-Anne's question was direct and without any particular interest.

"No." Bootsie studied his daughter with surprise. She had Carol's trick of cutting to the core of a thing. "She asked if *we'd* like to meet *her* there. I guess there's a difference. Is that what you meant?"

"Yes." Carol-Anne faced him. "And I don't want to go to New York, do you?"

Bootsie held out his hand, and when she took it a little reluctantly he pulled her to a perch on the chair's arm. She leaned against him comfortably.

"No." He spoke slowly. "I don't particularly want to go to New York."

"Then I don't think we should." She was quietly emphatic. "We did, once before. Remember? It was ghastly." That was a word currently enjoying her favor. She repeated it. "Just ghastly. We didn't know what to say to each other. It was like putting three strangers in a room and expecting them to be friends just because they're together. It was ghastly."

She slid from the chair's arm and walked to the French doors opening on a terrace. He studied the fine trimness of her adolescent figure. She was in her favorite dress, jodhpurs and a boy's flannel shirt.

"Don't you have any dresses?" He was mildly curious.

She turned. "Of course, Aunt Martha keeps buying them all the time. There's a whole closetful. That's another reason I don't want to go to New York. Dresses! The only thing I like about New York is Abercrombie & Fitch."

"Do you have everything you need for school?" He reached for his pipe, thinking how he was going to miss her.

"I guess so." She was indifferent. "Do you and Carol love each other?"

The directness of the question startled him. Slowly he unfolded

290

the pouch of oiled silk and worked the tobacco into the pipe's bowl. She was waiting for an answer.

"That's a hard question to answer, honey."

"I wouldn't think so. Either you do or you don't. I'd know if I was in love."

"The word doesn't mean just one thing. It's like, maybe, the way you make a stew. A lot of stuff goes into it." He winked at her. "That's the old armchair philosopher a-talkin'."

"You're funny." She smiled. "You're funny, sometimes, and nice to be with and I'd think any woman would be glad to have you for a husband. I would. Did you and Carol go off on dates when you were young, dancing and smooching around in a car? Did you like each other?"

"Yes, honey." He drew upon the pipe, tasting the rich bite of the tobacco. "I think we liked each other better than any two persons in the world. We still do. Maybe that's as far as it ever went. Maybe that's as far as it was supposed to go. With someone like Carol you never really know."

"When you're together, do you and Carol love each other. Like man and wife, I mean. You know."

He jerked himself upright in the chair and stared at her. "I know what you mean." His voice was almost sharp. "But I'm damned if I know how you do."

"Girls talk about things." She was undisturbed. "You said I could have Cajun Girl at Stuart Hall. Did you mean it?"

He understood this was no unconscious irrelevancy. She had changed the subject deliberately because she sensed her question had disturbed and troubled him. He found himself in the ridiculous position of being grateful. In so many ways she was like Carol. This trick of maneuvering so deftly that the other person was always a little off balance. He rose from the chair.

"I told Finley. He'll have Cajun Girl sent up to Staunton in a trailer the day you leave. Let's walk down to the track."

She listened to the scratching of a branch on the side of the house now as the wind worried it. They had strolled down to the eight-furlong oval where the exercise boys had the yearlings out. Davie, she remembered, was working Starlight, breezing her easily for the mile. When he brought her in to be blanketed and walked, she had moved away from her father and Mr. Finley, the trainer, to stand beside the gate. She always liked Davie best when he came off a horse. He had the animal's sweat, a sharp, sweet odor that made the nose tingle. He hadn't paid any attention to her but then he never did when he was working.

She twisted now in the bed, locking her legs at the ankles and feeling her body grow limp and sort of sleepily heavy. It was a strange feeling and she lay in the darkness for a long time enjoying it before she went to sleep.

Carol lay back, her head pillowed on a small square of foam rubber encased in a crisply laundered cover, and thought someone ought to tell the airlines that these damn reclining seats, in which you neither sat nor fully reclined, were a fancy delusion. Within the long cabin most of the passengers were asleep. Somewhere below lay the great, flat land of Kansas. Now and then, small grapelike clusters of lights marked a town or village. The big commercial transport chewed steadily at the miles on its night flight from San Francisco to New York.

She tried to close her eyes, wanting desperately to sleep. She thought she had never been so tired, so physically and mentally drained. It seemed impossible she could stay awake this way. The brain, though, was an infuriating trickster. It kept working no matter how weary the body became. It raced up and down innumerable dead-end channels like a blind mouse seeking an exit. Nothing was ever resolved, no thought completely pursued to a conclusion, but the mind seemed unable to crouch within its cavity and rest.

She reached up to touch the button which would light a small bulb in the compartment shared by the two stewardesses. When the girl, trimly efficient and smilingly pretty, came she asked for some water and an empty glass.

In the overnight case beside her was a pint flask of brandy. She poured herself a big drink and swallowed just a little water as a chaser. It was a hell of a way to treat good brandy but this was medicine, a sedative. She lay back again and waited for its effect.

She had gone to the Pentagon itself to get a priority on an Air Force plane out of Manila. They had bumped an irate lieutenant colonel for her, but he was out of Special Services and not the lines so she felt no twinge of conscience in seeing him left behind.

Her premature discharge from the hospital had been easier. She made herself so completely unpleasant that they were glad to see her go. Only one of the weary doctors took the trouble to stop by her bed after she was dressed.

"You're sicker than you think, Miss Warrington. The blood count shows a liver virus, hepatitis. You've had malaria, the common dysentery, and God alone knows what other stuff is crawling around inside you. You really ought to stay here for a while."

She worked at the snap at the waist of her skirt. "I'm going to take that priority. If they hadn't brought my clothes I would have gone out of here naked." She glanced at her hands in which the bones and veins showed clearly, and half smiled. "Not that seeing me in this condition would be much of a treat for man or beast. Or," she managed a grin, "are they the same thing? My Aunt Julia used to say they were." She stopped short and stared at the doctor. "What made me say that?" she wondered aloud. He had no idea what she meant and, after a moment, nodded pleasantly and moved on down the ward.

She sat on the edge of the bed, still puzzled that the name of Julia should have come to mind. She hadn't thought of the woman in twenty years; didn't know whether she was alive or dead. What, she asked herself, am I doing, rummaging around in that dark closet of my life? Only the very old turned to look back down the long, dim corridor for once-familiar figures. I may feel that old, she confided to herself, but I'm damned if I am.

Honolulu, Guam, Wake, San Francisco. They were blurred spots on a map. She had moved, talked and gone through the necessary motions of walking and sleeping without being completely aware of where she was or what she was doing. In San Francisco she had checked in at the Mark Hopkins and for four days didn't leave her room or answer a telephone call. The hotel had engaged a private maid for her and the girl slept in one of the two bedrooms of the suite.

Meals, at which she barely picked, were sent in and the cleaning maid daily took out an empty fifth of Scotch in the wastepaper basket. The doctors had told her alcohol could be little short of poison with her liver in the condition it was, but it was the only way she could sleep and she drank herself into a semistupor every night.

Then, she awoke one morning and the frightening lassitude was gone, the rubbery feeling in her legs miraculously strengthened. She was tired but no longer helpless. She called a shopping service and told the young buyer what she needed in the way of clothing. The house physician came up and after a talk, gave her intravenous shots of glucose and B complex. When this went to work she felt almost cheerful again. She nodded absently to the physician's suggestion that she ought to have the shots regularly. She was unimpressed. Hepatitis was only a fancy name for yellow jaundice.

On the bedside table there were half a dozen telephone call slips. Martin Baker, the managing editor of the Hillyard paper in San Francisco, had called. Reporters had picked her name up as a VIP arriving on the air transport. She had shaken them off wearily and asked that no pictures be taken.

"I look like hell and I know it. Give me a few days. I'll be at the Mark. I've already written everything I know." No, she didn't think it unusual for a publisher to cover a war as a reporter. She managed a small laugh. "If Roy Howard can do it, I can."

She had another drink of the brandy now and shook the flask to find out how much was left. The damn stuff didn't have much effect. On the adjoining seat were all the San Francisco papers. She had intended to look through them but it was too much effort. Baker had come to dinner and they had talked shop, the competition in San Francisco, Bridges and the Longshoremen's Union, and President Truman's Fair Deal. It disturbed her to realize she was listening more than she was talking. It wasn't her way. She was politely attentive to Baker but at the moment it didn't make a hell of a lot of difference whether the paper was making or losing money, gaining circulation or dropping it. Now and then she had caught him regarding her a little wonderingly. She smiled to herself now thinking of their conversation.

"Are you wondering about the 'dynamic, vividly forceful' Carol Warrington, Mr. Baker? Isn't that what *Time* called me once?"

He was embarrassed. "Well, I . . ." He all but stammered.

She leaned forward confidentially. "I have bugs in my guts and I'm so tired my tail drags when I walk. I don't feel dynamic at the moment. Anyhow, there isn't any need for my putting on an act. I've always thought you were doing a good job here in San Francisco. I don't crawl up my people's backs just for the exercise. I know I'm supposed to be red hell on wheels but if I am, right now I only want to coast."

Baker had arranged her flight transportation out, sent a corsage and a couple of current novels to the plane. Thinking of him now, she was irritated by the knowledge she still unconsciously measured every man on her papers by Chris Chandler. He was a stubborn bastard but one hell of a good man on a desk.

She glanced up now as the stewardess stood beside her. There was a faint shadow of concern on the girl's face.

"I have a Nembutal capsule, Miss Warrington, if you think it would help get you to sleep?"

Carol shook her head. "I'll stick with the booze. It usually works." She smiled understandingly. "Don't worry about me. I never get noisy or try to take up with the male passengers."

The girl's eyes crinkled with faint amusement and she went back to her compartment. A note for special attention had been appended to her passenger list from the executive offices. If Miss Warrington wanted to get herself potted, it was going to be all right with the airline.

Carol shifted the pillow. She wished now she hadn't wired Bootsie. The way she felt she would like to skip New York and Washington, charter a private flight out of La Guardia and go direct to Court House. She was in no humor for a family reunion.

It surprised her a little to realize she had been thinking of the house Mark had built as home, a place of quiet refuge. She would lie in the autumn sun and do nothing. When she was stronger she would try to ride again, get acquainted with her daughter, know the easy, undemanding companionship of Bootsie. It was odd, she mused, she never thought of him as a husband or even a lover. He was Bootsie, charming, easy to understand, neither deferential nor demanding. There were no complications with him. He had the uninhibited honesty of a child. The whole world pleased him just as it was. He had used the Hillyard fortune but was not impressed by it. If it vanished tomorrow it would make no real difference, for he was as adaptable as one of those French dolls which, thrown on a bed or couch, somehow manage a certain sprawling attractiveness.

She had a real curiosity about Carol-Anne. Children, as such, had never particularly interested her. They were absorbed in their own small world of make-believe and with them she had never found a medium of communication. Babies were nothing more than little animals, no better and no worse than puppies which tumbled about your feet and wet the rugs until housebroken. It was only after they had reached a certain degree of intelligence that a basis of companionship could be achieved.

At thirteen Carol-Anne would be someone in whom she could take pleasure. She was old enough to be entertaining, young enough to be malleable. It was a good time to come home. Now they could plan her schooling and the creation of a suitable background. When she had recovered from this damn malaise, they would take a house in Washington. There, for a generation or more, would be the world's capital. With the proper guidance, Carol-Anne would move effortlessly into the official and diplomatic circles. She would have an opportunity to become familiar with a society of many levels. As she moved into young womanhood the background would be invaluable.

She lit a cigarette and poured herself another drink. She was feeling pleasantly hazy now. It occurred to her she hadn't the slightest idea what Carol-Anne looked like. Was she tall, pretty, or awkwardly gangling and hoydenish? Thirteen was a bad age sometimes, a graceless interlude between girl and woman when teeth needed ugly braces and arms and legs seemed to have no connection with the body. She tried to remember what she had been like at thirteen and couldn't. No image came to mind. She, Mark and Aunt Julia had been somewhere in Texas. The old man had either made or was on the point of making his first big strike.

It disturbed her a little to realize how often during the past few weeks she had thought of Mark. It was as though she tried to recreate a time beyond capture. Old Mark would have liked what she had done. The newspapers which had been tottering on the cliff of failure were vigorous money-makers. That was the way he would have measured their success. Actually, their financial position did furnish the only yardstick. It was as simple as that. She had no inclination to be a voice in the wilderness. The public had listened and paid for the privilege.

A blessed numbness began to creep upon her. The brandy was at work. She twisted into a more comfortable position. Mark, she thought, would have been disappointed in not having a grandson. Maybe not, though. He had raised one girl. Anyhow, she'd do the best she could for him with Carol-Anne. She certainly didn't intend to go any further.

When the stewardess moved down the aisle on one of her periodic passenger checks she saw Miss Warrington was asleep. In repose the weary lines in her face seemed deeper, shadowed by illness and seemingly etched permanently into a mask.

XXII

STEPHEN KEITH made an attempt to conceal the shocked surprise he felt at her appearance and knew he had failed when a small, wan smile hovered for a moment about her mouth and she shook her head as though to say he didn't have to pretend.

She waited as he came quickly across the apartment's living room from the foyer, and then with a grimace put out her hand.

"It's beginning to look a little like a vulture's claw but it's the best I can offer."

"For God's sake, why aren't you in a hospital!" He was so startled that the words exploded almost angrily.

"Because I don't feel like dying just now and that's what would

happen if I went to a hospital. Sit down. It's good to see you again."
She indicated a tray on a table. "Drink?"

"It's been years since I've taken a drink in the middle of the day
but I think I need one. Why didn't you let me know you were this
ill?"

"Letting you know wouldn't have had the slightest effect on the
bugs inhabiting this poor carcass. They are singularly unimpressed
by authority. Pour me a small drink of the brandy, Stephen." She
looked up with an expression of astonishment. "That is the first time
in all these years I have called you anything but Mr. Keith. I guess
we are entering upon an irreverent and undisciplined era."

He handed her a pony of brandy doubtfully. "Should you be
drinking this?"

"No." She swallowed half of the liquor. "At least the doctors say
not, but they say no to everything as a matter of general principle."

A cold, damp wind swept up the street outside, tearing the fog
apart as it tried to gather. Here the soft lights and pleasantly crack-
ling fire made the apartment a cheerful retreat. Keith took a chair
on the opposite side of the hearth and held the Scotch and soda
in his hand without tasting it.

"I would have met you. Why didn't you let us know you were
coming? More to the point, why have you driven yourself this
way?"

"Because there wasn't any other way to do the job, Stephen."
She leaned back against the cushions. "I didn't let you know because
I hate being met or seen off." She didn't tell him she had strained,
almost eagerly, for a sight of Bootsie and Carol-Anne at La Guardia
Airport and of the sudden and unexpected feeling of empty loneliness which chilled her when she realized they had not come. It had
been a momentary weakness of which she was now ashamed. "Anyhow, I'm going down to Virginia in the morning if I can charter
a small private plane that will drop me right in the back yard. I did
want to see you. I'm tired, Stephen. Just so goddamned tired." Her
eyes closed and her breath was expelled softly.

"Is there anything I can do, take care of for you?"

She opened her eyes to shake her head. "No, I'll be all right.
Everything is such an effort. Just brushing my teeth comes under
the head of manual labor. I had planned to stop off at Washington
but I don't feel like it. I have definite plans for the paper there.
I want to make it a completely local paper, as personal as a country

298

weekly. We'll have to carry national news, of course, and the syndicated features, but I want everything and everyone in Washington to be of interest to us. Truman will run for another term. I don't like him or the men about him. I want to go after them. This may teach us all to be a little more careful when we come to the nomination of a Vice-President. It isn't just an empty office. Something like this happens and we're stuck with our own indifference." She paused. "I want Chris Chandler for the Washington city desk, Stephen. Get him back for me."

"I don't think it's possible." Keith didn't meet her eyes. "I had luncheon with him last week. He's had an offer from Hearst. I think he's going to take it."

"I'll double any offer Hearst has made." She snapped the statement. "He's the man I need in Washington."

"It isn't a question of money, Mrs. Warrington." Keith was being as gentle as possible. "I think you know that."

"Oh, for God's sake!" she exploded, but without any real vehemence. "Let's stop talking about bleeding hearts. This has nothing to do with sentiment." She sagged wearily and her eyes met his. "I was very much in love with him, Stephen." The words were whispered. "And I was so very, very young and ignorant; so certain I knew best. What should I do?"

"Take a long rest, get your health back. Forget about everything else." He put the untasted Scotch on the floor, locked his hands and bent forward, studying her with intent sympathy. "I don't think you are in any shape to make decisions."

She nodded indifferently. "I feel so old, as though I had compressed a hundred years into the last five or six. I'm only thirty-seven or so and yet, time after time, I catch myself looking back over my shoulder to see where everyone has gone. If I learned anything from covering this war it is that man's greatest fear is not that he may be killed or torn apart, his guts ripped out by a grenade. Those possibilities are always there of course. But what really scares him is the idea of suddenly finding himself alone. I used to see it in the faces of assault troops or men pinned to a strip of beach. They kept looking, not for the Japs or the Germans, but for the man at their side." She reached for a cigarette and lit it before he could offer a lighter. "Once, early in the war in London, I saw it on the faces of the people there. They looked a little bewildered and frightened, not because of the bombs and the fires but because there were no longer children around. They had all been evacuated. You never saw a youngster. The adults went through the mechanics of living and defending themselves but they were scared. It was as though they said, What happens if you and you and you and you get it and I'll be alone in an empty city and there are no children to grow up and take your places? I tried to write it."

"I remember." Keith nodded, not understanding the compulsion which drove her to talk this way. "It was a fine story. It surprised me because I had never suspected the compassion which made you write it."

"Oh, hell!" She forced a yawn and an indifference. "I guess it was just one of those sticky things you write now and then."

She laughed shortly and Stephen Keith thought he had never seen such sadness in a person's eyes.

The small plane cut high over Washington and across the Potomac. From her seat in the little cabin behind the pilot, Carol looked down with quickening interest as the countryside of Virginia began to unroll below.

A private plane had been difficult to find. Stephen Keith had finally made the arrangements for her at a field in New Jersey. Before leaving she had telephoned Court House. Neither Bootsie nor Carol-Anne was at home. She put in a call for Harkness and talked for a moment with Martha, who was deliberately and infuriatingly vague as to Bootsie's whereabouts. She left word at both places as to her expected arrival time and told Martha Harkness she could damn well go to hell. It was a childish exhibition of temper of which she was immediately ashamed.

She was unreasonably angry with Bootsie. He had her wire from San Francisco. He knew she had wanted him to meet her in New York. But she couldn't help admitting to herself, why in hell should he have come running? It had been a long time. Why did she imagine Bootsie would just sit and hold the reins until she came back? She was almost smugly pleased with herself for being so understanding under the circumstances. She felt she was generously and worldly tolerant. Maybe it was all those damn vitamins the doctors had been shooting into her; a synthetic milk of human kindness. She lay back and closed her eyes but the plane's rackety single motor permitted her to drowse only fitfully.

Nothing had really been accomplished by her stopping over in

New York. Keith had been firmly courteous in his refusal to make Chris Chandler an offer. She had brought herself to the point of looking his number up in the telephone book and then slamming the receiver down angrily just before dialing. The Washington paper could wait until she felt better and Chris Chandler could go to the devil or Hearst, whichever he considered more attractive. If necessary, until the paper was whipped into the shape she had conceived for it, she could sit on the desk herself. Who knew better than she how she wanted it run?

She slept for a while and when she awoke, the pilot was letting down for a look at the airstrip she had told him he would find. She looked for it herself from the window and it was barely discernible beneath a heavy growth of weeds.

The pilot called back over his shoulder. "Are you sure that strip will hold us, Miss Warrington?"

"I'd think so. It's solid concrete. I had it put down myself for a heavier plane than this. No one has used it in years, though."

He nodded and began a wide turn over the river for a new approach. He would be glad to get down. He had wondered about his passenger. She looked as though she ought to be making the trip in an ambulance. The wheels bit through the green matting and rolled easily. From the corner of his eye he caught sight of an open car drawn to one side of the strip and a girl standing beside it. He spun the ship about at the end of the runway and taxied back.

Carol, also, had seen the car and the figure of Carol-Anne. It had been no more than a flashing glimpse as they rolled past but she was certain the girl was alone. When the plane halted and the pilot dropped out and down to the ground, pulling the folding metal step for her, Carol paused for a moment to study her daughter from this distance.

She stood with her back to the car's door, arms stretched out on either side. She made no move to come forward nor did she smile or lift a hand in greeting. Carol felt a sudden tight anger. This was a contrived indifference close to insolence. She bent from the cabin, took the pilot's hand and put a not-too-steady foot on the step. Only then did she see that Carol-Anne was coming forward.

Carol studied her. The slender legs in well-fitting jodhpurs, the small waist and good hips. For a second she felt a stab close to jealousy. No one had a right to look that fresh and vital when she felt so lousy. She took a tentative step forward.

The pilot had his back to them, reaching in for the light bags. The two halted, almost warily, and regarded each other for an uncomfortable moment. Carol smiled and put out her hand. Instinctively, she realized any demonstrative greeting would be completely false.

"Hello, Carol-Anne." It seemed pitifully inadequate.

"Hello." Carol-Anne's eyes were faintly questioning. Then, because she was not quite so poised as she pretended, she hurried an explanation. "Bootsie is at Harkness. Starlight hurt a leg during the morning workout. He said you'd understand."

Carol nodded as though it made no difference and turned to the pilot.

"Would you like to come up to the house for a drink?"

"No thanks, Miss Warrington." He stared at her and then continued, "Are you that Warrington? Carol Warrington?"

"I suppose so, if you mean what I think you do." She noticed, for the first time, he walked with an obvious stiffness in one leg as though it were artificial or had been badly torn and never completely healed. "Here." Impulsively she reached for the lightest of the two bags he carried. "Let me take that."

He shook his head without embarrassment and swung the luggage into the rear seat.

"I used to read your stuff, after I was shipped back with this." He touched his leg and then grinned. "Or without it, to be more exact. Did you know Ernie Pyle?"

"Not well."

He held the door for her but she delayed getting in, feeling a little ashamed of her self-pity because she had returned with a few tropical bugs while this boy had left a leg.

"You wrote a lot alike." The pilot ran a hand through the tight, black hair with a self-conscious smile. "I mean you made it seem like a fight between some guys you knew and some others you didn't, but you had a feeling for them all—the little scared Jap and the fellow from Millersburg, Kentucky. I guess it was a real big war but you managed to make it personal. I'm real glad to meet you." He offered his hand awkwardly.

"Thank you." She took the hand, understanding she was almost childishly pleased by what he had said. "I'm going to need a private pilot again, soon I hope."

He shook his head. "Thanks just the same. I have this small

operation going now in Teterboro, just a couple of old ships. But if it works out, I'll get hold of some surplus equipment and build it up to a freight-carrying line. You won't have any trouble finding a pilot. They're going to come tumbling out of the wild blue yonder looking for any sort of a flying job that'll save them from going back to being clerks, bookkeepers or whatever they did before. A war sort of spoils you for anything else." He closed the door as she moved into the seat and then touched his forehead in a half-salute. "So long, Miss Warrington."

Watching him walk back to the plane, Carol-Anne had the awful feeling she was going to cry. It had nothing to do with the man or the fact he had lost a leg in a war which was incomprehensibly vague to her. She was going to cry for herself and Carol Warrington beside her because they should have so much to say to each other and couldn't or didn't know how. Because she was emotionally unprepared for this sensation, she was engulfed in a vast loneliness, an uncharted region of the heart. What she cried so silently for was such a simple, childish thing. She wanted Carol to turn, put an arm about her shoulders and say: Baby, I've missed you. I'm glad to be home. I'm proud of the way you look. We'll make it up to each other now that I'm back. I want to love you and have you love me. None of these things was going to be said. The terrible, empty feeling in her stomach told her so. They'd just sit here like a couple of polite strangers. Because she didn't want to bawl this nonsense and make an idiot of herself, she took refuge in a flippant avenue of escape.

"He's real cute-looking." She started the motor. "How do you think it is to lose a leg? Do you suppose he has a wife and how do you imagine she feels, getting into bed with a one-legged man?"

"I imagine his wife feels a damn sight better with her two legs than he does with his one. What made you ask such a question?" She was angered by the child's triviality.

"I just wondered." Carol-Anne fought down a wave of shame. It would have been better to have said nothing and she was miserably aware of her mother's contempt. "I wanted to know what you'd say." With her eyes straight ahead she put the car through its change of gears. "That's all."

Carol stared at her with growing astonishment. She suspected Carol-Anne had thrown up the words as a shield, now that they were alone, against any attempt on her part to establish a mother-daughter relationship. If so, the child's canny instinct was almost frightening. She studied the clear innocence of the profile and wondered if that was really a tear dangerously close to falling. Hesitantly she put out a hand to cover the white knuckles on the wheel and the sudden braking of the car all but pitched them into the windshield.

"Mother!" The word was cried in bewildered anguish.

The slender body in her arms was wracked and the tears against her cheek were real enough. Carol found herself making small, ineffectual sounds.

"Baby. Baby. Don't do this. I know it is a hard time. Bootsie shouldn't have let you come alone. Everything is going to turn out all right."

"It's just that I wanted you so for my mother but you never were." The sobs quieted but the body still remained half nestled, burrowing away from an unpleasant world. "Nothing you ever said or did made me think you wanted me. So I pretended I didn't care, but that only seemed to make it worse." She sniffled, straightened up, took a handkerchief from her shirt pocket and blew noisily. Her smile was misty, tentative. "I had it planned, what I was going to do and say when the plane landed. Instead, we just said hello to each other and it was awful." She leaned back, her head half touching Carol's shoulder, and stared at the sky. "When I began to read and saw something with your name on it in a paper, I cut it out. I have a shoebox full. I wanted to tell everyone: That's my mother. But I was afraid you wouldn't like it if I did. I never let Bootsie, Uncle John or Aunt Martha know what I felt. I just kept sort of hugging it to myself and saying: If she ever comes home again maybe we can start out by being friends, at first."

"I'd like that, Carol-Anne."

She lit a cigarette and thought how inadequate were those words. Why did she always stop short of an honest expression of emotion? She could write of it well enough but her lips seemed incapable of forming the words. I'm a wolf bitch, she told herself, without the instinct for motherhood. She caught herself thinking of Old Mark. He had gone on about the thing he must do, leaving her as a child wherever it suited his convenience or whim. When he took her with him, it was as though she were a piece of luggage mysteriously left in his care, the exact purpose of which he had never quite figured out. Once, she remembered she must have been about Carol-

304

Anne's age, he had said: *You'll damn well have to take me as I am because I ain't likely to change.* This, in softer words, she wanted to say now to her own daughter as a warning not to expect more than she could honestly give.

"Bootsie says we're a lot alike." Carol-Anne straightened up. "So it probably won't be too hard to be friends at first."

There was a quiet radiance in the girl's face and Carol touched her finger tips against the cheek.

"Why didn't you meet me in New York?"

"I was afraid it would be awful, the way it was once before. I guess Bootsie felt the same way." She started the car again, driving slowly. "Why didn't you and Bootsie ever make things together, the way other married people do?" There was no accusation, no rebuke. It was an honest question.

"I'm not sure I can or should try to answer that." She paused. "You get an itch and you have to scratch. That's pretty elementary, isn't it? I had an itch. It wouldn't let me stay here in Virginia. It won't now. If we're going to start as friends you'll have to understand I'm not sorry for anything—leaving you to grow up as you have, not being what you imagine a wife to be. Bootsie and I took each other for what we were. No one was tricked into or out of anything. I don't feel a damn bit guilty."

Carol-Anne nodded gravely. "Bootsie said you wouldn't. He said the greatest thing about you was your honesty." She laughed quietly. "He said a lot of people probably had a hell of a time living with it because no one could explain Carol better than Carol. I don't really know what that means but I guess it is that Carol always has a reason for Carol."

They were into the sweeping driveway now. Nothing had changed. The beauty Old Mark had seen rise here had only been enhanced by the years. As Carol-Anne came to a halt at the steps a Negro man came down quickly to open the door and hold it.

"Miz Warrington, ma'am."

"I don't remember you." The statement was a pleasant inquiry.

"William, ma'am. I'm new since you bin away."

He followed them with the bags up the steps and inside. Standing once again within the familiar hall with the floating curve of the staircases winding in a beautiful sweep to the second story, she experienced a sense of relief at homecoming. This was permanent, something which would be here forever. She had lived too long in an unstable world in which you could awake and find nothing as it had been.

At the landing she turned down to what had once been her room and halted on the threshold. It had been changed. It was a man's room now. Two or three of Bootsie's pipes were in a rack beside a humidor. There were scattered copies of *Field and Stream* on a desk. The curtains had yielded to formal draperies hanging in motionless columns. She wondered why he had taken her room when there were so many others available.

"Take my things down to the south wing, William." She turned to Carol-Anne. "Which is your room?"

"Next door. We haven't lived here much but when we did, Bootsie liked this one. It was yours, wasn't it? I guess he's sentimental about things. It's funny because I never thought of him that way."

Carol didn't answer. There was within her an unfamiliar sensation of wanting to cry a little. I must be getting old, she thought, or I'm a damn sight sicker than I imagined.

She turned and walked down the long gallery with the odd feeling she was, somehow, completing a cycle. The rooms where William waited had been Old Mark's. They were as he had used and left them—the high, canopied bed, and floor-to-ceiling windows looking down upon the river. She crossed and opened one, standing to stare with troubled concentration. Then, when she was certain her voice and emotions were under control, she turned to the waiting William.

"Bring me up some ice water with bourbon, Scotch or whatever we have in the house." She dropped into a chair, sagging with an abrupt weariness. "Find out if Dr. Earle Warren is still practicing in Court House. If he is, tell him Miss Hillyard—Mrs. Warrington—would like to have him come up right away." She closed her eyes.

XXIII

BECAUSE she had the feeling all of this had happened to her exactly this way before but at a time beyond reckoning, she kept her eyes closed against the presence of the others in the room.

When she opened them, Old Mark would be lying in this bed, but the voice when he spoke would be hers. Somehow she was inhabiting his wasted body here beneath the light covering and she knew a sudden terror that this could be so.

She knew she was not alone. There was the faint, molasses odor of pipe tobacco. That would be Bootsie. She felt, rather than saw, the shadow of a movement beside her as Earle Warren shifted. The tiny snicking of a latch would be Carol-Anne closing one of the French doors.

She looked first at her hands. They were her own. The swell of breast under chiffon belonged to her. Only then did she have the courage to open her eyes fully to meet the face above hers.

"How about it, Earle?" Her voice sounded harsh and unnatural. "Am I dying?"

"Not unless you want to."

She watched him put the stethoscope away. It was as though everything being said and done were repeated because they must move through precise channels already grooved for them. Then she turned her head slightly and stared at Bootsie.

"Hello." The voice was stronger, pitched normally. "When did you get here?"

"In time to put you in bed and wait for Dr. Warren." He came over and stood above her until she had to throw back her head to see him. "You're a lot skinnier than I remembered." His smile was quiet and gentle.

She pulled herself upright and stuffed some pillows at her back. Carol-Anne was still in jodhpurs and an obscene old man's words came winging from the years.

"Sister. You've got the prettiest behind in Virginia. If I wasn't your mother, and a man, I'd snatch me a handful of it."

The expression of complete astonishment on her daughter's face made her laugh until tears smeared a dirty course of mascara down her cheeks. How was the child supposed to know what she was talking about?

"Why did you call me that? Sister?" Carol-Anne was puzzled and interested. "You never did before."

"I know." Carol nodded, wiping at her eyes. "It's a private word. I don't know what made me remember it. I'd like a drink and a cigarette." She glanced at the empty bedside table and then at Earle Warren.

"I said you weren't going to die unless you wanted to. I didn't say you couldn't kill yourself, though."

She shrugged. "Give me a cigarette then. I'll have a drink after you leave if I feel like it."

He lit one for her and then indicated a large envelope. "These records from the Manila hospital were in your bags when they were unpacked. You've picked up a little of everything, haven't you? I looked through them."

The taste of the cigarette was foul but she wouldn't admit it. Her glance strayed from Warren to Bootsie to Carol-Anne at the window. What a lovely child she was, what a breath-takingly beautiful young woman she would be. She made this silent admission with a tinge of envious regret. By some miracle she had escaped an ungainly adolescence. She had a repose which was almost a detachment and it gave her a serene beauty. Her voice carried the soft accent of this part of Virginia. She had Bootsie's effortless charm and the easy grace of movement. What in her was there of Carol Hillyard Warrington?

She turned again to Warren. "If I'm not sick enough to die then I'm sure not sick enough to be kept lying in a bed this way. What did I do? Pass out in a chair? That's the last thing I remember. All right. I've been traveling. I was tired."

Warren halted in the act of closing his bag and leveled a finger at her. "You do as you damn well please. I went through this once before with your father. I'm too busy now to take it again with you. Take my advice or get someone else." The bag's catch snapped with an angry snick.

She leaned back against the pillows. Just the small effort of attempting to sit up defiantly straight had made her unaccountably weary. For the first time she was actually a little frightened by the relentless ferocity of the demons possessing her.

"All right." She made the concession reluctantly. "I won't take a drink. I'd like one but I won't take it. When can I get up and out of here?"

"When you really feel like it. You need a lot of rest. We'll try and clean up one thing at a time. Blood counts, analyses, shots for your liver, shots for everything I can think of. This is going to be a small gold mine. I haven't had one like it since old Mark Hillyard used to lie there and yell. Yes sir, it's a bonanza."

"Make it while you can." She winked at him and put out her hand with a friendly gesture. "It's good to see you again, Earle, even if I had to do it this way."

"I'll be in tomorrow." He paused. "You'd be better off in a hospital right now, Carol."

"No!" The word was explosive. "And, I don't want any nurse sneaking around with a phony smile and that silly business of saying: How are we this morning? Why is it nurses always use the plural? Why do they have to talk as though you were two-headed or something?"

Warren looked down at her with a quizzical expression of wonder and amusement. He shook his head and then spoke to Bootsie as though she weren't there.

"She even sounds like Old Mark, doesn't she? Sort of takes you back. Down memory lane with Carol Hillyard. I hope to God I'm not around to take care of her twenty years from now."

"You go to hell." Carol issued a friendly invitation.

After Warren had left there were uncomfortable moments of silence in the room which accumulated and became unbearable. Carol-Anne sat on the arm of a chair by the window, swinging a booted foot. She divided a cautious glance between her parents and then stood up with an affected yawn of boredom.

"I think I'll take a walk or something." She waited expectantly.

"Why don't you do that, honey." Bootsie managed to make it sound like an exceptional idea.

"I don't really want to go." Carol-Anne smiled at Carol.

"Come back later. We'll have a talk if you like. Maybe you can wheel the old lady around the room, move her into the afternoon sun." Carol smiled.

When the door closed, Bootsie pulled a chair across the room and near the bed's side. He knocked out his pipe and refilled it.

"She's beautiful, Bootsie. Not just on the outside. She has a radiance. When I'm well again I'm going to take a house in Washington. I have a new paper. Not so new, really, but it needs attention. She can go to school there and get the background she deserves."

He had halted in the act of filling the pipe to stare at her. She was conscious of his astonishment. Then he folded up the pouch.

"I think you really mean that." He struck a match.

"Of course I mean it. She's at the age when each year can be shiningly valuable to her."

He shook his head. "No. What I mean is, you really believe you can come back this way and take over, to possess and shape Carol-Anne into the image of Carol. Well, child," the fact that he purposely drawled the words only added to their determination, "I'll tell you now it isn't going to be that way at all. No sir, not at all that way."

The anger flared quickly. "I'm her mother. I have a right to an interest in her future. She's not going to grow up without the advantages I can give her, the doors I can open for her."

"The hell you say?" Bootsie was amiably interested.

"I'm not going to argue with you about it, Bootsie. Later we can talk it over."

"This is about as good a chance as we're going to get, honey." He drew reflectively upon the pipe. "Carol-Anne is already entered at Stuart Hall, in Staunton. She's due there next week. She has friends going, girls she has known most of her life. Her background will be all right. We're going to give her some time to mature, then she can make up her mind whether she wants to go through any of those doors you can open."

"Don't be so ridiculously provincial. You're talking this way, being stubborn, only because you want me to feel guilty. I should have stayed home, changed her diapers, burped her when she had gas. Any damn fool can do that. Now is the time when I can give her something of value." She halted the angry flow of words abruptly and stare incredulously at him. "You really mean it, don't you, Bootsie?" The question was softly, unbelievingly asked. "I don't think we ever spoke angrily to each other before."

Bootsie rubbed the pipe's bowl against his nose and admired the oily sheen. He stretched out his legs and studied his feet contentedly. When he spoke again his voice was softly sympathetic.

"This here whole thing is likely to come as a shock, child. I'm going to leave you."

"What?" Sheer astonishment jerked her upright and she sat there staring at him.

"Leave. Like go away." He was explaining something to a child. "I don't mean run off with another woman. I mean just leaving you, this place, the Hillyard Enterprises. I may only go as far away as Harkness but distance, miles, aren't what I'm talking about." He did a curious thing then, leaning forward to take one of her hands in his. "You're too smart not to know what I mean."

She said nothing, made no attempt to withdraw her fingers from his, but studied the handsome, almost regretful, face.

"I want to tell you a little about Harkness." He continued. "It's doing all right. A lot of the money has been paid back to Hillyard Enterprises. We have a two-year-old that may be a million-dollar horse and a couple of yearlings almost as good."

"You know I never gave a damn about the money spent on Harkness." Oddly enough she felt on the defensive. "I never asked. It was something you wanted to do."

"Let's say it was a part of something I wanted. The other part had to do with you, Carol-Anne. If," he continued slowly, "we ever had much between us it was a sort of honesty. It's decent and I want to hang on to it. When I married you, I got what I always knew was the best. I think maybe you married me and settled for a little less, but even then you were honest about it. Not even in bed—and you know good and well that's a time when the words come real easy and no one really expects them to mean more than sounds—did you ever say: I love you. I used to wonder about that, God knows you said a lot of other things nice girls aren't supposed to know and do. But you kept love to yourself like it was some sort of an admission of surrender or weakness."

"You're trying to make me a monster," she protested feebly. "We've been friends." The tone was close to vehement. "That's a damn sight more than most married persons can say."

"Child," he sighed, "I'm not saying we shouldn't be friends. What I'm trying to say is we're not going to be friends who go to bed with each other every now and then. I don't have the disposition for it. Well," he amended with a grin, "I don't have the kind of mental agility to switch from friend to husband or a good bounce in the hay. I've got a real simple mind, I guess. I can understand only one thing at a time. When my wife, right in the middle of it, looks at her watch and says, 'Honey, I've got to catch a plane for Rome' or 'There's a newspaper in Seattle I want to buy,' it confuses me, particularly when she never says. 'Come with me. We'll have fun and I need to be with you.'" He drew on his pipe and blew the smoke in a fine, pensive line down the stem. "You see," he wrestled with this for a moment, "it gets real complex, particularly since I wouldn't want to go to Rome or Seattle, but only would like her to say, 'Screwin' makes me real hungry. Let's go fix a sandwich and open a bottle of beer and come back and do it again.'"

She laughed. She had to laugh and then the sound bubbled away. She studied the handsome, untroubled face. The smile which made it seem that of a freshly scrubbed boy. She understood him well enough to know he was serious. He intended to do just what he said. He was going to leave her and she wondered how it would be, not to come home to Boothby Warrington when she needed the quiet assurance of his conviction that very little really mattered beyond this world of Virginia where persons he knew moved with an inherent grace and charm. She thrust the moody speculation aside. She was ill and because of that depressed. It produced an unnatural melancholia. Why should Carol Warrington suddenly find herself thinking of a time alone? The small, undefinable terror persisted.

"Do you want a divorce, Bootsie?" She thought the question suddenly ugly.

"That I'll sort of leave up to you."

He uncurled himself from the chair, went to the intra-house telephone, called the pantry and ordered a bottle of bourbon, ice and water. He came back and sat down.

"I've always had the idea," he spoke ruminatively, "you once got yourself involved with a man who didn't love you, or who maybe didn't love you enough. Or," he thought this over, "was just plain scared. If you can still get him or want him, then we can arrange a divorce."

"What about you?" She was curious.

He shook his head with an almost embarrassed grin. "It's safer just to leave you and let things as they are. In a pinch I can always say, 'Honey, you know I'm real crazy about you but my wife won't give me a divorce.'"

It startled her to realize she had never thought of Bootsie making love to another woman. Yet he was a healthy, normal animal. He must have during the years she was away.

"Would you marry again?" The question was so completely feminine, so conventional, she was ashamed of it.

"I don't think so. Without working at it you sort of spoil a man for any other woman. We could have had a hell of a fine life together, Carol. Different from what you know and live for but it could have been good. The big trouble was I thought I could change you enough to make it work. But I guess I would have wanted you even if I'd known it was going to end this way."

There was a soft knock on the door and William came in with a tray, glasses, ice and a bottle. He put them down on a table and left quickly. Bootsie uncurled himself and measured out some of the amber whisky.

"I'll have one with you."

He nodded. "I figured you would. I was thinking of your papa and how he used to lie there and yell for his whisky and cigar even though poor Earle told him it was poison." He swung about with curiosity. "What made you take this, his, room?"

"You had mine." That wasn't the reason. The truth was hidden somewhere in her subconscious. She had had the eerie feeling of being Mark and Carol-Anne Carol. The idea frightened and fascinated her. "This was handy. I like the view. What difference does it make?" She had the suspicion Bootsie knew and it made her angry.

He brought whisky and a glass of water, made a tall drink for himself and dropped again into the chair. She swallowed hers straight with an involuntary shudder.

"You know"—he appeared slightly surprised—"I've been doing an awful lot of talking, more than I generally do. But this may be the last good chance we'll have. I'm going back to Harkness in the morning."

"You're being pretty goddamned casual about the whole thing, aren't you?" She was infuriated by his almost cheerful acceptance of an accomplished fact.

He swallowed part of the drink, chewed an icecube with satisfaction.

"Honey," he confided, "I just don't know how we could do it any other way. You're not going to change. Just as soon as you're well again, or at least well enough to take an interest in things, you'll have a couple of telephones put in here. You'll be talking all over the world and Western Union might just as well put in a branch office downstairs. I don't say it's bad. It's the thing you have to do. The way your papa kept wanting to make money long after he had more than anyone could use. You know," he added with a softly reminiscent smile, "I asked him about that one time. He said, 'Goddamn it, boy, there ain't never enough of anything as long as there's still excitement in makin' it.' That's the way it was with him and I guess that's the way it is with you. Maybe you like the feeling of power—although that's kind of a nasty word. Maybe you just purely love what you're doing, the way a man goes crazy about a woman until nothing else has a meaning. I guess it's what set a Caesar, a Hannibal, an Alexander the Great off. They're pretty fascinating to read about but I'll bet they were hell to get along with at home. I keep thinking, though, your papa was a real lonely man around the end of things. He shouldn't have been but he was. Don't let that happen to you. Make a little room for love somewhere down the line. That's a word kicked around a lot but its hard to get along without."

"Pour me another drink." She was abrupt because he had frightened her a little. "A big one." This was an added defiance.

He made no comment but bent over the tray, and while his back

314

was turned a small shiver passed through her. She caught herself thinking, curiously enough, of BillJo Adams and the man's uncanny clairvoyance. One of these days you'll run out of men to fight at your weight. Something like that. Settle for a good sparring partner who'll let you be flashy. She half laughed. The sparring partner had wearied of the punches. She took the drink from Bootsie's hand without looking at him.

"I don't want Carol-Anne to go to Stuart Hall." She swallowed the drink.

"I know you don't." He didn't disagree.

"I'll get a house in Georgetown, enter her in a good school there. When she's ready she can finish her education abroad. She's entitled to everything I can do for her. If you want to leave that's one thing. Carol-Anne needs me now. I can open a whole world for her."

He shook his head. "She's going to Staunton the way I planned. It's the only thing I'll fight you all down the line for. She isn't a piece of property for you to pick up at a bargain price and make over." He regarded the stubborn, angry set of her jaw. "We've been pretty nice to each other so far, Carol. But I know this. If she had been ugly, crippled, colorless, you'd be only too glad to leave her with me. There was a time when she needed you but you're not going to take her off. Right now you're still something pretty special. She's mixed up about you with pride and uncertainty. You're the bright star on top of the Christmas tree. I'm not going to have her wake up some morning and discover someone has taken away the ornament. Right now you're glamor, excitement, the spangled bareback rider. She doesn't think I know it, but she has a box full of stuff—pictures, stories about you, clippings. She wants desperately to love and be loved by you. The kind of love that sends a child into a mother's bed to snuggle and be warmly secure, confident that everything is going to be all right. I want you to love her but at a distance. I'm not going to let you feed upon your young."

"You mean you'll try to stop me from seeing her?" Without realizing it, her voice had become shrill.

"No. But you're not going to take her because she's lovely, a showpiece, someone of whom you can be proud and say: Look what I did. If you think about it for a minute you'll know I'm right. You'll be off on some new interest. She'll be in school or living in that house you're going to pick up in Georgetown. She'll get a cable: MEET ME IN HONG KONG FOR CHRISTMAS. Or maybe you'll be busy and forget to cable or that it is even Christmas or that you have a house in Georgetown."

The words slapped her across the face. She was white with anger and her hands shook. She hid them beneath the covers.

His expression softened as he realized how ill she was. This was a women he had loved so deeply and still loved. He didn't want to hurt her.

"You know"—he smiled understandingly—"I don't honestly think you want the responsibility. If you do, though, I may have to go back to my tennis sneakers instead of Peale boots and shoes. Haney could call in the notes on Harkness. Everything I have done there and want to do could go on the block. That I can't or won't try to stop but I'll fight you for Carol-Anne."

She stared at him. "You scare me a little, Bootsie. You have no right to do it when I'm ill."

He bent down and kissed her gently on the cheek and she didn't turn away.

"You'll be all right," he reassured her. "The real wonderful thing about you is that you'll never be alone. Carol will always have Carol."

For a long time she had been lying there and the shadows lengthened and grew in hushed purple outside. She didn't answer the knock when it sounded. Then the door opened and Carol-Anne was framed with the gallery light behind her.

"Are you awake?" The question was whispered.

"Yes. Come in."

She moved within the room, closing the door behind her, and stood uncertainly.

"It's dark in here. Don't you want some light?" The question was tentative.

"Turn them on if you like."

One by one the softly shaded lamps glowed and Carol studied her daughter. Carol-Anne saw the whisky and her eyes widened. "Dr. Warren said you shouldn't."

"Earle Warren is an idiot." The voice was sharp. She pulled herself upright, sitting straight against the pillows.

Carol-Anne hesitated and then sat in her favorite position on the arm of a chair, one neatly booted foot swinging.

"Bootsie says you're going to Stuart Hall."

Carol-Anne made a small face and then laughed. "I keep pretending I don't want to but I really do."

"Bootsie's going back to Harkness in the morning. I'd like to have you stay here with me until you have to leave for Staunton." This was a question but not spoken so.

"Of course." The response was immediate and the lamplight made a golden aura about her face. "I'd like that."

"There's so much I want to know about you."

"Well"—she made a game of it, ticking the items off on her fingers—"I won a blue at the Warren County show. I'm in love with a jockey, he's really only an apprentice jockey, or maybe just now only an exercise boy. I think I'll marry him and then when Bootsie and Uncle John are ready to quit, we'll run Harkness."

"When I'm better I'm going to live in Washington for a while. Wouldn't you like to go to school there?" She watched for the expression of pleasure and it didn't come.

"No." Carol-Anne was quietly emphatic. "I'll like Stuart Hall, I guess. Besides, I wouldn't like to be too far away from Harkness and Bootsie."

"You love Bootsie a great deal, don't you?"

"Of course." There was astonishment in the answer, and then a curious shade of doubt and wonder. "Why don't you?" She hesitated with a natural reluctance, talking intimately with a stranger who was not actually a stranger but her mother. "It could have been real wonderful for us all if you had."

"I'm sorry about that, baby. But then, maybe I'm not really." She half smiled, feeling tired and so old as she felt the bright presence of this child who was almost a woman. "Sometimes it's hard to know whether you're sorry about something or just for yourself."

"The exercise boy's name is Davie Morton." She confided this only for something to say. Then, because she was a little uneasy, feeling a mood in her mother she couldn't understand, she walked to the window and stood looking out upon the evening.

"Sister, get me a drink and a cigarette." The words came and it seemed she had no part in speaking them.

Carol-Anne turned. "Why do you call me Sister?"

"An old man told me to." She felt a weariness tug at her eyelids. When she opened them Carol-Anne was at the bedside, the whisky held doubtfully. Carol took it and watched as her daughter lit the cigarette with a complete air of self-possession and then put it to her lips. She took a deep inhalation.

"When," she spoke slowly, "you marry your exercise boy, which you probably won't do, and take over Harkness, let him help you run it."

"What would Davie know about running Harkness?" Carol-Anne scoffed tolerantly. "By the time I'm ready I'll have learned what I need to know and I'll run it myself and better than anyone else could."

I'm lying here, Carol thought wonderingly, listening to myself talk, watching myself pour a glass of whisky, light a cigarette instead of a cigar, and it scares the hell out of me.

"I'd better get my bath and change for dinner." Carol-Anne turned questioningly.

"You do that." The voice, to her ears, seemed to quaver faintly. "Then come back here and we'll have a drink before we eat."

Carol-Anne stared. By some curious, immediate physical change the figure beneath the light covers suddenly seemed pitifully wasted and the eyes without recognition. She thought she had better call Dr. Warren and Bootsie.

At the door she turned. "What would you like to eat?"

Carol smiled then. She laughed and the tone was normal, the eyes brightly intelligent. Color flooded her face and Carol-Anne saw how really beautiful she was.

"Sister." The accent was rasping, twanging with vitality, and Carol-Anne recognized it as some play-acting on her mother's part. "Sister"—it was triumphant and assured now—"I want some fried chicken with gravy on it and not any of that goddamned puke Earle Warren ordered."